That Unfortunate Marriage by Frances E

IN THREE VOLUMES

Frances Eleanor Trollope, née Ternan, was born in August 1835 on board a paddle steamer in Delaware Bay in the United States.

After an introduction by Charles Dickens she became the governess to the child of Thomas Adolphus Trollope, the brother to the more famed Anthony. Within months they had married and settled on a new life together in Rome. It was from here that Frances elevated her talents to become a full member of the Trollope writing dynasty

Her fiction is peopled by eccentric cosmopolitan Londoners, Italian and French visitors, and motherless, bright, and educated young women trying to carve out niches for themselves within the boundaries of the middle and upper-middle classes, with varying degrees of success.

Although her work was fashionable at the time it fell into obscurity after her death but is now becoming the subject of growing interest and deservedly so.

Index of Contents

CHAPTER I.

Augustus Cheffington had made an unfortunate marriage. That was admitted on all hands. When he was a Cornet in a cavalry regiment quartered in the ancient Cathedral City of Oldchester, he ran away with pretty Susan Dobbs, the daughter of his landlady. Augustus's friends and family—all the Cheffingtons, the Dormer-Smiths, the Castlecombes—deplored this rash step. It was never mentioned, either at the time or afterwards, without expressions of deep commiseration for him.

Nevertheless, from one point of view there were compensations. This unfortunate marriage was made responsible for a great many shortcomings, which would otherwise have been attributed more directly to Augustus Cheffington himself. For example, it was said to account for his failure in his profession. He had chosen it chiefly because he very much liked the brilliant uniform of a certain crack regiment (it was in the days before competitive examinations); and he had no other aptitude for it than a showy seat on horseback, and a person well calculated to set off the works of the regimental tailor. But when years had passed, and he had remained undistinguished, his friends said, "What could one expect after Augustus's unfortunate marriage?"

After a time he sold out of the Army, and went to live on the Continent, where very shortly he had squandered nearly all his money, and fallen into shady paths of life; and again there was a chorus of "I told you so!" and a general sense that all this was due to the unfortunate marriage.

Finally, his wife died, leaving him with one little girl, the sole survivor of five children; and he came to England with the idea of securing some place which should be suited to his birth, his abilities, his habits, and his inclinations. No such place was found. Several members of the Peerage were applied to, to exert their influence with "Government" on behalf of so well-connected a personage as Augustus Cheffington. But "Government" behaved very badly, "Government" was insensible to his claims. His claims, it is true, were not small. They required a maximum of remuneration for a minimum of labour. He was unable, also, to furnish any proofs of his fitness for one or two posts which happened to be vacant, except the undeniable fact of his cousinship with all the Cheffingtons and Castlecombes in England; and to this kind of qualification "Government," it appeared, attached no importance at all.

He paid a round of visits at country houses, and renewed his long-disused acquaintance with a score of more or less distant relations. But he was not popular. It has been observed that unsuccessful men very often are not popular. "Gus Cheffington has dropped out of the running," men said. "A fellow naturally gets forgotten when he has kept out of sight for years—and besides, he makes himself so deuced disagreeable! He's always grumbling."

This latter accusation was true. If England had shown no maternal affection for her long-absent son, the son returned her hard-heartedness with interest. Indeed, in his case, it turned into active resentment. He got tired of country houses and town mansions where he was received but coolly. He was sarcastic and bitter on the failure of his connections to procure him a lucrative sinecure. He considered that the country was travelling downhill at break-neck speed, and, for his part, he did not feel inclined to move his little finger to impede that fatal course. Moreover, the black coffee was, nine times out of ten, utterly undrinkable. One day he shook the dust of England's inhospitable shores from off his feet, and returned to his shady haunts on the Continent—its irresponsibility, its cafés, its boulevards, and its billiards. And when he was fairly gone, all the Cheffingtons, and the Dormer-Smiths, and the Castlecombes were softened into sympathy; and with much shrugging of shoulders and shaking of heads declared that it was a heartrending spectacle to behold such a man as Augustus Cheffington ruined, crushed, eclipsed, destroyed by his unfortunate marriage.

When he went back to Belgium, he left behind him at school in Brighton his little motherless girl Miranda, familiarly called May. The Honourable Mrs. Cheffington, Augustus's mother, had advised her son to give the little girl a first-rate education, so as to mitigate as far as possible one disastrous effect of the unfortunate marriage, which was, that May had a plebeian mother. Mrs. Cheffington, known throughout all the ramifications of the family as "the dowager," was a hard-featured, selfish old woman, with a black wig, a pale yellow skin, and frowning eyebrows. She lived on a pension which would cease at her death, and she was supposed by some of her relations to be making a purse. They thought it would turn out that the dowager had considerable savings to leave behind her; and they founded this supposition on her never giving away anything during her lifetime. Mrs. Dormer-Smith, Augustus Cheffington's sister, declared that her mother made one exception to her rule of refusing assistance to any of them. She believed that Augustus, who had always been her favourite child, profited by the dowager's indulgence, and managed to extract some money from her tightly-closed purse. And it certainly was true that the old lady had paid May's school bills—so far as they had been paid at all.

But one day the Honourable Anne Miranda Cheffington took off her black wig for the last time, and relaxed her frowning eyebrows. The announcement of her death appeared in the first column of the Times, there was a brief obituary notice in a fashionable journal, and her place knew her no more.

Augustus hastened home to England on the receipt of a telegram from his sister. That is to say, he said he hastened; but he did not arrive in town until some hours after the funeral was over. Mr. Dormer-Smith was somewhat irritated by this tardiness, and observed to his wife that it was just like Augustus to keep out of the way while there was any trouble to be taken, and only arrive in time to be present at the reading of the will. Any expectations that Augustus might have founded on his mother's reluctance to give during her lifetime were quite disappointed. The dowager had no money to bequeath. She had spent nearly the last shilling of her quarter's income. In fact, there was not enough to cover the expenses of the funeral, which were finally paid several months afterwards by Mr. Dormer-Smith.

It seemed almost superfluous, under the circumstances, to have made a will at all. But the will was there. The chief item in it was a quantity of yellow old lace, extremely dirty, and much in need of mending, which was solemnly bequeathed by Mrs. Cheffington to her daughter, Pauline Augusta Clarissa Dormer-Smith. It was set forth at some length how that the lace, being an heirloom of the Cheffingtons, should have descended in due course to the wife of the eldest son, or, failing that, to the eldest daughter of the eldest son; and how this tradition was disregarded in the present case by reason of peculiar and unprecedented family circumstances. This was the dowager's Parthian dart at the unfortunate marriage. There was little other property, except the dingy old furniture of Mrs. Cheffington's house at Richmond, and a few books, treating chiefly of fortification and gunnery, which had belonged to Lieutenant-General the Honourable Augustus Vane Cheffington, the dowager's long-deceased husband.

"What the—What on earth my mother did with her money I can't conjecture!" exclaimed Augustus, staring out of the window of his brother-in-law's drawing-room the day after the funeral.

"She didn't give it to us, Augustus," returned Mrs. Dormer-Smith plaintively. "Even when my boy Cyril went to see her at the end of the holidays, just before returning to Harrow, she never tipped him. Once I think she gave him five shillings. But it's a long time ago; he was a little fellow in petticoats."

"Then what did she do with her money?" repeated Augustus, with an increasingly gloomy scowl at the gardens of the Kensington square on which his eyes rested.

"I believe that, with the exception of what she paid for May's schooling, she spent it on herself."

"Spent it on herself? That's impossible! It was a very good income indeed for a solitary woman, and she lived very quietly."

"You may get through a good deal of money even living quietly, when you don't deny yourself anything you can get. For instance, she never would drive one horse; she had been accustomed to a pair all her life."

Augustus checked an oath on his very lips, and, instead of swearing according to his first impulse, observed with solemnity that he knew not how his mother had been able to reconcile such selfishness with her conscience, and hoped her last moments had not been troubled by remorse.

"Oh, I don't think mamma felt anything of that kind," said Mrs. Dormer-Smith in her slow, gentle tones; "she was always complaining of other people's unreasonable expectations."

The brother and sister fell silent for a while after this, each being immersed in private meditation. That very morning a circumstance had occurred which had put the last touch to Augustus's disappointment and exasperation. The Brighton schoolmistress had sent Miss Miranda Cheffington to London in the charge of a maid-servant, and the little girl had arrived at her aunt's house in a cab with her worldly possessions, namely, a small black trunk full of clothes, and a canary-bird in a cage. The schoolmistress wrote civilly, but firmly, to the effect that, after the lamented decease of the Honourable Mrs. Cheffington, she could not undertake to keep May any longer; feeling sure, by repeated experience, that all applications for payment made to Captain Cheffington would be in vain, and understanding that Mrs. Dormer-Smith declined to charge herself with her niece's education. Captain Cheffington had been violently angry, and had denounced the schoolmistress—Mrs. Drax—as an insolent, grasping, vulgar harpy. But Mrs. Drax was out of his reach, and there was May, thirteen years old, with a healthy appetite, and limbs rapidly outgrowing her clothes.

Augustus continued to glare moodily at the square for some minutes. His sister leaned her cheek on her hand, and looked at the fire. At length Augustus, composing his face to a less savage expression, turned away from the window, sat down opposite to his sister, and said, pensively—

"We must arrange something for May, Pauline."

"You must, indeed, Augustus."

"We ought to consider her future."

"Yes; I think you ought, Augustus."

"The girl is at a hobbledehoy age. It's a perplexing position. So difficult to know what to do with her."

"There is no age at which it is so awkward to dress a girl. I have sometimes regretted not having daughters; but upon my word there must be a dreadful amount of harass about their clothes between twelve and fifteen—or in some cases sixteen."

"It's impossible for me to have her with me in Brussels. The way I live—am obliged to live malgré moi—she'd upset all my arrangements and habits. In short, you can see for yourself, Pauline, that it would be out of the question."

"No doubt it would be very bad for the girl."

"Of course! That's what I mean. Wouldn't it be the best plan after all, Pauline, to leave her here with you? She could have private masters—"

Mrs. Dormer-Smith shook her head.

"At my expense, of course," added Augustus. "I must screw and scrape and make some sacrifices no doubt, but—"

"It really won't do, Augustus. I assure you it won't do. Frederick will not have it. He talked to me after luncheon. It isn't the least use."

Mrs. Dormer-Smith continued plaintively to shake her head as she spoke, and to look with gentle melancholy at the fire.

"H'm! Frederick is very kind. But let us discuss the thing in a friendly spirit. If I pay for her clothing and education, surely the expense of her board wouldn't ruin you and Frederick!"

"No; but the butcher and the baker are the least part of the matter. It isn't as if May were the daughter of one's housekeeper or one's governess. She is a Cheffington, you know. So many things are required for a girl with her connections; and as to your paying for her masters, of course we know you wouldn't, Augustus."

"Upon my soul you are civil and sisterly!"

"Well, I dare say you would mean to pay, but you wouldn't. It would be sure to turn out so, don't you know? Things always have been like that with you, Augustus."

"Then what the devil do you think I'm to do?"

"Pray don't be violent! I really cannot bear any display of violence. You should remember that it is scarcely a week since poor mamma was taken from us."

"I don't see what that has to do with it. Miranda hasn't been taken from us; that's the point."

Mrs. Dormer-Smith making no answer, her brother continued, after a moment or two—

"You are fertile in objections, but you don't seem to have any plan to suggest."

"Well, an idea did occur to me. I don't know whether you would like it."

"Like it! Probably not. But I am used to sacrifice my inclinations."

"Well, I thought that you might put May into a school in France or Germany, or somewhere, letting her give lessons in English in return for her board and so on. There are plenty of schools where they do that sort of thing. It wouldn't so much matter abroad, because people wouldn't know who she was. You might tide over a year or two in that way."

Augustus got up from his chair. "My daughter a drudge in a Continental school?" he exclaimed indignantly.

"If you chose a place little frequented by English, I don't think people would know."

There was a short silence. Then Augustus said angrily, "I'll take the girl back with me. She must share my home, such as it is. We will neither of us trouble you or Frederick much longer. I shall start for Ostend by the morning mail to-morrow." And he dashed out of the room emitting a muffled roll of oaths, and jarring the door in a way which made Mrs. Dormer-Smith clasp her forehead with both hands, and lean back shrinkingly in her chair.

But when the morrow came, Captain Cheffington and his daughter did not go to Ostend. When they had got out of sight of the Dormer-Smiths' house, he ordered the cabman to drive to the Great Western Railway Station, and started by an express train for Oldchester.

CHAPTER II.

Amongst the minor grievances reckoned up by the deceased dowager as accruing from Augustus's unfortunate marriage was the fact that his wife had borne the plebeian name of Dobbs. One of her most frequent complaints against poor little May was that the child was "a thorough Dobbs." And when she was out of temper—which was very often—she would prefer this charge as indignantly as though Dobbs were synonymous with the most disgraceful epithets in the English language.

And yet the sound of it awoke very different associations in the city of Oldchester, where Augustus's mother-in-law had lived all her life. Mrs. Dobbs was the widow of a tradesman. The ironmonger's business, which her husband had carried on, had long passed into other hands; but his name still met the eyes of his fellow-townsmen in the inscription, "J. Brown, late Dobbs," painted over the shop.

Oldchester is a city in which two streams of life run side by side, mingling but little with each other. At a certain point in the existence of Oldchester, its ancient course of civil and ecclesiastical history had received a new tributary—a strong and ever-growing current of commerce. Commerce built wide suburbs, with villa residences in various stages of "detachment" and "semi-detachment" from one another. Commerce strewed the pleasant country paths and lanes with coal-dust, and blackened the air with smoke. Commerce set up Art schools, founded hospitals (and furnished patients for them), multiplied railways for miles round, and scored all the new streets, and some of the old, with tramway lines. Commerce bought estates in the neighbourhood, was conveyed to public worship in splendid equipages, sent its sons to Eton, and married its daughters into the Peerage. But, for all that, the fame of Oldchester continued to rest on its character as a cathedral city. The old current surpassed the new one in length and dignity, if in nothing else. The gray cathedral towers rose up majestically above the din and turmoil of forge and loom and factory, with a noble aspiration towards something above and beyond these; while the vibrations of their mellow chimes shed down sweet suggestions of peace and goodwill among the homes of the toilers.

Mrs. Dobbs particularly loved the sounds of the cathedral chimes; and she sat with closed eyes listening to them in the twilight of a certain autumn evening. Her house was in a narrow street, called Friar's Row, which turned out of the High Street. A monastery had once stood on the site of it, but all trace of the ancient conventual buildings had long since disappeared. The houses were solid brick dwellings, from one to two hundred years old. Mrs. Dobbs's husband had bequeathed her a long lease of that which she occupied. Most of the other houses in Friar's Row were used as offices or warehouses, the wealthier kind of tradespeople who once lived in them having migrated to the suburbs. On her husband's death some of Mrs. Dobbs's friends had urged her to remove to a newer and more cheerful part of the town, but she had resisted the suggestion with some contempt.

"I know what suits me," she would say. "And that's a knowledge the Lord doesn't bestow on all and sundry. This house suits me. It's weather-proof for one thing. And you needn't be afraid of putting your foot through the floor if you walk a little heavy, as I do. When I go to see the Simpsons in that bandbox they call Laurel Villa, I daren't lean my umbrella against the wall, for fear of bringing the whole concern down like a pack of cards."

She might easily have increased her income by letting her house and removing to one in the suburbs; for its position was central, and the tenements in Friar's Row were in great request for business purposes. But she resisted this temptation. There were reasons of a more impalpable kind than the solidity of its floors and roofs, which made Mrs. Dobbs constant to her old home. She had lived there all the days of her married life. Her daughter had been born there. Her husband had died there. The somewhat narrow and dingy street had in her eyes the familiar aspect of a friendly face. She loved to hear the rattle and bustle of the High Street, slightly softened by distance. Those common sounds were full of voices from the past: the common sights around were associated with all the joys and sorrows of her life. Mrs. Dobbs never said anything to this effect, but she felt it. And so she stayed in Friar's Row.

The parlour in which she sat was comfortably and substantially furnished. A competent observer would have perceived evidences of permanence and respectability in the solid, old-fashioned chairs and tables, the prints after Morland on the walls, and the corner cupboard full of fine old china. The bookshelves which filled one end of the room contained the accumulations of successive generations. There was a square pianoforte with a pile of old music-books on the top of it; and a big family Bible in massive binding had a place of honour all to itself on a side-table covered with green baize. On this special autumn evening, owing to the hour, and partly to the narrowness of the street, which shut out some of the lingering daylight, the parlour was very dim. A red fire glowed in the grate, a large tabby cat blinked and purred on the hearthrug, and in a spacious easy-chair at one side of the fireplace sat Mrs. Dobbs, listening with closed eyes to the cathedral chimes.

Presently the door was softly opened, and there came into the room Mrs. Dobbs's life-long friend and crony, Mr. Joseph Weatherhead. This person was her brother-in-law, and a childless widower. He had carried on the trade of bookseller and stationer in Birmingham for many years; but had sold his business on the death of his wife, and come to live in Oldchester, near the Dobbs's. Mr. Weatherhead was a tall, lean man, with a benevolent, bald forehead, and mild eyes. The only remarkable feature in his face was the nose, which was large, slightly aquiline, brownish red in colour, and protruded from his face at a peculiar angle. The forehead above, and the chin below, sloped away from it rather rapidly. The nose had thus a singularly inquisitive air of being eagerly in the van, as though it thrust itself forward in quest of news.

As he closed the door behind him, Mrs. Dobbs opened her eyes.

"I thought you were asleep, Sarah," said Mr. Weatherhead.

"Asleep!" ejaculated Mrs. Dobbs, with all the indignation which that accusation is so apt mysteriously to excite. "Nothing of the kind! I was listening to the chimes. They always make me think—"

"Of poor Susy," interrupted Mr. Weatherhead, nodding. "Ah! And so they do me. Poor Susy! How pretty she was!"

"She had better have been less pretty for her own happiness. The great misfortune of her life wouldn't have happened but for her pretty face."

Mr. Weatherhead nodded again, and sat down opposite to Mrs. Dobbs in a corresponding armchair to her own. He then took from his pocket a black leather case, and from the case a meerschaum pipe, which he proceeded to fill and light and smoke.

"What an infatuation!" sighed Mrs. Dobbs, pursuing her own meditations. "To think of Susy throwing herself away on that extravagant, selfish, good-for-nothing fellow without any principles to speak of, when she might have had an honest tradesman in a first-rate way of business! She had only to pick and choose."

"Humph! Honest tradesmen are not as plentiful as blackberries, though," observed Mr. Weatherhead, reflectively.

Mrs. Dobbs ignored this parenthesis, and went on: "It was a bad day for me and mine when he first came swaggering into this house."

From which speech it will be seen that the Dobbs side of the family coincided with the Cheffingtons in considering Augustus's to have been an unfortunate marriage; only each party arrived at the same conclusion by a different road.

"Have you heard from him lately, Sarah?" asked Mr. Weatherhead, after a pause.

"From my precious son-in-law? Not I!"

"Oh!"

"Not a word from him till he wants something. You may take your oath of that, Jo Weatherhead."

"Oh, I thought you might have heard from him, because—"

"Well?" (very sharply).

"Well, because I see something has been putting old times into your head; and I thought it might be that."

"Something been putting old times into my head? I should like to know when they're out of my head! Much you know about it!"

Mr. Weatherhead apparently did know something about it; for after another long silence, during which he puffed at his pipe and stared into the fire, Mrs. Dobbs justified his penetration by saying—

"The truth is, I have been turning things over in my mind a good deal since yesterday."

Mr. Weatherhead was too wary to expose himself to another snub, so he merely nodded two or three times in an oracular manner.

"I'm worried out of my mind about that child. She went off yesterday as bright and happy as possible, and looking so pretty and genteel—fit for any company in the land."

"Ah! She went off, you say, to—?"

"To the Hadlows'. She is to stay there over Sunday."

"Oh! But I don't quite see—"

"Go on! What is it that you don't quite see?"

"I don't quite see what there is to worry you in that. The Hadlows are very good sort of people."

"I should think they were very good sort of people! Canon Hadlow is one of the best men in Oldchester; or in all England, for the matter of that. And he's a gentleman to the marrow of his bones. But what sort of a position has my grand-daughter among the Hadlows and their belongings?"

"A very nice position, I should say."

"A very nice position!" exclaimed Mrs. Dobbs, who seemed determined to repeat all poor Mr. Weatherhead's speeches in a tone of disdainful irony. "That's so like you, Jo! She thinks it a very nice position, too, poor lamb. She knows nothing of the world, bless her innocent heart. And, for all her seventeen years, she is the merest child in some things. But you might know better. You are not seventeen years old, Jo Weatherhead."

"Certainly not," assented he emphatically.

"The fact of the matter is that, whether by good luck or bad luck, May does not belong to my sphere or my class. She's a Cheffington. She has the ways of a lady, and the education of a lady, and she has a right to the position of a lady. If that father of hers gives her nothing else he might give her that; and he shall, if I can make him."

"Perhaps it might have been better, after all, if you had not sent the child back to her old school, but just brought her up here, under your own eye, in a plain sort of way. It would have been better for you, anyhow."

"I don't know that."

"Why, you'd have been spared a good many sacrifices. There's not another woman in England would have done what you've done, Sarah."

"Nonsense; there are plenty of women in England as big fools as me. Even that wooden old figurehead of a dowager—Lord forgive me, she's dead and gone!—had the grace to pay the child's schooling as long as she lived."

"She!" exclaimed Jo Weatherhead, firing up suddenly, and tapping his meerschaum sharply against the hob. "That's a very different pair of shoes. She could afford it a precious sight better than you. What did she ever deprive herself of? I say there's not another woman in England would have done what you've done, and it's no good your contradicting."

"There, bless the man! Don't let us quarrel about it."

"But I shall quarrel about it, unless you give in. Here's the case fairly put:—A young spark runs away with your only daughter, and pretty well breaks your heart. He takes her wandering about into foreign parts, and you only get news of her now and then, and never good news. He's too fine a gentleman to do a stroke of work for his family, but as soon as he has run through his bit of money he's not too fine a gentleman to fall into disreputable ways of life, nor yet to let who will look after his motherless little girl, and feed, and clothe, and educate her. When his own mother dies—leaving two quarters' school-bills unpaid, which you have to settle, by-the-by—the rest of the family, including his own sister, refuse to advance a sixpence to save the child from the workhouse."

"I say, Jo, that's putting it a little too strong, my friend! There was no talk of the workhouse."

"Let me finish summing up the case. I say they wouldn't spend sixpence to save that child from starvation—there, now! When the dowager is dead, and the rest of them button up their breeches' pockets, and the schoolmistress sends away the poor little girl because she can't afford to keep her and teach her for nothing, what does my gentleman do? Does he try in any one way to do his duty by his only child? Not he. He coolly shuffles off all trouble and responsibility on other folks' shoulders. He hasn't taken any notice of you for years, except writing once to borrow fifty pounds—"

"Which he didn't get, Jo."

"Which he didn't get because an over-ruling Providence had ordained that you shouldn't have it to lend him. Well, after years of silence and neglect, he turns up in Oldchester one fine morning, and walks into your house bringing his little girl 'on a visit to her dear grandmother.' Talk of brass! What sort of a material do you suppose that man's features are composed of?"

"Gutta percha, very likely," returned Mrs. Dobbs, who now sat resting her head against the cushions of her chair, and listening to Mr. Weatherhead's eloquence with a half-humorous resignation; "that's a good, tough, elastic kind of stuff."

"Tough! He had need have some toughness of countenance to come into this house as he did. And that's not the end. He swaggers about Oldchester for a week or two, using your house as an inn, neither more nor less—except that there's no bill;—and then one day he starts off for the Continent, leaving little May here, and promising to send for her as soon as he gets settled. From that day to this, and it's four years ago, you have had the child on your hands, and her precious father has never contributed one shilling towards her support. You sent the child back to school. You pinched, and saved, and denied yourself many little comforts to keep her there. You have never let her feel or guess that she has been a burthen on you in your old age. And I say again, Sarah Dobbs, that, considering all the circumstances of the case, there's not another woman in England would have done what you've done. No, nor in Europe!"

"Well, having come to that, I hope you've finished, Jo Weatherhead."

"I hope I have," returned Mr. Weatherhead, mopping his flushed face with a very large red pocket-handkerchief. "I hope I have, for the present. But if you attempt to contradict a word of what I have been saying, I'll begin again and go still further!"

"There, there, then that's settled. But I am thinking of the future. Supposing I died to-morrow, what's to become of May? I have nothing to leave her. My bit of property goes back to Dobbs's family, and all right and fair, too. I've nothing to say against my husband's will. But people like the Hadlows, who invite May, and make much of her, have no idea that she has no one to look to but me. I don't say they'd give her the cold shoulder if they did know it; but it would make a difference. As it is, they talk to her about her aunt, Mrs. Dormer-Smith, and her cousin, Lord This, and her connection, Lady T'other, and a kind of a—what shall I say?—a sort of atmosphere of high folks hangs about her. She's Miss Miranda Cheffington, with fifty relations in the peerage. If she was known only as the grandchild of Mrs. Dobbs, the ironmonger's widow, she would seem mightily changed in a good many eyes. Sometimes it comes over me as if I was letting May go on under false pretences."

"Why, she has got fifty relations in the peerage, hasn't she?"

"A hundred, for all I know. But folks are not aware that her father's family take no notice of her. She hardly knows it herself."

"But her aunt, Mrs. Dormer-Smith, writes to her, doesn't she?"

"Oh, a line once in a blue moon, to say she's glad to hear May is well, and to complain of the great expense of living in London."

"The selfish meanness of that woman is beyond belief."

"Well—I don't know, Jo. She's a poor creature, certainly. But I feel more a sort of pity for her than anything else."

"Do you? It's only out of contradiction, then."

"Not altogether," said Mrs. Dobbs, laughing good-humouredly. "I made her out pretty well that time I took May up to London before she went back to school."

"Ah! I remember. You tried if the aunt would do anything to help."

"Yes, I tried. It was right to try. But I very soon saw that there was nothing to be hoped for from that quarter. Mrs. Dormer-Smith has been brought up to live for the world and the world's ways. To be sure her world is a funny, artificial little affair compared with God Almighty's: pretty much as though one should take a teaspoonful of Epsom salts for the sea. But, at any rate, I do believe she sincerely thinks it ought to be worshipped and bowed down to. It's no use to tell such a woman that she could do without this or that useless finery, and spend the money better. She'll answer you with tears in her eyes that it's impossible; and, what's more, she'll believe it. Why, if some Tomnoddy or other, belonging to what she calls "the best people," was to ordain to-morrow that nobody should eat his dinner unless he was waited on by a man with a long pigtail, that poor creature would know no peace, nor her meat would have no relish until a man with a pigtail stood behind her chair. That's Mrs. Dormer-Smith, Jo Weatherhead."

Mr. Weatherhead drew up his lips into the form of a round O, as his manner was when considering any matter of interest, and appeared to meditate a reply. But the reply was never spoken; for a brisk ring at the street door gave a new turn to his thoughts and those of his sister-in-law.

"Dear me!" exclaimed Mrs. Dobbs, putting up her hands to settle her cap, and stretching out her feet with a sudden movement which made the old tabby on the hearthrug arch her back indignantly. "Why, that must be the Simpsons! I didn't think it was so late. Just light the candles, will you, Jo? I hope Martha has remembered the roasted potatoes."

CHAPTER III.

The Simpsons were old friends of Mrs. Dobbs. Mr. Simpson was organist of the largest parish church in Oldchester, where his father had been organist before him. To this circumstance he owed his singular Christian name. The elder Simpson, whose musical enthusiasm had run all into one channel, insisted on naming his son Sebastian Bach. Some men would have felt this to be a disadvantage for the profession of organist and music-teacher, as involving a suggestion of ridicule. But Mr. Sebastian Bach Simpson was not apt to be diffident about any distinguishing characteristic of his own. His wife had been a governess, and still gave daily lessons in sundry respectable Oldchester families. By an arrangement begun during her late husband's lifetime, this couple came every Saturday evening to sup with Mrs. Dobbs, and to play a game of whist for penny points before the meal.

The two guests entered the parlour just as Mr. Weatherhead was lighting the candles.

"Dear me," exclaimed Mrs. Simpson, "are we too early? I had no idea! Surely the choir practice was not over earlier than usual, Bassy?"

She was a large stout woman of forty, with a pink-and-white complexion and filmy brown curls; and she wore spectacles. She had once been very slim and pretty, and still retained a certain girlishness of demeanour. It has been said that a man is as old as he feels, and a woman as old as she looks. Mrs. Simpson had innocently usurped the masculine privilege; and, not feeling herself to be either wiser or less trivial than she was at eighteen, had never thought of trying to bring her manners into harmony with her appearance. Her husband was a short, dark man, with quick black eyes, and thick, stubby, black hair. His voice was singularly rasping and dissonant, which seemed an unfortunate incongruity in a professor of music. Such as he was, however, his wife had a great admiration for him, and considered his talents to be remarkable. Her marriage, she was fond of saying, had been a love-match, and she had never got beyond the romantic stage of her attachment.

"Good evening, Mrs. Dobbs," said the organist, advancing to shake hands, and taking no notice of his wife's inquiry.

"How are you, Weatherhead? I suppose you were napping—having forty winks in the twilight, eh?"

"No, Mr. Weatherhead and I were chatting," said Mrs. Dobbs.

"Chatting in this kind of blind man's holiday, were you? I should have thought you could hardly see to talk!"

"See to talk! Oh, Bassy, what an expression! You do say the drollest things!" exclaimed Mrs. Simpson with a giggle. "Doesn't he, Mrs. Dobbs? Did you ever hear—?"

Mrs. Dobbs, for all reply, hospitably stirred the fire until it blazed, helped Mrs. Simpson to remove her bonnet and cloak, and placed her in a chair near her own. Mr. Simpson took his accustomed seat, and the four persons drew round the fire, whilst Martha, Mrs. Dobbs's middle-aged servant, set out a little card-table, and disposed the candles on it in two old-fashioned, spindle-shanked, silver candlesticks. It was all done according to long-established custom, which was seldom deviated from in any particular.

"And how are you, dear Mrs. Dobbs?" asked Mrs. Simpson, taking her hostess's hand between both her own. "And dear May—where's May?"

"May has been away from home on a visit since yesterday morning. She won't come back before Monday."

"And may one ask where she is? It is not, I presume, a Mystery of Udolpho!"

"She is at the Hadlows'."

"The Hadlows'? Canon Hadlow's?" cried Mrs. Simpson, clasping her hands with a gesture of amazement. Then she added rather inconsistently, "Well, I'm not surprised. I know they have lately taken a great deal of notice of her. Miss Hadlow and she having been at school together, of course created an intimacy which—ah, the friendships of early youth, where they are genuine, have a warmth, a charm—"

"Now, Amelia!" interposed her husband's rasping voice. (This ejaculation was his habitual manner of recalling Mrs. Simpson's attention to the matter in hand, whatever it might be; for the good lady's mind was discursive.) "If you'll be kind enough to leave off your nonsense, we can begin our game. Come and cut for partners."

An earnest whist player would have been outraged by the performances of the four persons who met weekly in Mrs. Dobbs's parlour. They chatted, they misdealt, they even revoked sometimes; and they overlooked each other's misdemeanours with unscrupulous laxity. In a word, they regarded the noble game of whist merely as a means and not as an end, and were scandalously bent on amusing themselves regardless of Hoyle. The only one of the party who had any pretensions to play tolerably was Mr. Weatherhead. But even his attention was always to be diverted from his cards by a new piece of gossip. And perhaps, it was as well that he did not take the game too much to heart—especially on the present occasion; for the fair Amelia fell to his lot as a partner, and her performances with the cards were calculated to drive a zealous player into a nervous fever.

The first hand or two proceeded in decorous silence. But by degrees the players began to talk, throwing out first detached sentences, and at last boldly entering into general conversation.

"Bassy had a great deal of trouble with the choir this evening," said Mrs. Simpson plaintively. "The sopranos were so inattentive! And inattention is so particularly—oh dear, I beg pardon, I have a diamond! Well, it does not much matter, for we couldn't have made the odd trick in any case."

"A nice business at Sheffield with those Trades Unions," said Mr. Weatherhead. "Some severe measures ought to be taken; but they won't be. That's what your precious Liberalism comes to!—Your lead, Simpson."

"Nonsense about Liberalism, Jo Weatherhead," replied Mrs. Dobbs. "I believe you'd like to accuse the Liberals of the bad weather. There!—Did you ever see such a hand? One trump! and that fell. Mrs. Simpson playing out her knave misled me."

"Oh, if you reckon on Amelia's having any sufficient motive for playing one card more than another—" exclaimed Amelia's husband. "Have you heard, Mrs. Dobbs, that Mr. Bransby is getting better?"

"What Bransby is that?" asked Mr. Weatherhead, thrusting his head forward inquiringly.

"Cadell and Bransby, Solicitors to the Dean and Chapter."

"Oh-o! He has been ill, then?"

"Very ill. But I hear he was pronounced out of danger on Wednesday."

"Is it not good news?" cried Mrs. Simpson. "Such a misfortune for his young family! I mean if he had died, you know."

"But I suppose he's a warm man, isn't he? Cadell and Bransby—it's a fine business, isn't it?" asked Mr. Weatherhead.

"It had need be," rejoined the organist, "to maintain that tribe of boys and girls, and an extravagant young wife into the bargain."

"Oh, Bassy, but they are such pretty children! And Mrs. Bransby is so truly elegant and interesting. All her bonnets come from Paris, I am told. And indeed there is a certain style—Eh? You don't mean to say that spades are trumps? What a disappointment! I thought I had all four honours."

This ingenuous speech might have called forth some remonstrance from Mrs. Simpson's partner, but that the latter was too much interested in the subject of the Bransbys to attend to it.

"The eldest son is provided for by his mother's fortune, isn't he?" he inquired.

"Well—'provided for;' I don't know that it is very much. But it was all tightly settled. Otherwise Bransby's second marriage would have been a greater misfortune for the young man than it is," replied the organist.

"I don't see that it is any misfortune at all," observed Mrs. Dobbs. "Theodore Bransby is quite well enough off for a young fellow. And why shouldn't his father marry again if he liked it?"

"He is an extremely gentleman-like young man, is Mr. Theodore Bransby," said Mrs. Simpson. "I have been imparting daily instruction to the younger children, and I saw him rather frequently when he was at home during the University vacation. He is now reading for the Bar, you know, and I believe—Was that your knave, Mr. Weatherhead? Really! Then I have thrown away my queen. However," smiling amiably, "one can but take the trick. I believe that Mr. Theodore Bransby means to go into Parliament later. There is really something of the statesman about him already, I think—a way of buttoning his coat to the chin, don't you know?"

"Is Theodore Bransby in Oldchester now?" asked Mrs. Dobbs, sorting her cards.

"Oh yes," replied Mr. Simpson. "I wonder you didn't know, for he is a great deal at Canon Hadlow's. They say he's making up to Miss Hadlow."

"O-ho! But there's Mrs. Hadlow's nephew, young Rivers," put in Mr. Weatherhead. "He's supposed to be dangling after his cousin, isn't he?"

"I should think young Rivers had better dangle after an employment that will give him bread and cheese. Miss Constance Hadlow won't have a penny."

"Oh, Bassy, but where there's real affection mercenary considerations must give way. True love—true love is above all!" As she uttered these words with great fervour, Mrs. Simpson flourished her arm enthusiastically, and in so doing swept off the table several coins which had served as counters to register her opponent's score. The silver discs rolled swiftly away into various inaccessible corners of the room, with the perversity usually observed in such cases. Fortunately the game had just come to an end, and Martha had announced that the supper was ready. This circumstance, and the fact that her husband was a winner, spared Mrs. Simpson a sharp reprimand.

Mr. Simpson uttered, indeed, a few sarcastic croaks. "Now, Amelia! There you go! Always up to some nonsense or other." But he watched Mr. Weatherhead and Martha as they crawled about on hands and knees to recover the missing shillings and sixpences, with considerable equanimity; merely observing that Amelia ought to be ashamed of herself for giving so much trouble.

When the supper was set on the table, three of the party, at least, were in high good humour, and disposed to enjoy it. Mr. Simpson had won, and was content. Mr. Weatherhead paid his losses without a murmur, conscious, no doubt, that they were due as much to his own wandering attention as to his partner's aberrations. As for Mrs. Simpson, the sweetness of her disposition was proof against far more souring circumstances than having spoiled Jo Weatherhead's game. She was not the least out of humour with him. Mrs. Dobbs alone was a little more silent and a little less genial than usual. The talk that evening with her old friend had awakened painful thoughts of the past and anxieties for the future. She very rarely mentioned her son-in-law's name, even to Mr. Weatherhead, who was thoroughly in her confidence; and, whenever she did speak of him, the result was invariably to irritate and depress her. However, her hospitable instincts roused her to shake off her cares in some degree, and to make her friends welcome to the fare set before them.

When the more substantial part of the supper was disposed of, and a jug of hot punch steamed on the board, Mrs. Simpson, delicately tapping with her teaspoon on the edge of her tumbler, observed, with an air at once penetrating and amiable—

"Well, I'm sure it will be very gratifying to Mrs. Dormer-Smith when she hears that dear May has been invited to the Hadlows'."

"H'm! I don't think Mrs. Dormer-Smith will lose her wits with joy," answered Mrs. Dobbs drily.

"No? Oh, but surely—! She must feel it agreeable that her niece should be noticed by persons of such eminent gentility."

Mrs. Dobbs would have dismissed the subject with a smile and a shake of the head, avoiding, as she always did, any discussion or even mention of her son-in-law's family; but Mr. Simpson interposed magisterially—

"If Mrs. Dormer-Smith isn't gratified, it must be because she is ignorant of the position held by Canon Hadlow's family in Oldchester."

Mrs. Dobbs faced about upon this, and said bluntly, "My dear good man, all the best society of Oldchester put together would seem mighty small beer to Mrs. Dormer-Smith."

"Oh, really!" returned Mr. Simpson, mortified and incredulous. "Such a very fine lady, is she? Well, 'Dormer-Smith' doesn't sound very aristocratic; but it may be, of course."

"Mrs. Dormer-Smith is a fine lady, and accustomed to mix with still finer ladies. It's no use shutting one's eyes to facts. If we won't look at them, we only bump up against them, because they're there, all the same. As to opinions, that's different. I suppose I needn't say anything about mine at this time of day. I'm a staunch Radical—always was, and always will be."

"Pooh, pooh! Call yourself a Radical!" said Mr. Weatherhead, laughing his peculiar laugh, which consisted of a series of guttural ho, ho, ho's. "You're convicted out of your own mouth of not being one. Whoever heard of a Radical that cared about facts?"

Mrs. Simpson put out her hand, and tapped him on the shoulder. "Now, now; that's very naughty of you," she exclaimed. "Politics are strictly forbidden on Saturday evenings by the ancient statutes of our society. Isn't it so, Mr. Dobbs? I appeal to the chair." And she threatened Mr. Weatherhead playfully with her forefinger, at the same time casting an arch look through her spectacles. Glasses are not favourable to any effective play of the eyes, and usually screen the most expressive of glances behind a ghastly glitter, void of all speculation. But of this consideration Mrs. Simpson was habitually oblivious. Then, by way of turning the conversation into more agreeable channels, she continued, "And, àpropos of May, dear Mrs. Dobbs, when did you last hear from her papa?"

This simple inquiry startled the company into absolute silence for a few moments. Mrs. Dobbs's resolute reserve on the subject of her son-in-law was so well known that none of her friends for several years past had ventured to mention him to her. Some refrained because they did not wish to hurt her; and many because they were afraid she might hurt them: for Mrs. Dobbs's uncompromising frankness of speech and force of character made her a hard hitter, when she did hit. But the specific levity of Mrs. Simpson's mind gave her a certain immunity from hard retorts—the immunity of a fly from a cannon ball. On the present occasion, however, she received no rebuke; for greatly to Jo Weatherhead's surprise, and somewhat to Mr. Simpson's, Mrs. Dobbs, after a brief pause, answered—

"I have not heard lately from Captain Cheffington. He is a bad correspondent. But we shall soon be obliged to communicate with each other. May is seventeen, and various arrangements will have to be made about her future."

"Goodness!" exclaimed Mrs. Simpson, clasping her hands. "You don't mean to say that May isn't to remain with you?"

"That will depend on what is agreed on in the family. May must take her place in the world as Miss Cheffington, you know, and not as my grand-daughter."

The Simpsons exchanged a glance of surprise. This was the first time they had heard Mrs. Dobbs assume any such position for her grandchild. Sebastian was inclined to resist her doing so now. But something in Mrs. Dobbs's manner checked him from expressing this feeling. It is generally found easier to criticize our friends' shortcomings when we are free from the disturbing element of their presence. The short remainder of the evening was passed in talking of other things. But on their way home Mr. and Mrs. Simpson discussed this new turn of affairs with some eagerness.

The organist considered that the notion of the Hadlows not being good enough company for the Dormer-Smiths was preposterous; and he feared that Mrs. Dobbs was giving herself airs. In reply to his wife's observations that Mrs. Dobbs was a "dear old soul," he pointed out that, dear and good though she might be, yet her husband had kept an ironmonger's shop, and publicly sold hardware therein behind his counter, to the knowledge of all Oldchester. This retort depended for its cogency on the understanding of an ellipsis; which, however, Mrs. Simpson was perfectly able to supply, for she answered immediately—

"Oh, I'm sure, Bassy, Mrs. Dobbs would never undervalue your position as a professional man. She knows very well that the Arts rank superior to trade."

On the other hand, when Mrs. Simpson proceeded to opine that if May were taken up by her father's family she would become quite a grand personage, Mr. Simpson declared, with a good deal of heat, that for his part he thought Mrs. Dobbs quite as good any day as the Cheffingtons, about whom nothing certain was known in Oldchester except that they were shabby in their dealings and "stuck-up" in their pretensions.

Mr. Weatherhead lingered behind the organist and his wife, to say a word to Mrs. Dobbs after their departure.

"I can tell you one thing, Sarah; what you said about May will be all over Oldchester by Monday."

"So I guess."

"O-ho! Then you mean it to be talked about?"

"I mean it to be known that May is to take her place in the world as Miss Cheffington."

"But is she? That's more than you can say, Sarah."

"I shall have a try for it, Jo."

Now whenever Mrs. Dobbs had said in that emphatic manner that she would "have a try" for anything, that thing, so far as Jo Weatherhead's experience went, had infallibly come to pass. But with all his faith in his old friend, he could not help doubting her success in the present case. He was eagerly curious to know how she intended to proceed; but Mrs. Dobbs refused to say any more on the subject, declaring that she must think things over quietly.

"I don't see it," said Mr. Weatherhead to himself, poking forward his nose, and pursing up his lips as he walked homeward. "Sarah Dobbs is a wonderful woman, but even she can't gather grapes from thorns. And in respect of justice or generosity—not to mention common honesty—I'm afraid all the Cheffingtons are rather thorny."

CHAPTER IV.

Among other features peculiar to itself, Oldchester possesses a quadrangular building with an inner cloister, commonly called College Quad. It is in the immediate neighbourhood of the cathedral, and is divided into small tenements inhabited by clergy forming part of the cathedral body. At the back of the houses on the south side of the quadrangle, pleasant gardens slope down towards the river Wend. The cloister is a very beautiful piece of Gothic work, with fretted roof and springing pillars. Peace and quiet reign within it. In summer there comes a sleepy sound of rooks from the Bishop's garden close at hand; and, towards sunrise and sunset, the chirp of innumerable sparrows mingled with the richer notes of thrush, blackbird, and nightingale in their season. At certain times of the day, too, the stillness is broken by the thrilling freshness of children's voices, as the scholars of the ancient Grammar School scatter themselves over the Cathedral Green, shouting and calling in the shrill silvery treble of boyhood. But these sounds are softened and subdued by distance and thick masonry before they penetrate within the precincts of College Quad. In autumn and winter there is a chill dampness on the greenish-gray paving-stones of the cloister, and the rain drips heavily from carven capitals into the resounding court. The very order and cleanliness of the place—its decorous, clerical, smooth-shaven air—seem sometimes under a watery sky, and when the winds are moaning and complaining, or thrumming like ghostly fingers on the fine resonant Gothic fret-work, to fill the mind with melancholy.

A rich contrasting note is seldom wanting:—firelight and the glimpse of a crimson curtain seen through lozenge-shaped window-panes; or an open door sending out a gush of warmth and spicy smells from the kitchen, and the sound of friendly voices. Yet even within doors there seems to be a haunting sense of the old, old times when hands long crumbled into dust built up that dainty cloister, and when patient monkish feet, long stilled for ever, paced its stones. It is not a wholly sad feeling. It may even give zest to the glance of living eyes, and the warm pressure of dear hands. But it has a peculiar pathos:—a pathos which, perhaps, is felt peculiarly by northern people, as the sad-sweet twilight belongs to northern climates, and which many of those, to the manner born, would not exchange for the unbroken garishness of golden-blue days and silver-blue nights.

The habitations on the south side of College Quad are considered the most desirable of all, by reason of the gardens before-mentioned running down to the Wend, although one or two houses on the west side may be a trifle larger. Canon Hadlow's family of three persons inhabited one of these coveted southern houses, and found it roomy enough for their needs; yet it was a small—a very small—dwelling. The front door opened on to the beautiful cloister. Immediately on entering the house you found yourself in a tiny entrance-hall, to the left of which a steep and narrow staircase of dark oak conducted to the one upper story. On the right, a massive oaken-door gave access to a long, low parlour, whose three latticed windows—darkened somewhat by a drooping fringe of jessamine and virginia-creeper—looked across the garden and the river to wide meadows. Opposite to the front door, a glass one, which in summer stood wide open all day long, led into the garden. In winter, swinging double-doors, covered with dark baize, shut out the cold air and the chill, damp mist which sometimes crept up from the river.

The exterior of the houses in College Quad was coeval with the Gothic cloister; within, the passing centuries had somewhat modified their aspect. The main features, however, were ancient, and most of the inhabitants had chosen to preserve this general air of antiquity. Only in some few cases had disastrous attempts at modernizing been made with paint and French wall-papers. It would have been needless to tell any Oldchester person that no such sacrilegious innovations deformed the fine oak beams and wainscoting in Canon Hadlow's house. There was a dark tone all through it, which, however, was not chill. It was rather the rich darkness of Rembrandt's shadows, which seem to have a latent glow in the heart of them. A deep red curtain here and there, or a well-worn Turkey carpet, with its kaleidoscope of subdued tints, relieved the general sombreness. Flowers in all manner of receptacles—from a precious old china punch-bowl to the cheapest of glass goblets—adorned every room in the house throughout the year. Even in winter there was ivy to be had, and red-berried holly, and the coral clusters of the mountain ash, and pale chrysanthemums. The garden furnished an ample supply of stocks, roses, carnations, holly-hocks, china asters, sweetwilliams, wallflowers, and the like old-fashioned blossoms with homely names. But as Mrs. Hadlow herself quaintly remarked, she cared more for the sight and smell of a flower than its sound.

One sacrifice the flowers cost; the Hadlows had no lawn-tennis ground. Mrs. Hadlow declared she could not spare the space. Her neighbours to the right and left boasted of lawns which, with their white lines, looked like tables chalked on the pavement for the popular street game of hop-scotch—and were very little bigger. But the Hadlows' garden was a mosaic of box-bordered flower-beds. Only quite at the lower end, where a clipped hedge divided it from a footpath on the river bank, there was a strip of green sward like a velvet carpet, spread completely across the garden. At one angle stood a yew-tree of fabulous age, and in its shadow were a garden bench and table, and a few rustic chairs. This was Mrs. Hadlow's drawing-room whenever the weather permitted her to be out-of-doors. There she sewed, and read, and received visits. The oak parlour, which served also as a dining-room, was the ordinary family living room. There was a small room called the study, lined with books from floor to ceiling; but drawing-room, properly so-called, there was none at all. Constance Hadlow was the only one of the family who regretted this circumstance. The canon was perfectly content with his abode. And as to Mrs. Hadlow, no one who valued her good opinion would have ventured to hint to her that her house lacked anything to make it convenient and delightful. An ill-advised stranger had once opined in her presence that the near neighbourhood of the river must make the south side of the College Quad damp and unhealthy during the autumn and winter, and Mrs. Hadlow's indignation had been boundless. That it was sometimes cold in College Quad she was willing to admit—just as it was sometimes cold on the Riviera or in Cairo. But that it could, under any circumstances, or for the shortest space of time, be damp, was what she would never be brought to acknowledge. As to the Wend, if any exhalations did arise from that gentle stream, they could not, she was sure, be unwholesome—above bridge. It was important to bear in mind this limitation, since below bridge, where the factories were, and where the poorer dwellings stood in crowded ranks, and the streets vibrated to the rumble of heavy waggons and tramway cars, the Wend must naturally incur such corruption of its good manners as came from evil communications. Mrs. Hadlow loved and admired Oldchester with enthusiasm. But Oldchester, in her mind, meant the cathedral and its immediate surroundings. Her admiration was bounded by the cathedral precincts; and, to judge from her words, so was her love also. But her heart was not to be imprisoned within any such confines. Prejudice might rule her speech, and warp her judgments, but her warm human sympathies went out towards those unfortunates who dwelt beyond the pale, even under the shadow of Bragg's factory chimney; nay, even in those vulgar suburban villas, with fine names, which were particularly abhorrent to Mrs. Hadlow's soul.

The sun shone brightly on a group of persons assembled in Mrs. Hadlow's garden on the Monday forenoon after Mrs. Dobbs's supper-party. It was a sun more bright than warm; and a little crisp breeze fluttered now and then among the scarlet and gold leaves of the virginia-creeper which draped the back of the house. Constance Hadlow, wrapped in a fleecy shawl, and sitting in a patch of sunshine outside the shadow of the yew-tree, declared it was "bitterly cold." Her opinion was evidently shared by a black-and-tan terrier that shivered convulsively at intervals with a sort of ostentation, as though to hint to the less sensitive bipeds that it was high time to retire to the shelter of a roof and the comforts of the hearthrug. Mrs. Hadlow's round, rosy face seemed to shed a glow around it like a terrestrial sun, as she beamed from behind a great basket piled with grey woollen socks belonging to the canon: which socks were never darned by any other than his wife's fingers. Her nephew, Owen Rivers, lounged on the bench beside her. Seated on a low chair, May Cheffington was winding a ball of grey worsted for the socks; and standing opposite to her, with his shoulder against the trunk of the yew-tree, was Mr. Theodore Bransby. This young gentleman had just said something which had startled the assembled company. He was not given to saying startling things. He would probably have pronounced it "bad form" to do so:—a phrase which, to his mind, carried with it the severest condemnation. He had merely observed, "You will all be sorry to lose Miss Cheffington, shall you not, Mrs. Hadlow?" quite unconscious of saying anything to cause surprise. Surprise, however, was plainly expressed on every countenance, including that of Miss Cheffington herself.

The fact was that rumour, speaking by the voices of Mr. and Mrs. Simpson, had already announced in Oldchester that May Cheffington was going away to live with her grand relations in London. The report had not yet penetrated College Quad, but it had been brought to the Bransbys' house that morning by Mrs. Simpson when she came to give her daily lesson to the children.

"Lose her! What do you mean?" asked Mrs. Hadlow.

"You're not going to be married, are you, May?" cried Miss Constance, dropping her parasol in order to look full at the other girl; while Mr. Rivers, on the other hand, raised himself on his elbow and stared at young Bransby.

May laughed and coloured at her friend's question. "Certainly not that I know of, Constance," she answered.

"Are you going away, then?"

"You must ask Mr. Bransby. He seems to know; I don't."

As she spoke, May turned a pair of bright hazel eyes full on the young gentleman in question, and smiled. The admixture of Dobbs blood with the noble strain of Cheffington had certainly not produced any physical deterioration of the race. Yet the dowager had been discontented with her grand-daughter's appearance, and had particularly lamented the absence of the Cheffington profile. Now the Cheffington profile was handsome enough in its way, in certain subjects and at a certain time of life; but with advancing years it was apt to resemble the profile of an owl: the nose being beaky, and the orbit of the eyes very large, with eyebrows nearly semi-circular; while the chin tended to disappear in hanging folds and creases of throat. The Cheffingtons, moreover, were sallow and dark-haired. May inherited her mother's fair skin and soft brown hair. Her slender young figure, not yet fully grown, was rather below than above the middle height. She had the healthy, though delicate, freshness of a field-flower; but, like the field-flower, she might easily pass unnoticed. There was nothing of high or dazzling beauty about May Cheffington, but she had that subtle attraction which does not always belong to beauty. A great many persons, however, thought she did not bear comparison with Constance Hadlow, her friend and schoolfellow. Besides a firm faith in her own beauty—which is a more powerful assistance to its recognition by others than is generally supposed—Miss Hadlow possessed a pair of fine dark eyes and eyebrows, a clear, pale skin, regular features, and white teeth. Those who were disposed to be critical observed that her face and head were rather too massive for her height; and that her figure, sufficiently plump at present, threatened to become too fat as she approached middle life. But at twenty years of age that would have appeared a very remote contingency to Constance Hadlow, supposing her to have ever thought about it. Although circumstances often prevented her from being dressed after the latest fashion, her hair—dark, wavy, and abundant—was always skilfully arranged in the prevalent mode, whatever that might be. It happened just then to be a becoming one to Miss Hadlow's head and face. The crimson colour of the shawl wrapped round her made a fine contrast with the creamy pallor of her skin and the vivid darkness of her eyes. Altogether, she looked handsome enough to excuse Owen Rivers for finding it difficult to remove himself from her society, supposing Mr. Simpson's statement to be true that the young man was "dangling after his cousin instead of minding his business."

Theodore Bransby, on being called upon to explain himself, answered that he understood Miss Cheffington was shortly going to London to reside with her aunt, Mrs. Dormer-Smith.

"Oh no, I'm not," said May promptly, before any one else could speak. "That is quite a mistake."

"Indeed!"

"Oh yes, indeed it is. I'm going to stay with granny."

"Indeed!" said Theodore Bransby once more. Then he added, "Are you quite sure? Because I had it from a person who had it from Mrs. Dobbs herself."

"From granny?" In her astonishment May let fall the ball of worsted. It rolled across the grass under the very nose of the toy terrier, who snapped at it, and then shivered more strongly than ever with an added sense of injury.

"Very likely nothing is positively settled yet," continued Theodore. "Mrs. Dobbs was speaking of family arrangements for the future."

"Then I suppose," said May, with an anxious look, "that she has heard from papa?"

"Yes, I believe so; something was said about a communication from Captain Cheffington."

There was a little pause. Then Mrs. Hadlow said, "Well, of course we shall be sorry to lose you, my dear, as Theodore says. But it is quite right that you should be amongst your own people, and be properly introduced."

"Granny is my own people," returned May in a low voice.

"Of course; and a most kind and excellent grandmother she is. But I mean—in short, since it is Mrs. Dobbs's own plan, we must suppose she thinks it best for you to go to town; and I must say I agree with her."

"It is obviously necessary," said young Bransby. "Miss Cheffington will have, of course, to be presented."

"Why, you look quite glum, May!" cried Constance laughing. "Oh, you little goose! I only wish I had the chance of going to town to be presented."

Owen Rivers, who had hitherto been silent, now addressed May, and asked her if she disliked her aunt.

"Dislike Aunt Pauline? Oh no; I don't dislike her at all. But I—I don't know her very well."

"I thought," said Bransby, "that you had been in the habit of staying with Mrs. Dormer-Smith during the school vacations?"

"No; before Grandmamma Cheffington died I used to go to Richmond, and I only saw Aunt Pauline now and then. Since that time I haven't seen her at all, for I've spent all my holidays with dear granny."

Constance began to question young Bransby as to who had given him the news about May's departure; what it was that had been said; whether the time of her going away were positively fixed; and so forth. May rose, and, under cover of picking up her ball of worsted, walked away out of earshot.

"Are you that phenomenon, a young lady devoid of curiosity, Miss Cheffington?" asked Owen Rivers, as she passed near him.

"Oh, there's nothing to be curious about," returned the girl, flushing a little. "Granny and I shall talk it all over together this evening. I need not trouble myself about what other people may say or guess."

Miss Hadlow had apparently forgotten that it was "bitterly cold:" for she continued to sit on the lawn talking with Theodore after the others had gone into the house. She moved at length from her seat at the summons of the luncheon-bell. Fox the terrier, more consistent, had availed himself of the breaking-up of the little party to hasten indoors and establish himself on the dining-room hearthrug:—a step which nothing but his unconquerable dislike to being alone, had prevented him from taking long ago.

When the two loiterers at length entered the dining-room, Mrs. Hadlow announced that May had gone home. Her grandmother had sent the servant for her a little earlier than usual, and May had refused to remain for luncheon. The young girl's absence gave an opportunity for discussing her and her prospects; and they were discussed accordingly, as the party sat at table.

Mrs. Hadlow expressed great satisfaction at hearing that May was to be received and accepted "as a Cheffington;" Constance inclined to think that May would not duly appreciate her good fortune; and Theodore Bransby observed stiffly, that Miss Cheffington's removal to town had always been inevitable, and that the date of it alone could have been matter for uncertainty to persons who knew anything of the Cheffington family.

"Well," said Rivers, "I suppose Constance is the only one of us here present who possesses that knowledge."

"No; I never knew much of them," answered his cousin. "I saw them occasionally when I was at school. Sometimes the dowager came down to stay at Brighton, and she used, now and then, to call for May in her carriage; but she never entered the doors. And once or twice Mrs. Dormer-Smith came. I remember we girls used to make game of old Mrs. Cheffington with her black wig and her airs."

"She was thoroughly grande dame, I believe," said Theodore Bransby.

"Very likely. The servants used to say she was dreadfully stingy, and call her an old cat. Mrs. Dormer-Smith had nice manners, and was always beautifully dressed."

"Your information is somewhat sketchy, my dear Constance; but no doubt the outline is correct as far as it goes," observed Rivers.

"Decidedly sketchy!" said Mrs. Hadlow, who was helping her guests to minced mutton.

"Miss Hadlow, however, is not the only one of us who knows anything about the Cheffingtons," said young Bransby, with his grave air.

"Oh, dear me, I had forgotten!" interposed Mrs. Hadlow, after a quick glance at the young man's face. "To be sure, Theodore has visited the family in town. The fact is, Theodore has been a stranger himself so long, that we have had no opportunity of hearing his report. Tell us what the Dormer-Smiths are like, Theodore, since you know them."

"Like? They are like people who move in the best society—like thoroughbred people," returned Theodore, drawing himself up, stiffly.

"Poor little May!" said Mrs. Hadlow, thoughtfully. "She's a sweet little thing. I hope they'll be kind to her."

"Do you know anything of Mrs. Dobbs, Aunt Jane?" asked Rivers. "I mean," he added, "of course, you know of her. But do you know her?"

"Oh yes. Once, many years ago, the canon had a tough battle with Mrs. Dobbs, when he was helping to canvas for the city member. We couldn't get her husband's vote for the right side. But he was a worthy man, and sold very good ironmongery. When Constance first asked leave to invite her schoolfellow here, I had an interview with Mrs. Dobbs. She came to the point at once. She said, 'Mrs. Hadlow, you need not be uneasy. My friends and equals are not yours; but neither are they my grand-daughter's. She belongs by her father's family to a different class. As for me, I am too old to make any mistakes about my place in the world, and too proud to wish to change it."

"Too proud!" repeated Bransby, with raised eyebrows.

"I thought it was very well said," answered Mrs. Hadlow. "I only wish all the people of her class had the same honest pride. But Mrs. Dobbs is a woman of great good sense, and of the highest integrity. All the same, of course, now that May is grown up, the girl's position in that house is too anomalous. Captain Cheffington no doubt feels that. He probably left his daughter there so long out of tenderness to Mrs. Dobbs's feelings; and perhaps also to help out the old lady's income. But now, naturally, it must come to an end. He can't sacrifice May's future. That is how I explain the state of the case; and it seems to me to be creditable to all concerned."

"At all events, it is creditable to Mrs. Dobbs, Aunt Jane," said Rivers.

"And why not, pray, to Captain Cheffington too?" asked Constance. "But Captain Cheffington has the misfortune to be born a gentleman, so, of course, Owen disapproves of him."

"Not at all, 'of course.' But I agree with you as to the misfortune—for the other gentlemen, at all events!"

"I think you're a little mistaken about Captain Cheffington, Rivers," said Theodore. "He's a friend of mine."

"In that case I'm very sorry," answered Owen drily.

Mrs. Hadlow here interposed, rising from the table with a show of cheerful bustle. "Come," said she, "you children must not loiter here all day. The canon comes home from Wendhurst by the three-forty train, and I am going to meet him; Constance has an engagement with the Burtons; and as for you two boys, I shall turn you out without ceremony."

The kind lady's intention had been to break off the discourse between the two young men, which threatened to become disagreeable. But as Bransby and Rivers walked away side by side through the fretted cloister of College Quad, the former, with a certain quiet doggedness which belonged to him, returned to the subject.

"You must understand," he said, "that I am not very intimate with Captain Cheffington; but I know him, and am his debtor for some courteous attentions. And I think you are a little—rash, if you don't mind my saying so, in condemning him."

"I don't at all mind your saying so."

"You see, there are a great many circumstances to be taken into account, in judging of Captain Cheffington's career. In the first place, there was his unfortunate marriage."

CHAPTER V.

When Augustus Cheffington had paid that sudden visit to his mother-in-law which resulted in leaving May on her hands, Theodore Bransby happened to be at home during a University vacation, and was flattered by Captain Cheffington's notice. The fact was that Augustus found himself greatly bored and out of his element in Oldchester, and was glad to accept a dinner or two from Mr. Bransby, the solicitor to the Dean and Chapter; for Mr. Bransby's port wine was unimpeachable. He had also condescended to play several games of billiards with Theodore upon a somewhat mangy old table in the Green Dragon Hotel; and to smoke that young gentleman's cigars without stint; and to hold forth about himself in the handsomest terms, pleased to be accepted, apparently, pretty much at his own valuation. Theodore Bransby was no fool. But he was young, and he had his illusions. These were not of a high-flown, ideal cast. He would have shrugged his shoulders at any one who should set up for philanthropy, or poetry, or socialism, or chivalry. But he was subdued by a display of nonchalant disdain for all the things and persons which he had been accustomed to look up to, from childhood. Mr. Bragg, the great tin-tack manufacturer, his father's wealthiest client, was dismissed by Augustus Cheffington in two words: "Damned snob!" and even the bishop he pronounced to be a "prosin' old prig," and spoke of the bishop's wife as "that vulgar fat woman." These indications of superiority, together with many references to the noble and honourable Castlecombes and Cheffingtons who composed Augustus's kith and kin, had greatly fascinated Theodore. And Augustus had completed his conquest over the young man by giving him a letter of introduction to his sister, Mrs. Dormer-Smith, which letter was delivered when young Bransby went to London to read for the Bar.

Although the brother and sister had parted not on the best terms with each other, yet Augustus had not hesitated to give the introduction. He believed that his sister would be willing to honour his recommendation by showing civilities which cost her nothing; and, moreover, he was quite indifferent (being then on the point of saying a long farewell to Oldchester) as to whether the Dormer-Smiths snubbed young Bransby or not. They did not snub him. Mrs. Dormer-Smith rather approved of his manners; and it was quite clear that he wanted neither for means nor friends. She was therefore inclined to receive him with something more than politeness. And, in justice to Pauline, it must be said that she was really glad of the opportunity to please her brother. She was not without fraternal sentiments; and she strongly felt that an introduction from a Cheffington to a Cheffington was not a document to be lightly dishonoured. As for Mr. Dormer-Smith, although his feelings towards his brother-in-law—never very cordial—had been exacerbated by having to pay the bill for the dowager's funeral expenses, yet his resentment had been to some degree soothed by Augustus's abrupt departure, and by his withdrawal of May from her aunt's house. For many years past the attachment of Augustus's relations for him had increased in direct proportion to the distance which divided him from them. In Belgium he was tolerated and pitied; had he gone to the Antipodes he would doubtless have been warmly sympathized with; and it might safely be prophesied that, when he should finally emigrate from this planet altogether, the surviving members of the family would be penetrated by a glow of affection.

"I think he's rather nice, Frederick," said Mrs. Dormer-Smith, with a little sigh of relief after young Bransby's first visit.

"We may be thankful," returned her husband, "that Augustus has sent us a possible person. One never can reckon on what he may choose to do."

"Mr. Bransby is quite possible. Indeed, I think he is nice. He shall have a card for my Thursdays."

In this way Theodore had been received by Mrs. Dormer-Smith, and had established himself in her good opinion on further acquaintance. "He was," she said, "so quiet and so safe." At this time May Cheffington was still at school, being maintained there, as has been recorded, by her grandmother Dobbs; and Pauline would occasionally speak of her niece to young Bransby. She always spoke kindly, though plaintively, of the girl, over whom there hung the shadow of the unfortunate marriage.

Theodore Bransby was an Oldchester person, and could not, therefore, be supposed to be ignorant of that lamentable event. The fact was, however, that he had never heard a word about it until he made Captain Cheffington's acquaintance in his native city. It had taken place before he was born; and, indeed, Oldchester had been less agitated by the marriage, even at the time when it happened, than any Cheffington or Castlecombe would have believed possible. But Pauline found young Bransby's sentiments on the subject all that they should be. No one could have expressed himself more shocked at the idea of a gentleman's marrying a person in Susan Dobbs's rank of life than did this solicitor's son. And Mrs. Dormer-Smith had not the least suspicion that he would have considered such a marriage quite as shocking a mésalliance for himself as for Captain Cheffington. "Misunderstanding" is used as a synonym for "discord;" but, perhaps, a great deal of social harmony depends on misunderstandings.

Theodore could not, of course, have the slightest personal interest in a schoolgirl whom he had never seen; but his sympathies were so entirely with the Cheffingtons on the question of the unfortunate marriage as to inspire him with an odd feeling of antagonism against Mrs. Dobbs, and a sense that she ought to be firmly kept in her place. He secretly thought Mrs. Dormer-Smith weakly indulgent in allowing Miss Cheffington to associate so freely with her grandmother, and was indignant at the idea of that plebeian exercising any authority over Lord Castlecombe's grand-niece. However, all that would doubtless come to an end when the girl left school, and was introduced into society under her aunt's protection. Theodore flattered himself that he thoroughly understood the position. As for Viscount Castlecombe, he certainly knew all about him—or, at least, what was chiefly worth knowing; for he had read about him in the Peerage.

Primed with this varied knowledge, young Bransby held forth to Owen Rivers as they walked together through College Quad, across the open green beyond it, and up to the house of Mr. Bransby, senior, in the Cathedral Close. Here they parted. Rivers declined a polite invitation from the other to enter, and pursued his way alone towards the High Street; and Bransby, as he waited for the door to be opened, stood looking after him for a few moments.

The two young men had known each other more or less all their lives, but theirs was a familiarity without real intimacy. The years had not made them more congenial to each other. People began to say that they were rivals in Constance Hadlow's good graces. But, whether this were so or not, the latent antagonism between them had existed long before they grew to be men. They had never quarrelled. The air is always still enough in a frost. They did not even know how much they disliked one another. As Theodore watched Owen's retreating figure, the thought uppermost in his mind was that his friend's shooting-coat was badly cut, and that he did not remember ever to have seen him wear gloves.

The home of Mr. Martin Bransby, of the old-established firm of Cadell and Bransby, was a luxurious one. The house was an ancient substantial stone building, with a spacious walled garden behind it, contiguous to the bishop's. The present occupant had made considerable additions to it. It is perhaps needless to say that he had been severely criticized for doing so, there being no point on which it is more difficult to content public opinion than the expenditure of one's own money. Several of Mr. Bransby's acquaintances were unable to reconcile themselves to the fact that he was not satisfied with that which had satisfied his father and grandfather (for Martin Bransby was the third of his family who had successively held that house and the business of solicitor to the Dean and Chapter of Oldchester). It would have been better, they opined, if, instead of building new rooms, he had saved his money to provide for the young family rising around him. If it were observed to this irreconcilable party that the presence of a numerous family necessitated more space to lodge them in than the original house afforded, they would triumphantly retort, "Very well, then, what business had Martin Bransby to marry a second time? Or, if he must marry, why did he choose a young girl without a penny instead of some person nearer his own age and with a little property?" Martin Bransby, however, marrying rather to please himself than to earn the approval of his friends, had chosen a remarkably pretty girl of twenty, a Miss Louisa Lutyer, of a good Shropshire family, whom he had met in London. They had now been married twelve years, during which time five children had been born to them, and they had lived together in the utmost harmony. Those persons who disapproved of the match (solely in Mr. Bransby's interests, of course) could find nothing worse to say than that Martin was absurdly in love with his wife, and treated her with weak indulgence. In short, the irreconcilables were driven, year by year, to put off the date at which their unfavourable judgments were to be corroborated by facts, much as sundry popular preachers have been compelled by circumstances over which they had no control, to postpone the end of the world.

Latterly they had had the mournful satisfaction of observing that Martin Bransby was looking far from well—harassed and aged. And when he was attacked by the severe illness which threatened his life, they solemnly hinted that the malady had been aggravated by anxiety about his young family; for although Martin had made, and was making, a great deal of money, yet, with three boys to put out in the world, two daughters to provide for, and an extravagant wife to maintain, even the excellent business of Cadell and Bransby must be somewhat strained to supply his needs.

At any rate, the evidences of wealth and comfort were as abundant as ever in the home which Theodore entered when he parted from his friend. There was plenty of solid furniture, dating from the dark ages before modern æstheticism had arisen to reform upholstery and teach us the original sinfulness of the prismatic colours. But these relics of the earlier part of the century were not to be found in the two spacious drawing-rooms, which had been arranged by the fashionablest of fashionable house-decorators from London. These rooms, together with a tiny cabinet behind them, which was styled "The Boudoir," were Mrs. Bransby's special domain. And here Theodore found her seated by the fireside. A book lay on her knees; but she was not reading it. She was resting in a position of complete repose, with her head leaning against the back of the chair, her hands carelessly crossed on her lap, and her feet supported on a cushion. She was enjoying the sense of bodily and mental rest which comes from the removal of a keen-edged anxiety; for during several weeks Mrs. Bransby had been the most devoted of sick-nurses, and had scarcely left her husband's room. But now the doctors had pronounced all danger to be over; the children's active feet and shrill voices were no longer hushed down by warning fingers; the housemaid sang over her brooms and dusters; and the mistress of the house had unpacked and put on a new "tea-gown," which had lain neglected for more than a fortnight in its brown-paper wrappings. From the golden-brown clusters of hair on her forehead to the tip of her dainty shoe every detail of her appearance was cared for minutely. Yet there was nothing of stiffness or affectation. She reminded one of an exquisitely-tended hothouse flower, and carried her beauty and her toilet with as perfect an air of unconscious refinement as the flower itself. Certainly Oldchester held no more lovely and graceful figure than Mrs. Bransby presented to the eyes of her stepson. Yet the eyes of her stepson rested on her with a glance of cool disapprobation. His manner of addressing her, however, was not more chilly than his manner of addressing most other persons—perhaps rather less so; and he was scrupulously polite.

"Did Hatch give a good account of my father this morning?" he asked, seating himself by the fire opposite to Mrs. Bransby.

"Excellent, thank goodness! He is to drive out on Wednesday, if the weather is favourable. I felt so soothed and comforted by Dr. Hatch's report, that I thought I would indulge myself with half an hour of perfect laziness," added Mrs. Bransby, with a deprecating glance at Theodore. She constantly reproved herself for assuming an apologetic attitude towards her stepson, but constantly recurred to it; she was so keenly conscious of his—always unexpressed—criticism.

"Mrs. Hadlow desired to send word that the canon means to call on my father this afternoon, if he is well enough to see him."

"Oh yes; a talk with Canon Hadlow will do him good." Then, after an instant's pause, Mrs. Bransby asked, "Have you been in College Quad, then?"

"I lunched with Mrs. Hadlow. Rivers was there; I parted from him just now. And Miss Cheffington."

"Oh, really? Mrs. Hadlow is very kind to that little May Cheffington."

Theodore made no answer, but looked stiffly at the fire.

Mrs. Bransby went on: "I saw her in the cathedral at afternoon service yesterday, with the Hadlows. It struck me she was growing quite pretty. Don't you think so?"

"I should not call her pretty—" began Theodore slowly.

Mrs. Bransby broke in: "Well, of course, she is eclipsed by Constance. Constance is so very handsome. But still—"

"I should not describe Miss Cheffington as pretty," pursued Theodore, in an inflexible kind of way. "She is something more than pretty. She looks thoroughbred."

"But that's exactly what she is not, isn't it?" exclaimed Mrs. Bransby impulsively.

"I am not sure that I apprehend you."

"I mean her mother was quite a common person, was she not?"

"A woman takes her husband's rank."

"Yes; but she doesn't inherit his ancestors. Besides, one really doesn't know much about the father, for that matter. To be sure, Simmy was making a great flourish about May's grand relations in London this morning. But then all poor dear Simmy's geese are swans." (The name of "Simmy" had been bestowed on Mrs. Simpson by the youngest little Bransby but one; and although the elder children were reproved for using it, the appellation had come to be that by which she was most familiarly known in the Bransby family.)

"Mrs. Simpson is a silly person, but her information happens, in this case, to be correct," returned Theodore. "The relations with whom Miss Cheffington is going to live in London are friends of mine."

"Oh! Then what Simmy said is true?" said Mrs. Bransby simply.

Theodore proceeded, with a scarcely perceptible hesitation, "I think you might invite Miss Cheffington here before she goes to town. I—I should be obliged to you for the opportunity of showing her some attention, in return for the Dormer-Smiths' kindness to me in London."

"Yes, I can ask the girl if you like," answered Mrs. Bransby, not quite as warmly as Theodore thought she ought to have answered such a suggestion from him; "but it will be rather stupid for her, I'm afraid. At the Hadlows' there is a young girl near her own age; but here, unless she likes to play with the children, I don't see how we are to amuse her."

"I did not contemplate Miss Cheffington's playing with the children. I meant that you should invite her to a dinner-party, or something of that sort."

"Invite May Cheffington to a dinner-party!" repeated Mrs. Bransby, opening her soft, brown eyes in astonishment.

"My father spoke of giving a dinner before I go back to the Temple, and he said he thought he should be well enough to see his friends by the end of next week."

"Yes. He talked of inviting the Pipers, and the Hadlows, and perhaps Mr. Bragg."

"Could you not include Miss Cheffington? Perhaps if you allowed me to see your list I might help to arrange it."

"Oh, I suppose one could; but wouldn't it seem a very strange thing to do?"

A little colour came into Theodore's pale fair face, and his chin grew visibly more rigid above his cravat, as he answered, "I don't know. But the social convenances are not to be measured by Oldchester's provincial ideas as to their strangeness. And—pardon me—I don't think you quite understand Miss Cheffington's position."

And then he entered on an explanation of the "position," much as he had explained it to Owen Rivers; with only such suppressions and variations (chiefly regarding the private history of Augustus Cheffington) as he thought the difference between his hearers demanded.

"Well, I'm sure if your father has no objection, I have none," said Mrs. Bransby at length. And so Theodore got his own way. It was a matter of course that he should get his own way so far as his step-mother was concerned. Mrs. Bransby had, indeed, successfully resisted him on many occasions; but always through the medium of her husband. If Theodore attacked her face to face, she never had the courage to oppose him. Not that in the present case she very much wished to oppose him. Nor, in truth, had their wills ever clashed seriously. But the secret consciousness of her weakness and timidity was mortifying: for Mrs. Bransby, although too gentle to fight, was not too gentle to wish she could fight. And after Theodore had left the room, she sat for some time imagining to herself various neat and pointed speeches which would doubtless have brought down her stepson's sententious, supercilious tone, if she had only had the presence of mind to utter them.

CHAPTER VI.

May Cheffington went back to her grand-mother's house, very eager to understand the origin of the rumours about herself which she had heard at the Hadlows'. Mrs. Dobbs had not calculated on this, and would have preferred to break the project to May herself, and in her own fashion. However, as it had been mentioned, she spoke of it openly. She merely cautioned her grand-daughter against rashly jumping at any conclusions: the future being very vague and unsettled.

"There's one conclusion I have jumped at, granny," said the girl, "and that is, that I don't mean to give you up for any aunts, or uncles, or cousins of them all. They are strangers to me, and I don't care a straw about them—how should I?—whilst you are—granny!"

"There is no question of giving me up, May. Perhaps I should not like that much better than you would. But if your father should think it right for you to stay for a while with his family, we mustn't oppose him. And I must tell you that I should think it right, too."

"Oh, if it's only staying 'for a while'—!"

"Well, at all events we needn't look beyond a 'while' and a short while, for the present."

Mrs. Dobbs found it more difficult than she had anticipated to put before May the prospect of being removed from Oldchester altogether, and, now that the idea of losing May out of her daily life fully presented itself, she felt a grip at the heart which frightened her. But she had one of those strong characters whose instinct it is to hide their wounds and suffer silently; and she resolutely put aside her own pain at this prospect—or rather, put it off to the solitary hours to come.

During the four years since her father had left her at Oldchester, May's life had been passed between her school at Brighton and her holidays in Oldchester. These had certainly been the happiest years she could remember in all her young life. Her grand-mother's house had been the first real home she had ever known. Her recollections of their life on the Continent were dim and melancholy. She remembered fragmentary scenes and incidents in certain dull Flemish towns; their strong-smelling gutters, their toppling gables, the carillons sounding high up in some ancient cathedral belfry. She had a vision of her mother's face, very pale and thin, with large bright eyes, and streaks of gray in the brown hair. May, as the youngest of Susan Cheffington's children, had come in for the worst part of their Continental life. The earlier years, when there was still some money to spend, and fewer debts to be run away from, had not been quite devoid of brightness. But poor little May's conscious observation had little to take note of at home save poverty, sickness, domestic dissensions, and frequent migrations from one shabby lodging to another. Then her mother died, and some six or eight months afterwards she was brought to England, and—Fate and the dowager so willing it—was sent to school to Mrs. Drax in Brighton. The choice of this school proved to be a very fortunate one for the little motherless stranger. And perhaps the credit of it ought fairly to be assigned rather to Destiny than the dowager. The latter would have selected a more fashionable, pretentious, and expensive establishment had she consulted merely her idea of what was becoming and suitable for Miss Miranda Cheffington. But she soon found out that whatever was paid for that young lady's schooling must, sooner or later, come out of her own pocket, and she therefore preferred to honour Mrs. Drax with her patronage, rather than Madame Liebrecht, who had been governess for years in a noble family, and was supposed to accept no pupil who could not show sixteen quarterings; or, of course, their equivalent in cash.

The choice made was, as has been said, very fortunate for May. Mrs. Drax had the manners of a gentlewoman, and more amiability than could perhaps have been reasonably expected to survive a long struggle with her special world—a world of parents and guardians, who held, for the most part, a liberal view of her duties and a niggardly one of her rights. Here little May Cheffington remained as a pupil for nearly eight years. During the first half of that time she sometimes spent her holidays with the dowager at Richmond, and sometimes in Brighton under the care of Mrs. Drax. She preferred the latter. Old Mrs. Cheffington did not treat the child with any active unkindness; but she showed her no tenderness. The little girl was usually left to the care of her grand-mother's maid—an elderly woman, to whom this young creature was merely an extra burthen not considered in her wages. The child passed many a lonely hour in the garden, or beside the dining-room fire with a book, unheeded. Her aunt Pauline she only saw at rare intervals. She had a confused sense of innocently causing much sorrow to Mrs. Dormer-Smith, who seemed always to be afflicted (why, May did not for several years understand) by the sight of her clothes; and who used to complain softly to the dowager that "the poor dear child was lamentably dressed." But, on the whole, she retained a rather agreeable impression of her aunt, as being pretty and gentle, and kissing her kindly when they met.

Then came the dowager's death, the sudden journey to Oldchester, and the first acquaintance with that unknown Grandmother Dobbs, whose very name she had heard uttered only in a reproachful tone by the dowager, or in a hushed voice by the dowager's elderly maid, speaking as one who names a hereditary malady. And to this taboo Grandmother Dobbs the neglected child soon gave the warm love of a very grateful and affectionate nature. May did not know or guess that she was a burthen on her grand-mother's means, nor would the knowledge have increased her gratitude at that time. It was the fostering affection which the child was thankful for. She nestled in it like a half-fledged bird in the warm shelter of the mother's wing. She was not timid or reserved by temperament; but the circumstances of her life had given her a certain repressed air. That disappeared now like hoar-frost in the sunshine. She was like a young plant whose growth had been arrested by a too chilly atmosphere. She burgeoned and bloomed into the natural joyousness of childhood, which needs, above all things, the warmth of love, and cannot be healthily nurtured by any artificial heat.

In her school there was no influence tending to diminish May's attachment to her grandmother, or her perfect contentment with the simple bourgeois home in Oldchester. Plain Mrs. Dobbs, who paid her bills punctually, and listened to reason, stood far higher in the schoolmistress's esteem than the Honourable Mrs. Cheffington, who was never contented, and required to be dunned for the payment of her just debts. As to her noble relations, May had no acquaintance with them, and never sighed to make it. She was ignorant of the very existence of many of them. When, at seventeen years of age, she was removed from school, she looked forward to living in the old house in Friar's Row, and she certainly desired no better home. Mrs. Drax, it has been said, had the manners of a gentlewoman, and she had not vulgarized May's natural refinement of mind by misdirecting her admiration towards ignoble things. The provincialisms in her grand-mother's speech, and the homely style of her grand-mother's household—although she clearly perceived both—neither shocked nor mortified May. On the other hand, she accepted it as a quite natural thing that she should be invited to Canon Hadlow's house as a guest on equal terms. As Mrs. Dobbs had said to Jo Weatherhead, May was very much of a child still, and understood nothing of the world. Her unquestioning acceptance of the situation as her grandmother presented it to her had something very child-like. She did not inquire how it came to pass that her aunt Pauline, who had taken very little notice of her during the past four years, should now desire to have her as an inmate of her home. She did not ask why her father, after so long a torpor on the subject, had suddenly awakened to the necessity of asserting his daughter's position in the world; neither did she, even in her private thoughts, reproach him for having delegated all the care and responsibility of her education to "granny." A healthy-minded young creature has deep well-springs of unquestioning faith in its parents, or those who stand in the place of parents.

But there was one person not so easily contented with the first statement offered; and that person was Mr. Joseph Weatherhead. Mr. Weatherhead was very fond of May, and admired her very much. His social and political theories ought logically to have made him regard her with peculiar interest and consideration as coming of such very blue blood—at least on one side of the house. But it so happened that these theories had nothing on earth to do with his attachment to May. That arose, firstly, from her being Sarah Dobbs's grandchild (Jo would have loved and championed any creature, biped or quadruped, that belonged to Sarah Dobbs), and, secondly, from her being very lovable. The poor man was often embarrassed by the conflict between his curiosity and his principles. His curiosity, which was as insatiable and omnivorous as the appetite of a pigeon, would have led him to cross-question May minutely about all she knew or guessed respecting her own future, and the probable behaviour of her father's family towards her; but his conscience told him that it would not be right to put doubts and suspicions into the girl's trusting young soul. Certainly he himself cherished many doubts and suspicions as to the future conduct of May's papa. He questioned Mrs. Dobbs, indeed; but there was neither sport nor exercise for his sharp inquisitiveness in that. When Mrs. Dobbs did not choose to answer him, she said so roundly, and there was an end. She had told him that she was in correspondence with Captain Cheffington, and that she believed he would share her views about his daughter. Jo, however, entertained a rooted disbelief as to Captain Cheffington's holding any "views" which had not himself for their supreme object.

"And this Mrs. Dormer-Smith, now, Sarah," said he. "What reason have you to suppose that she will be willing to take charge of her niece now, when she would have nothing to say to her before?"

"A pretty girl of seventeen is a different charge from a lanky child of twelve, Jo. Mrs. Dormer-Smith couldn't have taken a schoolgirl in short frocks out into the world with her."

"Humph! You don't know that she will take May out into the world with her?"

"I have written. I shall have an answer in a few days, I dare say. I don't expect matters to be settled like a flash of greased lightning, as Mr. Simpson says. There's a deal to be considered. Hold your tongue, now; here's May."

Similar conversations took place between them nearly every day. And when they were not interrupted by any external circumstance, Mrs. Dobbs would resolutely put an end to them by declining to pursue the subject.

One afternoon, about a week after May's return from her visit to the Hadlows', the young girl was seated at the old-fashioned square pianoforte, singing snatches of ballads in a fresh, untrained voice; Mr. Weatherhead had just taken his accustomed seat by the fireside; and Mrs. Dobbs was opposite to him in her own armchair, with the old tabby purring in the firelight at her feet, when Martha opened the parlour door softly, shut it quickly after her, and announced, with a slight tone of excitement in her usually quiet voice, that there was a gentleman in the passage asking for Miss May.

"For me, Martha?" exclaimed May, turning round at the sound of her own name, with one hand still on the keys of the pianoforte. "Who is he?"

"He said 'Miss Cheffington.' I don't know him, not by sight. But here's his card."

Mrs. Dobbs took the card from the servant, and put on her spectacles, bending down to read the name by the firelight. "Bun—Brun—oh, Bransby! Mr. Theodore Bransby. Ask the gentleman to walk in, Martha."

As Martha left the room, Mr. Weatherhead pointed to the door with one thumb, and whispered, "Wonder what he wants!" To which Mrs. Dobbs replied by lifting her shoulders and slightly shaking her head, as much as to say, "I'm sure I can't guess." The next moment Mr. Theodore Bransby was ushered into the parlour.

The room was rather dim, and Theodore did not immediately perceive May, who still sat at the piano. "Miss Cheffington?" he said interrogatively, with a stiff little gesture of the head towards Mrs. Dobbs, which might pass for a bow.

Mrs. Dobbs had risen from her chair, and now motioned her visitor to be seated. "My grand-daughter is here. Pray sit down, Mr. Theodore Bransby," she said. Then May got up, and came forward, and shook hands with him.

"I don't think you know my grandmother, Mrs. Dobbs," she said, presenting him.

Theodore, upon this, began to hold out his hand rather slowly; but, as Mrs. Dobbs made no answering gesture, but merely pointed again to a chair, he was fain to bow once more—a good deal more distinctly, this time—and to sit down with the sense of having received a little check.

"I hope I have not interrupted you, Miss Cheffington?" said he, clearing his throat and settling his chin in his shirt-collar. "You were singing."

"Oh no; you haven't interrupted me at all. And, even if you had, it wouldn't matter. My singing is not worth much."

"Pardon me if I decline to believe that. From some sounds which reached me through the door, I am sure you sing charmingly."

May laughed. "Ah," said she, "the other side of the door is the most favourable position for hearing me. I really don't know how to sing. Ask granny."

"No; May doesn't know how to sing," said Mrs. Dobbs quietly, but very decisively. (For she had caught an expression on Mr. Theodore Bransby's pale, smooth face, which seemed to wonder superciliously what on earth she could know about it.) Whereupon his pale, smooth eyebrows raised themselves a hair's breadth more, but he said nothing.

"My grandmother is a great judge of singing, you must know," went on May innocently. "She has heard all the best singers at the Oldchester Musical Festivals for years and years past, and she used to sing herself in the choruses of the oratorios."

"Oh, I see!" said Theodore, with a little contemptuous air of enlightenment.

Jo Weatherhead looked across at him uneasily. He had a half-formed suspicion that this young spark with the smooth, rather closely-cropped blonde head, severe shirt-collar, faultlessly-fitting coat, and slightly pedantic utterance, showed a tendency to treat Mrs. Dobbs with impertinence. But he checked the suspicion, for, he argued with himself, young Bransby had had the training of a gentleman. And what gentleman would be impertinent to a worthy and respected woman, and in her own house, too? He thought, as he looked at him, that Theodore bore very little resemblance to his father, Martin Bransby, who was altogether of a different and more massive type.

"You don't favour your father much, sir," said Jo blandly.

The young man turned his pale blue eyes upon him with a look studiously devoid of all expression. "I had the honour of knowing your worthy father well, some five-and-twenty—or it may be thirty—years ago."

Theodore, continuing to stare at him stonily, said, "Oh, really?" in a low monotone.

"Yes; I knew him in the way of business. He was a customer of mine when I was in the bookselling business at Brummagem, as we called it. Your father was, even at that time, very highly thought of by some of the leading legal luminaries. We had no assizes at Birmingham, as no doubt you're aware; but I used to go over to Warwick Assizes pretty reg'larly in those days, having some dealings there in the stationery line—which I afterwards gave up altogether, though that isn't to the point—and I used to frequent a good deal of legal company. Mr. Martin Bransby was thought a good deal of, among 'em, I can tell you, and was taken a great deal of notice of by some of the county families—quite the real old gentry," added Mr. Weatherhead, pursing up his mouth and nodding his head emphatically, like a man enforcing a statement which his hearers might reasonably hesitate to accept.

"Oh, how is Mr. Bransby?" asked May.

"Thanks; my father is going on very well indeed. He has driven out twice, and, in fact, is nearly himself again. He purposes asking some friends to dine with him next week. Indeed, that furnishes the object of my visit here. I—Mrs. Bransby—of course, you understand that my father's long illness has given her a great deal to do."

"Truly it must!" broke in Mrs. Dobbs, thinking at once sympathetically of the wife and mother threatened with so cruel a bereavement, and now almost suddenly relieved from overwhelming anxiety. "I'm sure most folks in Oldchester have been feeling greatly for Mrs. Bransby."

"And so," continued Theodore, addressing himself exclusively to May, "she has not really been—been able to see as much of you as she would have liked, Miss Cheffington."

May looked at him in surprise. "Why of course?" said she. "Mrs. Bransby hasn't been thinking about me! How should she?"

"That is the reason—I mean my father's illness, and all the occupations resulting from it—which has induced Mrs. Bransby to make me her ambassador on this occasion."

As he spoke, Theodore took a little note from his pocket-book, and handed it to May. She glanced at it, and exclaimed with open astonishment, "It's an invitation to dinner! Look, granny!"

Mr. Weatherhead poked forward his head to see. It was, in fact, a formal card requesting the pleasure of Miss Cheffington's company at dinner on the following Saturday. Mrs. Dobbs once more put on her spectacles and read the card.

"I hope you will be disengaged," said Theodore, severely ignoring "granny."

"Oh, I couldn't go to a grand dinner-party. It would be ridiculous!"

"May! That's not a gracious fashion of receiving an invitation, anyhow," said Mrs. Dobbs, smiling a little.

"It's very kind indeed of Mr. and Mrs. Bransby, but I would much rather not, please," said May, endeavouring to amend her phrase.

"Oh, that's dreadfully cruel, Miss Cheffington!"

"You don't think I ought to go, do you, granny?"

"That," replied Mrs. Dobbs, "depends on circumstances."

"I assure you," said Theodore, turning round with his most imposing air, "that it would be quite proper for Miss Cheffington to accept the invitation. I should certainly not urge her to do so unless that were the case."

Jo Weatherhead's suspicions as to this young spark's tendency to impertinence were rather vividly revived by this speech, and his forehead flushed as dark a red as his nose. But Mrs. Dobbs, looking at Theodore's fair young face made up into an expression of solemn importance, smiled a broad smile of motherly toleration, and answered in a soothing tone—

"No, no; to be sure, you mean to do what's right and proper; only young folks don't look at everything as has to be considered. But youth has the best of it in so many ways, it can afford to be not quite so wise as its elders."

This glimpse of himself, as Mrs. Dobbs saw him, was so totally unexpected as completely to dumfounder Theodore for a moment. Never, since he left off round jackets, had he been so addressed: for the behaviour of our acquaintances towards us in daily life is generally modified by their idea of what we think of ourselves.

"I—I can assure you," he stammered; and then stopped, at a loss for words, in most unaccustomed embarrassment.

"There, there, we ain't bound to say yes or no all in a minute," pursued Mrs. Dobbs. "Any way, we couldn't think of making you postman. That's all very well for your step-mother, of course; but May must send her answer in a proper way. Meanwhile, will you stay and have a cup of tea, Mr. Bransby? It's just our teatime. The tray will be here in a minute."

Theodore had risen as if to go. He now stood hesitating, and looking at May, who certainly gave no answering look of encouragement. She wanted him gone, that she might "talk over" the invitation with her grandmother.

With a pleasant clinking sound, Martha now brought in the tea-tray; and in another minute had fetched the kettle and placed it on the hob, where, after a brief interval of wheezing and sputtering, consequent on its sudden removal from the kitchen fire, it resumed its gurgling sound, and made itself cheerfully at home.

If Mrs. Dobbs had urged him by another word,—if she had shown by any look or tone that she thought it would be a condescension in him to remain, Theodore would have refused. But she began placidly to scoop out the tea from the caddy, and awaited his reply with unfeigned equanimity. There was an unacknowledged feeling in his heart that, to go away then and so, would be to make a flat kind of exit disagreeable to think of. He would like to leave this obtuse old woman impressed with a sense of his superiority; and apparently it would still require some little time before that impression was made.

"Thanks," he said. "If I am not disturbing you—"

"Dear no! How could it disturb me? Martha, bring another cup and saucer."

And then Theodore, laying aside his hat and gloves, drew a chair up to the table and accepted the proffered hospitality.

Having found the method of supercilious reserve rather a failure, the young man now adopted a different treatment for the purpose of awaking Mrs. Dobbs, and that objectionably familiar person with the red nose, to a sense of his social distinction and general merits. He talked—not volubly, indeed: for that would have been out of his power, even had he wished it, but he talked—in a succession of short speeches, beginning for the most part with "I." His efforts were not, however, exclusively aimed at Mrs. Dobbs and Jo Weatherhead. He watched May a good deal, and spoke to her of the Dormer-Smiths as though that were a topic between themselves, from which the profane vulgar (especially profane ex-booksellers, with red noses) were necessarily excluded. As the others said very little—with the exception of an occasional question from Jo Weatherhead—Theodore's talk assumed the form of a monologue spoken to a dull audience.

He was conscious, as he walked away from Friar's Row, of being a little surprised at his own conversational efforts, and half-repentant of his condescension. He had been obliged to take his leave without obtaining any definite answer to the dinner invitation. But, perhaps, the feeling uppermost in his mind was irritation at May's perfectly simple acceptance of her position as Mrs. Dobbs's grand-daughter, and her perfectly filial attachment to her grandmother. "It is really too bad! Cheffington ought never to have allowed his daughter to be got hold of by those people. Mrs. Dormer-Smith cannot have the least idea what sort of a milieu her niece lives in!" he said to himself.

The worst was that May was so evidently contented! If she had been at all distressed by her surroundings, Theodore could have better borne to see her there.

CHAPTER VII.

Persons like the Simpsons, who knew Mrs. Dobbs intimately, allowed her to have a strong judgment, and asserted her to have a still stronger will. She was far too bent on her own way ever to take advice, they said. It certainly did not happen that she took theirs. But Mrs. Dobbs's judgment was stronger than they knew. It was strong enough to show her on what points other people were likely to know better than she did. She would undoubtedly have followed Amelia Simpson's counsels as to the best way of dressing the hair in filmy ringlets—if she had chanced to require that information.

On the morning after Theodore Bransby's visit to her house, Mrs. Dobbs put on her bonnet and set off betimes to College Quad. There she had an interview with Mrs. Hadlow, who, it appeared, was going to the Bransbys' dinner-party, and willingly promised to take charge of May.

"It seemed to me it wouldn't be the right thing for my grand-daughter to go alone to a regular formal party," said Mrs. Dobbs. "But, as I don't pretend to be much of an authority on such matters, I ventured to ask you to tell me."

"Of course you were quite right, Mrs. Dobbs."

"And you think she had better accept the invitation? She doesn't much want to do so herself, being shy of going amongst strangers. But, to be sure, if she may be under your wing, and in company with Miss Hadlow, that would make a vast difference."

"Oh yes, let her go, Mrs. Dobbs. Sooner or later she will have to go into the world, and it may be well to begin amongst people she is used to. Is it true that she is to go to her aunt's house in London very soon?"

"Nothing is settled yet. If there had been, you and Canon Hadlow should have been the first to know it—as it would be only my duty to tell you, after all your kindness to the child. Nothing is settled. But I am in favour of her going myself."

"You take the sensible view, Mrs. Dobbs, as I think you always do—except at election time," added Mrs. Hadlow, smiling.

The elder woman smiled back, with a little resolute setting of the lips, and begged her best respects to the canon as she took her leave. The canon was a great favourite with Mrs. Dobbs; and, on his part, their political struggle in that long past election had inspired him with a British respect for his adversary's pluck and fair play.

The prospect of going with Mrs. Hadlow and Constance greatly reconciled May to the idea of the dinner-party. But she did not look forward to it with anticipations of enjoyment.

"I would much rather dine in the nursery with the children," she said, unconsciously echoing Mrs. Bransby's suggestion.

Mr. Weatherhead, who was present, took her up on this, and said, "Why, now, May, you will enjoy being in good society! Mr. Bransby is a very agreeable man, and used to some of the best company in the county. Mrs. Bransby, too, is very pleasant and very pretty; a Miss Lutyer she was, a regular beauty, and belonging to a good old Shropshire family. And young Theodore—" Jo Weatherhead pausing here, and hesitating for a moment, May broke in, "Come now, Uncle Jo," she exclaimed, "you can't say that he's pretty or pleasant!"

"He's not bad-looking," returned Mr. Weatherhead, rather doubtfully. "Though, to be sure, he isn't so fine a man as his father."

"No; this lad is like his mother's family," said Mrs. Dobbs. "I remember his grandfather and grandmother very well."

"Do you? Do you, Sarah? Who were they? What sort of people, now, eh?"

"Common sort of people; Rabbitt, their name was. Old Rabbitt kept the Castlecombe Arms, a roadside inn over towards Gloucester way. He ran a coach between his own market-town and Gloucester before the branch railway was made, and they say he did a good deal of money-lending; any way, he scraped together a goodish bit, and his wife came in for a slice of luck by a legacy. So altogether their daughter—the first Mrs. Martin Bransby that was—had a nice fortune of her own. She was sent to a good school and well educated, and she was a very good sort of girl; but she had just the same smooth, light hair, and smooth, pale face as this young Theodore. Martin Bransby had money with his first wife—he's got beauty with his second."

"O-ho!" exclaimed Jo Weatherhead, eager and attentive. "Rabbitt, eh? I never knew before who the first Mrs. Bransby was."

"Not a many folks in Oldchester now do know. I happened to know from being often over at Gloucester, visiting Dobbs's family, when I was a girl. Many a day we've driven past the Castlecombe Arms in the chaise. Dear, dear, how far off it all seems, and yet so plain and distinct! I couldn't help thinking of those old times when the lad was here the other day; he has such a look of old Rabbitt!"

Thus Mrs. Dobbs, rather dreamily, with her eyes fixed on the opposite houses of Friar's Row—or as much of them as could be seen above a wire window-blind—and her fingers mechanically busy with her knitting. But she saw neither the quaint gables nor the gray stone-walls. Her mind was transported into the past. She was bowling along a smooth highroad in an old-fashioned chaise. A girl friend sat in the little seat behind her, and leaned over her shoulder from time to time to whisper some saucy joke. Beside her was the girl-friend's brother, young Isaac Dobbs:—A personable young fellow, who drove the old pony humanely, and seemed in no hurry to get home to Gloucester. She could feel the moist, sweet air of a showery summer evening on her cheek, and smell the scent of a branch of sweetbriar which Isaac had gallantly cut for her from the hedge.

Theodore Bransby did not guess that Mrs. Dobbs had treated him with forbearance and indulgence; still less did he imagine that the forbearance and indulgence had been due to reminiscences of her girlhood, wherein his maternal grandfather figured as "Old Rabbit."

The question of May's dress for the dinner-party gave rise to no debate. Mrs. Dobbs had been brought up in the faith that the proper garb for a young girl on all festive occasions was white muslin; and in white muslin May was arrayed accordingly. The delicate fairness of her arms and neck was not marred by the trying juxtaposition of that dead white material. It served only to give value to the soft flesh tints, and to the sunny brownness of her hair. When she had driven off in the roomy old fly with Mrs. Hadlow and the canon and Constance, who called to fetch her, Mrs. Dobbs and Mr. Weatherhead agreed that she looked lovely, and must excite general admiration. But the truth was that May's appearance did not seem to dazzle anybody. Mrs. Hadlow gave her a comprehensive and approving glance when she took her cloak off in the well-lighted hall of Mr. Bransby's house, and said, "Very neat. Very nice. Couldn't be better, May." Canon Hadlow—a white-haired venerable figure, with the mildest of blue eyes, and a sensitive mouth—smiled on her, and nodded in confirmation of his wife's verdict. Constance, brilliant in amber, with damask roses at her breast and in her hair, thought her friend looked very school-girlish, and wanting in style. But she had the good-nature to pay the one compliment which she sincerely thought was merited, and to say, "Your complexion stands even that blue-white book muslin, May. I should look absolutely mahogany-coloured in it!"

May felt somewhat excited and nervous as she followed Mrs. Hadlow up the softly carpeted stairs to the drawing-room. But she had a wholesome conviction of her own unimportance on this occasion, and comforted herself with the hope of being left to look on without more notice from any one than mere courtesy demanded. Her first impression was one of eager admiration; for just within the drawing-room door stood Mrs. Bransby, looking radiantly handsome. May thought her the loveliest person she had ever beheld; and her dress struck even May's inexperienced eyes as being supremely elegant. Constance Hadlow's attire, with its unrelieved breadth of bright colour and its stiff outline, suddenly appeared as crude as a cheap chromo-lithograph beside a Venetian masterpiece. Behind his wife, seated in an easy-chair, was Martin Bransby, a fine, powerfully built man of sixty, with dark eyes and eyebrows, and a shock of grizzled hair. His naturally ruddy complexion was pallid from recent illness, and the lines under his eyes and round his mouth had deepened perceptibly during the last two months. Theodore stood near his father, stiffly upright, and with a cravat and shirt-front so faultlessly smooth and white as to look as though they had been cast in plaster of Paris. Standing with his back to the fire, was Dr. Hatch:—a familiar figure to May, as to most eyes in Oldchester. He was a short man, rather too broad for his height; with benevolent brown eyes, a wide, low forehead, and a wide, firm mouth, singularly expressive of humour when he smiled. No other guest had arrived when the Hadlows entered the drawing-room.

After the first greetings, the party fell into little groups: the canon and Mr. Bransby, who were very old friends, conversing together in a low voice, whilst Theodore advanced to entertain Mrs. Hadlow with grave politeness, and Constance made a minute and admiring inspection of Mrs. Bransby's dress.

May thus found herself a little apart from the rest, and sat down in a corner half hidden by the protruding mantelpiece of carved oak, which rose nearly to the ceiling; an elaborate erection of richly carved pillars, and shelves and niches holding blue-and-white china, in the most approved style.

"Well, Miss May, and how are you?" asked Dr. Hatch, moving a little nearer to her, as he stood on the hearthrug.

"Quite well, thank you, Dr. Hatch," said May, looking up with her bright young smile.

"That's right! But don't mention to any member of the Faculty that I said so. There's a professional etiquette in these matters; and I shouldn't like to be quoted as having given any encouragement to rude health."

"I'll take care," returned May, falling into his humour, and assuming a grave look. "And I will always bear witness for you that you gave me some very nasty medicine when I had the measles, Dr. Hatch. I'm sure the other doctors would approve of that, wouldn't they?"

"Nice child," murmured Dr. Hatch. "Understands a joke. It would be as much as my practice is worth to talk in that way to some young ladies I could mention. Well, and so this is your first entrance into the gay and festive scene, eh?"

"Yes; I have never been to a regular dinner-party before. I am so glad Mr. Bransby is quite well again," said May, looking across the room at their host.

"Are you? Well, I believe you are glad. Yes; it is much to be desired that he should be quite well again." Dr. Hatch's eyes had followed the girl's, and rested on Martin Bransby with a thoughtful look. Then, after a minute's pause, he went on: "Now, as you are not quite familiar here, I'll give you a map of the country, as the French say. Do you know who that is who has just come in? No? That is Mr. Bragg. He makes millions and billions of tin-tacks every week. You've heard of him, of course?" May nodded. "Of course you have. Couldn't live long in Oldchester without hearing of Mr. Bragg. That handsome, elderly man, now bowing to Mrs. Bransby, is Major Mitton, of the Engineers. Ever hear of him? Ah, well; I suppose not. He's a very good-natured, kindly gentleman, and an excellent soldier, who distinguished himself greatly in the Crimea. But no one will ever hear him say a word about that. What he is proud of is his reputation as an amateur actor. I have known more reprehensible vanities. Ah, and here come the Pipers, Miss Polly and Miss Patty; and I think that makes up our number."

Dr. Hatch did not think of asking May whether she had ever heard of the Miss Pipers. The fact was she had heard of them very often. They were Oldchester celebrities quite as much as Mr. Bragg was. But their fame had not extended beyond Oldchester; whereas Bragg's tin-tacks were daily hammered into the consciousness of the civilized world.

Miss Mary and Miss Martha Piper (invariably called Polly and Patty) were old maids between fifty and sixty years old. They were not rich; they had never been handsome; they were not, even in the opinion of their most partial friends, brilliantly clever. What, then, was the cause of the distinction they undoubtedly enjoyed in Oldchester society? The cause was Miss Polly Piper's musical talent—or at least her reputation for musical talent, which, for social purposes, was the same thing. Miss Piper had once upon a time, no matter how many years ago, composed an oratorio, and offered it to the Committee of a great Musical Festival, for performance. It was not accepted—for reasons which Miss Piper was at no loss to perceive. The reader is implored not to conclude rashly that the oratorio was rejected because it failed to reach the requisite high standard. Miss Piper knew a great deal better than that. She had been accustomed to mix with the musical world from an early age. Her father, an amiable Oldchester clergyman, rector of the church in which Mr. Sebastian Bach Simpson was organist, was considered the best amateur violoncello player in the Midland Counties. When the great music meeting brought vocal and instrumental artists to Oldchester, the Reverend Reuben Piper's house was always open to several of them; and Miss Polly had poured out tea for more than one great English tenor, great German basso, and great Scandinavian soprano. So that, as she often said, she was clearly quite behind the scenes of the artistic world, and thoroughly understood its intrigues, its ambitions, and its jealousies. Thus she was less mortified and discouraged by the rejection of her oratorio than she would have been had she supposed it due to honest disapproval. The work, which was entitled "Esther," was played and sung, however;—not indeed by the great English tenor, German basso, and Scandinavian soprano, but by very competent performers. It was performed in the large room in Oldchester, used for concerts and lectures, and called Mercers' Hall. Admission was by invitation, and the hall was quite full, which, as Miss Patty triumphantly observed, was a very gratifying tribute on the part of the town and county. Miss Polly did not conduct her own music. Ladies had not yet wielded the conductor's bâton in those days. But she sat in a front row, with her father on one side of her and her sister Patty on the other, and bowed her acknowledgments to the executants at the end of each piece.

It was a great day for the Piper family, and that one solitary fact (for the oratorio was never repeated) flavoured the rest of their lives with an odour of artistic glory, as one Tonquin bean will perfume a whole chest full of miscellaneous articles. Truly, the triumph was not cheap. The rehearsals and the performance had to be paid for, and it was said at the time that the Reverend Reuben had been obliged to sell some excellent Canal Shares in order to meet the expenses, and had thereby diminished his income by so many pounds sterling for evermore. But at least the expenditure purchased a great deal of happiness; and that is more than can be said of most investments which the world would consider wiser. From that day forth, Miss Polly held the position of a musical authority in certain circles. Long after a younger generation had grown up, to whom that famous performance of "Esther" was as vague an historical fact as the Heptarchy, people continued to speak of Miss Polly Piper as a successful composer. The lives of the two sisters were shaped by this tradition. They went every year to London for a month during the season; and, for a longer or shorter time, to some Continental city,—Leipsic, Frankfort, or Brussels: once, even, as far as Vienna,—whence they came back bringing with them the latest dicta in musical fashions, just as Mrs. Clarkson, the chief Oldchester milliner, announced every year her return from Paris with a large and varied assortment of bonnets in the newest styles. It has been written that "they" brought back with them the newest dicta on musical matters; but it must not be supposed that Miss Patty set up to interpret the law on such points. She was, as to things musical, merely her sister's echo and mouthpiece. But sincerity, that best salt for all human communications, preserved Miss Patty's subservience from any taint of humbug. However extravagant might be her estimate of Polly's artistic gifts and attainments, you could not doubt that it was genuine.

These circumstances were, broadly speaking, known to every one present. But May was acquainted with another aspect of the legend of Miss Piper's oratorio: a seamy side which the poor good lady did not even suspect. That famous oratorio had been a fertile source of mirth at the time to all the performers engaged in it. There were all sorts of stories current as to the amazing things Miss Piper did with her instrumentation: the impossible efforts she expected from the "wind," and the anomalous sounds she elicited from the "wood." These were retailed with much gusto by Jo Weatherhead, who, in virtue of a high nasal voice, and a power (common enough in those parts) of reading music at sight, had sung with the tenors through many a Festival chorus, and known many professional musicians during his sojourn in Birmingham. One favourite anecdote was of a trombone player who at rehearsal, in the very climax and stress of the overture, when he was to have come in with a powerful effect, stretched out his arm at full length, and produced the most hideous and unearthly noise ever heard; and who, on being rebuked by the conductor, handed up his part for inspection, observing, amid the unrestrained laughter of the band, that that was the nearest he could come to the note Miss Piper had written for him, which was some half octave below the usual compass of his instrument. Of this, and many another similar story, Miss Piper and Miss Piper's friends knew nothing. But May, remembering them, looked at the two old ladies as they marched into the room with an interest not so wholly reverential as might have been wished.

They were both short, fat, snub-nosed little women, with wide smiling mouths, and double chins. Miss Patty was rather shorter, rather fatter, and rather more snub-nosed than her gifted sister. But the chief difference between the two, which struck one at first sight, was that whereas Miss Piper's own grey locks were disposed in a thick kind of curl, like a plethoric sausage, on each side of her face, Miss Patty wore a pale, gingerbread-coloured wig. Why, having all the wigmaker's stores to choose from, she should have chosen just that particular hue, May secretly wondered as she looked at her. But so it was. And if she had worn a blue wig, it could scarcely have been more innocent of any attempt to deceive the beholder. Both ladies wore good substantial silk gowns, and little lace caps with artificial flowers in them. But the remarkable feature in their attire was the extraordinary number of chains, beads, and bracelets with which they had festooned themselves. And, moreover, these were of a severely mineralogical character. Round Miss Patty's fat, deeply-creased throat, May counted three necklaces:—One of coral, one of cornelian, and the third a long string of grey pebble beads which dangled nearly to her waist. Miss Polly wore—besides a variety of other nondescript adornments which rattled and jingled as she moved—a set of ornaments made apparently of red marble, cut into polygonal fragments of irregular length. Their rings too, which were numerous, seemed to be composed for the most part of building materials; and each sister wore a mosaic brooch which looked, May thought, like a bit out of the tesselated pavement of the smart new Corn Exchange in the High Street.

It did not take that young lady's quick perception long to make all the foregoing observations. Indeed, she had completed them within the minute and a half which elapsed between the Miss Pipers' arrival, and the announcement of dinner.

CHAPTER VIII.

The order of the procession to the dining-room had been pre-arranged not without some difficulty. Mrs. Bransby had pointed out to Theodore that his whim of inviting Miss Cheffington must cause a solecism somewhere in marshalling their guests.

"Constance will, of course, expect you to take her," said Mrs. Bransby, "and then what is to be done with little Miss Cheffington? I really think I had better invite two more people, and get some young man to take her in to dinner. Perhaps Mr. Rivers would come."

But Theodore utterly opposed this suggestion, and said that the simple and obvious course was for him to give his arm to Miss Cheffington, and for Dr. Hatch to escort Miss Hadlow.

"Oh, well, if you don't mind," said Mrs. Bransby, looking a little surprised. And so it was settled. But at the last moment, in arranging her table and disposing the cards with the guest's name before each cover, Mrs. Bransby found that it would be necessary, for the sake of symmetrically alternating a lady and gentleman, to divide one couple, and place them on opposite sides of the table. She decided that Dr. Hatch and Miss Hadlow would endure this sort of divorce with equanimity; and thus it came to pass that when Theodore took his seat at table he found himself in the enviable and unexpected position of sitting between the two young ladies of the party—Constance and May.

Mr. Bransby led out Mrs. Hadlow, the hostess bringing up the rear with Canon Hadlow. Major Mitton had the honour of escorting Miss Piper, while Miss Patty fell to Mr. Bragg. There was, as is usual on such occasions, very little conversation while the soup and fish were being eaten. Miss Piper, indeed, who was constitutionally loquacious, talked all the while to Major Mitton, though in a comparatively low tone of voice; but the rest of the company devoted themselves mainly to their plates; or at least said only a fragmentary sentence now and then. But by degrees the desultory talk swelled into a continuous murmur, across which bursts of laughter were wafted at intervals. May had the satisfaction she had hoped for, of being allowed to be quiet; for her neighbour on the one hand was the canon, who contented himself with smiling on her silently, whilst Theodore was greatly occupied by his neighbour, Miss Hadlow. Being seated between him and Major Mitton, she monopolized the younger gentleman's attention with the undoubting conviction that he enjoyed being monopolized.

Mr. Bragg, a heavy, melancholy-looking man, found Miss Patty Piper a congenial companion on a topic which interested him a good deal—cookery. Not that he was a gastronome. He had a grand French cook; but he confided to Miss Patty that he never tasted anything nowadays which he relished so much as he had relished a certain beef-steak pudding that his deceased "missis" used to make for him thirty years ago, and better. Miss Patty had, as it happened, some peculiar and special views as to the composition of a beef-steak pudding; and Mr. Bragg—borne backwards by the tide of memory to those distant days when his missis and he lodged in one room, and before he had learned the secret of transmuting tin-tacks into luxury and French cooks—enjoyed his reminiscences in a slow, sad, ruminating way.

Presently, when the dessert was on the table, there came a little lull in the general conversation, and the husky contralto voice of Miss Piper was heard saying, "My dear Major, I tell you it was the same woman. You say you heard her at Malta fifteen years ago. Very well. That's no reason; for she might have been only sixteen or seventeen then. These Italians are so precocious."

"More like six or seven-and-twenty, Miss Piper. Bless you, she had long outgrown short frocks and pinafores in those days. Fourteen—fifteen—yes; it must be fully fifteen years ago. It was the season that we got up the 'Honeymoon' for the garrison theatricals. I played the Duke. It has been one of my best parts ever since. And there was a scratch company of Italian opera-singers doing wretched business. We got up a subscription for them, poor things. But fancy 'La Bianca' still singing Rosina in the 'Barber!'"

"She looked charming, I can tell you. I don't say that her voice may not be a little worn in the upper notes—"

"I wonder there's a rag of it left," put in the Major.

"Yes; a little worn. But she knows how to sing. If one must listen to such trivial, florid music, that's the only way to sing it."

"Ah, there we shan't agree, Miss Piper! No, no; I always stand up for Rossini. I don't pretend to be a great swell at music, but I have an ear, and I like a toon. Give me a toon that I can remember and whistle, and I'll make you a present of Wagner and the other fellows, all howlings and growlings."

"Major, Major," called out Dr. Hatch from the opposite side of the table, "this is terribly obsolete doctrine! We shall have you confessing next that you like sugar in your tea, and prefer a rose to a sunflower!"

Mr. Bransby, wishing to avert any unpleasant shock of opinions on such high themes, here interposed. He turned the conversation back to the Italian singer, who could be abused without ruffling anybody's amour proper.

"But who is this prima donna you're talking of, Major?" said he.

Miss Piper struck in before Major Mitton could reply. "It's a certain Moretti:—Bianca Moretti. We heard her last summer in a minor theatre at Brussels, with a strolling Italian Opera Company. Don't you remember, Patty?"

"Moretti?" said Miss Patty, instantly breaking off in the middle of a sentence addressed to Mr. Bragg, at the sound of her sister's voice.

"The woman with the fine eyes? Oh yes. I remember her particularly, because of the awful scandal there was afterwards about her and that Englishman."

Several heads at the table were now turned towards Miss Patty, who shook her ginger-bread-coloured wig with a knowing air.

"I was just telling the Major," said Miss Piper. "We might never have known of it, if it had not been for the Italian Consul, who was a friend of ours. It was quite a sensation! A bit out of a French novel, eh?—Oh yes; quite ready, Mrs. Bransby."

The last words had reference to a telegraphic signal from the hostess, who immediately rose. Mrs. Hadlow had been looking across at her rather uneasily during the last minute or so. The fact was that the Miss Pipers were reputed in Oldchester to have a somewhat unconsidered and free way of talking. Some persons attributed this to their annual visit to the Continent: others thought it connected rather with Miss Piper's artistic experiences, which in some mysterious way were supposed to have had a tendency to make her "a little masculine." The implication would seem to be that to be "masculine" involves a lax government of the tongue. But as no Oldchester gentleman was ever known to protest against this imputation, it is not necessary to examine it here more particularly. "When she began to talk about a French novel, my dear, there was no knowing what she might say next," said Mrs. Hadlow afterwards to Mrs. Bransby. So the latter hurried the departure of the ladies as we have seen.

When they rose to go away, May, of course, went out last; Theodore holding the door open with his air of superior politeness.

"Who is that pretty little girl? I don't think I know her face," said Major Mitton, when the young man had resumed his seat, and the chairs were drawn closer together.

"That is Miss Miranda Cheffington."

"Cheffington? I knew a Cheffington once—a terrible black sheep. Very likely it's not the same family, though. What Cheffingtons does this young lady belong to?"

"The family of Viscount Castlecombe."

"The man I knew was a nephew of old Castlecombe. Gus Cheffington his name was, I remember now."

Theodore moved a little uneasily on his seat, and, after a moment's reflection, said gravely, "Captain Augustus Cheffington is this young lady's father; he is a friend of mine. Miss Cheffington is going to town to be presented next season by her aunt, Mrs. Dormer-Smith. She is a very thoroughbred woman. Do you know the Dormer-Smiths, Major Mitton? They are in the best set."

The Major did not know the Dormer-Smiths, and had no interest in pursuing the subject. He turned to join in the conversation going on between Mr. Bransby, the canon, and Dr. Hatch, and then Theodore slipped out of his place and went to sit nearer to Mr. Bragg, who was looking a little solitary. Mr. Bragg had a great many good qualities, but he was usually considered to be heavy in hand from a conversational point of view. Theodore, however, did not find him dull. He talked to Mr. Bragg with an agreeable sense of making an excellent figure in the eyes of that millionaire. Theodore had a strong memory, considerable powers of application, and had read a great many solid books. He favoured Mr. Bragg now with a speech on the subject of the currency, about which he had read all the most modern theories up to date. The currency, he felt, must be a peculiarly interesting subject to a man who sold millions and billions of tin-tacks in all the markets of the world. Mr. Bragg drank his wine, keeping his eyes on the table, and listened with silent attention. Theodore, warmed by a mental vision of himself speaking in a breathless House of Commons, rose to parliamentary heights of eloquence. He had already addressed Mr. Bragg as "Sir," and had sternly inquired what he supposed would be the consequence if the present movement in favour of bimetallism should be still further developed in the United States, when he was interrupted by his father's voice saying—

"Come, shall we ask Mrs. Bransby for a cup of coffee?"

Mr. Bragg lifted his eyes and rose from his chair, and Theodore and he moved towards the door side by side.

"It ought to be boiled in a basin, oughtn't it?" said Mr. Bragg thoughtfully. "Ah, no; it wasn't you. I remember now, it was Miss Patty Piper who was mentioning—I'll ask her again when we get upstairs."

Meanwhile the elder ladies had been deep in the discussion of Miss Piper's interrupted story. Constance and May had got close together near the pianoforte, and Mrs. Bransby asked Constance to play something "soft and pretty." Constance opened the instrument and ran her fingers over the keys in a desultory manner, playing scraps of waltzes or whatever came into her head, and continuing her chat with May to that running accompaniment. Mrs. Bransby, Mrs. Hadlow, and the Miss Pipers grouped themselves near the fireplace at the other end of the room, and carried on their talk also under cover of the music.

"It was odd enough that on my happening to mention the name of the Moretti to Major Mitton he should remember her at Malta so many years ago," began Miss Piper.

"Yes; and you see now that I was right, and she can't be so young as you thought her, Polly," said her sister.

"Lord, what does that matter? I only said she looked young, and so she did. And besides, I dare say the Major exaggerates her age. When a woman becomes a celebrity, or comes before the public in any way, her age is sure to be exaggerated. Many people who only know me through my works suppose me to be eighty, I dare say. They never imagine a woman so young as I was at the time composing a serious work like 'Esther.'"

"Is she handsome, this Signora Moretti?" asked Mrs. Bransby, who was always interested in, and attracted by, beauty.

"Very handsome—in that Italian style. Great black eyes, and black eyebrows, and a fine profile. Too thin, though. But, oh yes; extremely handsome. And a very clever singer."

"And a very worthless hussey," added Miss Patty severely.

"What a pity!" exclaimed Mrs. Hadlow. "It does seem so sad when one finds great gifts, like talent and beauty, without goodness!"

"Well, I don't know that she was so very bad either," replied Miss Piper.

"Goodness, Polly! How can you talk so!" cried her sister. "Why, she was living openly with that Englishman!"

"Some people said she was married to him, you know, Patty."

"Stuff and nonsense!" returned Miss Patty, who, whilst undoubtedly accepting her sister's views about music, tenaciously reserved the right of private judgment as to the character of its professors, and was, moreover, chronically incredulous of the virtue of foreigners in general. "No sensible person could believe that. And as to her 'not being so very bad'—what do you make of that nice story of the gambling, and the police, and all the rest of it?"

"The police!" echoed Mrs. Hadlow, in a low shocked voice.

"What was that?" asked Mrs. Bransby.

"Now, just let me tell it, Patty," said the elder sister. "If I am wrong you can correct me afterwards. But I believe I know more about it than you do. Well, there was an Italian Opera Company singing in a minor theatre of Brussels when we were there, and doing very well; for the prima donna, Bianca Moretti, was a great favourite. They had previously been making a tour through Belgium. One night we were in the theatre with some friends, expecting to hear her for the second time in the 'Barbiere,' when, some time after the curtain ought to have risen, a man came on to the stage, and announced that the Signora Moretti had been suddenly taken ill, and there would be no performance. But the next day we learned that the story of the Moretti's illness was only an excuse—or, at least, that if she was ill, it was only from the nervous shock of having her house searched by the police."

"I think that was quite enough to make her ill! But why did they search her house?" said Mrs. Bransby.

"Well, you see, it was in this way," continued Miss Piper, lowering her voice, and drawing a little nearer to her hostess, while Mrs. Hadlow cast a glance over her shoulder to assure herself that the girls were occupied with their own conversation. "It seems that a set of men were in the habit of meeting every night after the opera in her apartment to play cards. There was the Englishman, and a young Russian belonging to a grand family, and a Servian, or a Roumanian, or a Bulgarian, or something," said Miss Piper, whose ideas as to the national distinctions between the younger members of the European family were decidedly vague, "and others besides. Now this man, the—the Bulgarian, we may as well call him, was a thorough blackleg, and bore the worst of characters. He led on the Russian to play for very high stakes, and won large sums from him. Well, to make a long story short, one night there was a terrible scene. The Russian accused the other man of cheating. They came to blows, I believe, and there was a regular esclandre. And next day the Bulgarian was missing. He had got away with a good deal of plunder."

"How shocking and disgraceful!" exclaimed Mrs. Hadlow, in whom this gossip excited far more disgust than interest; and who thought Polly Piper showed very bad taste in selecting such a topic.

"But why did the police search the Italian singer's apartment? It was not her fault, was it?" asked Mrs. Bransby.

"Why, you see, the gambling had gone on in her rooms. And the Bulgarian turning out to be connected with a regular gang of swindlers, the search was made for any letters or papers of his that might be there. We were told that the Russian ambassador had something to say to it; for the young Russian was connected with very high people indeed. Nothing was found, however."

"Nothing was found that could be laid hold of," put in Miss Patty. "But there could be no question what sort of a person that woman was after all that!"

"Well, really, Patty," said her sister, "it seems to me that the Englishman was a deal more to blame. Nobody pretended that the Moretti wanted to gamble for her own amusement, or profit either! It was the ruin of her in Brussels; at any rate for that season. There was a party made up to hiss her whenever she appeared; and there were disturbances in the theatre; and, in short, the performances had to cease. I was sorry for her."

"Upon my word, Polly, I don't see why you should be," cried Miss Patty. "She deserved all she got. I have no patience with bestowing pity and sympathy on such creatures. If she had been an ugly washerwoman, instead of a painted opera-singer, nobody would have had a soft word for her."

"Oh, surely there are plenty of people who would be gentle to an ugly washerwoman, if she needed gentleness," put in Mrs. Hadlow. "And you know, my dear Miss Patty, we are taught to pity all those who stray from the right path."

"As to that, I hope I can pity error as well as my neighbours—in a religious sense," returned Miss Patty with some sharpness. "But this is different. I was speaking as a member of society."

"And the Englishman—was he implicated?" asked Mrs. Bransby, rather from a desire to divert the conversation from a direction fraught with danger to the general harmony than from any special curiosity on the subject.

"No; not exactly implicated," replied Miss Piper. "That is to say, he was not suspected of any unfair play, or anything of that sort; but it was considered disgraceful for him to have been mixed up in these gambling transactions; especially as he was a much older man than the others. And then—"

"And then," continued Miss Patty, "it was not considered exactly creditable, I believe—although perhaps Polly thinks it was; I'm sure I don't know,—it wasn't, most people would say, exactly creditable for a man of family, an English gentleman, to be strolling about the world with a parcel of foreign singers. And he had been doing just that. We heard of his being at Antwerp, and Ghent, and Ostend with them."

"A man of family, do you say? A really well-born man?" said Mrs. Hadlow, sitting suddenly very upright in the energy of her feelings. "How shocking! That really seems to be the worst of all!"

"Well, I suppose we must pity his errors," observed Miss Patty, with some causticity. But Mrs. Hadlow was insensible to the sarcasm; or, at all events, her sense of it was swallowed up by a stronger feeling. "I do think it's a public misfortune," she went on, "when a person on whom Providence has bestowed gentle birth derogates from his rank and forgets his duties. It grieves me."

"You must suffer a good deal in these days, I'm afraid," said Miss Patty, grimly.

"Not on that account," replied Mrs. Hadlow. "No; truly not. There may be exceptions—I won't deny that there are some. But, on the whole, I thoroughly believe that bon sang ne peut mentir."

"Well, perhaps Mr. Cheffington's blood is not so good as he says it is; that's all," said Miss Patty, with a short laugh.

Mrs. Hadlow and Mrs. Bransby uttered a simultaneous exclamation of amazement; and then the former said in a breathless whisper, "Hush, hush, my dear, for mercy's sake! Did you say Cheffington? That is—Cheffington is the name of that girl! Don't turn your head."

"Oh, it can't be the same!" said Mrs. Bransby, nervously.

"No, no; I dare say not. But the name—it must, I fear, be a member of the family," answered Mrs. Hadlow.

"How lucky it wasn't mentioned in her hearing," said Miss Piper. "Poor little thing, I wouldn't for the world—! She's very pretty and bright-looking. I don't think I ever saw her before."

Mrs. Bransby hurriedly explained how May came to be there, and as much of her story as she was acquainted with—which was, in truth, very little. The Miss Pipers listened eagerly, and Mrs. Hadlow sat by with a cloud of anxious perplexity on her usually beaming face. They all admitted that of course the person spoken of might be no relation of May's at all; but it was evident that no one believed that hypothesis. To the Miss Pipers the whole matter was simply a relishing morsel of gossip. They dwelt with gusto on "the extraordinary coincidence" of Miss Cheffington's being there just that very evening, and "the singular circumstance" that Major Mitton should remember Bianca Moretti, and enjoyed it all very much. Mrs. Bransby's prevalent feeling was one of annoyance, and resentment against Theodore, who had brought this girl into the house. Mrs. Bransby detested a "fuss" of any sort; and shrank, with a sort of amiable indolence, from the conflict of provincial feuds and the excitement of provincial gossip. And now, she reflected, this story would be spread all over Oldchester, and she would be "worried to death" by questions on a subject about which she knew very little, and cared less.

"We won't say another word about this horrid story," she said, looking appealingly at the Miss Pipers. "Silence is the only thing under the circumstances. Don't you think so? It would be so dreadful if the girl should overhear anything, and make a scene; wouldn't it?"

Miss Polly and Miss Patty readily promised to be most guardedly silent—for that evening, and so long as May should be present; declaring quite sincerely that they would not for the world risk hurting the poor child's feelings. And then Mrs. Bransby began to flatter herself that the subject was done with, so far as she was concerned. But Fate had decided otherwise.

When the gentlemen came into the drawing-room, Miss Hadlow was playing one of her most brilliant pieces, to which Miss Polly Piper was listening with an air of responsible attention, and gently nodding her head from time to time in an encouraging manner; Miss Patty Piper and May were looking over a large album full of photographs together; while Mrs. Bransby was narrating to Mrs. Hadlow, Bobby's latest witticisms, and Billy's extraordinary progress in the art of spelling:—these juvenile prodigies being her two younger children.

Constance did not interrupt her performance on the entrance of the gentlemen, and Major Mitton went to stand beside the pianoforte, gallantly turning over the music leaves at the wrong moment, with the best intentions. Canon Hadlow sat down near Miss Piper; the host with Dr. Hatch crossed the room to speak to Mrs. Hadlow, and Mr. Bragg and Theodore approached the table, at which Miss Patty and May Cheffington were seated. Mr. Bragg drew up a chair close to Miss Patty at once, and began to talk with her in a low voice, and with more appearance of animation than his manner usually displayed. Theodore, as he observed this, remembered with satisfaction that his friend Captain Cheffington had formerly pronounced old Bragg to be a d—d snob. A man must indeed be on a low level who could prefer Miss Patty Piper's culinary conversation to a luminous exposition of the currency question as set forth by Mr. Theodore Bransby. He bent over May, who was still turning the leaves of the photograph book, and said, "I'm afraid you are not having a very amusing evening, Miss Cheffington."

"Oh yes, thank you," returned May, making the queerest little grimace in her effort not to yawn. "I am very fond of looking at photographs."

"I don't suppose there are many portraits there that you would recognize. A little out of your set," said Theodore. "In fact, I don't know many of them myself, I have been so much away. By the way, have you any commands for your people in town? I go up the day after to-morrow."

"Shall you see Aunt Pauline?"

"Certainly. I suppose Lord Castlecombe is not likely to be in town at this season?" went on Theodore, raising his tone a little so as to be heard by the others. Constance's playing had now come to an end, and there was a general lowering of voices, occasioned by the cessation of that pianoforte accompaniment.

"I don't know, I'm sure. I don't know where he lives," answered May innocently.

"Ahem! He is at this season, in all probability, at Combe Park, his place in Gloucestershire."

May had never heard of her great-uncle's place in Gloucestershire; but now, when Theodore said the words, her thought flashed through a chain of associations to Mrs. Dobbs's mention of the Castlecombe Arms on the Gloucester Road, kept by "Old Rabbitt," and she blushed as though she had done something to be ashamed of.

"The last time I had the pleasure of seeing your father, he was talking to me about Combe Park," continued Theodore, with a complacent sense of superiority to the rest of the company in these manifestations of familiar intercourse with members of the Castlecombe family. Lord Castlecombe was a very important personage in those parts. As May did not speak, Theodore went on: "Grand old place, Combe Park, isn't it?"

"Is it?" returned May absently. She was looking with great interest at the portrait of a superb lace dress, surmounted by a distorted image of Mrs. Bransby's head and face, which were quite out of focus. But the lace flounces had "come out splendidly," as the photographer remarked. And, if the truth must be told, May admired them greatly.

"Is it?" repeated Theodore, with a little smile. "But you have lived so long abroad, that you are quite a stranger to all these ancestral glories. I hope, however, that you have not the same preference for the Continent that your father has?"

"Oh, I'm sure I should always love England best. But I don't know the most beautiful parts of the Continent—Switzerland or Italy. We were always in Belgium, and Belgium isn't beautiful. At least I don't remember any beautiful country."

Thus May, with perfect simplicity, still turning over the photographs, and all unconscious that the Miss Pipers had simultaneously interrupted their own conversation, and were staring at her.

"No; Belgium is not beautiful—except architecturally," replied Theodore. "But there is very nice society in Brussels, and a pleasant Court, I believe. No doubt that's one reason why Captain Cheffington likes it."

"Is Brussels your home, then? Do you live there?" asked Miss Patty, leaning eagerly forward.

May looked up, and perceived all at once that every one was gazing at her. The Miss Pipers' sudden attention to what she was saying had attracted the attention of the others—as one may collect a crowd in the street by fixedly regarding the most familiar object. In her inexperience she feared she had committed some breach of the etiquette proper to be observed at a "grown-up dinner party." Perhaps she ought not to have devoted so much attention to the photographs! She closed the book hurriedly as she answered—

"No, I don't live in Brussels, but papa does—at least, generally."

Mrs. Bransby rose from her chair, and came rather quickly across the room. "My dear," she said, "I want to present our old friend, Major Mitton, to you;" and taking May by the arm, she led her away towards the pianoforte.

Theodore observed this proceeding with a cool smile, and sense of inward triumph. Mrs. Bransby began to understand, then, what a very highly connected young lady this was, and was endeavouring, although a little late, to show her proper attention. Another time Mrs. Bransby would receive his introduction and recommendation with more respect. In the same way, he felt gratification in the eager questions with which Miss Patty plied him. Miss Patty left the millionaire Mr. Bragg in the lurch, and began to catechize Theodore on the subject of the Cheffington family.

That fastidious young gentleman said within himself that the snobbery of these Oldchester people was really too absurd; and mentally resolved to cut a great many of them, as he gained a firmer footing in the best London circles. Nevertheless he did not check Miss Patty's inquiries. On the contrary, he condescendingly gave her a great deal of information about his friends the Dormer-Smiths, the late lamented Dowager, the present Viscount Castlecombe, his two sons, the Honourable George and the Honourable Lucius, as well as some details respecting the more distant branch of the Cheffington family, who had intermarried with the Scotch Clishmaclavers, and were thus, not remotely, connected with the great ducal house of M'Brose.

This was all very well; but Miss Patty was far more interested in getting some information about Captain Cheffington which would identify him with the hero of the Brussels story, than of following the genealogy of the noble head of the family into its remotest ramifications. And, notwithstanding that Theodore was much more reticent about the Captain, she did manage to find out that the latter had lived abroad for many years—chiefly in Belgium—and that his pecuniary circumstances were not flourishing.

"I'm quite convinced it's the same man, Polly," she said afterwards to her sister. And, indeed, all the inquiries they made in Oldchester confirmed this idea. The Simpsons gave anything but a good character of May's absentee parent. And subsequent conversation with Major Mitton elicited the fact that Augustus Cheffington had been looked upon as a "black sheep" even by not very fastidious or strait-laced circles many years ago. The story of the Brussels scandal was not long in reaching the ears of every one in Oldchester who had any knowledge, even by hearsay, of the parties concerned.

Theodore Bransby, who left Oldchester on the Monday following the dinner-party, and spent the intervening Sunday at home, was one of the few in the above-named category who did not hear of it.

CHAPTER IX.

The correspondence between Mrs. Dobbs and Mrs. Dormer-Smith on the subject of May's removal to London was not voluminous. It consisted of three letters: number one, written by Mrs. Dobbs; number two, written by Mrs. Dormer-Smith; and number three, Mrs. Dobbs's reply to that. Mrs. Dobbs always went straight to the point, both with tongue and pen; and Mrs. Dormer-Smith, although by no means so forcibly direct in her dealings, had a dislike to letter-writing, which caused her to put her meaning tolerably clearly on this occasion, so as to avoid the necessity of writing again.

Mrs. Dobbs had proposed that May should become an inmate of her aunt's house in London—at all events for a time—in consideration of an annual sum to be paid for her board and dress. The said sum was to be guaranteed by Mrs. Dobbs, and was so ample as to make Pauline say plaintively to her husband, "Just fancy, Frederick, how deplorably imprudent Augustus has been in offending and neglecting this old woman as he has done! You see she has plenty of money. I had no idea what her means were; but it is clear that, for a person in her rank of life, she may be called rich. And Augustus might have obtained solid pecuniary assistance from her, I've no doubt, if he had played his cards with ordinary prudence. But there never was any one so reckless of his own interests as Augustus—beginning with that unfortunate marriage."

Whereunto Mr. Frederick Dormer-Smith thus made reply, "I don't know what you may call 'solid pecuniary assistance,' but it seems to me pretty solid to keep Augustus's daughter, and clothe her, and pay for her schooling, for four years and upwards. As to Augustus's disregard of his own interests, it does not at any rate lie in the direction of refraining from borrowing money, or remembering to pay it back; that much I can vouch for."

Pauline put a corner of her handkerchief to her eyes. "Oh, Frederick," she said, "it pains me to hear you speak so harshly. Remember, Augustus is my only brother."

"Mercifully! By George, if there was another of 'em I don't know what would become of us."

Mrs. Dormer-Smith declined to consider this hypothesis, but contented herself with saying that she should like to do something for poor Augustus's girl, and asking her husband if he didn't think they could manage to receive her. Mr. Dormer-Smith thought they could on the terms proposed, which, he frankly said, were handsome. And Pauline added softly—

"Yes; and it is satisfactory that she offers to keep the arrangement strictly secret. It would scarcely do to let it be known that Mrs. Dobbs pays for May. It would be inconvenable. People would ask all sorts of questions. It would put the girl herself in an awkward position. 'Grandmother!' people would say. 'What grandmother?' and the whole story of that wretched marriage would be raked up again.

But, on the conditions proposed, I do think, Frederick, it could do no harm to receive May. I am glad you consent. It will be a comfort to me to feel that I am doing something for poor Augustus's girl, and acting as mamma would have wished."

So a favourable reply was dispatched to Mrs. Dobbs's application. Mrs. Dormer-Smith suggested that May should come to town a little before the beginning of the season, so as to give time for preparing her wardrobe—a task to which her aunt looked forward with dilettante relish. And in answer to that, Mrs. Dobbs wrote the third and last letter of the series, assenting to the date proposed for May's arrival, and entering into a few minor details.

She had also, meanwhile, received a letter from Captain Cheffington, elicited, after a long delay, by three successive urgent appeals for an immediate answer. It was a scrawl in a hasty, sprawling hand, and ran thus:

"Brussels, Nov. 1, 18—.

"DEAR MRS. DOBBS,

"I think it would be very desirable for Miranda to be presented by her aunt, if she is to be presented at all, and to be brought out properly. I have no doubt that my sister will introduce her in the best possible way. Since you seem to press for my consent, you have it herewith, although I hardly feel that I can have much voice in the matter, being separated, as I have been for years, from my country, my family, and my only surviving child. I am a mere exile. It is not a brilliant existence for a man born and brought up as I have been. However, I must make the best of it.

"Yours always,

"A. C."

This was sufficient for Mrs. Dobbs. She had made a point of obtaining Augustus's authority for his daughter's removal to town; not because she relied on his judgment, but because she knew him well enough to fear some trick, or sudden turn of feigned indignation, if, from any motive of his own, he thought fit to disapprove the step. As to the tone of his reply, that neither troubled nor surprised her. But Mr. Weatherhead was moved to great wrath by it. Mrs. Dobbs had tossed the note to him one day, saying—

"There; there's my son-in-law's consent to May's going to town, in black and white. That's a document."

Mr. Weatherhead eagerly pounced on it. "What a disgusting production!" he exclaimed, looking up over the rim of the double eyeglass which he had set astride his nose to read the note.

"Is it?" returned Mrs. Dobbs carelessly.

"Is it? Why, Sarah, you surprise me, taking it in that cool way. It is the most thankless, unfeeling, selfish production I ever read in my life."

"Oh, is that all? Well, but that's just Augustus Cheffington. We know what he is at this time of day, Jo Weatherhead. It 'ud be a deal stranger if he wrote thankfully, and feelingly, and unselfishly."

But Mr. Weatherhead refused to dismiss the matter thus easily. He belonged to that numerous category of persons who, having established and proclaimed a conviction, appear to be immensely astonished at each confirmation of it. He had years ago pronounced Augustus Cheffington to be a heartless scoundrel. Nevertheless he was shocked and amazed whenever Augustus Cheffington did anything to corroborate that opinion.

The letter from Mrs. Dormer-Smith was not shown to him. Mrs. Dobbs meant to keep the amount she was to pay for May a secret even from her faithful and trusted friend Jo. He might guess what he pleased, but she would not tell him. The means, too, by which she meant to raise the money would not, she knew, meet with his approval. And, since she had resolved to use those means, she thought it best to avoid vain discussion beforehand, and therefore said nothing about them.

Accident, however, revealed a part of the secret in this way:

Mr. Weatherhead, calling one afternoon at Laurel Villa to see Mrs. Simpson, who had been kept at home by a cold, found other visitors there. Miss Polly and Miss Patty Piper were drinking tea out of Mrs. Simpson's best cups and saucers, and chatting away with their usual cheerfulness and volubility. The Miss Pipers, as they would themselves have expressed it, "moved in a superior sphere" to that of the music-teacher and his wife; but they did not consider that they derogated from their gentility by occasionally drinking tea and having a chat with the Simpsons. They liked to condescend a little, and opportunities for condescension were rather rare. Then, too, they had a certain interest in Sebastian Bach Simpson, inherited from the long-ago days when Sebastian Bach's father played the organ in their father's church, and Miss Polly and Miss Patty wore white frocks and blue sashes at evening parties, and were the objects of a good deal of attention from the Reverend Reuben's curates. Besides the sisters there was present Dr. Hatch, who had come to pay a professional visit to Mrs. Simpson, and who was just going away. It was a peculiarity of Dr. Hatch to be always just going away. He had a very large practice, and was wont to aver that his professional duties scarcely left him time to eat or sleep. Yet Dr. Hatch's horses stood waiting through many a quarter of an hour during which their master was engaged in conversation not of a strictly professional nature.

When Mr. Weatherhead entered the best parlour of Laurel Villa, Dr. Hatch had a cup of tea in one hand, and his watch in the other, and greeted the new arrival with a friendly nod, and the assurance that he was "just off." Mrs. Simpson shook hands with Mr. Weatherhead, and the Miss Pipers graciously bowed to him. He, too, was connected in their minds with old times. Miss Polly specially remembered seeing him on her visits to the Birmingham Musical Festivals, when her father would take the opportunity of turning over Weatherhead's stock of books, and making a few purchases. And once the Pipers had lodged during a Festival week in the rooms over Weatherhead's shop.

"Glad to see you better, Mrs. Simpson," said Jo, taking a seat after having saluted the company.

"Oh yes, thank you, I'm quite well now. I know Dr. Hatch will scold me if he hears me say so"— (with an arch glance baulked of its effect by the unsympathetic spectacles)—"because he tells me I still need great care. But my cough is gone. It is, really!"

Mrs. Simpson girlishly shook back her curls, and proceeded to pour out a cup of tea for Mr. Weatherhead.

"And how is Simpson?" asked the latter.

"Bassy is very well, only immensely busy. He has three new pupils for pianoforte and harmony; the daughters of Colonel —, tut, I forget his name,—recommended by that kind Major Mitton. Or at least it would be more proper to say that Major Mitton recommended Bassy to them! Not very polite to say that the young ladies were recommended—oh dear! I beg pardon. I'm afraid I've over-sweetened your tea?"

She had, in fact, put in half a dozen lumps, one after the other. But Mr. Weatherhead fished the greater part of them out again with his teaspoon, and deposited them in the saucer, saying it was of no consequence.

"I am so sadly absent-minded!" said Mrs. Simpson, smiling sweetly. "Bassy would scold me if he were here."

"Serve you right, if he did!" said Dr. Hatch, rising from the table. "You should pay attention to what you're doing. I expect to hear that you have swallowed the embrocation and anointed your throat with syrup of squills."

"Oh, doctor! You do say the drollest things!" exclaimed the amiable Amelia, with an enjoying giggle.

"Ah, no; not the drollest! Thank Heaven, I hear a great many droller things than I say! That's what mainly supports me in my day's practice."

Mrs. Simpson, not in the least understanding him, giggled again. Dr. Hatch had the reputation of being a wag; and Amelia Simpson was not the woman to defraud him of a laugh on any such selfish ground as not seeing the point of his joke.

"Well, Mr. Weatherhead," said Miss Patty Piper, blandly, "so we are to have your sister-in-law for a neighbour, I hear."

Jo poked his nose forward, and pursed up his mouth. "O-ho! my sister-in-law, Mrs. Dobbs? How do you mean, ma'am, 'as a neighbour'?"

"We understand that Mrs. Dobbs has been looking after Jessamine Cottage; the little white house with a garden on the Gloucester Road," returned Miss Patty. Dr. Hatch paused with his hand on the latch of the parlour door to hear.

"Oh dear no," said Jo Weatherhead decisively. "Quite a mistake. Sarah Dobbs is too wedded to her old home. Nothing would induce her to leave Friar's Row. You must have been misinformed, ma'am."

"As to leaving Friar's Row," put in Miss Polly, "she must do that in any case; for she has let the premises as offices; and at a high rent, too, I hear. Friar's Row is considered a choice position for business purposes."

Jo had opened his mouth to protest once more, when a sudden idea made him shut it again without speaking. "Oh!" he gasped, and then made a little pause before proceeding. "Ah, well—she—it wasn't quite settled when I heard last. Would you mind stating your authority, ma'am?"

"The best—Mr. Bragg told us himself. His managing man at the works has made the arrangement. Mr. Bragg has been looking out for a more central office for some time."

"I told Mrs. Dobbs long ago that she was living at an extravagant rental by sticking to Friar's Row," observed Dr. Hatch, turning the handle of the door. "Depend on it, she has let it at a swinging rent; and quite right, too. Now I really am off."

Jo Weatherhead sat very still after the doctor's departure, with his cup of tea in his hand, and a pondering expression of face. The Miss Pipers were not sufficiently interested in him to observe his demeanour very closely. If they did chance to notice that he was unusually silent, that was accounted for by his sense of the superior company he found himself in. They always spoke of him as "a good, odd creature, with sound principles—a very respectable man, who knew his station." As for Amelia Simpson, she was habitually unobservant, with an inconvenient faculty, however, of suddenly making clear-sighted remarks when they were least expected.

"I'm sure this is very good news for us!" she exclaimed. "Jessamine Cottage is so near! At least, it was quite close to us when we lived in Marlborough Terrace."

"It will be a good move for Mrs. Dobbs. The air in our neighbourhood is so much better than in her part of the town," said Miss Patty, with a certain complacency, as who should say, "The merit of this atmospheric superiority is all our own; but we are not proud."

"And yet I am surprised, too, at Mrs. Dobbs moving," replied Amelia. "She always declared that she hated the suburbs, with their little slight-built houses."

"That cannot apply to our house," said Miss Polly. "Garnet Lodge stood in its own ground many a long year before those new houses sprung up between Greenhill Road and the Gloucester Road."

"But Mrs. Dobbs isn't going to live in Garnet Lodge!" returned Amelia, with one of her sudden illuminations of common sense. "And Jessamine Cottage is a mere bandbox."

"I remember Mrs. Dobbs among the trebles in 'Esther,'" observed Miss Polly. "She had a fine clear voice, and could take the B flat in alt with perfect ease."

"And her husband sold capital ironmongery. We have a coal-scuttle in the kitchen now which was bought at his shop—a thoroughly solid article," added Miss Patty.

These appreciative words about the Dobbses, which at another time would have gratified Jo Weatherhead, now fell on an unheeding ear. He took his leave very shortly, and walked straight to Friar's Row.

"Well, Sarah Dobbs," said he, on entering the parlour, "I didn't think you would steal a march on me like this! I did believe you'd have trusted me sooner than a parcel of strangers, after all these years!"

He did not sit down in his usual place by the fireside, but remained standing opposite to his old friend, looking at her with a troubled countenance. Mrs. Dobbs gave him one quick, keen glance, and then said—

"So you've heard it, Jo? Well, I didn't mean that you should hear it from any one but me. But who shall stop chattering tongues? They rage like a fire in the stubble. And the poorer and lighter the fuel, the bigger blaze it makes. It was settled only this very morning, too."

"It is true, then, Sarah? I had a kind of a hankering hope that it might be only trash and chit-chat."

"You mean about my letting my house, don't you? Yes; that's true."

"And me never to know a word of it!—To hear it from strangers!"

"Now look here, Jo; let us talk sensibly. Sit down, can't you?"

But Jo would not sit down; and after a minute's pause, Mrs. Dobbs went on—

"I'll tell you the truth. I didn't say a word to you of my plan beforehand, because I was afraid to—there!"

"Afraid! You, Sarah Dobbs, afraid of me! That's a good one!" But his face relaxed a little from its pained, fixed look.

"Yes; afraid of what you'd say. I knew you wouldn't approve, and I knew why. You wouldn't approve for my sake. But, thinks I, when once it's done, Jo may scold a little, but he'll forgive his old friend. And I never thought of chattering jackdaws cawing the matter from the house-tops. I meant to tell you myself this very afternoon; I did indeed, Jo."

Jo drew a little nearer to his accustomed chair, and put his hand on the back of it, keeping his face turned away from Mrs. Dobbs. "Of course, you're the mistress to do what you like with your own property," he muttered.

"Nobody's mistress, or master either, to do what's wrong with their own property. I mean to do what's right if I can. I was never one to heed much what outside folks think of me; but I do heed what you think, Jo, and reason good. And I want you to know my feeling about the matter once for all, and then we can leave it alone."

Mr. Weatherhead here slid quietly into the armchair, and sat with his face still turned towards the fire.

"You know," continued Mrs. Dobbs, "I told you some weeks ago that I was troubled about the child's position here. She is a real lady, and ought to be acknowledged as such. That's the only good that can come now from poor Susy's marriage, and I do hold to it. There was only one way, that I could see, of managing what I wanted. I could do it at a sacrifice—after all, a very small sacrifice."

Jo Weatherhead shook his head emphatically.

"Yes, really and truly a very small sacrifice," persisted Mrs. Dobbs. "I don't see why I shouldn't be just as happy and comfortable in Jessamine Cottage as here—provided, of course, that my old friends don't cut me and sulk with me. I shall be lonely enough when once the child's gone; and you and me'll have to cheer each other up, and keep each other company, as well as we can. You won't refuse to do that, will you, Jo? Come, shake hands on it!"

Jo slowly put out his hand and grasped her proffered one. He then took out, filled, and lighted his meerschaum, and smoked in silence for some quarter of an hour, Mrs. Dobbs, meanwhile, knitting in equal silence. All at once she said—

"Hark! There's May's step coming downstairs. Now you'll please to understand that when my moving from this house is mentioned to the child, it's because I find Friar's Row too noisy, and think the air in Greenhill Road will agree better with my health. I trust you for that, Jo Weatherhead, mind!"

May at this moment came gaily into the room, and Mr. Weatherhead thus solemnly addressed her: "Miranda Cheffington, you have been to a first-rate school, and have read your Roman history and all that, haven't you?"

"Not much, I'm afraid, Uncle Jo."

"You have read about Lucretia, and Portia, and the mother of the Gracchi" (pronounced "Gratch-I;" for Jo's instruction had been chiefly taken in by the eye rather than the ear, in the shape of miscellaneous gleanings from his own stock-in-trade), "and other distinguished women of classical times, whose virtues were, in my opinion, not wholly unconnected with bounce?"

Mary laughed and nodded.

"Well, allow me to tell you that there are Englishwomen at the present day whom I consider far superior, in all that makes a real good woman, to any Roman or Grecian of them all. Englishwomen to whom bounce in every form is foreign and obnoxious. Englishwomen who do good by stealth and never blush to find it Fame, because Fame is a great deal too busy with rascals and hussies ever to trouble herself about them! Your grandmother, Mrs. Sarah Dobbs, whom I'm proud to call my friend, is one of those women. And what's more—and I'll have you bear it in mind, Miranda Cheffington—I believe you'd be puzzled to find her equal in Europe, Asia, Africa, or America—not to mention Australasia and the 'ole of the islands in the Pacific Ocean."

With that, Mr. Weatherhead walked gravely out; his nose somewhat redder than usual, and his eyes glistening.

CHAPTER X.

About a year before that dinner-party at which May Cheffington had made her début in Oldchester society, Mrs. Hadlow had begun to think it probable that Theodore Bransby might wish to marry her daughter, and to consider the desirability of his doing so. On the whole she did not disapprove the prospect. Constance was very handsome, but she was also very poor. Her ambition might not be satisfied by a match with Martin Bransby's son; but on the other hand, Theodore was a young man of good abilities, and apt to rise in the world. Moreover, he had sufficient property of his own to facilitate his rising—a little ballast of that sort being as useful in the melée of this world as the lead in a toy tumbler, and enabling a man, if not to strike the stars with his sublime head, at least to keep right side uppermost.

Certainly Theodore had appeared much attracted by Miss Hadlow. Not only her beauty but her self-assertion approved itself to him; for a man's wife should be able to justify his taste; and there would be no distinction in winning a woman whose meekness made it doubtful whether she could have had the heart to say "No" to an inferior suitor. They had been playfellows in childhood, but school and Cambridge had separated them. But after Theodore began to read for the Bar, and, during the two last vacations, which he had spent chiefly at home, a great intimacy had sprung up between the young people. Theodore's frequent visits to the old house in College Quad did not pass unobserved. One or two persons thought his partiality for the Hadlows—especially when contrasted with the lukewarm politeness he bestowed on other families, such as Raynes the brewer, or the Burtons who lived in a park, and had had nothing to do with retail for two generations—was creditable to Theodore's heart. "He was not one to neglect old friends," said they, candidly confessing at the same time that it was more than they should have expected of him. But the majority felt sure that nothing short of being in love with Constance Hadlow could induce young Bransby to prefer the canon's old-fashioned parlour to Mrs. Raynes's red and gold drawing-room, or the Burtons' æsthetic upholstery. Oldchester folks did not guess that Theodore intended to frequent a style of society in which neither the Rayneses nor the Burtons would be able to make any figure, nor did they know that he set a considerable value on Mrs. Hadlow's connections. That lady had been a Miss Rivers, and her family ranked among the oldest landed gentry in the kingdom. There were not many Oldchester magnates to whom Theodore Bransby thought it worth while to be more than coolly civil. Mr. Bragg was an exception, but then Mr. Bragg was a man of very great wealth; and as mere size is held in certain cases to be an element of grandeur, so money, Theodore thought, is capable in certain cases of inspiring veneration—that is to say, when there is enough of it.

As to Miss Constance's state of mind about young Bransby, it was too complex to be described in a word. She liked Theodore, and thought him a superior person; if not quite so superior as he thought himself. She had faith, too, in his future. It would be agreeable to be the wife of a distinguished M.P. or Q.C., or perhaps of both combined in one person. Theodore would certainly settle nowhere but in London, and to live in London had been Constance's dream ever since she was fifteen. Her visions of what her life would be if she married Theodore Bransby concerned themselves chiefly with their joint-entry into some fashionable drawing-room, her presentation at Court, her name in the Morning Post, herself exquisitely dressed driving Theodore down to the House in a neat victoria, and returning the salutations of distinguished acquaintances as they passed along Whitehall. All more serious questions regarding their married life Constance set at rest by a few formulas. Of course, she should do her duty. Of course, Theodore would always behave like a gentleman. Of course, they should never condescend to vulgar wrangling. Of course, her husband would give way to her in any difference of opinion;—particularly since she was pretty sure to be always right. And then Constance knew herself to be so very charming, that a man of taste could not fail to delight in her society.

Yet it must not be supposed that she had fully made up her mind to marry Theodore. That Theodore would be very glad to marry her she did not doubt at all. There had been a time—nay, there were moments still—when her visions of herself as Mrs. Theodore Bransby had been blurred by the disturbing element of her cousin Owen's presence. He had shown an attractive appreciation of her attractions; and had, to use Mr. Simpson's phrase, "dangled after his cousin" a good deal. Owen Rivers had reached the age of three and twenty without ever having earned a dinner, and without any serious preparation to enable him to earn one. He had had an expensive education, and had done fairly well at Oxford. His mother had died in his infancy; and his father, a country clergyman, had allowed the young man to lounge away his life at the parsonage, under the specious pretext of taking time to make up his mind what career he would follow. Owen had fished, and shot, and walked, and boated, and cricketed; but he had also read a good deal, having an intellectual appetite at once robust and discriminating. His friends and relatives agreed in thinking him very clever; and, when they reproached him with wasting his fine abilities and leading a purposeless existence, he would answer jestingly that he should be sorry to belie their judgment by subjecting his talents to the dangerous touchstone of action. His father died before he had determined on a profession. But, fortunately as he thought, and unfortunately as was thought by some other persons, including his Aunt Jane, he inherited wherewithal to live without working, and, with a hundred and fifty pounds per annum, could not lack bread and cheese. On his father's death he went to travel on the Continent. He walked wherever walking was possible, carrying his own knapsack, spending little, and seeing much. After more than two years' absence, he returned to England and made his way to Oldchester to see his Aunt Jane, with whom he had maintained an intermittent correspondence. There he found Constance, whom he last remembered as a sallow, self-sufficient schoolgirl, grown to a beautiful young woman. Her sallowness had turned into a creamy pallor, and her self-sufficiency was mitigated, to the masculine judgment, by the depth and softness of a pair of fine dark eyes. Owen, on his part, made a decidedly favourable impression on his cousin. He was not handsome—which mattered little—nor fashionably dressed—which mattered more; but he was well made, and had the grace which belongs to youthful health and strength. And he had, too, that indefinable tone of manner which ensured his recognition as an English gentleman. Constance was by no means insensible to this attraction. If she had not the sentiments which originate the finest manners, she had the perceptions which recognize them. When Mary Raynes and the Burnet girls criticized the roughness of Owen's demeanour, comparing it with Theodore Bransby's "polish," she knew they were wrong. Theodore always behaved with the greatest propriety; but between his manners and Owen's there was the same sort of difference as between a native and a foreigner speaking the same language. The foreigner may often be more accurately correct of the two on minor points, but it is an affair of conscious acquirement, and must inevitably break down now and then; whereas the native talks as naturally as he breathes, and can no more make certain mistakes than an oak tree can put forth willow leaves. Then Owen was very amusing company when he chose to be so,—and he usually did choose to be so when at his Aunt Jane's; and he had good old blood in his veins. This latter fact gave a certain piquancy, in Constance's opinion, to his political theories, which were opposed to the staunch Tory traditions of his family. Constance frequently took her cousin to task on this subject; but with the comfortable conviction to sweeten their controversy that a Rivers could afford to indulge in a little democratic heresy, just as Lord Castlecombe could afford to wear a shabbier coat than any of his tenants.

All these considerations, together with the crowning circumstance that he evidently admired her a good deal, caused Owen to fill a large place in his cousin's mind. She even asked herself seriously more than once if she were in love with Owen, but failed to answer the question decisively. She did, however, arrive at the conviction that falling in love lay much more in one's own power than was commonly supposed; and that no Romeo-and-Juliet destiny could ever inspire her with an ungovernable passion for a man who possessed but a hundred and fifty pounds a year. Mrs. Hadlow had at one time felt some uneasiness—nearly as much on Owen's account as on her daughter's, to say the truth. But she had satisfied herself that there was nothing more than a fraternal kind of regard between the young people—wherein she was wrong; and that there was no danger of their imprudently marrying—wherein she was right.

Mrs. Hadlow had, indeed, made up her mind that Constance would accept Theodore Bransby whenever he should offer himself; and she privately thought it high time that the offer were made. What did Theodore wait for? His means (according to Mrs. Hadlow's estimate of things) were sufficient to allow him to marry at once. But even supposing that he did not choose to marry until he had fairly entered on his career as a barrister, still there ought to be at least some clear understanding between him and Constance. All Oldchester expected to hear of their engagement, and it was not fair to the girl to leave matters in their present uncertain condition. When, at the end of the vacation, young Bransby left Oldchester again without having made any declaration, Mrs. Hadlow was not only surprised, but uneasy; and she opened her mind to her husband on the subject, invading his study at an unusual hour for that purpose.

"Edward," said Mrs. Hadlow, "don't you think that Theodore Barnsby ought to have spoken before he went to town this last time?"

"Spoken, my dear?"

"To Constance; or to us about Constance."

The canon leaned his head on his hand, keeping the thumb of the other hand inserted between the pages of his Plato as a marker, and looked absently at his wife.

"Well? Don't you think he ought?" she repeated impatiently.

The good canon meditated for a few moments. Then he said—

"I—I don't feel quite sure that I understand. What ought he to have said, Jane?"

"Said! Goodness, Edward! He ought to have declared his intentions, of course. It is high time that something was understood clearly."

The canon's gentle blue eyes lost their abstracted look, and a little sparkle came into them as he answered, "I hope—nay, I am sure—Jane, that you would not think of taking any step, or saying any word, which might compromise our dear child's dignity. Let it not appear that you are eager to put this interpretation on the young man's visits."

"My dear Edward, Theodore has been paying Conny marked attentions for more than a year past; but during this last summer and autumn he has been in our house morning, noon, and night. He doesn't come for our beaux yeux."

"H'm, h'm, h'm! But, Jane, an attachment of that sort between two young creatures should be treated with the greatest delicacy. It is shy and sensitive. Let us beware of pulling up our flower by the roots to see if it is growing."

This trope by no means corresponded with Mrs. Hadlow's conception of the relations between Theodore Bransby and her daughter. She was an affectionate mother, but she did not delude herself into thinking Constance peculiarly sensitive or romantic. In fact, she was wont to say that her daughter was twenty years older than herself on some points. But the canon erroneously attributed to his daughter a quite poetical refinement of feeling. His views on most subjects were romantic and unworldly, and his ideas about women were peculiarly chivalrous. They frequently irked Constance. She was not without respect as well as affection for her father; and it was sometimes difficult to bring these sentiments into harmony with her deep-seated admiration for herself. However, she usually reconciled all discrepancies between what he expected of her and what she knew to be the fact, by declaring that "Papa was so old-fashioned!"

"Tell me, Jane," said the canon, after a little pause, "do you think Conny's feelings are seriously engaged? Do you think this matter is likely to make her unhappy?"

"Unhappy? Well, no; I hope not unhappy," answered Mrs. Hadlow slowly.

"Then all is well. We will not let our spirits be troubled."

"But, Edward, although she may not break her heart—"

"Heaven forbid! Break her heart, Jane?"

"Well, I say of course there's no fear of that; but it is detrimental to a girl to have an affair of this kind dragging on in a vague sort of way. It might spoil her chance in other directions; and people will talk, you know."

"Tut, tut! As to 'spoiling her chance'—which is a phrase very distasteful to me in this connection—if you mean that any eligible suitor would be discouraged from wooing Conny because another man is supposed to admire her too, that's all nonsense. Do you think I should have been frightened away from trying to win you, Jenny, by any such impalpable figment of a rival?"

"You?" exclaimed Mrs. Hadlow, with a sudden flush and a proud smile. "Oh, that's a very different matter, Edward. I don't see any young men nowadays to compare with what you were."

The canon laughed softly. "Thank you, my dear. No doubt your grandmother said much the same sort of thing once upon a time; and I hope your grand-daughter may say it too, some day. But set your heart at rest as to this matter. That Theodore Bransby, whom we have known from his birth, should be a frequent guest in our house, can surprise no one. There is youthful society to be found here. Without reckoning Constance, there's Owen Rivers, the Burton girls, little May—we may reasonably suppose this to be attractive to a young man who has no companions of his own age at home, without attributing to him any such intentions as you speak off. In fact," added the canon simply, "we must believe you are mistaken; since, if Theodore loved our daughter, there's nothing to prevent his saying so!"

Of all which speech, two words chiefly arrested Mrs. Hadlow's attention and stuck in her memory—"little May." It was true, now she came to think of it, that the increased frequency of Theodore's visits coincided with May Cheffington's presence in Oldchester. Then she suddenly remembered it was by Theodore's influence that May had been invited to Mrs. Bransby's dinner-party, and many words and ways of his with reference to Miss Cheffington occurred to her in a new light. But then, again, came a revulsion, and she told herself that the idea was absurd. It was out of the question that Theodore Bransby, with his social ambition, should think seriously of marrying insignificant little May Cheffington, who was not even handsome (when compared with Constance), who had childish manners, no fortune—and, worst of all, was Mrs. Dobbs's grand-daughter! "Besides," said Mrs. Hadlow to herself, "he must be fond of Conny. It's quite an old attachment; and, though Theodore may not have very ardent feelings, I don't believe he is fickle."

Nevertheless, she was not entirely reassured. After Theodore's departure from Oldchester she observed her daughter solicitously for some time; but she finally convinced herself that Conny's peace of mind was in no danger. She had sometimes been provoked by Conny's matter-of-fact coolness, and had felt that young lady's worldly wisdom to be an anachronism. But she admitted that in the present case these gifts had their advantage; for, when Oldchester friends showed their interest or curiosity by hints and allusions to Theodore, which made Mrs. Hadlow quite hot and uncomfortable, Constance met them all with perfect calmness, and she discussed the young man's prospects with an almost patronizing air that puzzled people.

In a few weeks more May Cheffington departed for London; Owen Rivers also went away, and life in the dark old house in College Quad resumed its usual quiet routine.

CHAPTER XI.

It was a raw, gusty afternoon towards the end of March when May and her grandmother arrived in London. There had been some difficulty about the journey, arising from Mrs. Dormer-Smith's objection to her niece's travelling alone, and insisting on her being properly attended. In reply to a suggestion that May would be quite safe in a ladies' carriage, and under the care of the guard, she wrote:—"It is not that I doubt her being safe; but I cannot let my servants see her arrive alone when

I meet her at the station. Why not send a maid with her?" To which Mrs. Dobbs made answer that she could not send a maid, having only one servant-of-all-work, but that she herself would bring her grand-daughter to London. "I shall go up by one train, and come down by the next," said she to Jo Weatherhead. And when he remonstrated against her incurring that expense and fatigue, she answered, "Oh, we won't spoil the ship for a ha'porth of tar. If I make up my mind to part with the child, I'll start her as well as I can."

The travellers found Mrs. Dormer-Smith awaiting them at the railway station. She greeted May affectionately, and Mrs. Dobbs amiably. "My servant has a cab here for the luggage," she said. "But"—hesitatingly—"how shall we manage about—? I'm afraid the brougham is too small for three." Mrs. Dobbs settled the question by declaring that she did not purpose going to Mrs. Dormer-Smith's house. She would get some dinner at the station, and return to Oldchester by an evening train. "Oh dear, I'm afraid that will be very uncomfortable for you!" said Pauline, politely trying to conceal her satisfaction at this arrangement. "Will you not come and—and lunch with us?" But Mrs. Dobbs stuck to her own plan.

While the footman was superintending the placing of May's luggage on the cab, her grandmother drew her into the waiting-room to say "good-bye." "God bless you, my dear, dear child! Write to me often, keep well, and be happy!" she said, folding the girl in her arms. Mrs. Dormer-Smith stood by, not unsympathetic, but at the same time relieved to know James was busy with the luggage, so that he could not witness the parting, nor hear May's exclamation, "Darling granny! darling granny!" Indeed, it might be hoped that he would never know the relationship between this stout, common-looking old woman and Miss Cheffington; nor be able to report it in the servants' hall. She felt that Mrs. Dobbs was behaving very properly, and said with gracious sweetness, "I'm sure we ought all to be very much obliged to you for the care you have taken of my niece. It was most good of you to undertake this tiresome journey."

Mrs. Dobbs looked up with a flash in her eyes. "I only hope," she returned hotly, "that you will take as good care of my grandchild as I have taken of your niece." The next moment she repented of her retort, and said quite humbly, "You will be kind to her, won't you? Poor motherless lamb! You will be kind to her, I'm sure!"

"Indeed I will," answered Mrs. Dormer-Smith, with unruffled gentleness. "I have always wished for a daughter, and she shall be like my own daughter to me." And, with a motherly caress, she drew May to her side.

"Don't be afraid for me, granny dear!" said May, smiling with tearful eyes. "I shall be very happy with Aunt Pauline. Besides, I shall see you again very soon."

Mrs. Dobbs laid her hand on the girl's shoulder and pushed her gently, but firmly, out of the waiting-room, standing herself in the doorway until May and her aunt had disappeared. Then she sat down by the fire, untied her bonnet-strings, pulled out her handkerchief, and sobbed unrestrainedly. The waiting-room attendant looked at her curiously; for she had noticed that Mrs. Dobbs did not belong to the same class as that elegantly dressed lady, attended by a servant in livery, with whom the young girl had gone away. Presently she drew near, on pretence of poking the fire, and said—

"You're very fond of the young lady, ain't you? But don't take on so. You'll see her again very soon, I dare say. Don't cry, poor dear!"

"I have cried," said Mrs. Dobbs, getting up and drying her eyes resolutely. "I have cried, and it's done me good. And now I'll go and get a bit of food."

But she only trifled with the modest dinner set before her; and, as she sat in a corner of the second-class carriage which conveyed her back to Oldchester, her handkerchief was soaked with silent tears.

To May the separation naturally seemed far less terrible than it did to Mrs. Dobbs. She had no idea that it was to be a long, much less a permanent, one. She found it agreeable to sit in the well-hung, neatly appointed brougham, with a cushion at her back and a hot-water tin under her feet, and to look through the clear glasses at the bustle and movement of London. Her aunt Pauline was very pleasant and sympathetic. May thought that she might come to love her father's sister very dearly. She admired her already. Mrs. Dormer-Smith's gentle manner, her soft, low voice, the quiet elegance of her dress, and even the delicate perfume of violets which hung about her, were all appreciated by May.

"My cousin is not at home, is he, Aunt Pauline?" she asked after a little silence.

"No; Cyril is at Harrow. There are only the children."

"Oh, children!" cried May, with brightening eyes. "I'm so glad! I love children. I didn't know you had any children besides Cyril."

Mrs. Dormer-Smith laughed her peculiar little guttural laugh, consisting of several ha, ha, ha's, slowly and softly uttered, and made no answer.

"Are they boys or girls? How many are there? How old are they?" questioned May eagerly.

"Two little boys. Harold is—let me see—Harold is six, and Wilfred five. It is very awkward having two little things in the nursery so many years younger than their elder brother. Cyril is turned fifteen. It is like beginning all one's troubles over again," said Pauline plaintively. The birth of these two children was, indeed, a standing grievance with her.

May thought this an odd way of talking, and said no more on the subject of her little cousins. But she looked forward to seeing them with pleasant expectation.

The sight of the house in Kensington brought back vividly to her mind the day after the dowager's funeral, when she had arrived there from school, feeling very strange and forlorn. She remembered, too, the abrupt departure next morning with her father, and her impression that the Dormer-Smiths had not behaved well, and that her father was very angry with them. May was shown into a bedroom at the back of the house, overlooking some gardens. The maid, having asked if she could do anything for Miss Cheffington, and having mentioned that the luncheon-gong would sound in ten minutes, withdrew, and left May alone. She examined the room with girlish interest. It was very pretty, she thought. Perhaps, in point of solid comfort, the old-fashioned furniture of her room in Friar's Row might be superior; but in Friar's Row there was no such ample provision of looking-glasses as there was here. She was still contemplating herself from head to foot in a long swing mirror, which stood in a good light near the window, when the gong sounded.

May ran downstairs, and in the dining-room she found her aunt and a heavy-looking man with grizzled, sandy hair, and dull blue eyes, who asked her how she did, and supposed she would hardly recognize him.

"Oh yes, I do, Uncle Frederick!" she answered.

And again an uncomfortable recollection of her father's angry departure from that house came over her. But whatever quarrels there might have been in those days, her aunt and uncle appeared to have forgotten all about them. Mr. Dormer-Smith told May more than once that he was pleased to see her.

"You're not a bit like your father, my dear," said he, with an approving air not altogether flattering to Augustus.

"Oh yes, Frederick!" interposed his wife. "There is a family expression."

"It's an expression I have never seen on your brother's face. No, nor any approach to it."

Mrs. Dormer-Smith laughed the soft little laugh which was habitual with her when embarrassed or disconcerted, and changed the conversation. "I hope you like your room, May?" she said.

"Oh yes, very much indeed, thank you, Aunt Pauline."

"I wish I could have come upstairs with you. But I am obliged to ménager my strength as much as possible."

"Are you not well, Aunt Pauline?" asked May with ready sympathy.

"I am not strong, dear."

"You would be better if you exerted yourself more," said Mr. Dormer-Smith. "Your system gets into a sluggish state from sheer inactivity."

"Ah, you don't understand, Frederick," answered his wife, with a plaintive smile.

And May felt indignant at her uncle's want of feeling. But the next minute she relented towards him when he said, as he rose from table—

"I'll go round to the chemist's myself for Willy's medicine, and bring it back with me, as I suppose you will be wanting James to go out again with the carriage by-and-by."

"Is one of the little boys ill?" asked May.

This time it was her aunt who replied calmly, "Oh no. The child has a little nervous cough; it is really more a trick than anything else."

"Huggins doesn't think so lightly of it, I can assure you. He tells me great care is needed," said Mr. Dormer-Smith.

"Can I—would you mind—might I see my little cousins?" asked May, with some hesitation. She was puzzled by these discrepancies of opinion between husband and wife.

Mr. Dormer-Smith turned round with a look almost of animation. "Come now, if you like. Come with me," he said. And May followed him out of the room, disregarding her aunt's suggestion that it would be better for her to lie down and rest after her journey.

The nursery was a large room—in fact, an attic—at the top of the house. May noticed how rapidly the elegance and costliness of the furniture and appointments decreased as they mounted. If the dining-room and drawing-rooms represented tropical luxury, the bedrooms cooled down into a temperate zone; and the top region of all was arctic in its barrenness. The nursery looked very forlorn and comfortless, with its bare floor, cheap wall-paper dotted with coarse, coloured prints, and its small grate with a small fire in it, which had exhausted its energies in smoking furiously, as the smell in the room testified. At a table in the middle of the room sat a hard-featured young woman, with high cheek-bones, and a complexion like that of a varnished wooden doll, mending a heap of linen; and in one corner, where stood a battered old rocking-horse and a top-heavy Noah's Ark, two little boys were kneeling on the floor, building houses with wooden bricks. On their father's entrance, they looked up languidly; but when they saw who it was, they scrambled to their feet with some show of pleasure, and came to stand one on each side of him, holding his hands. They were both like him, blue-eyed and sandy-haired, and both looked pale and sickly. Harold, the elder, seemed the stronger of the two. Wilfred was a meagre, frail-looking little creature, with a half-timid, half-sullen expression of face. Their father kissed them both, and, sitting down, drew the younger child on his knee, whilst Harold stood pressing close against his shoulder.

"Well, do you know who this is?" asked Mr. Dormer-Smith, pointing to May.

Apparently they had no wish to know, for they nestled closer to their father, and sulkily rejected May's proffered caresses.

"Oh, come, you mustn't be shy," said their father. "This is your cousin May; kiss her, and say, 'How d'ye do?'"

But nothing would induce either of the boys to give May his hand, nor even to look at her; and at length she begged her uncle not to trouble himself, and hoped they would all be very good friends presently.

"And how do we get on with our lessons, ma'amselle?" asked Mr. Dormer-Smith of the hard-featured young woman, who, beyond rising from her chair when they came in, had hitherto taken no notice of them.

"We haven't had no lessons to-day," put in Harold, with a lowering look at "ma'amselle."

"No, monsieur, it has been impossible till now; I have had so much sewing to do for madame. See!" and she pointed to the heap of linen. "But we will have our lessons in the afternoon."

"I don't want lessons; I want to go out with papa. Take me with you, papa," cried Harold. Whereupon little Wilfred lisped out that he too would go out with papa, and set up a peevish whine.

"It is too cold for you, my man," said the father. "The sharp wind would make you cough. Harold will stay with you, and you can play together, and do your lessons afterwards, like good boys."

But the children only wailed and cried the louder, whilst mademoiselle, with her eyes on her needlework, monotonously repeated in her Swiss-French, "What is this? Be good, my children," and apparently thought she was doing all that she was called upon to do under the circumstances.

May thought her little cousins peculiarly disagreeable children; but she could not help feeling sorry for them and for their father, who looked quite helpless and distressed. "Would you like me to tell you a story?" she said. "I know some very pretty stories."

A wail from Wilfred and a scowl from Harold were all the answer she received from them. But her uncle caught at the suggestion eagerly.

"Oh, that would be very kind of Cousin May," he said. "A pretty story! You'll like that, won't you?"

"No, I shan't! I want to go with papa," grumbled Harold.

"I want to go wis papa," sobbed Wilfred.

"It is always so when monsieur comes to the nursery," said the Swiss, coolly going on with her sewing. "The children are so fond of monsieur."

"Poor little fellows!" cried May.

Then kneeling down beside her uncle, she began softly to stroke Wilfred's hair, and to speak to him coaxingly. After a while, the child glanced shyly into her face, and ceased to sob. Presently he allowed himself to be transferred from his father's knee to May's. The Noah's Ark was brought into requisition. May ranged its inmates—all more or less dilapidated—on the floor, and began to perform a drama with them, making each animal's utterances in an appropriate voice. A smile dawned on Wilfred's pale little face, and Harold drew near to look and listen with evident interest.

"Now, Uncle Frederick, if you have to go out, I will stay and play with the children, until lesson-time. They are going to be very good now; ain't you, boys?"

"Ve'y good now," assented Wilfred, his attention still absorbed by the Noah's Ark animals.

"Well, if you'll make the pig grunt again, I will be good," said Harold, with a Bismarckian mastery of the do ut des principle.

Mr. Dormer-Smith's face beamed with satisfaction. "It's very good of you, my dear," said he. "If you don't mind, it would be very kind to stay with them a little while; that is, if you are not too tired by your journey?" And as he went away, he repeated, "It's very good of you, my dear; very good of you!"

But May found that her aunt took a different view.

"Dear May," said she, when she learned where her niece had been spending the two hours after luncheon, "this is very imprudent! You should have lain down and taken a thorough rest instead of exerting yourself in that way."

"Oh, I'm not in the least tired, Aunt Pauline."

"Dear child, you may not think so; but a railway journey of three or four hours jars the nerves terribly."

"Oh, I was very glad to amuse the children, Aunt Pauline. They were crying to go out with their father, so I tried to comfort them. They got quite merry before I left them."

Mrs. Dormer-Smith slowly shook her head and smiled. "You will find them extremely tiresome, poor things!" said she placidly. "They are by no means engaging children. Cyril was very different at their age."

"Oh, Aunt Pauline! I think they might be made—I mean I think we shall come to be great friends. I couldn't bear to see them cry, poor mites!"

"That is all very sweet in you, dear May, but I fancy it is best to leave their nursery governess to manage them. Her French is not all that I could wish. But a pure accent is not so vitally important for boys. It is much if an Englishman can speak French even decently. And Cecile makes herself very useful with her needle."

Pauline then announced that she would not go out again that afternoon, but would devote herself to the inspection of May's wardrobe. "Of course you have no evening dresses fit to wear," she said; "but we will see whether we cannot manage to make use of some of your clothes. Smithson, my maid, is very clever."

"Why, of course granny would not have sent me without proper clothes!" protested May, opening her eyes in astonishment. "And I have an evening frock—a very pretty white muslin, quite new."

To this speech Aunt Pauline vouchsafed no answer beyond a vague smile. She scarcely heard it, in fact. Her mind was preoccupied with weighty considerations. As she seated herself in the one easy-chair in May's room, and watched her niece kneeling down, keys in hand, before her travelling trunk, she observed with heartfelt thankfulness that the girl's figure was naturally graceful, and calculated to set off well-cut garments to advantage.

"Oh!" exclaimed May suddenly, turning round and letting the keys fall with a clash as she clasped her hands, "above everything I must not miss the post! I want to send off a letter, so that granny may have it at breakfast time to-morrow for a surprise. Have I plenty of time, Aunt Pauline?"

"No doubt," answered her aunt absently. She was debating whether the circumference of May's waist might not be reduced an inch or so by judicious lacing.

"Perhaps I had better get my letter written first, Aunt Pauline. I wouldn't miss writing to granny for the world, and any time will do for the clothes."

To which her aunt replied with solemnity, and with an appearance of energy which May had never witnessed in her before, "Your wardrobe, May, demands very serious consideration. April is just upon us. You are to be presented at the second Drawing-room. Dress is an important social duty, and we must not lose time in trifling."

CHAPTER XII.

It was a great comfort to Mrs. Dormer-Smith to find her niece so pretty ("not a beauty," as she said to herself, "but extremely pleasing, and with capital points"), and so entirely free from vulgarisms of speech or manner. In fact, May's outward demeanour needed but very few polishing touches to make it all her aunt could desire. But a more intimate acquaintance revealed traits of character which troubled Mrs. Dormer-Smith a good deal.

"I suppose," she observed to her husband, with a sigh, "one had no right to expect that poor Augustus's unfortunate marriage should have left no trace in his children. But it is dreadfully disheartening to come every now and then upon some absolutely middle-class prejudice or scruple in May. Now, Augustus, whatever his faults may be, always had such a thoroughbred way of looking at things."

"Certainly, no one can accuse your brother of having scruples," said Frederick.

"Besides, it is terribly bad form in a girl of her age to set up for a moralist."

"It doesn't seem much like May to set up for anything: she is always so childish and unpretending."

"Oh yes; and that ingénue air is delicious: it goes so perfectly with her physique. But there are so many things which one cannot teach in words, but which girls brought up in a certain monde learn by instinct."

"What sort of things do you mean?" asked her husband after a little pause.

"Well, on Thursday, for instance, I was awfully annoyed. Mrs. Griffin was here, and seemed pleased with May, and talked to her a good deal. You know that is very important, because the duchess invites people or leaves them out pretty much as her mother dictates. So I was naturally very much gratified to see May making a good impression. In fact, Mrs. Griffin whispered to me, 'Charming! So fresh.' Presently Lady Burlington came in, and they began talking of those new people, the Aaronssohns, who have a million and a half a year. Lady Burlington had been at a big dinner there the night before, and she told us the most astonishing things of their vulgarity and their pushing ways. When she was gone Mrs. Griffin said, 'I do like Lady Burlington,' and began praising her manners and her air of grande dame. And, very kindly turning to May, she said, 'Do you know, little one, that that is one of the proudest women in England?' 'Is she?' said May. 'I should never have guessed that she was proud.' Something in her way of saying it caught Mrs. Griffin's attention; and she pressed her and cross-questioned her, until May blurted out that she thought it despicable to accept vulgar people's hospitality only because they were rich, and then to ridicule them for being vulgar. I never was so shocked; for, you know, the duchess and Mrs. Griffin both went to the Aaronssohns' ball last season. Now you know," pursued Mrs. Dormer-Smith almost tearfully, "that kind of thing will never do. You must allow that it will never do, Frederick."

"It would be awkward," assented Frederick, looking grave. "Couldn't you tell her?"

"Of course, I spoke to her after Mrs. Griffin had gone away. But she only said, 'What could I do, Aunt Pauline? The old lady insisted on my answering her, and I couldn't tell her a story.' You see what a difficult kind of thing it will be to manage, Frederick."

Mr. Dormer-Smith had become a great partisan of May's. He was genuinely grateful for her kindness to his children, and would willingly have taken her part had it been possible. But he felt that his wife was right; it would really never do to carry into society an enfant terrible of such uncompromising truthfulness. And this feeling was much strengthened by the recollection of sundry remarks which May had innocently made to himself—remarks indicating an inconvenient assumption on her part that one's principles must naturally regulate one's practice. However, as he told his wife, they must trust to time and experience to correct this crudeness.

"She is but a schoolgirl, after all," he said.

Pauline did not pursue the subject, but she reflected within herself that there are schoolgirls and schoolgirls.

There had been some discussion as to who should present May. Mrs. Dormer-Smith was of opinion that had there been a Viscountess Castlecombe, the office would properly have devolved on her ladyship; but old Lord Castlecombe had been a widower for many years. At length it was decided that May should be presented by her aunt.

"I know it is a great risk for me to go out décolletée on an English spring day," said that devoted woman. "And Lady Burlington would do it if I asked her. But I wish to carry out the duty I have undertaken towards Augustus's daughter, as thoroughly as my strength will allow. Under all the circumstances of the case, it is important that she should be publicly acknowledged, and, as it were, identified with the family. Of course, I shall feel justified in buying my gown out of May's money."

"May's money" had come to be the phrase by which the Dormer-Smiths spoke of the payment made by Mrs. Dobbs for her grand-daughter.

But besides the comforting sense of duty fulfilled, there were other compensations in store for Mrs. Dormer-Smith. May's presentation dress was pronounced exquisite, and was ready in good time; and May herself profited satisfactorily by the instructions of a fashionable professor of deportment, in the difficult art of walking and curtsying in a train. To be sure, she had alarmed her aunt at first, by going into fits of laughter when describing Madame Melnotte's lessons, and imitating the impressive gravity with which the dancing-mistress went through the dumb show of a presentation at Court. But she did what she was told to do, not only with docility, but with an unaffected simplicity which Aunt Pauline's good taste perceived to be infinitely charming. And she said to her husband that she really began to hope May would be "a great success."

The great day of the Drawing-room came and went, as do all days, great or small. But whether she had been a success or a failure, in her aunt's sense of the words, May had not the remotest idea. Indeed, the various feelings on the subject of her presentation which had filled her breast beforehand (including a genuine delight in her own appearance as she stood before the big looking-glass, while Smithson put the finishing touches to her head-dress), were all swallowed up in the supreme feeling of thankfulness that it was over; and that she had not disgraced herself by tumbling over her train, or otherwise shocking the eyes of august personages. Also, in a minor degree, she was thankful that Aunt Pauline's antique lace-flounce—a portion of the dowager's legacy lent for the occasion—had escaped destruction. On their drive homeward, she sat silent, trying to extricate some definite image from her confused impressions of the ceremony, and finding that her most distinct recollection recorded the pressure of a persistent and ruthless elbow against her ribs. Mrs. Dormer-Smith, too, was too much exhausted to say much. She leaned back in the carriage with closed eyes, wrapping her furs round her, and sniffing at a bottle of salts.

But when refreshed by a glass of wine, and seated in a well-cushioned chair before a blazing fire, Mrs. Dormer-Smith felt very well satisfied with the result of the day. Mrs. Griffin had been there, and had nodded approvingly across a struggling crowd of bare shoulders; and Mrs. Griffin's approbation was worth having. Mr. Dormer-Smith came home from his club a full hour earlier than usual, in order to hear the report—a proof of interest which May, not being a whist-player, was unable fully to appreciate.

"Well," said Pauline, with a kind of pious serenity, "we have accomplished this somewhat trying social duty."

"Trying, indeed," exclaimed May. "I'm afraid you are dreadfully tired, Aunt Pauline. And the crowd and closeness made your head ache, I saw. How is your head now?"

"It is better, dear, much better."

"Well?" said Mr. Dormer-Smith, looking interrogatively with raised eyebrows at his wife.

"Oh yes, Frederick; very nice indeed, very satisfactory. I was very much pleased. I had been a little anxious about the effect of the corsage, but Amélie has done herself great credit. And, mercifully, white suits our dear child to perfection. She really looked very well."

"Did I, Aunt Pauline? Well, I'm sure it didn't much matter how I looked."

"Didn't matter!" echoed Mrs. Dormer-Smith in a shocked tone.

"Oh, come, May!" cried her uncle. "I thought you were above that sort of nonsense. Do you mean to tell me that you don't care about looking pretty?"

"Oh no! I mean—well, I did think my dress was lovely when I looked at myself in the big glass upstairs; but in that crush who could see it? And I was awfully afraid that Aunt Pauline's lace flounce would be torn completely off the skirt."

Her uncle laughed. "You don't appear to have altogether enjoyed your first appearance as a courtier," said he.

"Enjoyed! Oh, who could enjoy it?" Then, fearful of seeming ungrateful, she added, "It was very, very kind of Aunt Pauline to take so much trouble, and to get me that beautiful dress."

May had not been accustomed to think about ways and means. It had seemed a matter of course that her daily wants should be supplied, and she had hitherto bestowed no more thought on the matter than a young bird in the nest. But it was impossible for her to live as a member of the Dormer-Smiths' family without having the question of money brought forcibly to her mind. There were small pinchings and savings of a kind utterly unknown in Friar's Row; elaborate calculations were made as to the possibility of this or that expenditure; Aunt Pauline frequently lamented her poverty; and yet, withal, there was kept up an appearance of wealth and elegance. May was not long in discovering the seamy side of all the luxury which surrounded her; and it amazed her. Why should her aunt so arrange her life as to derive very little comfort from very strenuous effort? And what puzzled her most of all at first was the air of conscious virtue with which this was done: the strange way in which Aunt Pauline would mention some piece of meanness or insincerity as though it were an act of loftiest duty. On one or two occasions May had innocently suggested a straightforward way out of some social difficulty; such as wearing an old gown when a new one could not be afforded, or refusing an invitation which could only be accepted at the cost of much bodily and mental harass. But these childish suggestions had been met by an indulgent smile; and she had been told that such and such things must be done or endured in order to keep up the family's position in society. Once May had asked, "Then why should we keep up our position in society?" But her aunt had shown such genuine consternation at this impious inquiry, that the girl did not venture to repeat it.

Another question, however, soon forced itself upon May—namely, how it came to pass that, under all the circumstances, so much money was spent on her dress. Besides the court train and petticoat, her aunt had provided for her a wardrobe which, to the young girl's inexperienced eyes, appeared absolutely splendid (for Pauline's conscience, although cramped and squeezed into artificial shape like a Chinese lady's foot, was alive and sentient; and she would on no account have failed to expend "May's money" for May's advantage): and yet all the while there were the two little boys in their comfortless nursery, wearing coarse clothing and shabby shoes; and there was Cecile toiling at needlework instead of attending to the children, in order that the cost of a seamstress might be saved! On this subject May felt that she had a right to interrogate her aunt; and accordingly she took courage to do so. Mrs. Dormer-Smith was considerably embarrassed, and made an attempt to fence off the subject. But May persisted.

"It's very, very good of you and Uncle Frederick to do so much for me," she said; "but I can't bear to take it all."

"Nonsense, May! Remember you are a Cheffington. You must appear in the world properly equipped."

"But, Aunt Pauline, it isn't fair to Harold and Wilfred!"

"Harold and Wilfred?" echoed her aunt, opening wide her soft dark eyes. "What do you mean, May?"

May coloured hotly, but stuck to her point. "Well," she said, "you know Uncle Frederick was saying the other day that Willy ought to have change of air; and you said you couldn't afford to send him to the seaside just now; and—and I think Cecile thinks they ought to have new walking suits; and all the while I have so many expensive new frocks. I can't bear it. It isn't really fair."

Then Mrs. Dormer-Smith found herself compelled to assure her niece that no penny of the cost of her toilet came out of Uncle Frederick's pocket, and reading a further question in the girl's face, she hastened to anticipate it by adding, "The arrangements made for you here, May, are in entire accordance with your father's wishes. There has been a correspondence with him on the subject, and he wrote quite distinctly; otherwise your uncle and I would not have undertaken to bring you out."

"I hope," said May, "that papa does not deprive himself of anything for me. He used not to be at all well off, I know. I can remember when I was a little thing in Bruges."

"Augustus deprives himself of nothing," answered Mrs. Dormer-Smith softly, but emphatically. "Pray say no more on the subject, my dear. This sort of thing makes my head ache."

Her conscience being thus relieved, May accepted and enjoyed her new finery and her new life. She found that "taking up one's position in society" involved pleasanter things than being presented at a Drawing-room. It was delightful to be tastefully and becomingly dressed. It was agreeable to be sure of plenty of partners at every dance. It was satisfactory to have so admirable a chaperon as Aunt Pauline. One could no more form a fair judgment of that lady from knowing her only in domestic life, than one could fully appreciate a swan from seeing it on dry land. In the congenial element of "society," her merits were exhibited to the utmost advantage. They were, indeed, greater than May had any idea of; Mrs. Dormer-Smith's tact in warding off ineligible partners, and securing as far as possible eligible ones for her niece, was masterly. But May admired her aunt's unruffled temper and gentle grace. She had been quick to find out—with some astonishment, but beyond the possibility of doubt—that fine people can be exceedingly rude on occasion; and she observed with pride that Aunt Pauline was never rude. Moreover, Aunt Pauline's softness of manner was a far more effectual protection against impertinence, than the brusquerie affected by sundry ladies who forgot the wisdom embodied in the homely saying, that "those who play at bowls must look out for rubbers;" and who were always liable to be vanquished by greater insolence than their own.

May soon began to be reticent of her real sentiments and opinions in speaking to her aunt and uncle. She felt that nine times out of ten she was not understood; or, which was worse, was misunderstood. But in writing to her dear granny, she frankly and fully poured out all her heart. These letters were the joy and consolation of Mrs. Dobbs's life. Every minutest detail interested her. She laughed over May's description of the Drawing-room, and read it out aloud to Jo Weatherhead by way of a wholesome corrective to his Tory prejudices.

But at the same time she secretly treasured a copy of the Morning Post containing Miss Miranda Cheffington's name, and a description of Miss Miranda Cheffington's toilet on that occasion. And she listened, with a complacency of which she was more than half ashamed, to Mrs. Simpson's ecstasies on the subject; and to the scraps of information which the good-natured Amelia quoted—generally incorrectly—from social gossip setting forth how Mrs. Dormer-Smith and her niece, Miss Miranda Cheffington, had been present at this or that grand entertainment. These things might appear frivolous; but was it not for this end, to put May in her right place in the world, to give her her birthright, that Mrs. Dobbs had made a great sacrifice? Jo Weatherhead understood this so well, that the "fashionable intelligence" in the local newspapers assumed a quite pathetic interest in his eyes. When he went to drink tea with his old friend in the parlour of her new abode with its trashy, stuccoed ceiling, miserably thin walls, and squeezed little fireplace, he felt it to be a positive comfort to pull from his pocket a copy of the Court Journal or other equally polite print, and read aloud to Sarah some paragraph in which May's name occurred. It was a consolation, too, to let himself be lectured and laughed at by Sarah for his absurd admiration of the aristocracy. And he took every opportunity of combating her Radicalism, in order that she might victoriously vindicate the steadfastness of her political principles.

Meanwhile, Captain Cheffington saw the accounts of his daughter's appearance in the fashionable world, and began to think that he had been too easy in giving his consent to it. He had got nothing by it; and perhaps something might have been got. He wrote twice to Pauline, urgently requiring her to tell him what was the exact sum which Mrs. Dobbs paid for her grand-daughter's maintenance. That it was handsome he did not doubt; knowing by experience that the Dormer-Smiths would not contribute a shilling. Pauline had replied evasively to the first letter, and not at all to the second, with the result that Augustus's imagination absurdly exaggerated Mrs. Dobbs's wealth. The old woman must be rolling in money after all! Had May's allowance been a small one, his sister would not have hesitated to tell him the exact sum. It was clear to his mind that the Dormer-Smiths were making an uncommonly good thing of it, and he was decidedly disinclined to leave all the profit to them. He wrote off to Oldchester a demand for money on his own account. It was refused; and his anger was very bitter. He even began to cherish a grudge against May. Why should she be surrounded by luxury, enjoying all the gaieties of London, and taking a social position to which her only claim was the fact of being his daughter, whilst he lived the life of an outcast? He went so far as to threaten to come to England and bring away his daughter: having some idea that Mrs. Dobbs might ransom May, and pension him off. But the energy which might once upon a time have enabled Augustus Cheffington to take this strong step had waned long ago. He had grown inert. And, above all, the circumstances of his private life rendered such independent action difficult, if not impossible.

It presently began to be reported amongst Mrs. Dormer-Smith's acquaintance, with other items of tea-table gossip, that "little May Cheffington had a rich old grandmother somewhere down in the country." Theodore Bransby, who was admitted as a familiar visitor at the Dormer-Smiths', and who made a parade of his intimacy with the Cheffingtons, was interrogated on the subject. He maintained a cautious reserve in his replies:—"He really could say nothing; he had no idea what the old lady's means might be; he could scarcely, in fact, be said to know her at all." Wishing, as he did, completely to ignore that objectionable old ironmonger's widow, it was irritating to find her existence known, and her means discussed, in London. To be sure, no one troubled himself to inquire "Who is she?" general interest being exclusively concentrated on the question, "What has she?" Theodore's reticence was by no means attributed to its real cause. People said that young Bransby was looking after the girl himself, and wanted to choke off possible rivals. Theodore did, indeed, push himself as far as possible into every house which May frequented. There were some still inaccessible to him; but he had patience and perseverance. And he was constantly meeting May in the course of the season. She was far more pleased to see him in London than she had ever been in Oldchester. He was associated with persons whom she loved: and on many occasions when ball-room lookers-on pronounced Miss Cheffington and young Bransby to be "spooning awfully," May was talking with animation of his half-brothers, Bobby and Billy, of the dear old canon and her friend Constance, or even of Mr. and Mrs. Sebastian Bach Simpson. Theodore had no relish for these topics; but it was better to talk with May of them, than not to talk with her at all. And to the girl, he seemed the only link between her present life and the dear Oldchester days.

At the beginning of June, however, he ceased to have this exclusive claim on her attention. One fine day Aunt Pauline, returning from an afternoon drive with her niece, found a large visiting card with "The Misses Piper" engraved on it with many elaborate flourishes, whilst underneath was written in pencil "Miss Hadlow."

"Piper!" said Pauline, languidly dropping her eyeglass, and looking round at May. "What can this mean?"

"Oh, it means Miss Polly and Miss Patty and my schoolfellow Constance Hadlow!" cried May, clapping her hands. "Fancy Conny being in town! I dare say the Pipers invited her on a visit. I'm so glad!"

Mrs. Dormer-Smith's countenance expressed anything but gladness; and she privately informed May that it would be impossible to do more than send cards to these ladies by the servant. "I can't have them here on my Thursdays, you know, May," she said plaintively, and with an injured air.

Three months ago May would have indignantly protested against this tone, and would have pointed out that it would be unfeeling and ungrateful on her part to slight her old friends. But she had by this time learned to understand how unavailing were all such representations to convince Aunt Pauline, in whose code personal sentiments of goodwill towards one's neighbour had to yield to the higher law of duty towards "Society."

"Perhaps," said May, after a pause, "if you cannot go yourself, Uncle Frederick would take me to Miss Piper's some Sunday after church, when we go for a walk with the children. You see they have written 'Sundays' on the corner of their card."

"Oh, do you think they would be satisfied with that sort of thing?" asked her aunt.

"They are most kind, good-natured old ladies," pursued May. "They wouldn't mind the children at all. Indeed, they like children. And as to coming to your Thursdays, Aunt Pauline, I really don't think they would care to do it. Music is their great passion—at least, Miss Polly's great passion—and when they are in London I think they go to concerts morning, noon, and night. Miss Hadlow is different. Her grandpapa was a Rivers," added May, blushing at her own wiliness, "and she is very handsome, and sure to be asked out a great deal."

But May's profound strategy did not end here. She coaxed Uncle Frederick by representing what a treat it would be to Harold and Wilfred to go out visiting with papa. Those young gentlemen, privately incited by hints of possible plum-cake, were soon all eagerness to go; and when, on the very next Sunday, May set off with her uncle and cousins to walk to Miss Piper's lodgings, she felt that she had achieved a diplomatic triumph.

CHAPTER XIII.

Those Oldchester persons who considered Miss Piper's artistic tendencies responsible for her occasional freedom of speech would have been confirmed in their opinion as to the demoralizing tendency of Art and Continental travel had they known how the daughters of the late Reverend Reuben Piper employed Sunday afternoon in London. Miss Patty herself had been startled at first by the idea of not only receiving callers, but listening to profane music on that day; and the sisters had had some discussion about it. When Patty demurred to the suggestion, Polly inquired whether she truly and conscientiously considered that there was anything more intrinsically wrong in seeing one's friends and opening one's piano on a Sunday than on a Monday.

"No; of course not that," answered Patty. "If I thought it wrong, I shouldn't discuss it even with you. I should simply refuse to have anything to do with it."

"I know that, Patty," said her sister. "And I hope I am not altogether without a conscience either."

"No, Polly; but would you do this in Oldchester?"

"Certainly not."

"Then that's what I say. We ought not to have two weights and two measures. If a thing is objectionable in Oldchester, it is objectionable in London."

"Not at all. Circumstances alter cases. I may think it a good thing to take a sponge-bath every morning; but I should not take it in public."

"Polly! How can you?"

"What I mean is, that, so long as we are not a stumbling-block of offence to other people, we have a right to please ourselves in this matter."

So Miss Polly's will prevailed, as it prevailed with her sister upon most occasions; and the Sunday receptions became an established custom.

The house in which the Miss Pipers lodged when they came to London was in a street leading out of Hanover Square. The lower part of it was occupied by a fashionable tailor—a tailor so genteel and exclusive that he scorned any appeal to the general public, and merely had the word "Groll" (which was his name) woven into the wire blind that shaded his parlour window. The rooms above were sufficiently spacious, and were, moreover, lofty—a great point in Miss Polly's opinion, as being good for sound. They were furnished comfortably, albeit rather dingily. But a few flower-pots, photographic albums, and bits of crochet-work, scattered here and there, answered the purpose—if not of decoration, at least of showing decorative intention. A grand pianoforte, bestriding a large tract of carpet in the very middle of the front drawing-room, conspicuously asserted its importance over all the rest of the furniture.

May and her uncle, accompanied by the two little boys, were shown upstairs, and, the door of the drawing-room being thrown open, they found themselves confronted by a rather numerous assembly. The last bars of a pianoforte-piece were being performed amidst the profound silence of the auditors, and the newly arrived party stood still near the door, waiting until the music should come to an end.

At the piano sat a smooth-faced young gentleman playing a series of incoherent discords with an air of calm resolve. Immediately behind him stood an elderly man of gentleman-like appearance, whom May found herself watching, as one watches a person swallowing something nauseous, and involuntarily expecting him to "make a face" as each new dissonance was crashed out close to his ear. But his amiable countenance remained so serene and satisfied, that the doubt crossed her mind whether he might not possibly be deaf. In the embrasure of a window stood a very tall, thin man, whose bald head was encircled by a fringe of grizzled red hair, and whose eyes were fast shut. But as he stood up perfectly erect, with his hands folded in a prayerful attitude on his waistcoat, it was obvious that he was not asleep. Miss Piper was seated with her back towards the door and her face towards the pianist, so that May could not see it. But the composer of "Esther" nodded her head approvingly at every fresh harmonic catastrophe which convulsed the keyboard. Her satisfaction seemed to be shared by a stout lady of majestic mien, who sat near her and fired off exclamations of eulogium, such as "Charming!" "Wonderful modulation!" "Intensely wrought out," and so on—like minute guns; and with a certain air of suppressed exasperation, as though she suspected that there might be persons who didn't like it, and was ready to defy them to the death. A dark-eyed girl, very plainly dressed, and holding a little leather music-roll in her hand, occupied a modest place behind this lady. Sitting close to the dark-eyed girl was a man of about thirty-five years old, well-featured, short in stature, and with reddish blonde hair and moustaches. This personage's countenance expressed a singular mixture of audacity and servility. His smile was at once impudent and false, and he listened to the music with a pretentious air of knowledge and authority. The rest of the company, with Miss Patty, were relegated, during the performance, to the back drawing-room, where tea was served; and the folding-doors were closed, lest the clink of a teaspoon, or the sibillation of a whisper, should penetrate to the music-room. But, in truth, nothing less than a crash of all the crockery on the table, and a simultaneous bellow from all the guests, could have competed successfully with the pianoforte-piece then in progress.

At length, with one final bang, it came to an end, and there was a general stir and movement among the company. The amiable-looking elderly man advanced towards Miss Piper with a most beaming smile, and said, in a soft refined voice—

"That is the right way, isn't it? One knows the sort of thing said by people who don't understand this school of music, the only music, in fact; but I have long been sure that this is the right way."

"Of course, it is the right way," exclaimed the stout lady, breathing indignation, not loud but deep, against all heretics and schismatics.

"We are so very, very much obliged to you, Mr. Turner," said the hostess. "That new composition of yours is really wonderful!" (And so, indeed, it was.)

As Miss Piper went up to the young gentleman who had been playing the piano, and who remained quite cool and unmoved by the demonstrations of his audience, she caught sight of the group near the door, and hastened to welcome them. May was received with enthusiasm, and her uncle with one of Miss Piper's best old-fashioned curtsies. Mr. Dormer-Smith began to apologize for bringing his little boys, and to explain that he had not expected to find so numerous an assembly; but Miss Piper cut him short with hearty assurances that they were very welcome, and that her sister in particular was very fond of children. Then, the doors being by this time reopened, she ushered them all into the back room, crying—

"Patty! Patty! Who do you think is here? May Cheffington!" and then Miss Patty added her welcome to that of her sister.

Harold and Wilfred had been shyly dumb hitherto, although once or twice during the pianoforte-playing Wilfred had only saved himself from breaking into a shrill wail and begging to be taken home, by burying his face in the skirts of May's dress; but on beholding plum-cake and other good things set forth on the tea-table, they felt that life had compensations still. They took a fancy also to the Miss Pipers, finding their eccentric ornaments a mine of interest; and before three minutes had elapsed Harold was devouring a liberal slice of cake, and Wilfred, seated close to kind Miss Patty, was diversifying his enjoyment of the cake by a close and curious inspection of that lady's bracelet, taken off for his amusement, and endeavouring to count the various geological specimens of which it was composed.

As soon as May appeared in the back drawing-room, Constance Hadlow rose from her seat in a corner behind the tea-table, and greeted her.

"Dear Conny," cried May, "I am so glad to see you! Then you are staying with the Miss Pipers! I guessed you were."

Mr. Dormer-Smith was then duly presented to Miss Hadlow. Constance was in very good looks, and her beauty and the quiet ease of her manner made a very favourable impression on May's uncle.

Miss Hadlow found a seat for him near herself; and then turned again to May, saying, "There is another Oldchester friend whom you have not yet spoken to. You remember my cousin Owen?"

May's experience of society had not yet toned down her manner to "that repose which stamps the caste of Vere de Vere." She heartily shook hands with the young man, exclaiming, "This is a day of joyful surprises. I didn't expect to see you, Mr. Rivers. Now, if we only had the dear canon, and Mrs. Hadlow, and granny, I think I should be quite happy."

"You are not a bit changed," said Owen Rivers, giving May his chair, and standing beside her in the lounging attitude so familiar to her in the garden at College Quad.

"Changed! What should change me?"

"The world."

"What nonsense!" cried May, with her old schoolgirl bluntness. "As if I had not been living in the world all my life!"

Mr. Rivers raised his eyebrows with an amused smile.

"Well, isn't it nonsense," pursued May, "to talk as if a few hundred or thousand persons in one town—though that town is London—made up the world?"

"It is a phrase which every one uses, and every one understands."

"But every one does not understand it alike."

"Perhaps not."

"What did you mean by it, just now?"

"What could I mean but the world of fashion, the world par excellence? Rightly so-called, no doubt, since it affords the best field for the exercise of the higher and nobler human faculties. Those who are not in it exist, indeed; but with a half-developed, inferior kind of life, like a jelly-fish."

May laughed her frank young laugh.

"You're not changed either!" she said emphatically.

"Did you enjoy the performance with which that young gentleman has been obliging us?" asked Rivers.

"I only heard the end of it."

"Very diplomatically answered."

"Are you fond of music, Mr. Rivers?"

"Yes, of music—very fond."

"So am I; but I know very little about it. Granny is a good musician."

"How fond you are of Mrs. Dobbs!" said Rivers.

"I am very proud of her, too," answered May quickly.

Owen Rivers looked at her with a singular expression, half-admiring, half-tenderly, pitying—as one might look at a child whose innocent candour is as yet "unspotted from the world."

"I suppose you know all the people here," said May, looking round on the assembly.

"I know who they are, most of them."

"That gentleman who was standing by himself at the window—the tall gentleman—who is he?"

"Mr. Jawler, a great musical critic."

"And the pleasant-faced man who seemed so delighted with the playing?"

"Mr. Sweeting. He is an enthusiastic admirer and patron of young Cleveland Turner, the pianist: a very kindly, amiable, courteous gentleman, with much money and leisure, as I am told."

"That stout lady talking to Miss Piper seems to be musical also?"

"That is Lady Moppett: a very good sort of woman, I dare say, but fanatical. She would bowstring all us dogs of Christians who believe in melody."

"And who is that disagreeable little man in the corner?"

"Disagreeable—?"

"The little man with moustaches. There. Close to the nice-looking, dark-eyed girl."

"Oh, that man? But he is not considered disagreeable by the world in general, Miss Cheffington! He is by way of being a rather fascinating individual: Signor Vincenzo Valli, singing-master, and composer of songs. I wonder why he condescends to favour Miss Piper with his presence."

"Is it a condescension?"

"A great condescension. Signor Valli is nothing, if not aristocratic."

At this moment there was a general movement in the other room. The young pianist seated himself once more at the instrument. The various groups of talkers dispersed, and took their places to listen. May whispered nervously to Miss Patty, that perhaps she and her uncle had better go, and take away the children before the music commenced.

"I am so afraid," she said naïvely, "that Willy may cry if that gentleman plays again."

Miss Patty found a way out of the difficulty by taking the children away to her own room. It was no deprivation to her, she said, not to hear Mr. Turner play.

So the two little boys, laden with good things, and further enticed by the promise of picture-books, trotted off very contentedly under Miss Patty's wing. Mr. Dormer-Smith had passed into the front drawing-room, where he was chatting with Lady Moppett, who proved to be an old acquaintance of his. May was following her uncle to explain to him about the children, when Miss Piper hurried up to her with an anxious and important mien.

"Sit down, my dear," she said; "sit down. Cleveland Turner is going to play that fine Beethoven, the one in F minor, the opera 57, you know. Mr. Jawler particularly wishes to hear him perform it."

May glanced round, and seeing no place vacant near at hand, returned to the other room, and took a seat close to the folding-doors, which were now left open.

"What is our sentence?" asked Rivers.

"Do you mean what is he going to play? A piece of Beethoven's."

"Ah! Well, at least he will have something to say this time. Remains to be seen whether he can say it."

Mr. Cleveland Turner performed the sonata appassionata correctly, although coldly, and with a certain hardness of style and touch. But the beauty of the composition made itself irresistibly felt, and when the piece was finished there was a murmur of applause. Mr. Jawler opened his eyes, inclined his head, opened his eyes again, and said, apparently to himself, "Yes, yes—oh yes!" which seemed to be interpreted as an expression of approval; for Miss Piper looked radiant, and even the icy demeanour of Mr. Cleveland Turner thawed half a degree or so. Signor Valli had applauded in a peculiar fashion—opening his arms wide, and bringing his gloved hands together with apparent force, but so as to produce no sound whatever. And as he went through this dumb show of applause, he was talking all the time to the dark-eyed girl near him, with a sneering smile on his face.

Miss Piper bustled up to them. "Dear Miss Bertram," she said, "you must let us hear your charming voice. Mr. Jawler has heard of you. He would like you to sing something. Signor Valli," with clasped hands, "might I entreat you to accompany Miss Bertram in one of your own exquisite compositions? It would be such a treat—such a musical feast, I may say!"

Miss Bertram unrolled her music-case in a business-like way, and spread its contents before the singing-master.

"What are you going to sing, Clara?" asked Lady Moppett, turning her head over her shoulder.

"Signor Valli will choose," answered the young lady quietly.

Valli selected a song and offered his arm to Miss Bertram to lead her to the piano. She did not accept it instantly, being occupied in replacing the rest of her music in its case; and with a sudden, impatient gesture, Valli wheeled round and walked to the piano alone. Miss Bertram followed him composedly, and took her place beside him. May looked at her with interest, as she stood there during the few bars of introduction to the song.

Clara Bertram was not beautiful, but she had a singularly attractive face. Her dark eyes were not nearly so large, nor so finely set, as Constance Hadlow's, but they were infinitely more expressive, and her rather wide mouth revealed a magnificent set of teeth when she smiled or sang. The song selected for her was one of those compositions which, if ill-sung, or even only tolerably sung, would pass unnoticed. But Miss Bertram sang it to perfection. Her voice was very beautiful, with something peculiarly pathetic in its vibrating tones, and she pronounced the Italian words with a pure, unaffected, and finished accent.

"Oh, how lovely!" exclaimed May, under her breath, when the song was over.

"Isn't it?" said Miss Piper, who happened to be near enough to catch the words. "I am so glad you are pleased with her! Do you think Mrs. Dormer-Smith would like her to sing now and then at a soirée? She wants to get known in really good houses."

Before May could answer the little woman had hurried off again, and in another minute was leading Miss Bertram up to Mr. Jawler, who spoke to the young singer with evident affability, keeping his eyes open for a full minute at a time.

Meanwhile Valli was left alone at the piano, and an ugly look came into his face as he glanced round and saw himself neglected. But his expression changed in an instant with curious suddenness when Miss Hadlow drew near, and, leaning on the instrument, addressed some words of compliment to him.

"Will you not let us hear you sing, Signor Valli?" she said presently.

Valli merely shook his head in answer, keeping his eyes fixed on Miss Hadlow's face with a look of bold admiration, and letting his fingers stray softly over the keys.

"Oh, that is a terrible disappointment!"

"I don't think so," replied the singing-master, speaking very good English.

"It is, indeed."

Again he shook his head.

"It is to me, at all events."

"Well, I shall sing for you; a little song sotto voce, all to ourselves."

"Oh, but that would be too selfish on my part, to enjoy your singing all to myself."

"It is a very good plan to be selfish," returned Valli; and forthwith he began a little Neapolitan love-song—murmuring, rather than singing it—and still keeping his eyes fixed on Miss Hadlow.

At the first sound of his voice, low and subdued though it was, Miss Piper held up her finger to bespeak silence. There was a general hush. Every one looked towards the piano, against which Constance was still leaning, with her back to the rest of the company. She made a little movement to withdraw to a seat, but Valli immediately ceased singing, and, under cover of a noisy ritournelle which he played on the piano, said to her, "I am singing for you. If you go away, my song will go away too."

"But I can't stand here by myself, Signor Valli," protested Constance, by no means displeased. At this moment Miss Piper approached to implore the maestro to continue, and Constance whispered to her in a few words the state of the case.

"Caprices of genius, my dear," said the little woman. "When you have seen as much of professional people as I have, you will not be astonished." Then to Valli, "Will you not continue that exquisite air? We are all dying to hear it."

"Yes; on condition that you both stay there and inspire me," answered he, with an unconcealed sneer.

Miss Piper, however, took him at his word, and, linking her arm in Constance's, remained standing close to the instrument. Valli, upon this, resumed his song. He gave it now at the full pitch of his voice, addressing it ostentatiously to Miss Hadlow, and throwing an exaggerated amount of expression into the love passages. Miss Piper was enchanted, and led off the applause enthusiastically. Valli was soon surrounded by a group of admirers, Mr. Dormer-Smith among them. May was conscious of a painful impression, which destroyed any pleasure she might have had in the song. And that Owen Rivers shared this impression was proved by his walking up to the piano, and unceremoniously putting his cousin's hand on his arm to lead her away.

"Oh, don't take Conny away, Mr. Rivers," cried Miss Piper. "Signor Valli is going to favour us with some more of his delicious national airs."

"Come and sit down, Constance," said Owen authoritatively. "Let me get you a seat also, Miss Piper," he added. "It can scarcely be necessary for the due exhibition of this gentleman's national airs to keep two ladies standing."

"Oh no, no; please don't mind me. I'm quite comfortable," said Miss Piper, with a shade of vexation on her good-humoured round face.

Constance remained perfectly calm and self-possessed; only a faint smile and a sparkle in her eyes revealed a gratified vanity as she took the chair near May, to which her cousin conducted her.

Miss Piper shrugged up her shoulders and pursed up her mouth. "He has no idea what artists are," she whispered in Lady Moppett's ear. "And, besides, poor dear young man, he's so desperately in love with his cousin that he can't bear her to be even looked at. I only hope Signor Valli won't take offence."

But Valli, finding himself now the object of general attention, was very gracious. He sang song after song without the inspiration of Miss Hadlow's handsome face opposite to him; and he sang far better than before;—with less exaggeration, and managing his naturally defective voice with singular skill and finesse. But the praise and flattery which his hearers poured forth unstintingly did not seem quite to satisfy him. His glance wandered restlessly, as though in search of something; and finally, after a very clever rendering of an old air by Carissimi, he addressed himself suddenly to Miss Bertram, who was standing somewhat apart in the background, and asked, in Italian—

"Is the Signorina content?"

"I always like your singing of that aria," she answered, in a quiet, matter-of-fact tone.

"Like it, indeed!" exclaimed Lady Moppett, with her severest manner. "I should think you did like it, Clara! And you ought to profit by it. To hear singing so finished—of such a perfect school—is a lesson for you."

Valli, upon this, made a low bow to Lady Moppett—a bow so low as to seem almost burlesque. As he raised his face again he turned it towards Miss Bertram with a subtle smile, saying, "Miladi is such a judge! Her praise is very precious." Clara, however, kept an impassive countenance, and declined to meet the glance he shot at her. Then Valli made a second and equally low bow to the hostess, and, cutting short her ecstatic compliments and thanks, left the room without further ceremony.

The party now broke up. Lady Moppett departed with Miss Bertram and Mr. Jawler, to whom she offered a seat in her carriage. Mr. Cleveland Turner and his patron, Mr. Sweeting, went away together. In a few minutes there remained Mr. Dormer-Smith, with his niece, and Owen Rivers. Miss Patty bustled in with the two children.

"Dear me," said she. "Is the music all over? Well, now let us be comfortable."

But Mr. Dormer-Smith declared he must reluctantly bring his visit to an end. "I don't know how to thank you," said he to Miss Patty, "for your kindness to my children. I hope you will forgive me for bringing them."

Miss Patty heartily assured him that there was nothing to forgive, and that she hoped he would bring them again. She had gathered from the artless utterances of Harold and Wilfred an idea of their home life, which made her feel compassionately towards them.

As for Miss Polly, she was in the highest spirits. Mr. Jawler and Signor Valli, both stars of considerable magnitude in the musical world, had shone for her with unclouded lustre. It had been, she thought, a highly successful afternoon. So also thought Harold and Wilfred. And perhaps these were the only three persons who had enjoyed themselves thoroughly and unaffectedly.

CHAPTER XIV.

The London season proceeded with its usual accumulation of engagements, its usual breathless chase after half-hours that have got too long a start ever to be recaptured, its usual fleeting satisfactions and abiding disappointments, its snubs, sneers, smiles, follies, falsehoods, and flirtations. The rushing current of fashionable life in London carried little May Cheffington on its surface, together with many brazen vessels of a very different kind. Constance Hadlow observed half-enviously to her friend that she was thoroughly "in the swim," a phrase which May found singularly inappropriate in her own case, feeling that there was no more question of a swim than in shooting Niagara! To her, especially, the whirl of society was confusing, phantasmagoric, and unreal. All the faces were new to her, most of the names awoke no associations in her mind. On the other hand, this peculiar inexperience gave freshness to her impressions and keenness to her insight. She had none of those social traditions which, nine times out of ten, supply the place of private judgment. She found her impression of many personages startlingly at variance with the label which the world had agreed to affix to them. It is possible to be at once simple and shrewd, just as it is possible to be both rusé and dull-witted.

May's simplicity was not of the blundering thick-skinned type; and her ingenuous freshness was admired by a great many persons, among whom was Mrs. Griffin. Far from being offended by May's moral indignation against those who accepted the hospitality of vulgar people, and then ridiculed them for being vulgar, Mrs. Griffin entirely approved her sentiments. Mrs. Griffin herself deplored, as she often said, "the servility towards mere money, which was degrading the tone of society." And whenever any new instance of it came to her knowledge, she would shake her head, and exclaim, softly, "Oh, Mammon, Mammon!" But this did not, of course, apply to her daughter the duchess, who sometimes went to the Aaronssohns'. Her daughter was so very great a lady as to be above ordinary restrictions. Other people worshipped Mammon; the duchess only patronized Mammon—which was, surely, a very different thing!

Aunt Pauline, however, derived no gratification from May's unconventional frankness. It was, on the contrary, a source of constant anxiety to her; and she felt daily more and more that it would be a relief to get May off her hands. Introducing her niece into society—even although the niece was a pretty girl, and a Cheffington to boot—had not proved so pleasing a task as she had anticipated. There was, to her thinking, a strange perversity in the girl's character, which made her callous where she should be sensitive, and sensitive where she might well be indifferent. For instance, she showed culpable coolness about her great-uncle Castlecombe and his family, and provoking warmth about her Oldchester friends. Not that May was apt to speak much of her life in Oldchester. In the natural course of things she would have talked freely and eagerly about her dear granny; but very soon after her arrival in London, her affectionate loquacity on this subject received a check. Aunt Pauline had hinted, with her usual mild politeness, that it would be desirable not to speak of Mrs. Dobbs before Smithson or any of the servants. Seeing the startled look in May's eyes, and the indignant flush on May's cheeks, her aunt added diplomatically, "Your father would not like it, May. I am trying to carry out his expressed wishes. That ought to be enough for you."

It was enough, at all events, to close May's lips. Her love and pride combined to make her silent. She tried to persuade herself that her father, at all events, had some good and reasonable motive for this prohibition, and that he, at least, was not ashamed of Mrs. Dobbs—ashamed of granny! The very thought made her hot with anger. But that Aunt Pauline was ashamed of her was too clear to May's honest mind. Painful as this conviction was, however, she came by degrees to hold it rather in sorrow than in anger, and to regard her aunt with something of the same indulgent toleration that Mrs. Dobbs had once expressed to Jo Weatherhead. For Mrs. Dormer-Smith's worldliness was not at all of a cynical sort. It was rather in the nature of a deep-rooted superstition conscientiously held.

To some points of her worldly creed Pauline clung with religious fervour. One of these was the duty incumbent on a dowerless young lady to marry well. To marry very well was to marry a man with birth and money; but to secure a husband with money only—provided there were enough of it—she allowed to be marrying well. She did not look at the matter with vulgar flippancy. It was, no doubt, a sacrifice for a well-born woman to become the wife of an underbred man, however wealthy. But well-born women were no less called upon than their humbler sisters to make sacrifices in a good cause.

None of the Castlecombes much frequented fashionable society, and Mrs. Dormer-Smith had hitherto resigned herself, without much difficulty, to seeing very little of her noble kinsfolk. But when May was introduced, her aunt thought it desirable to cultivate them. Lord Castlecombe's big, gloomy, family mansion in town had been let ever since his wife's death many years ago; and whenever his lordship came to London to give his vote in the House of Peers—which was almost the sole object that had power to bring him up from the country—he occupied furnished lodgings. Of his two sons, both bachelors, the elder was governor of a colony on the other side of the globe, and the younger held a permanent post under Government. This Lucius Cheffington occasionally met Mr. Dormer-Smith at the club, and exchanged a few words with him. Captain Cheffington, on his penultimate visit to England, when his ungrateful country declined to provide for him, had quarrelled with all the Castlecombes, and had made himself particularly obnoxious to Lucius; for Lucius, whom his cousin considered a solemn ass, held a lucrative place, whilst Augustus, who knew himself to be a remarkably clever fellow, with immense knowledge of the world, was relegated to poverty and obscurity. But Pauline had not quarrelled with them. She would not willingly have quarrelled with any one, least of all with her Uncle Castlecombe and his family. And as to Mr. Dormer-Smith, it chanced that the one point of sympathy between himself and his cousin-in-law Lucius was the latter's cordial dislike to Gus. Nevertheless, the dislike did not descend to Gus's daughter. Lucius was pleased to approve of his young kinswoman, none the less, perhaps, that it was evident her father troubled himself little about her.

Mr. Dormer-Smith knew very well that the most effectual way of winning Lord Castlecombe's goodwill for his grand-niece was to assure his lordship that he would not be called upon to do anything for her. He, therefore, confidentially informed Lucius that the girl's grandmother in Oldchester was defraying her expenses, and would, no doubt, eventually provide for her altogether. The sagacity of this course was proved soon afterwards, when Lucius announced that his father would come and dine with Pauline the next time he should be in town, and make Miranda's acquaintance.

This was well. And even as to May's Oldchester friends matters turned out better than her aunt could have hoped. In the first place, the Misses Piper showed no disposition whatever to force themselves on Mrs. Dormer-Smith. That being the case, there was no objection to May's going to see them every Sunday with her uncle and the children. To Harold and Wilfred these Sunday visits were such a delightful break in the dull routine of their lives that their father would have endured considerable boredom and discomfort rather than deprive them of it. But, in fact, he was not bored. Whenever the music became too severe, he could withdraw into the tea-room, where he always found some one to chat with. Possibly he, too, felt these Sundays to be a break in the monotony of his daily life. There was a cordial, hearty tone about the hostesses which was decidedly pleasant, although he was aware that Pauline would pronounce it sadly underbred. But Pauline was not there to be shocked, and there were some red drops in Mr. Dormer-Smith's veins (he was not quite so blue-blooded as his wife) which warmed to this plebeian kindness. Sometimes even the moisture would come into his eyes when he watched his little boys clinging familiarly about Miss Patty as they never clung about their mother. The good-natured old maid had won the children's hearts completely. They were overheard one day in a lively discussion as to which was the prettier, Miss Patty or Cousin May: Wilfred inclining, on the whole, to award the palm of beauty to his cousin, but Harold powerfully arguing in favour of Miss Patty that she had such "beautiful curls" (an ingenuous, and probably unique, tribute to the ginger-bread coloured wig!) and a "shiny brooch like a butterfly."

Then Constance Hadlow, whom Mrs. Dormer-Smith had unwillingly invited to lunch one day with her former schoolfellow, proved to be in every respect "most presentable," as Aunt Pauline herself candidly admitted. So presentable was she in fact, so handsome, self-possessed, and even (on the mother's side) well connected, that there might have arisen objections of a different sort against receiving her, as being a dangerous competitor for that solemn duty of marrying well. But a chance word of May's to the effect that young Bransby had long been an admirer of Constance, and that they were supposed by many persons in Oldchester to be engaged to each other, relieved Aunt Pauline's mind on that score.

"It would be very suitable," she said approvingly. "I think Mr. Bransby a very nice person; so quiet."

The subject of this glowing eulogium had not appeared at Mrs. Dormer-Smith's receptions for some time. He had been ordered into the country, to cure a violent cold by change of air; and although he much disliked leaving town at that moment, he never thought of neglecting his physician's advice. Theodore's mother had been consumptive; and the fear that he inherited her constitution made him anxiously careful of his health. Immediately on his return to London he presented himself, about half-past five o'clock one Thursday afternoon, in Mrs. Dormer-Smith's drawing-room, and experienced a shock of disagreeable surprise on finding Constance Hadlow seated near May at the tea-table. May, innocently supposing that she was doing him a good turn, gave him her place, and went to another part of the room. But Constance coolly greeted him with a "How d'ye do, Theodore?" in a tone of the politest insipidity, which he sincerely approved of. Nevertheless, he would rather not have found her there. On glancing round he was struck by several innovations. In the first place, the pianoforte—usually a dumb piece of furniture in Mrs. Dormer-Smith's house—stood open, with some loose sheets of music lying on it; and Signor Vincenzo Valli sat, teacup in hand, smiling his false smile beside Mrs. Griffin. Theodore knew perfectly well who Signor Valli was; and it needed not Mrs. Griffin's gracious demeanour to instruct this rising young man that Valli was sufficiently the fashion to be worth being civil to. But he was surprised to find him there. His surprises, however, were not at an end; for whom should he behold in familiar conversation with a gentleman at the opposite side of the room but Owen Rivers? And near them was—he could hardly believe his eyes—Mr. Bragg! It seemed to Theodore as if there had been a conspiracy amongst his acquaintance to make all sorts of fresh combinations on the social chess-board during his brief absence. He felt that it was necessary for him to take an accurate survey of the new positions. But he saw no immediate opportunity of doing so; for there was no one at hand to interrogate, except Constance Hadlow, who, of course, knew nothing. She must be spoken to, however; but he would cut the conversation as short as possible.

Thoughts—even the weighty thoughts of a diplomatically-minded young gentleman—move quickly, and there was scarcely any perceptible pause between Constance's greeting and his gravely polite remark that it was quite an unexpected pleasure to see her there.

"Yes; I came up a few weeks ago with the Pipers."

"Oh! you are staying with them?" (This with a strong flavour of his superior manner; for the Pipers were really nobodies.)

"And what have you been doing with yourself? I haven't seen you anywhere," said Constance coolly.

"I have been out of town. But in any case we might possibly not have met. Have you been going out much?"

"Oh, as much as most people, I suppose. I was at the Aaronssohns' dance last night."

"The Aaronssohns!" exclaimed Theodore. (This time he was so astonished that he spoke quite naturally.) "I didn't know that you knew them."

"Oh, I don't know them."

"Then how did you get—I mean—"

"How did I get there? Dear me, Theodore, your visit to the country has given you a refreshing buttercup-and-daisy kind of air! Do you suppose that the Aaronssohns' ball-room was filled with their personal friends and acquaintances? Mrs. Griffin got me an invitation."

Now to be presented to Mrs. Griffin and to be invited to the Aaronssohns' were pet objects of Theodore Bransby's social ambition, and he had not yet compassed either of them.

"Oh, indeed!" said he, struggling, under the disadvantage of conscious ill-humour, to maintain that air of indifference to all things in heaven and earth which he imagined to be the completest manifestation of high breeding. "I suppose that was achieved through Mrs. Dormer-Smith's influence."

"Not altogether. It was May Cheffington who first introduced me to Mrs. Griffin. She's just the same dear little thing as ever—I don't mean Mrs. Griffin! But Mrs. Griffin found out that she had known my grandfather Rivers. I believe they were sweethearts in their pinafores a hundred years ago; so she has been awfully nice to me."

While Constance was speaking, Theodore's eye lighted on Mr. Bragg, solid and solemn, wearing that look of melancholy respectability which is associated with the British workman in his Sunday clothes.

"Oh, and Mr. Bragg was at the Aaronssohns', too," said Constance, following the young man's glance. "Fancy Mr. Bragg at a ball!"

"Did Mrs. Griffin know his grandfather?" asked Theodore, with a sneer.

It was clear to Constance that he had quite lost his temper. Otherwise he would not, she felt sure, have said anything in such bad taste. But she replied calmly—

"I don't think Mr. Bragg ever had a grandfather. But he is rich enough to do without one. It is poor persons like you and me who find grandfathers necessary—or, at all events, useful."

Theodore understood the sarcasm of this quiet speech, and it helped him to master his growing irritation. There are some natures on which a moral buffet acts as a sedative.

"Was it your friend Miss Piper who brought Mr. Bragg here?" he asked, showing no sign of having felt the blow, except a slight increase of pallor.

"Oh dear, no! The Pipers have never been here themselves, except to leave a card at the door. This is not the kind of society they care for, you know. I saw Mr. Bragg come in to-day with May's cousin, Mr. Lucius Cheffington, but I can't say whether he first introduced him or not."

"Is that Mr. Lucius Cheffington?"

"That man talking to Owen?—Yes."

"Mrs. Dormer-Smith has rather a mixed collection this afternoon. I see Valli over there. You know who I mean? That short, foreign man near—"

"Oh yes; Signor Valli is a great ally of mine. He's delightful, I think. His airs and graces are so amusing. I can tell you how he comes to be here, if you like," returned Constance placidly. She was secretly enjoying Theodore's discomfiture. He had expected to play the part of town mouse, and to patronize and instruct her. "The fact is," she continued, "that Lady Moppett begged Mr. Dormer-Smith to induce his wife to have her protégée, Miss Bertram, to sing here on Thursday afternoons, promising, as a kind of bait, to get Valli to come too. I don't think Mrs. Dormer-Smith particularly wished to have Miss Bertram; but she thought it would be nice to have Valli, who is run after by the best people, and is very difficult to get hold of. So the negotiation succeeded. It is too funny how one has to ménager and coax these professional people. If you don't want any more information just now, I think I will go and speak to Mrs. Griffin." Whereupon Constance glided away, self-possessed and graceful, and with a becoming touch of animation bestowed by the consciousness that she had been mistress of the situation.

Theodore looked decidedly blank for the moment. No one bestowed any attention on him. As he sat watching, he was struck by the evidently familiar way in which Owen Rivers and Mr. Cheffington were talking together. He himself particularly desired to be introduced to Lucius Cheffington, but a secret, grudging feeling made him unwilling to owe the introduction to Rivers. Presently Rivers moved away to join May and Miss Bertram, who were turning over some music together, and Mr. Bragg took his place near Mr. Cheffington. This was the opportunity which Theodore had wished for. He at once rose and walked up to them. Theodore's manner was never servile, but there was an added gravity in his demeanour towards certain persons, intended to show that he thought them worth taking seriously; and this tribute he rendered to Mr. Bragg. For, although the young man had by no means forgotten Mr. Bragg's deplorable insensibility to an enlightened view of the currency question, yet he prided himself on thoroughly understanding that the great tin-tack maker's claims to consideration rested on a solid basis quite apart from culture or intelligence.

"I wish," said Theodore, after the first salutations, "that you would do me the favour to make me known to Mr. Lucius Cheffington. I know so many members of his family, but I have not the pleasure of his personal acquaintance."

Mr. Bragg eyed him with his usual heavy deliberation. "Oh," said he slowly, "this is Mr.—I don't call to mind your Christian name—eh? Oh yes—Mr. Theodore Bransby."

Mr. Lucius Cheffington made an unusually low bow, his pride being of the sort which manifests itself in the most ceremonious politeness.

He was a small, lean man, with a pale face deeply lined by ill-health and a fretful temperament. He had closely shaven cheeks and chin; heavy, grizzled moustaches; and very thick, grizzled hair, which he wore rather long. His voice was harsh, though subdued, and he spoke very slowly, making such long pauses as occasionally tempted unwary strangers to finish his sentences for him. A double eyeglass with tortoise-shell rims was set astride his nose; and behind the glasses two dark, near-sighted eyes looked out, somewhat superciliously, upon a world which fell sadly short of what a Cheffington had a right to expect.

"I have the pleasure of knowing your cousin, Captain Augustus Cheffington, very well indeed," said Theodore.

Lucius bowed again and adjusted his eyeglass. A shade of surprise and annoyance passed over his face. His Cousin Augustus had been a sore subject with the family for years; and latterly such rumours as had reached England about him had not made the subject more agreeable.

"I have often thought," pursued Theodore, quite unaware that his listener was regarding him with a mixture of astonishment and disfavour, "that it is a great pity a man of Captain Cheffington's abilities and accomplishments should live out of England; unless, indeed, he held some diplomatic appointment abroad. In my opinion these are times in which the great old families should hold fast by the public service. As I ventured to say to one of our county members the other day—" And so on, and so on. Having thus happily launched himself, Theodore proceeded in his best Parliamentary style: holding forth with a power of self-complacent and steady boredom beyond his years. A sensitive person would have been petrified by the unsympathizing stare from behind those tortoise-shell-rimmed glasses; but Theodore was not sensitive to such influences: being fortified by the à priori conviction that he must naturally make a favourable impression. And since Lucius Cheffington could not, compatibly with his own dignity, plainly tell him that he considered him a presumptuous young ass, there was nothing to check his flow of eloquence.

But at length the cold stare was softened, and the pale, peevish, furrowed face turned to Theodore with a faint show of interest. Some casual word of this intrusive young man's seemed to show that he came from Oldchester.

"Do you know—a—Mrs.—a—Dobbs?" asked Lucius, speaking for the first time, and edging in this point-blank question between two of Theodore's neatly-turned sentences setting forth a political parallel between the late Lord Tweedledum and the present Right Honourable Tweedledee.

It was a shock; but Theodore bore it stoically.

"Not exactly. I have spoken with her. Mrs. Dobbs is not precisely—in our set," he answered, with a slight smile at one corner of his mouth, intended to demolish Mrs. Dobbs.

"I thought that, being a native of Oldchester, you might—a—be—" begun Mr. Cheffington in his low, harsh tones.

"Be acquainted with her? Really—"

"I thought that, being a native of Oldchester, you might—a—be able to tell me something about her."

"Not much, I fear," replied Theodore. He felt tempted to add that in Oldchester there were natives and natives.

"She's—a—rich, isn't she?" pursued Mr. Cheffington.

"Not that I know of," answered Theodore, staring a little.

"Rich is, perhaps, too much to say. At any rate, she is—a—quite well—"

"Well off? Oh, as to that—"

"At any rate, she is quite well-to-do, I presume!"

Theodore had never considered the question, but he said, "Oh yes," at a venture; and then suddenly a light flashed upon his mind. Perhaps Mrs. Dobbs was rich, after all. Though she lived in so humble a style she might, perhaps, have laid by money.

"She appears to be a person of—a—great—good sense," said Mr. Lucius Cheffington, remembering how Mrs. Dormer-Smith had stated that she declined to give any money-assistance to Augustus. And after that he made a second very low bow, and brought the interview to an end.

Little had Theodore Bransby expected to hear Mrs. Dobbs discussed and approved by a member of the noble house of Castlecombe. He had noticed that Mrs. Dormer-Smith systematically avoided any mention of the vulgar old woman. But then Mrs. Dormer-Smith was a person of the very finest taste. And, to be sure, it could scarcely be expected that Mr. Lucius Cheffington should feel Augustus's mésalliance as acutely as it was felt by Augustus's own sister. Besides, if, as really seemed possible, the ironmonger's widow turned out to be a moneyed person—! But it must be recorded of Theodore, that not even the idea of her having money reconciled him to Mrs. Dobbs. He said to himself afterwards, when he was meditating on what he had heard, that nothing so convincingly proved how much he was in love with Miss Cheffington, as his being ready to forgive her even her grandmother!

CHAPTER XV.

George Frederick Cheffington, fifth Viscount Castlecombe, was, in many ways, a very clever old man. He was extremely ignorant of most things which can be taught by books. But he had a thorough acquaintance with practical agriculture, considerable keenness in finance, and a quick eye to detect the weaknesses of his fellow men. On the other hand, his overweening self-esteem led him to think that what he knew comprised what was chiefly, if not solely, worth knowing, and his avarice occasionally overrode his native talent for business. In his youth he had been idle and extravagant. The former vice gave him the reputation of a dunce at school and college, and, by a reaction which belonged to his character, made him defiantly contemptuous of bookish men, with one single exception, presently to be noted. As to his extravagance, that was effectually cured by the death of his father. From the moment that he came into possession of the family estates, which he did at about thirty years of age, his income was administered with sagacious economy, and by the time his two sons arrived at manhood Lord Castlecombe was a very rich man.

If he had a soft place in his heart, it was for his son Lucius, who resembled his dead mother in features, and also, unfortunately, in the delicacy of his constitution. George, his heir, was like himself—strong, tough, and hardy. Lord Castlecombe secretly admired Lucius's talents very much, and had been highly gratified when his second son took honours at his University. That this success had not been followed by any particularly brilliant results later, and that Lucius had, as it were, stuck fast in his career, had even decidedly failed in Parliament, and had finally been shelved in a Government post which, although lucrative, was inglorious, his lordship attributed to the increase of folly, incapacity, and roguery which he had observed in the world during the last twenty years or so. That a Cheffington of such abilities as Lucius should remain undistinguished was part of the general decadence. In politics Lord Castlecombe was a Whig of the old school; and though he continued to vote with his party, yet the only point on which he was thoroughly in sympathy with the Liberals—a word, by the way, which he had come greatly to dislike, as covering far too wide a field—was that they fought the Tories.

The person whom Lord Castlecombe most detested in all the world was his nephew Augustus. He disliked his extravagance, his poverty, and the biting insolence of his tongue. This antipathy had latterly added poignancy to the old man's desire that his son should marry, and transmit the Castlecombe title and estates in the direct line; for Augustus was the next heir after his two cousins. It was true that the contingency of Captain Cheffington succeeding seemed remote enough. George Cheffington was only his senior by a couple of years, and Lucius was his junior. But neither of them had married; and they were well on in middle life. Lucius, indeed, seemed to have settled down into incorrigible old bachelorhood. And although George, in answer to his father's exhortations on the subject, always replied that he really would think seriously of looking for a wife on his next visit to England (persons suitable for that dignity not being to be found, it appeared, in the particular portion of the globe where his official duties lay), yet the years went by, and still there came no daughter-in-law, no grandson to inherit the coronet and enjoy the broad acres of Castlecombe. The idea that Augustus Cheffington might ever come to enjoy them was gall and wormwood to their present owner. But he had never breathed a word on this subject to any human being.

Mrs. Dormer-Smith was gratified by her uncle's gracious acceptance of an invitation to dine with her, soon after his arrival in town, about the middle of June. Lord Castlecombe did not visit her often; but that was from no ill-will on his part. In fact, he was rather fond of Pauline. He considered her a bit of a goose. But he thought it by no means unbecoming in a woman to be a bit of a goose. And she had thoroughbred manners, a gentle voice, and was still agreeable to look upon. The old lord disliked ugly women, and maintained that the sight of them disagreed with him like bad wine.

This consideration influenced Pauline in the choice of her guests to meet her uncle. It was understood there was to be no large party. It had been agreed that they should invite Mr. Bragg, who had bought a good deal of land in Lord Castlecombe's county, was director of a company of which the noble viscount was chairman, and of whom his lordship was known to entertain a favourable opinion, as being a man who made no disguise about his humble origin, and was free from the offensive pretensions of many nouveaux riches. For, although Lord Castlecombe willingly admitted that money could buy everything on which most people valued themselves, he greatly disliked the notion that it could be supposed to buy the things on which he most valued himself.

"Well, then, Frederick," said Mrs. Dormer-Smith, "that makes four men: my uncle, Lucius, Mr. Bragg, and yourself. Then May and I; and I thought of having that handsome Miss Hadlow. Uncle George likes to see pretty faces. We want another woman, but really I don't know who there is available at this moment. There are so few odd women who ain't frights," pursued the anxious hostess plaintively. "If it were a man, now—There are plenty of odd men to be had." Then, struck by a sudden inspiration, she said, "Why shouldn't we have an odd man instead of another woman? Uncle George gives me his arm, of course. You take Miss Hadlow, Mr. Bragg takes May, and Lucius and the odd man go in together. Positively, I think it would be the best arrangement of all."

"I suppose Lucius wouldn't mind, eh?"

"It certainly would be the best arrangement for me, at all events; for if there are only those two girls, I can simply put my feet up on a sofa when we go into the drawing-room, shut my eyes, and be quiet for half an hour, which, of course, would be out of the question if there was any woman who required to have civilities paid her; and in all probability I shall be in a state of nervous prostration by Friday. This season with May has tried me severely."

Mr. Dormer-Smith offering no objection, there only remained to make choice of the "odd man," and, after a moment's reflection, Pauline decided on young Bransby.

"Bransby!" exclaimed Mr. Dormer-Smith. "He's a dreadful prig."

"I think he's very nice, Frederick. But really that is not the point. He's engaged, or wants to be engaged, or something of the sort, to Miss Hadlow, so of course—"

"What? You don't mean to say that handsome girl would have such an insignificant fellow as Bransby?"

"I mean to say nothing about it. The subject has only a faint interest for me, Frederick. But what is important is that, in any case, he will help to take her off."

Mr. Dormer-Smith stared; he understood his wife's phrase, but not her allusion. "Why, you don't suppose there's any danger of her setting her cap at Lucius?" said he.

"I should have no objection to her doing so."

"Well, there's nobody else."

"We need not discuss it, Frederick. Please give your best attention to the wine; you know that Uncle George is terribly fastidious about his wine, and the worst is that if he is discontented, he will not hesitate to say so before everybody."

That really did seem to her the worst. Most of the evils of life, she thought, might be more endurable if people would but be discreet, and say nothing about them.

The evil of Uncle George's public reprobation of her wine did not, however, befall her. Lord Castlecombe was content with his dinner, and looked round him approvingly as he sat on his niece's right hand.

"A couple of uncommonly pretty girls those," said his lordship. "They've got on pretty frocks, too; I like a good bright colour."

Pauline had begged Miss Hadlow beforehand not to wear black, or any sombre hue, her uncle having a special dislike to such; and Constance, perfectly willing to please Lord Castlecombe by looking as brilliant as she could, had arrayed herself in her favourite maize-colour.

"You have a very nice gown on, too, Pauline," added his lordship graciously.

Mrs. Dormer-Smith privately thought her own toilette detestable. It was a gaily-flowered brocade (a gift from her husband soon after Wilfrid's birth), which had been hidden from the light for several years. But she had self-denyingly caused Smithson to furbish it up for the present occasion, and was gratified that her virtue did not go unrewarded.

"I knew you liked vivid colours, Uncle George," said she softly.

"Of course I do. Everybody does, that has the use of his eyes. Don't believe the humbugs who tell you otherwise. Your upholsterer now will show you some wretched washed-out rag of a thing, and try to persuade you to cover your chairs with it, because it's æsthetic! Parcel of fools! Not that the fellows who sell the things are fools. They know very well which side their bread is buttered." Then glancing across the table with his keen, sunken, black eyes, he continued, "That little Miranda—what is it you call her? May? Well, May is a very good name for her—is remarkably fresh and pretty. Good frank forehead. Not a bit like her father. Different type. But the other girl is the beauty. Uncommonly handsome, really."

"I'm glad you think May nice," said Mrs. Dormer-Smith. "Of course I was anxious that you should like her. She is poor Augustus's only child—only surviving child. You know there were five or six of them, but the others all died in babyhood."

Lord Castlecombe did know it, and remembered it now with grim satisfaction. At least Augustus had no male heir to come after him.

"Ah! Gus made a pretty hash of it altogether," said the old man.

But he did not say it unkindly. He would not willingly have been harsh or brutal towards Pauline. She really was a very sweet creature, and had, he thought, almost every quality that he could desire in the women of his blood. For, it must be observed, Lord Castlecombe did not know that Pauline admired æsthetic furniture, nor that she considered Augustus to have been rather hardly treated by the Castlecombes.

"Of course," replied that gentle lady. "My poor brother's unfortunate marriage—"

"Oh! Ah! Yes. But that, at all events, seems to have turned out better than could have been expected. Lucius tells me there is a grandmother who has money, and is generous."

"Not to Augustus, Uncle George; Mrs. Dobbs positively refuses to assist Augustus."

"H'm!" grunted Uncle George, his opinion of Mrs. Dobbs's good sense taking a sudden leap upward. "Well, my dear, people have to think of their own interests, you know." Then, in a louder tone, "Frederick, send me that white Hermitage. It's a very fair wine, as times go—a very fair wine indeed."

When the ladies had left the table, young Bransby felt what he would have called, in speaking of any one else, "a little out of it." My lord talked with Mr. Bragg, Lucius and Frederick were discussing some item of club politics, in the midst of which the host would now and again interpolate some parenthetical observations addressed to young Bransby, obviously as a matter of duty. At length, in declining the claret which Mr. Dormer-Smith pushed towards him, Theodore took the opportunity to say—

"Do you think I might venture to go upstairs? I have a message for Mrs. Dormer-Smith about a little commission with which she entrusted me."

"No more wine, really? Oh, my wife will be charmed to see you," replied Frederick, with alacrity. And, thereupon, the young man quietly left the room.

It was true that he had undertaken a commission for Mrs. Dormer-Smith; but he would not have prematurely withdrawn himself from the company of a peer and a millionaire, on that account. He was moved by a far weightier purpose. He had made up his mind to propose to Miss Cheffington; and, if the Fates favoured him, he might do it that very evening. For some time past—before May left Oldchester—Theodore had been sure that he wished to marry her. There were drawbacks. She had no money (or at all events he had not reckoned on her having any money), and she had connections of a very objectionable kind. But he rather dwelt on these things, as proving the disinterested nature of his attachment. He was so much in love with May, that he liked to fancy himself making some sacrifices on her account. As to her feelings towards him, he was not without misgivings. But he watched her in society at every opportunity, and had convinced himself that she was, at all events, fancy-free. She did not even flirt; but enjoyed herself with child-like openness:—or was bored with equal simplicity and sincerity. As to her aunt, Theodore did not doubt that his suit would be favourably received by Mrs. Dormer-Smith. She must, long ago, have perceived his intentions; and he felt that his being invited to that intimate little dinner—almost a family dinner—was strong encouragement.

Theodore was fortifying himself with this reflection as he mounted the stairs to the drawing-room. His foot fell more and more lingeringly on the soft, soundless carpet as he neared the door. He was on an errand which can scarcely be undertaken with cool self-possession, even by a young gentleman holding the most favourable view of his own merits and prospects. One can never certainly reckon on one's soundest views being shared. A servant carrying coffee, preceded him, and opened the drawing-room door just as he arrived on the landing; and Theodore felt positively grateful to the man for, as it were, covering his entrance, and relieving him from the embarrassment of walking in alone. He entered close behind the footman, and was, for a few moments, unperceived by the ladies.

The room was a little dim; all the lamps being shaded with rose-colour. Mrs. Dormer-Smith was reclining on a sofa, with closed eyes. But she was not asleep; for beside her in a low lounging-chair, and talking to her in a subdued voice, sat Constance Hadlow. May was at the other side of the room, leaning with both elbows on a little table which stood in a recess between the fireplace and a window, and apparently absorbed in a book. Theodore thought she made a charming picture, with the soft light falling on her fair young face and white dress; and his pulse, which had been beating a little quicker than usual all the way upstairs, became suddenly still more accelerated.

May looked up.

"Is that you?" she said. "Where are the others?"

It was not a very warm or flattering welcome; but Theodore was scarcely conscious of her words. He was thinking what a fortunate chance it was which left May isolated, so far away from the other ladies as to be out of earshot, if one spoke in a suitably low tone. At the sound of her niece's voice Mrs. Dormer-Smith languidly turned her head.

"Oh, please don't move, Mrs. Dormer-Smith," said Theodore, speaking in a quick, confused way, very different from his accustomed manner. "If I am to disturb you, I must go away at once. But I—I don't take much wine, and he said—Mr. Dormer-Smith said he thought I might—if you don't mind my preceding the other men by a few minutes, I will be as quiet as a mouse."

He crossed the room and sat down by May in the shadow of a heavy window-curtain.

The hostess murmured a gracious word or two and then closed her eyes again. She had been a little vexed by the young man's premature arrival; but if he was content to be quiet, and whisper to May, she need not stand on ceremony with him. The fact was, she was listening with great interest to Constance's account of a feud which had arisen between Lady Burlington and Mrs. Griffin's daughter, the duchess. Constance had the details at first hand, from Mrs. Griffin herself, on the one side, and from Miss Polly Piper on the other: for the feud had arisen about Signor Vincenzo Valli. The fashionable singing-master had thrown over one of the great ladies for the other, on the occasion of some soirée musicale; and the quarrel had been espoused by various personages of distinction, whose sayings and doings with regard to it Mrs. Dormer-Smith considered to be at once important and entertaining. She mentally contrasted with a sigh the intelligence, tact, and correctness of judgment which Constance brought to bear on this matter, with the nonchalance—not to say downright levity and indifference—displayed by May. It was impossible to get May to interest herself in the bearings of the case. In fact, she had abandoned the discussion, and gone away to her book; whereas this provincial girl, with not one quarter of May's advantages, understood it perfectly, remembered the names of all the people concerned, had a very sufficient knowledge of their relative importance, and was able to impart to her hostess a variety of minute circumstances, narrated in a low, quiet tone, free from emphasis or emotion, which was delightfully soothing.

May, for her part, was by no means pleased to have her reading interrupted; but politeness, and the sense that she was, in her degree, responsible for the hospitality of the house, impelled her to close her book at once, and to turn a good-humoured countenance towards her companion.

"Isn't Uncle Frederick coming?" she asked, finding nothing better to say at the moment.

"Presently. Are you in a great hurry to see him?" returned Theodore.

"Oh no; I was amusing myself very well."

"Are you angry with me, for interrupting you?"

"Oh no," answered May again. But this second "Oh no" was not quite so hearty as the first.

"May I see what you have been reading?"

She pushed the book towards him.

"'Mansfield Park.' Whose is it?"

"Good gracious! You don't mean to say that you don't know?"

"I don't read novels," said Theodore loftily, but not severely. It was all very well for women to have that weakness.

"But this is an English classic! Mr. Rivers says so. You really ought to know who wrote 'Mansfield Park,' even if you have never read it. It is one of Jane Austen's works."

"Ah! Do you—do you like it?" said Theodore, scarcely knowing what he said. He was playing nervously with a little ivory paper-knife which lay on the table, and his whole aspect and manner—had not both been to some extent concealed by the shadow of the velvet curtain—would have betrayed to the most indifferent observer that he was agitated and unlike himself. He felt that the precious minutes of this chance tête-à-tête were passing swiftly; he longed to profit by them; and yet, now that the moment had come, he feared to stand the hazard of the die, and kept deferring it by idle words.

"Oh yes! I like it, of course," answered May. "Not so much, perhaps, as 'Emma,' or 'Pride and Prejudice.' Mr. Rivers advised me to read it."

It was the second time she had mentioned Rivers's name, and this fact stung Theodore unaccountably. It acted like a touch of the spur to a lagging horse. He burst out, still speaking almost in a whisper, but with some heat—

"Rivers is a happy fellow! What would I give if you cared enough about me to follow my advice!"

"You have only to advise me to do something which I like as much as reading Jane Austen," replied May archly. But his tone had struck her disagreeably. She peered at him furtively as he sat in the shadow, trying in vain to see his countenance clearly. The idea crossed her mind that he might have taken too much wine at dinner. But it was so repulsive an idea to her, that she felt she ought not to entertain it without better foundation.

"It is a most fortunate chance for me to have this—this blessed opportunity," pursued Theodore. (He had hesitated for the epithet, and was not by any means satisfied with it when he had got it). "I have long been wanting to speak to you."

"To me? Well, that need not have been very difficult," answered May, edging a little away, and trying to obtain a good view of his face.

"Pardon me. It is not easy to have the privilege of a private word with Miss Cheffington. When we meet in society, you are surrounded, as is but too natural. And latterly, in your own home, you have been a good deal engrossed. I could not say what I have to say before—"

He glanced over at Constance Hadlow as he spoke. This was an immense relief to May who had been growing more and more uncomfortable, and vaguely apprehensive. She thought she understood it all now. Conny had been treating him with coolness and neglect. She herself had noticed this, and now he wanted to enlist the sympathies of Conny's friend.

"Oh, I see!" she exclaimed. "It's something about Constance that you wish to say to me."

"About Constance? Ah, May, you are cruel! You know too well your power!" he said, endeavouring to give a pathetic intonation to his voice, but producing only an odd, croaking, throaty sound. Then May decided, in her own mind, that he had been taking too much wine; and, angry and disgusted, she tried to rise from her chair and leave him. But she was hemmed in by the little table, and on her first movement, Theodore took hold of the skirt of her dress to detain her. May turned round upon him with a pale, indignant face, and flashing eyes.

"Don't touch my dress, if you please. I wish to go away."

"Miss Cheffington—May—you must hear what I have to say now. You must know it without my saying, for I have loved you so long and so devotedly. But I have a right to be heard."

May was thunderstruck. But she perceived in a moment that she had, in one sense, done him injustice—he had not drunk too much wine. But this—! This was worse! How far easier it would have been to forgive Theodore if he had even got tipsy—just a little tipsy—instead of making such a declaration! She supposed she had no right to be disgusted; she had heard that properly behaved young ladies always took an offer of marriage to be a great honour. But she was disgusted, nevertheless; and so far from feeling honoured, she was conscious of a distressing sense of humiliation. She tried, however, to keep up her dignity, and at the same time to say what was right to this—this dreadful young man, who had suddenly presented himself in the odious light of wanting to make love to her.

"Oh, please don't say any more. I'm very much obliged to you. I mean I'm extremely sorry. But I beg you won't say another word, and forget all about it as quickly as possible."

"Forget it! Nay, that is out of the question. I could not if I would."

Theodore began to recover his self-command as May lost hers. She was agitated and trembling. Well, he would not have had her listen to his words unmoved. She was very young and inexperienced. And he had, it seemed, taken her by surprise.

"Is it possible," he continued softly, "that you were quite unprepared to hear—"

"Quite unprepared. But that makes no difference. And you really must allow me to go away. I'm very sorry, indeed, but I can't stay here another moment."

"Am I so repulsive?" said he, with a sentimental beseeching glance. But he met an expression in her face which made him add quickly, in quite another tone, "Well, well, I will prefer your wishes to my own," at the same time drawing himself and his chair to one side.

She had looked almost capable of leaping over the table to escape. May brushed past him, and darted away out of the room without another word.

Theodore seized hold of the book she had left behind her, and bent his head over it. He saw not one word on the printed page beneath his eyes, but it saved him from appearing as confused as he felt. Had he been rejected? And, if so, was it a rejection which he was bound to consider final? Or had he received no real answer at all? Gradually, as his throat grew less dry, his head less hot, and his brain more clear, he arrived at the conclusion that he had virtually had no answer. May was little more than a child, and he had startled her. Then he remembered that word of May's, "It is about Constance you wish to speak to me." Could she be under any misapprehension as to his position with regard to Constance? The idea was fraught with comfort. That, at least, he could set right, and without delay. He rose and walked across the room at once to Mrs. Dormer-Smith's sofa.

At this moment the procession of men, headed by Lord Castlecombe, arrived from the dining-room. Constance glided away, leaving her vacant chair for Theodore, who immediately occupied it, thus cutting off Mrs. Dormer-Smith from the rest of the company. That lady looked anxiously across his shoulder.

"Would you," she said to Theodore, "would you be so very good as to ask my husband to inquire where Miss Cheffington is? My uncle would like to talk to her, I know; and—Oh, there she is! Thanks. Don't trouble yourself."

May had returned to the drawing-room; but instead of going near her noble grand-uncle, she perversely seated herself in a remote nook beside Mr. Bragg, with whom she presently began a conversation, keeping her face persistently turned away from every one else. Her noble grand-uncle did not seem to care. His lordship marched straight up to Miss Hadlow, and stood before her, coffee-cup in hand, with his curious air of perfectly knowing how to behave like a fine gentleman whenever he should think it worth while. Lucius and Frederick were continuing their club discussion, which possessed the advantage—for persons of leisure—of having neither beginning nor end, and of being indefinitely elastic. Pauline took in the whole room with one comprehensive glance, and then leant back against her cushions with a sigh, which, if not contented, was resigned. She made no effort to recall May to her duty towards Lord Castlecombe.

"You must forgive me, Mr. Bransby," she said graciously, "if I have been selfish in engrossing Miss Hadlow. If you don't take care, my uncle will do the same! Lord Castlecombe admires her very much."

Theodore cleared his throat, settled his cravat with a rather unsteady hand, and looked at her as solemnly as if he were about to commence an oration. But all he managed to say was—

"There has been a mistake, Mrs. Dormer-Smith."

"A mistake?"

"Yes. I have some reason to believe that you are under a wrong impression about me."

His hostess faintly raised her eyebrows, and answered with a smile, "I hope not: for all my impressions of you are very pleasant."

Theodore bowed gravely. "You are very kind," said he. "It is important to me to set this matter right. You perhaps imagine—some one may have told you that I and Miss Hadlow—there has been, I believe, some idle gossip coupling our names together."

"Not very unnaturally," said Mrs. Dormer-Smith, still smiling. But she began to wonder what he could be driving at.

"Well, I do think it hard that one cannot be on friendly terms with a person one has known all one's life without being supposed to be engaged to her."

"Or him," put in Pauline quietly.

"Of course. I mean, of course, that it is particularly unfair to the lady. But it puts a man in a false position too. I have just been speaking to May—"

Then, in an instant, the true state of the case flashed on Mrs. Dormer-Smith, to her unspeakable consternation. This, then, was her model young man, whom she had pronounced to be so "nice" and so "quiet;" and who, moreover, had always expressed the most proper sentiments on the subject of unequal marriages! She felt herself to be of all ladies the most persecuted by fate.

"Oh," she said, coldly interrupting him; "it was scarcely necessary to say anything to Miss Cheffington on the subject."

But Theodore was beyond taking heed of any snub or check of that kind. "One moment," he said, breathing quickly. "If you will allow me to finish what I was saying, you will see—I am, as you must have perceived, deeply attached to your niece."

"No, no," protested Mrs. Dormer-Smith faintly. "I never perceived it."

"Then that must have been because you were looking in a wrong direction. You were misled about Constance Hadlow; otherwise, the nature of my attentions could scarcely have escaped you."

"And you say that you have been speaking to—to my niece?"

"I have this evening told her how devotedly I love her."

"Good heavens!" whispered Mrs. Dormer-Smith, letting her head sink back among the sofa-cushions. "And what was her reply?"

"Her reply was—well, practically, it was no reply at all. May was agitated and startled, and I think she had believed that foolish gossip about my engagement to Miss Hadlow. But I trust to you to explain—"

"Pray, Mr. Bransby, say no more. I regret extremely that this should have happened."

"Oh, but I don't know that I have any reason to despair," he answered naïvely.

This was almost more than Pauline could endure. She got up from the sofa, and plaintively murmuring, "Say no more; pray say no more. I really am not equal to it at present," fairly walked away from him.

That night when the guests were gone, Mrs. Dormer-Smith sent for her husband to her dressing-room, and revealed to him what young Bransby had said. His indignation at the young man's presumption was equal to her own: although not wholly on the same grounds.

"You will have to talk to him, Frederick," she said. "When he went away he said something about requesting an early interview. I cannot stand any more of it. It upsets me too frightfully. Of course, you won't quarrel with him. Just give him politely to understand that it is out of the question. Fortunately, May appears to have been as much outrée by this preposterous proposal as I could desire. May behaved very nicely to-night altogether. I was pleased with her."

"H'm! Oh yes; but I thought she might have paid a little more attention to your uncle. She never went near him after we came upstairs. I think she talked to old Bragg more than to any one else."

"Frederick," said his wife slowly, "do you know that Lady Hautenville is making a dead set at Mr. Bragg for Felicia?"

"Is she?"

"Yes. Mrs. Griffin told me all about it. They are moving heaven and earth to catch him."

"Really? Well, bonne chance!"

"It would be mauvaise chance for him, poor man! Felicia has a frightful temper, and incredibly extravagant habits. She must be over her eyebrows in debt. But I fancy Mr. Bragg has better taste."

Her meaning tone made her husband look at her with sudden earnestness. "What do you mean?" he asked brusquely.

Mrs. Dormer-Smith put her hand to her forehead. "Let me entreat you not to raise your voice!" she said. "I have had quite enough to try my nerves this evening. I mean that I think Mr. Bragg is interested in May. It would be a splendid match for her."

"What?" cried Frederick, disregarding his wife's request, and raising his voice considerably. "Old Bragg!"

Pauline turned on him impressively. "Frederick," she said, speaking with patient mildness, as one imparting higher lore to some untutored savage, "Mr. Bragg is barely fifty-four; and his income—entirely within his own control—is over sixty thousand a year."

CHAPTER XVI.

Theodore did not take his rejection meekly. In his interview with Mr. Dormer-Smith he pressed hard to see May again, and insinuated that she was under undue influence. Moreover, he conveyed, with stiff civility, that he considered himself to have been badly treated by the whole family, who had first encouraged his attentions and then rejected them.

"He really is a fearful young man!" said May to her aunt on hearing the report of the interview. "What does he mean by insisting on 'an answer from my own lips'? Could he not believe what Uncle Frederick said? Besides, he has had his answer from me. The truth is, he is so outrageously conceited that he can't believe any young woman would refuse him of her own free will."

"The idea of his dreaming for an instant that I encouraged him is too preposterous," said Mrs. Dormer-Smith, shaking her head languidly. "I am sadly disappointed. I thought him quite a nice person. I fancied he had sufficient savoir vivre to understand—However, it is one more proof that one can never reckon on half-bred people who don't know the world."

It was privately a great relief to May to know that her aunt took her part in this affair. Aunt Pauline's motives and views were still very mysterious to May on many points. She did not even now fully understand the grounds of her aunt's virtuous indignation against Theodore Bransby, although she was thankful for it. "Aunt Pauline thought him good enough for Conny," said May to herself innocently; "and Conny is so beautiful, and so much admired!"

It was true that—thanks, in the first place, to Mrs. Griffin—Constance had enjoyed a more brilliant season than she had ever ventured to dream of. Fashionable houses, of which she had read in the newspapers, but which had appeared to her as unattainable as though they were in another planet, had opened their doors to her; and old connections of her mother's family, finding her in the aforesaid houses, discovered that she was a charming girl, and were delighted to open their doors to her. She had accepted several invitations to country houses, and would probably not be at home again until late in the autumn.

Mrs. Griffin watched this young lady's progress with considerable interest. She opined that Miss Hadlow was a shining instance of the advantages of "race."

"In spite of having been brought up in the pokiest way in some provincial town, as I understand, that girl has a thoroughbred self-possession quite remarkable," said Mrs. Griffin. "She never makes a blunder. You are never nervous about her. She has no trace of that loud, bouncing style, which I detest, and which so many underbred-people take up nowadays, mistakenly imagining it to be the proper thing. She doesn't 'go in' for anything. And," added Mrs. Griffin musingly, "there's a wonderful look of her grandfather, poor Charley Rivers, about the brow and eyes."

The season was rapidly drawing to a close when Mrs. Dobbs received two letters; one from her grand-daughter, and the other from Mrs. Dormer-Smith. Jo Weatherhead, arriving one evening at his usual hour in Jessamine Cottage, was told by his old friend that she had had a letter from May, and that she meant to read him a portion of it. No proposition could have been more welcome to Mr. Weatherhead. He drew his chair up to the grate—filled now with fresh boughs instead of hot coals; but Jo kept his place in the chimney-corner winter and summer—and prepared to listen.

Mrs. Dobbs read as follows:—"You must know, dear granny, that I told Aunt Pauline yesterday that I really must go home at the end of this season. She has been very kind and so has Uncle Frederick; but granny is granny, and home is home."

Here Mr. Weatherhead slapped his leg with his hand, and took his pipe out of his mouth as though about to speak; but on Mrs. Dobbs holding up her hand for silence, he put his pipe back again, and slowly drew his forefinger and thumb down the not inconsiderable length of his nose.

Mrs. Dobbs read on: "To my amazement, Aunt Pauline answered that it was my father's wish that I should remain with her altogether! That is not my wish. And it isn't yours—is it, granny dear? And if we two are agreed, I cannot think my father would object. I mean to write to him about it. I should have done so already, but I have not his address, and Aunt Pauline can't or won't give it to me. Please send it. I shall tell my father just what I feel. I don't care for what Aunt Pauline calls Society. I was happy enough as long as it was only like being at the play, with the prospect of going home when it was over, and living my real life. But to go on with this sort of thing and nothing else, year in, year out—it would be like being expected to live on wax fruit, or those glazed wooden turkeys I remember in a box of toys you gave me long ago. Please answer directly, directly. There's an invitation for me to go in August to a place in the Highlands, where Mrs. Griffin's daughter has a shooting-box. At least, I suppose it is Mrs. Griffin's daughter's husband who has the shooting-box. Only nobody talks much about the duke, and everybody talks a great deal about the duchess." ("Fancy our Miranda among the dukes and duchesses!" put in Jo Weatherhead, softly. And he smacked his lips as though the very sound of the words had a relish for him.) "Aunt Pauline wants to go to Carlsbad; Uncle Frederick is to join a fishing-party in Norway; the children are to be sent to a farmhouse; and Mrs. Griffin has offered to take care of me in the Highlands. But I would far, far rather come back to dear Oldchester, and be amongst people who know me, and care for me, and whom I love with all my heart. Do write and ask for me back, granny darling! And mind you give me papa's address. I am resolved to write to him, whatever Aunt Pauline may say. He is my father, and I have a right to tell him my feelings."

"That's all of any consequence," said Mrs. Dobbs, slowly refolding the letter. "Oh, of course she writes at the end 'Love to Uncle Jo.' She never forgets that."

There was a brief silence. Mr. Weatherhead, who was very tender-hearted, blew his nose and wiped his eyes unaffectedly. "Of course you'll have the child down, Sarah," said he; "anyway, for a time. She's pining, that's where it is; she's pining for a sight of you."

Mrs. Dobbs sat choking down her emotion. She had cried privately over that letter herself, but she was resolved to discuss it now with judicial calmness; and it was provoking that Jo endangered her judicial tone of mind by that foolish, soft-hearted way of his, which was terribly catching. But she loved Jo for it, nevertheless, and scolded him so as to let him know that she loved him.

"It's a good thing your feelings are righter and kinder than most folks', Jo Weatherhead, for you're sadly led by 'em, my friend. If you'd wait and hear the whole case, you might help me with your advice." Then Mrs. Dobbs pulled another letter from her pocket, and handed it to her brother-in-law. This second epistle was from Mrs. Dormer-Smith, and ran thus:—

"DEAR MRS. DOBBS,

"I think it right to let you know how very important it is for May not to miss her visit to Glengowrie. There will be among the guests there a gentleman who has been paying her a good deal of attention—a man of princely fortune. I have some reason to think that May is disposed to look favourably on this gentleman; but he must be allowed time and opportunity to declare himself. No better opportunity could possibly be found than at Glengowrie; and I may tell you, in confidence, that the duchess has, at my friend Mrs. Griffin's request, invited them both on purpose. I trust, therefore, that, in my niece's interests, you will induce her not to relinquish this chance. As to her writing to her father, it is absurd, and would only irritate my brother after his giving me carte blanche to do the best I can for her. If the visit to Glengowrie turns out as we hope, I shall have procured for her a settlement which many a peer's daughter will envy. My husband and I have such confidence in your good sense, that we are sure you will second our efforts as far as you can. Of course you will consider this letter strictly private, and will not, above all, mention it to May.

"I am, dear Mrs. Dobbs,

"Yours very truly,

"P. DORMER-SMITH."

"You see that alters the case, Jo," said Mrs. Dobbs, when he had finished reading the letter.

Jo nodded thoughtfully, and rubbed his nose. "Of course, what you want, Sarah, is for the child to be happy. That's the main thing," said he.

"Of course I want her to be happy. And I want her to have her rights," answered Mrs. Dobbs, setting her lips firmly.

"Ah! Yes, to be sure! Her rights, eh?"

"My son-in-law brought no good to any of us in himself. If his name can do any good to his daughter, she ought to have the benefit of it—and she shall."

"Ay, ay. Her rights, eh? To be sure. Only—only it ain't always quite easy to know what a person's rights are, is it?"

"I know well enough what May's rights are," answered Mrs. Dobbs sharply.

"Nor yet it ain't quite easy to be sure whether they'd enjoy their rights when they got 'em," pursued Jo, with a thoughtful air. "Everybody likes to be happy. There can be no manner of doubt about that. And somehow the dukes and duchesses don't seem to be enough to make Miranda quite—not quite happy, humph?"

"I wonder you should confess so much of your dear aristocracy!" returned Mrs. Dobbs with some heat.

"Why, you see, Sarah, it may be—I only say it may be—that the way Miranda has been brought up, living here in the holidays in such a simple kind of style, and all that, makes her feel not altogether at home among these tip-top folks."

"If you mean she isn't good enough for them, that's nonsense; downright nonsense. And I wonder at a man with your brains talking such stuff! If you mean they're not good enough for her, that's another pair of shoes. As to manners—why, do you imagine that that aunt of hers, who—though she is a fool, is a well-born fool, and a well-bred one—would be taking May about, presenting her at Court, and introducing her to the grandest society, if the child didn't do her credit? Not she! I'm astonished at you, Jo! I thought you knew the world a little bit better than that."

Mrs. Dobbs leant back in her chair, and fanned her flushed face with her handkerchief. Mr. Weatherhead, having smoked his pipe out, put it in its case, and then sat silent, slowly stroking his nose, and casting deprecating glances at his hostess. At length the latter resumed, in a calmer tone, "But May's future is what I've got to think of. I'm an old woman. I can leave her next to nothing when I die. I want her to marry. All women ought to marry. Nobody in my own walk of life would suit her. And what gentleman fit to match with her was ever likely to come and look for her in my parlour in Friar's Lane? You ought to know all about it, Jo Weatherhead. We've gone over the whole ground together often enough."

They had done so. But Jo Weatherhead understood very well that his old friend was talking now, not to convince him, but herself. "Well, Sarah," he said, "there seems a good chance for May to marry well, according to this good lady. 'Princely fortune,' she says. That sounds grand, don't it?"

"Ah! And it isn't a few thousands that Mrs. Dormer-Smith would call a princely fortune."

"Not a few thousands you think, eh, Sarah? Tens of thousands I shouldn't wonder, humph?" And Mr. Weatherhead pursed up his mouth, and poked forward his nose eagerly.

"Not a doubt of it."

"Bless my stars! To think of our little Miranda!—and her aunt says that May is disposed to look favourably on the gentleman."

"So she says. But I can tell you that May doesn't care a button for him at present."

"Lord! How do you know, Sarah?"

"How do I know? That's so like a man! No girl in love would give up the chance of meeting her lover, as May wants to give it up. If she'd rather come to Oldchester than go to Scotland, it is because—so far, at any rate—she doesn't care a button for him."

"I never thought of that. But perhaps, Sarah, she doesn't know that he is to be invited."

Mrs. Dobbs seemed struck by this remark. "Well now, that's an idea, Jo!" said she, nodding her head. "It may be so. They seem to have had the sense not to talk to her about the matter. May's just the kind of girl to fling up her heels and break away, if she suspected any scheming to make a fine match for her. But she might come to care for him in time. There's no reason in nature why a rich man shouldn't be nice enough to be fallen in love with. And by his taking to May—and she without a penny—I'm inclined to think well of the young man."

After some further consideration it was agreed that Mrs. Dobbs should write and propose a middle term: in the interval between her aunt's departure for Carlsbad, and the date of her invitation to Glengowrie, May should come down to Oldchester, on condition that she afterwards paid her visit to the Duchess. This arrangement would be a joy to Mrs. Dobbs, would satisfy May's affectionate longing, and could not prejudice the girl's future prospects. A letter to May was written, as well as one to Mrs. Dormer-Smith. This letter was very short, and may as well be given.

"DEAR MRS. DORMER-SMITH,

"I have to acknowledge yours of the 5th. I agree with you that it would be a pity for my grand-daughter not to accept the invitation you speak of. Some good may come of it, and I do not think that any harm can come. If May spends the three or four weeks with me after you start for the Continent, I will undertake for her to meet the lady who is to take charge of her to Scotland, at any place that may be agreed upon. I wrote to May by this post, and she will tell you what I propose. With regard to her father's address, I have had none for some time past, except, 'Post-Office, Brussels.' This much I shall tell her, as I think she has a right to know it. You need not disturb yourself about her writing to her father, as I think, from what I know of Captain Cheffington, that he is not likely to answer her letter.

"I am, dear Mrs. Dormer-Smith,

"Yours truly,

"SARAH DOBBS."

The proposal was accepted, and within a fortnight after the despatch of this letter, May Cheffington was in Oldchester once more.

VOLUME II.

CHAPTER I.

Four months in their passage leave traces, more or less perceptible, on us all. On the first evening of May's arrival, her grandmother drew her to the window, where the rosy light of a fine summer evening shone full on her face, and scrutinized her long and lovingly. Then she kissed her grand-daughter's cheek, and tapping her lightly on the forehead, said, "This is not the big baby I parted from. You're a woman now, my lass. God bless thee!" May stoutly declared that she was not changed at all; that she had returned from all the pomps and vanities just the same May as ever. But on her side she found changes.

On her first view of it in the glow of a rosy sunset, Jessamine Cottage had been looking its best. The little parlour was fragrant with flowers, and May's tiny bedroom was a pleasant nest of white dimity, smelling of lavender and dried rose-leaves. She thought the house delightful. But a very brief acquaintance showed it to be badly built and inconvenient—one of those paltry "bandboxes" of which Mrs. Dobbs had been wont to speak with contempt. Moreover, there was an indefinable air of greater poverty than she remembered in Friar's Row; and—last and worst of all—she thought granny herself looking ill. When she hinted this privately to Uncle Jo, he scouted the idea. Ill? No, no; Sarah was never ill. There was nothing amiss with Sarah. But the suggestion made him look at his old friend with new observation, and he was forced to acknowledge to himself that she was not quite so active as formerly. But he still would not admit the idea of illness. "She'll be all right now she's got you back again, Miranda," said Mr. Weatherhead, incautiously. "It's the sperrit, you see—the sperrit has been preying on the body. There's where it is."

The idea that granny had been fretting at her absence strengthened May in her resolution not to return to London. If it were absolutely insisted upon she must, she supposed, keep the compact and pay her visit to Glengowrie. But after that she would resume her place by her grandmother's side—the place to which duty and affection equally bound her. She wrote to her father announcing this intention. And she suggested that the money spent on her expenses in London would be far better employed in paying granny handsomely for her board. "I do not think she is so well off as she used to be," wrote May in simple good faith. "And I am sure, my dear father, you will feel with me that we are bound to do anything in the world we can to help her, after all her goodness to me."

The subject which mainly occupied Mrs. Dobbs's waking thoughts after May's arrival was the unknown "gentleman of princely fortune" who might turn out to be May's fate. But, try as she would, she could find no clue to May's feeling about this individual, nor could she discover who he might be. Once she tried a joking question of a general kind about sweethearts and admirers, but May's response was as far as possible from the tone of a lovelorn maiden.

"Oh, for goodness' sake, granny, don't talk of such things. It makes me sick!" was her very unexpected exclamation. And then, with a little judicious cross-questioning, the story of Theodore Bransby's wooing came out.

"Well, well, well, child, you needn't be so fierce! Poor young man! I can't help feeling sorry for his disappointment," said Mrs. Dobbs.

"Don't waste your sorrow on him, granny; he ought to have known better."

"Well, as to that, May—" began her grandmother, with a slow smile spreading over her face.

"Now, granny dear, only listen! At any rate he might have known better when he was told, mightn't he? But he would not take 'no' for an answer; and when Uncle Frederick spoke to him the next day, he was quite rude, and declared—it makes me so hot when I think of it!—declared he had been encouraged! The idea of his daring to say such a thing! And, you know all the time I quite thought he was as good as engaged to Conny Hadlow. Everybody said so in Oldchester."

"'Everybody' is a person who makes a good many mistakes about his neighbours' affairs, May. Mrs. Simpson says that young Bransby is not coming down here this summer."

"So much the better! However, in any case, he would not honour you with one of his condescending visits now. Do you remember that evening when he called in Friar's Row? How little we thought—"

May chatted with as much apparent candour and frankness as ever. But in all her descriptions of the people whom she met in London there was not one who seemed to fit Mrs. Dormer-Smith's unknown.

"Maybe her saying no word is a sign she likes him," reflected Mrs. Dobbs; "girls will keep a secret of that kind very close. They are shy of it even in their own thoughts. If I saw him and her together, I could make a shrewd guess as to how things are."

But there was no chance of her seeing them together, and the gentleman of princely fortune remained wrapped in mystery.

Meanwhile, May went to see her old friends, and was pronounced by most of them to be quite unspoiled by her London season. But one critical spirit, at least, there was in Oldchester, who did not look on Miss Cheffington with unmixed approbation: Mr. Sebastian Bach Simpson declared that she gave herself airs.

One of the first visits which May paid was to the old house in College Quad. The Canon received her with his former paternal benevolence; but, at first, a slight indefinable chill was perceptible in Mrs. Hadlow's usually cordial manner. A little maternal jealousy on the subject of Theodore Bransby rankled in her mind. It was true that Constance did not seem to care for him; would not probably have accepted him had he asked her. But, under all the circumstances, Mrs. Hadlow was strongly of opinion that he ought to have asked her. And then a rumour reached Oldchester of Theodore's attentions to Miss Cheffington. But there was no resisting May's warm and single-minded praises of her friend. It seemed that Conny's prospects had grown unexpectedly brilliant. Mr. Owen Rivers, who had recently reappeared in Oldchester after his own erratic fashion, walking in one morning unexpectedly to his aunt's quaint old sitting-room, pronounced his cousin to have made a great social success. "You know my opinion of the worth of that game, Aunt Jane," said he. "But, such as it is, Conny has won. Old Lord Castlecombe is in love with her. And—which is far more important—so is Mrs. Griffin. You and I always knew she was handsome. But there are certain people to whom the evidence of their senses is as nothing compared with the evidence of peers, and griffins, and such-like heraldic creatures."

"My Aunt Pauline is in love with Conny, too," declared May. "I ought to be jealous; for Aunt Pauline is always quoting Constance Hadlow to me as an example of everything that is delightful in a girl. But I knew it before. I didn't wait for the heraldic creatures, did I, Mrs. Hadlow?"

And so the old affectionate, familiar intercourse was resumed, and May was welcomed in the old way. The Canon missed his daughter, and had not consented easily to her prolonged absence. He liked to see young faces around him; and May's face was particularly pleasant to him. At first May had refused to leave her grandmother. But Mrs. Dobbs urged her to spend some hours every day with the Hadlows. "I have my own occupations in the daytime," she said; "and when you come home of an evening, and tell me all your sayings and doings, I can enjoy it comfortably. I don't want you hanging about this poky little place all day, my lass."

The girl was the more easily persuaded to do as her grandmother wished in this matter from her own secret resolve to fix herself in Oldchester. She did not grudge the hours given to her friends. There would be plenty more time to be spent with granny. So she thought; reckoning on the morrow with the assurance of youth. Day after day she sat during the hot afternoon hours under the black shadow of the old yew tree in the Canon's garden; sometimes volunteering to do some task of needlework for Mrs. Hadlow, sometimes winding wool for the Canon's grey socks, sometimes making up posies for the adornment of the sitting-room. And there was Fox, the terrier, dividing his attentions between her and his mistress; the peaceful Wend flowing by on the other side of the hedge; the garden blooming, the birds twittering, the distant schoolboys shouting, the sweet cathedral bells chiming,—everything as it had been last summer.

And yet not quite as it had been. There was some subtle difference between these afternoons and the afternoons of last summer.

It was not merely that Constance was missed, nor that Theodore Bransby no longer made one of the group beneath the yew tree. Of these changes one was scarcely to be regretted—for Conny was enjoying herself extremely, and only desired to prolong her leave of absence—and the other was undoubtedly satisfactory. But this could not surely suffice to make it a deep delight to sit silent and wind balls of gray worsted for half an hour at a stretch! Was it the negative joy of Theodore's absence which caused May to look forward with her first waking thoughts to those hours in the garden, and to live them over again in her mind when she lay down to rest at night? It seemed as if the London season, far from spoiling her for simple things, had marvellously enhanced the quiet pleasures of her home life, and given them a new intensity.

They were very quiet pleasures, truly. Mary Rayne and the Burton girls seldom appeared in College Quad now that Constance was away. Mrs. Hadlow had no lawn-tennis court, as has already been set forth; and persons who gave up their garden-ground to the frivolous purpose of growing flowers could not expect their younger friends to spare them many minutes out of a summer's day. Visitors of the sterner sex were chiefly represented by Major Mitton and Dr. Hatch, with a liberal sprinkling of the elder cathedral clergy.

The eldest Miss Burton said to May once, "I can't imagine how you stand the dull life down here after your aunt's house in town! But I suppose you are simply resting on your oars. We hear you are to go to Glengowrie in the autumn. How delicious! The Duchess is sure to have her house filled with nice people."

May emphatically denied that she was dull in Oldchester. Dull! She had never, she thought, been so happy in her life. "I wonder," said she to Mrs. Hadlow that same afternoon, "whether Violet Burton feels Oldchester to be dull. And if not, why should she assume that I do?"

"Violet has a serious object in life, you know. She is the best tennis player in the county. One cannot be dull with an absorbing pursuit of that sort," answered Mrs. Hadlow, who, with all her genial benevolence, had an occasional turn of the tongue which proved her kinship with her nephew Owen.

"The fact is," observed the latter, who was lying under the yew tree with a pipe in his mouth, and an uncut magazine in his hand, "that each of us carries his own supply of dulness about with him independently of external circumstances. Not but what there are conceivable cases where external circumstances would have a tremendous dulness-producing power; such as being banished to a desolate shore beyond the reach of 'baccy;' or having to read the Parliamentary debates right through every day."

"Or being obliged to attend a musical afternoon at Miss Piper's London lodging three times a week," put in May, laughing. "You don't know what a hopeless heretic he is, Mrs. Hadlow. Even amiable Mr. Sweeting gave him up in despair. And Lady Moppett thinks he ought to be excommunicated."

"Well, I suppose he need not have gone to Miss Piper's unless he had chosen to do so," said Aunt Jane. "Owen is rather fond of being pitied for having his own way. He ate his cake in the shape of enjoying Miss Piper's music, and had it in the shape of declaring himself a victim."

"Enjoying—? Good heavens!" exclaimed Owen, waving his pipe in protest.

"Why did you go, then?"

To this simple query Owen made no other response than muttering, with his pipe between his teeth again, that there were "compensations."

"Owen," said his aunt abruptly, after a long silence, "you are a most unsatisfactory spectacle to behold."

"That's disappointing, Aunt Jane. I flattered myself that I was a thing of beauty and a joy for ever."

"I shouldn't care about your not being ornamental, if only you were useful. But it is dreadful to see you wasting your life."

"I assure you I am employing my life in a very agreeable manner just now," answered Owen, resting on his elbow, and glancing up from under the shadow of his straw hat.

"Agreeable! That is not the point."

"It's my point."

"Ah! Well, we won't begin a wrangle, Owen; but—"

"My dear Aunt Jane! Do I ever wrangle with you?"

"You do worse. I'm afraid you are incorrigible. But every one else sees that I am right. Ask May what she thinks."

May started, and coloured violently; but she kept her eyes on the needlework in her hand, and said nothing.

"No; I shall not ask Miss Cheffington. She is a partisan, and would be sure to side with you."

"Not at all. May has her own opinions; haven't you, May?"

"One can't help having opinions," returned May shyly.

"Good gracious! Miss Cheffington, what an extraordinarily wild assertion! 'Can't help having opinions—'? One might suppose you had been nurtured among sages, and had never heard of Mr. Thomas Carlyle's celebrated majority."

"I have been nurtured by Granny," rejoined May, lifting her eyes for the first time with a bright, brief glance.

"Ay," exclaimed Mrs. Hadlow, "I'd advise you to ask Mrs. Dobbs what she thinks of a young man with your education and talents—oh, you need not disclaim having brains, it only makes your case so much the worse!—sitting lazily in his form, and letting all sorts of dunderheaded tortoises win the race."

"Bravo, Aunt Jane! I like 'dunderheaded tortoises.' 'Mobled Queen is good.'"

"You wouldn't enjoy hearing Mrs. Dobbs's opinion, I can tell you. I know very well what she would say," pursued Mrs. Hadlow, more than half angry.

"I should like to ask her myself," said Owen, rising to his feet. "Do you think I might, Miss Cheffington?"

"Of course! If you have courage!" answered May, looking up with a smile.

"I'm quite in earnest; I have long wished to know Mrs. Dobbs. Do you think she would consider it a liberty if I were to call?"

May cast her eyes down again, and became very busy with her needlework. "No," she answered; "I don't think Granny would consider it a liberty; she knows about you. I mean she knows you are Mrs. Hadlow's nephew."

Mrs. Hadlow gave no more thought to this conversation, and May, although she gave many thoughts to it, told herself that Mr. Rivers had only been jesting, and that nothing was more unlikely than that he should fulfil his words. She told herself so, with all the more insistence because at the bottom of her heart she longed that he and "Granny" should know each other.

Nevertheless, on the very next afternoon, when May was absent, Owen Rivers did call at Jessamine Cottage.

He was at once received with cordiality for his aunt's sake, but he soon earned a welcome for his own. Jo Weatherhead took to him amazingly. "That's what I call a gentleman," said he, "a real gentleman—sterling metal, and not Brummagem electro-plating. What a difference from that young Bransby! A stuck-up, impudent—but, Lord! what could one expect from an old Rabbitt's grandson! There's where it is."

"Mr. Rivers is a good Radical, Jo," Mrs. Dobbs answered slyly. Whereupon Jo nodded his head with undiminished complacency, and declared that if it wasn't for such Radicals as them, Radicalism might soon shut up shop altogether; concluding with his favourite apophthegm that many good things came down from above, but very few mounted up from below.

CHAPTER II.

Owen Rivers was greatly attracted by Mrs. Dobbs. He admired her uprightness of character, and downrightness of speech; her shrewd common sense, combined with unpretending simplicity; her indomitable strength of purpose, tempered by broad good nature. At the very beginning of their acquaintance, he told her that he had been recommended by his aunt Jane to take her (Mrs. Dobbs's) opinion as to his mode of life. And when Mrs. Dobbs tried to put him off by declaring that

Mrs. Hadlow must have been joking, he answered that he, at any rate, was not joking; and begged her to speak candidly.

"If I speak at all, I shall speak candidly, you may depend," said Mrs. Dobbs.

And, in truth, Owen soon found that he had no cause to complain of her lack of plain speaking. Mrs. Dobbs was wholly and heartily on the side of Aunt Jane, and held many a stout argument with the young man.

"But, pray, how is one to manage?" asked Owen. "My aunt says, 'Go into a profession.' Easier said than done! Besides, although I might not object to be Lord Chancellor—or even, perhaps, Admiral of the Fleet—I have no relish for the intermediate stages, which makes a difficulty."

"That's all stuff and nonsense," said Mrs. Dobbs bluntly. "It's a shame to see a gentleman with your book-learning, and good gifts, wasting the advantages God has given him."

"Wasting my advantages! That's Aunt Jane's pet phrase. But those are mere words, you know."

"Words are words, for certain. And nuts are nuts. Only some of 'em hold sound kernels, whilst others have got nothing inside but dust."

"Well, come now, let us get at the kernel," said Owen, half earnest, half amused. "What would you have me do, Mrs. Dobbs?"

"Do! Any honest work that's of use to your fellow creatures."

"Such as stone-breaking, for instance?"

"Better than nothing."

"And my 'advantages' would not then be wasted, I presume?"

"You might be getting a quarter per cent. for 'em—or maybe less—instead of doubling your capital. But that would be better than keeping all you've got in a stocking, like some ignorant old woman, and pulling out a shilling at a time whenever you happen to want it."

Many such passages of arms did they have; and Owen told himself that Mrs. Dobbs was a very interesting study. Meanwhile, from the superior vantage ground of her seniority, she had been making one or two studies of him; and the result of them induced her to give him a hint as to May's prospects. "I shall let him know how the land lies," said she to herself. "Very likely he's in no danger. So much the better. But I'll act fair by the young man. He's one of them quiet-looking sort that feels very deeply; though, for all his humble-mindedness, he's a deal too proud to show it."

Accordingly Mrs. Dobbs took her opportunity one afternoon when Owen strolled in somewhat earlier than usual. He and his hostess were tête-á-tête; for May had gone to lunch with Mrs. Martin Bransby, and to enjoy a romp afterwards with the children, who adored her.

"Do you know this Duchess my grand-daughter is going to visit, Mr. Rivers?" began Mrs. Dobbs abruptly.

"To the best of my belief I never saw her in my life. My acquaintance among duchesses is not extensive."

"Nor yet her mother—Mrs. Griffin?"

"Mrs. Griffin I have seen; and I make her a bow when we meet. That's about all."

"They are very kind to May."

"Small blame to them! And yet I don't know; it is to their credit, when one comes to think of it."

"May talks of wishing to give up her visit."

"She is unwilling to leave you, I believe."

"Yes; bless her! But I mustn't give in to that." Then with a little air of hesitation very unusual with her, Mrs. Dobbs proceeded: "I want you and Mrs. Hadlow and all her friends not to encourage her in that idea. The fact is, it is very important that May should not miss going to Glengowrie this autumn. More important than she knows."

Owen Rivers leant forward with a sudden attentive contraction of the brows. "What is it?" he asked brusquely. Then, remembering himself, he added, "I beg your pardon. I didn't mean to put a conversational pistol to your head; nor to demand any secrets from you."

"I don't know that there are any secrets, Mr. Rivers. But you understand there are certain—certain opportunities which I am bound to give May, if I can. I'm not one for forcing buckets of water down any horse's throat, but unless you take him to the water he can't drink if he would. The truth is, that I am anxious about my grandchild's future. When I am gone, she will be left very desolate, poor lamb!" She paused suddenly, and pressed her lips together. Then, after a minute's silence, she went on more firmly, "God knows I never wished my poor daughter to marry above her station; her marriage was a sore stroke to me. But now, whatever you and me may think about distinctions of rank, it's certain that May has a right to a lady's place in the world, through her father's birth and family. I sacrificed a good deal in parting from her at all—sacrificed my feelings, I mean—and I don't want it all to be wasted. I want the child to get some good out of it, do you see, Mr. Rivers?"

"I see."

"And don't you think I'm right?"

"Yes; the horse ought to have his choice in that matter of drinking."

"I'm glad you agree with me. My dear old friend Jo Weatherhead is half inclined to think me wrong. He says I ought to consider the child's happiness first and foremost, and that, if being with fine folks don't make her happy, I ought to let her give them up. But May is very young still—barely eighteen; she hasn't had time to judge. I wouldn't have her think, later on, that this or that good thing might have befallen her if she had had her chance and seen more of the world. It's bitter to look back on opportunities lost or wasted, and that," added Mrs. Dobbs, changing her tone, and shaking hands with the young man, who had risen to go away, "is why I take the liberty of scolding you now and then. But I hope an old granny like me may speak her mind without offence? That's one of our privileges."

It seemed clear that Owen Rivers, at all events, was not offended. His visits to Jessamine Cottage grew longer and more frequent. It became an established custom for him to drop in at tea-time. Very often when May had been spending the afternoon at the Canon's house, he would escort her home through the fields. That was a longer way than by the streets; but so much pleasanter, that their preference for it was surely very natural.

Oh, those rambles by the Wend, with the pearly evening sky above them, the dewy, flower-speckled grass under foot, and in their ears the sound of the sweet chimes, which seemed but to accompany some still sweeter melody, felt not heard. May gave herself no account of the charm which encompassed her. She looked not "before and after," but was happy, as youth alone can be happy, in the intense sweetness of the present. Later life has happiness of its own; but not that. It may be more or less, but it is different. Those young delights can no more return than a rose can furl itself again into a rosebud. And as to Owen, if his day-dream was sometimes pierced by a sharp ray of common sense from the work-a-day world, he turned his eyes away, and plunged still deeper into the rainbow-tinted cloudland of young love.

It could not hurt her, he argued. It could hurt no one but himself, and he was prepared to suffer. She was sweet and kind; but she had not—she could not have—any special feeling of tenderness for him. If, indeed, that could be possible—! But what was there in him to attract so lovely and lovable a creature as May Cheffington? A strongly-marked trait in Owen's character was what Mrs. Hadlow, being hotly provoked by some manifestation of it, had once designated as "pig-headed modesty!" It was obstinate enough, truly, at times; and it had a warp of inflexible pride in the woof of it. But it was genuine modesty for all that. Still he would not so resolutely have shut his eyes to the possibility that this matter of falling in love might be mutual, but for Mrs. Dobbs's well-meant words of warning. May was going away in a week or two—away out of his reach, perhaps for ever. Since she was in no danger, he need, surely, have no scruple in enjoying these few happy moments in her company. They would probably be the last. No one suspected his feeling, and he could keep his own counsel.

He honestly believed that no one suspected him. His Aunt Jane, whose observation might have been the most to be dreaded, was in truth blind to what was going on under her eyes. In the first place, it was nothing new or unusual for Owen to spend his afternoons under the yew tree in her garden; nor for May Cheffington to be there also. And it did not occur, it scarcely could have occurred, to Conny's mother, that Conny was being a second time supplanted by this girl so much her inferior in beauty. And then, too, it must be acknowledged, that neither May nor Owen thought it necessary to trouble Mrs. Hadlow with any detailed report of the number of visits which her nephew paid to Jessamine Cottage; nor with a chronicle of their many evening strolls beside the Wend. Such strange tricks does love play with all: making the simple cunning, and the straightforward wily, almost in spite of themselves! While as for Mrs. Dobbs, her usual keenness with regard to her grand-daughter was baffled by a vision of "the gentleman of princely fortune" on whom May had been said to look favourably; and there were but few opportunities for other eyes to note the behaviour of Owen and May towards each other.

The custom of the Saturday evening whist-parties, at which Mr. and Mrs. Simpson and Mr. Weatherhead were the only guests, had been unavoidably broken through at the time of Mrs. Dobbs's removal from Friar's Row: and, although efforts had been made to renew it, it had somehow languished, like a plant whose roots have been disturbed. Sometimes two or three weeks would elapse without the Simpsons appearing at Jessamine Cottage on the accustomed Saturday evening. The amiable Amelia tried to compensate for these gaps in their social intercourse by running in at odd moments to see Mrs. Dobbs. She would frequently call on her way home from Mrs. Bransby's, or some other house where she gave lessons, and chat in her discursive style: smilingly unconscious, for the most part, whether Mrs. Dobbs vouchsafed her any attention or not; but always too sweet-tempered to resent it, if she chanced to discover that Mrs. Dobbs had not heard three sentences of all she had been saying. On one topic she was, at any rate, sure of being listened to: the words "our dear Miranda" were certain to arouse Mrs. Dobbs from her deepest fit of musing; and fits of musing had become more and more frequent with her of late.

It was not clear whether Mrs. Simpson had taken to call May "Miranda" by way of ceremoniously acknowledging her place in the world as a young lady who had been presented at Court; or whether she considered three syllables to be intrinsically more genteel than one; or whether she had simply caught the word from the fashionable journals which had chronicled the appearance of Miss Miranda Cheffington at various festivities of the season. Mrs. Simpson's reasons for doing or leaving undone were usually of a tangled kind, and an endeavour to extricate one of them often resulted in pulling up a number of others by the roots. At all events, Mrs. Simpson had taken to speak of May as "our dear Miranda," and the words infallibly insured her an attentive hearing from Mrs. Dobbs for whatever might follow them. If Mr. Weatherhead chanced to be present at any of Amelia's erratic visits, he listened willingly to all the gossip she might pour forth. It was always good-natured gossip. Sebastian might bear a grudge here and there, and might impute shabby motives to the conduct of his fellow-creatures; but Amelia never. There seemed to be an excess of saccharine matter in her disposition which flavoured every word she said. This species of excess being somewhat uncommon, many persons pronounced poor Mrs. Simpson to be an arrant humbug. But, had she been consciously a humbug, she would assuredly have distributed her sweet speeches with more discretion; for nothing is less popular than uncritical eulogy—of other people.

There was an unusual air of excitement about her when she appeared one afternoon in Jessamine Cottage. She found its mistress knitting in her accustomed arm-chair, with Jo Weatherhead seated opposite to her reading aloud paragraphs from a local newspaper.

"My dear Mrs. Dobbs," cried Amelia, bursting in breathlessly, "how do you do? And Mr. Weatherhead! Now this is quite against rules—or, at least, against custom; for I am sure you would never make such a rule. You are far too hospitable. But as I was passing—so nice to be neighbours instead of Friar's Row, though I shall ever look on Friar's Row with affection for the sake of old times. What is it the poet says about 'portions and parcels of the dreadful past'? Only there was nothing dreadful in our little suppers; and Martha's stewed tripe beyond praise."

"I hope you are going to eat some of our little supper to-night," said Mrs. Dobbs, composedly. "It's Saturday, you know."

"How odd you should say that! It is exactly the remark I made to Bassy this morning! Oh yes; certainly. And, as I was saying just now, it's quite hors ligne, as the French express it, to inflict myself on you twice in one day."

"You know you are very welcome."

"You're always so kind, dear Mrs. Dobbs! I have been busy teaching all the morning. This very moment I have come from Miss Piper's and—"

"You are not giving her lessons, are you?" asked Mrs. Dobbs, looking up with a smile.

"Oh dear, no! Not, I'm sure, that she would not be an excellent pupil; indeed, both of them in their different styles. One the accomplished musician, and the other so domesticated. No doubt you will hear of it from our dear Miranda, for of course she will be invited. But I thought I would mention it."

"Mention what?—eh?" asked Jo Weatherhead, with impatient curiosity.

"The party. They are going to give a musical party. Though really I might omit the adjective, for who could imagine the Miss Pipers giving a party that wasn't musical? To be sure some persons find it rather trying. Bassy, for instance, cannot altogether approve the new school. But then he was brought up in the strictest classical principles, and he is so very clever himself, that of course—!"

Some native gift of incoherency which distinguished Mrs. Simpson's mind enabled her to reconcile the most conflicting claims on her admiration.

"Ho, ho! a party, eh? A musical party?" said Mr. Weatherhead.

"Yes; but of course there is nothing remarkable in that," replied Mrs. Simpson, very unexpectedly.

"Nothing at all remarkable, I should think," assented Mrs. Dobbs.

"Ah! But the point is—oh, pussy! Poor old pussy, did I hurt her? Dear, dear, dear!"

In the act of throwing herself forward from her place on the sofa, in order to touch Mrs. Dobbs's arm, and thus emphasize her communication, Amelia had accidentally set her foot on the tail of the old tabby cat, who at once protested in the frankest manner.

"I'm so sorry! I am so very nearsighted. Poor old pussums! Come and let us make it up—won't you, like a dear?"

Poor old pussums, however, declined these advances, and took up her position on the other side of her mistress's ample skirts; whence for some time she glared distrustfully at every fresh manifestation of Mrs. Simpson's playful vivacity.

"Well, for goodness' sake tell us the point, if there is one!" cried Mr. Weatherhead, who had been irritably rubbing his nose during this episode.

"Ah! Naughty impatience! That is so like a gentleman! Gentlemen are dreadfully impatient in general; don't you agree with me, Mrs. Dobbs? However, it really will be quite a musical treat. Mr. Cleveland Turner is one of the most rising musicians of the day; I believe nobody can understand his compositions without severe preliminary training. Mr. Sweeting, too, is most amiable; he has taken a country house in the neighbourhood. And Miss Piper has invited a young lady down to stay with her who sings divinely—quite divinely, Miss Piper says; and, indeed, I have no doubt she does, for I saw her name mentioned in the Morning Post at a very aristocratic soirée. And Bassy and I are to be invited!"

"Are you, now? Well, I'm glad of it," said Mrs. Dobbs heartily. She knew this was a distinction which would give her friends pleasure.

"Yes; Bassy is to accompany the young lady's songs on the piano. Mr. Cleveland Turner will not accompany;—or, at least, not anything of a tuneful sort. He doesn't like it. Well, you know, there's no accounting for tastes, is there? Most people think strawberries delicious. But I have known a person who couldn't touch them—invariably produced a rash!"

With which lucid illustration Mrs. Simpson rose, and declared she must positively be going. After an effusive leavetaking—in the course of which the old tabby leaped on to the back of Mrs. Dobbs's chair, where she sat arching her spine and growling—the good lady set forth on her way down the little garden-path in front of the house. But scarcely had she reached the gate, when she turned and tripped back again with a girlish step, which neither increase of years nor flesh had much sobered. "I never delivered my message," she said; "and really it is an extraordinary instance of my absence of mind, for that was the chief reason why I came at all at this hour. I was at Mrs. Bransby's about four o'clock, and left our dear Miranda there."

Here she paused so long that Mrs. Dobbs replied, "Yes; I knew May was going to call there."

"Now I dare say you will scarcely credit it," said Amelia, with her head on one side, her spectacles glistening, and an arch smile illumining her countenance, "but, for the moment, I had totally forgotten again what I was going to say!"

"Lord bless the woman!" muttered Jo Weatherhead, in a tone not, perhaps, quite so inaudible as politeness required.

"But I have it now. This is the message; our dear Miranda begged me to tell you that she will remain at Mrs. Bransby's for afternoon tea, and come home in the cool of the evening. Mrs. Bransby—indeed, all the family—are most kind to her. Of course I don't mean to say that after the brilliant scenes of London society it can be any particular treat to her, although anything more truly elegant than Mrs. Bransby's new cream broché I never beheld in my life. However, they pressed our dear Miranda to stay. And she remarked to me that 'Granny would not be left alone, for she knew Mr. Weatherhead was coming.' And now"—looking at her watch—"I must fly, or I shall be too late for tea; and then what would Bassy say?" She tripped once more down the garden path, stopped at the gate to wave her hand, and at length finally departed.

CHAPTER III.

Meanwhile, May was playing with Mrs. Martin Bransby's children, in the delightful old walled garden; and Mrs. Martin Bransby herself was looking on from the shade of a trellised arbour. These two had become very good friends. Whether Mrs. Bransby was or was not aware of her stepson's rejected suit, May had no means of knowing; but she felt instinctively that Mrs. Bransby was not likely to be super-sensitive on her stepson's behalf, nor to bear her a grudge for having refused him. Theodore's absence was not lamented in his own home. His young half-brothers and sisters openly rejoiced at it; and even his father felt that life went on more pleasantly without him.

May's popularity with the children was a sure passport to their mother's heart; while on her side Mrs. Bransby had developed a most endearing trait of character: she liked Owen Rivers, and was always happy to welcome him to her house. Although Owen admired her beauty and elegance extremely, there was no alloy of coquetry in the preference she showed for his company. Indeed, Owen told his Aunt Jane that Mrs. Bransby's delight in adorning her graceful person came nearer to being a pure case of l'Art pour l'Art than any he had ever witnessed. Nevertheless, the most transcendental of artists enjoys appreciation. So it chanced that on this special afternoon, Mr. Rivers being announced just when she was urging May to remain and drink tea with her, Mrs. Bransby at once suggested that perhaps Mr. Rivers would stay too, and be kind enough to see Miss Cheffington home. Mr. Rivers handsomely acceded to the proposal; and these three persons passed a very agreeable afternoon together.

The romping, happy children, with that disregard for any "plurality of worlds" theory which belongs to their age, accepted the whole arrangement as being ordained for their sole and peculiar enjoyment. Under this impression they declined to allow Owen to remain lounging beside their mother in the shade, but imperiously required him "not to be lazy," but to "come and play." He withstood the clamour of the boys for some time; but when three-year-old Enid toddled up to him, and gravely seized one of his hands with both hers, evidently under the conviction that she was quite able to drag him off with her by main force, it was impossible to resist any longer. A very noisy game—known to the younger Bransbys under the alliterative appellation of "Tiggy, Tiggy, touchwood," and which involved a great deal of confused rushing about, and shrill vociferation—was proceeding in the liveliest manner, when forth from the long window of the drawing-room stepped a figure at sight of whom Martin, the eldest boy, stopped short in a headlong course, and Bobby and Billy were so surprised that they checked a wild halloo in their very throats.

It was Theodore. He was dressed in travelling garb (Theodore had appropriate costumes for every department of life; and adhered to them as punctiliously as a Chinese), and was advancing with his usual erect gravity towards his step-mother, when, catching sight of May and Owen, he stopped, surprised in his turn.

"Dear me, Theodore, is that you?" said Mrs. Bransby, rising and coming forward. "When did you arrive? We did not expect you. You did not write, did you?"

"No; I took a sudden resolution to run down for a week. I wished to consult my father about a little matter of business, and I wanted change of air besides."

In answer to Mrs. Bransby's nervous inquiries whether the servants had attended to him, and whether she should order his room to be prepared, he replied—

"Thanks; I have given the necessary orders. My valise has been carried upstairs. I will go and wash my hands, and then I shall ask you for a cup of tea, if you please," glancing at the table already spread beneath the trees. Then he marched up to May, who was standing on the lawn, with a look of little less dismay than the children ingenuously exhibited. He raised his hat with one hand, and shook her reluctant hand with the other, saying in his deliberate accents—

"This is truly an unexpected favour of Fortune. I knew you were in Oldchester, but I scarcely hoped to find you here. How do you do, Rivers?" (This in an indefinable tone of condescension.) Then again addressing himself to May, he said, "You have not had any communication from town this morning?"

"No."

"Nor from Combe Park?"

"Oh no!"

"Ah! I imagined not. May I beg the favour of a word with you presently? I am only going to get rid of some of the dust of travel. You will still be here when I return?"

May was tempted to declare that she positively must go home immediately. But before she could speak Mrs. Bransby answered for her: "Oh, of course Miss Cheffington will be here still. I do not mean to let her run away just yet."

Then, with another formal bow, Theodore returned to the house and disappeared through the drawing-room window.

There was an awkward silence, broken by Martin's exclaiming, in a solemn tone, "He's just like the vampire."

The laugh which followed came as a relief to the embarrassment of the elders.

"Martin!" exclaimed his mother reprovingly.

"Well, mother, he is," persisted Martin, who was unspeakably disgusted at the sudden quenching of the festivities. "What does he come stalking and prowling like that for? He's exactly like the vampire!"

May and Owen avoided each other's eye, feeling a guilty consciousness that Martin had in a great measure expressed their own sentiments. Certainly, the whole party appeared to have been suddenly iced. The three younger children were dismissed to the nursery; and Martin and his sister Ethel voluntarily withdrew, feeling that all the fun was over. A large slice of cake apiece was looked upon as very inadequate amends, and accepted under protest.

"I should think he might have stayed in London when he was there," grumbled Martin, as he walked away, viciously digging his heels into the turf at every step by way of a vent to his injured feelings. "Nobody wants stalking, prowling vampires here. Why couldn't he stop in London?"

As though "stalking, prowling vampires" were generally admitted to be popular members of society in the metropolis.

Mr. Rivers and the two ladies beguiled the time until Theodore should return, by drinking tea and discussing Miss Piper's forthcoming musical party. Curiously enough no one said a word about young Bransby. They all seemed to avoid the topic by a tacit understanding. But though out of sight, he was not out of mind—at any rate, he was not out of May's mind. She was secretly wondering what he could have to say to her. Could he possibly intend to renew his offer of marriage? The idea seemed a wild one; nevertheless, it darted through her mind. One could never tell, she thought, what his obstinate self-conceit might lead him to do. However, May resolved, come what might, to cling tightly to Mrs. Bransby's sheltering presence so long as she remained in that house; and in going home she would have the protection of Mr. Rivers's escort. Even Theodore Bransby could scarcely propose to her before these witnesses!

At length Theodore reappeared, brushed and trim, in speckless raiment. He took his place at the tea-table; and after the exchange of a few commonplace remarks, silence stole over the company. Theodore seemed to be waiting for something; and from time to time he looked at Owen as though expecting him to take his leave. Finally he cleared his throat, and said gravely, "Miss Cheffington, I see you are not taking any more tea; may I crave the favour of a few words with you?"

"Oh, please, I think I will have some more tea," said May, hastily pushing her cup towards Mrs. Bransby. Theodore, who had half risen from his chair, bowed, resumed his seat, and folded his arms in a waiting attitude. Then May added, with desperate resolution, "Will you not be kind enough to say what you have to say, now? I must be going home immediately; and I'm sure there can be no secrets to tell." She buried her face in her teacup to hide the colour which flamed into her cheeks as she said the words.

"If you desire it," returned Theodore stiffly, "of course I shall obey. I merely thought you might prefer to receive painful tidings in—"

"Painful!" cried May, turning pale, and suddenly interrupting him. "Is anything the matter with Granny?"

A glance at his raised eyebrows reassured her, for the next moment she said, "Oh, how stupid I am! Of course you could know nothing, you have only just arrived. It isn't—it isn't my father, is it?"

"Pray do not alarm yourself, Miss Cheffington. Captain Cheffington is, so far as I know, perfectly well."

"Wouldn't it be better to speak out?" said Owen. As soon as he had spoken, he felt that he had no right to put in his word. But he could not help it; Theodore's self-important slowness was too exasperating.

"Yes; do, please," said May.

"There is no cause for alarm, as I said," returned Theodore, trying to look as if he had not heard Owen's suggestion. "But a shock—a slight shock—is apt to be felt at the announcement of sudden death, even in the case of a total stranger."

"Sudden death!"

"Yes; I regret to inform you that your cousin, George Cheffington, has been killed by the accidental discharge of a gun, when he was on a shooting expedition up the country."

All three of his listeners drew a deep sigh of relief.

"Oh!" sighed May, the colour returning to her cheeks and lips, "I felt a horrible fear for the moment about Aunt Pauline!"

"This is a very important event," said Theodore, looking over his cravat with his House-of-Commons air, and indicating by his tone that the fate of Aunt Pauline was a matter of comparative insignificance.

"I am sorry for poor old Lord Castlecombe," said May.

"It will, of course, be a severe blow to your great-uncle; all the more so that Mr. Lucius Cheffington is in deplorably weak health."

"Lucius is never very strong, is he?"

"He is never robust, but this season he has been extremely delicate. I have reason to believe that a very high medical authority has expressed considerable anxiety about him."

"Does Aunt Pauline know?—I mean about George Cheffington's death?"

Theodore drew himself up even more stiffly than usual as he answered, "I am not aware what means Mrs. Dormer-Smith may have had of hearing the news; but my impression is that it can scarcely yet have been communicated to her. The original telegram to Lord Castlecombe only reached him yesterday."

"Did they—Lucius, or any of them—ask you to tell me?" inquired May. It now for the first time struck her as being odd that Theodore Bransby should have been selected for such an office.

"Ahem! No. I was not precisely commissioned to inform you. But I was anxious to spare you the shock of hearing of this disaster accidentally."

The fact was that Theodore had seen the telegram in a London newspaper of that morning.

There ensued a short silence. Then Theodore said to his step-mother, with an elaborate shivering movement of the shoulders, "Don't you think it grows very damp and chilly? I cannot consider it prudent to remain here whilst the dews are falling."

No one was sorry for this excuse to break up the sitting. Mrs. Bransby made a move towards the house; and May said it was time for her to be going home.

"With your permission, I will have the pleasure of escorting you, Miss Cheffington," said Theodore.

"Oh no, please!—thank you. Mr. Rivers said—"

"I have undertaken to see Miss Cheffington safe home," said Rivers. And Mrs. Bransby suggested that Theodore must be tired with his journey; and, moreover, that dinner would be ready at eight. But he disregarded both suggestions. "I shall enjoy a stroll at this cool hour; and I don't mean to dine. I lunched rather late, and will have something light cooked for my supper about ten. Do you mean to go, Rivers? Oh! well, I'll join you as far as Mrs. Dobbs's house."

Of course, under the circumstances it was impossible for May to say a word to prevent him. And accordingly he walked from his father's door on one side of her, while Owen strode on the other. As for May, she had been ready to cry at first with vexation and resentment; but after a while the sense of something ludicrous in the behaviour of her bodyguard so overcame her, that she was very near bursting out into a fit of almost hysterical laughter.

The two young men were full of smouldering animosity towards each other. But they both manifested this feeling chiefly by a severe, and almost sullen, demeanour towards May. She felt that she was being marched along between them more like a detected malefactor than a young lady whom one of them, at least, had besieged with tender proposals. If she addressed a word to Owen, he answered her in dry monosyllables; if she spoke to Theodore, he replied as from a lofty pinnacle of freezing politeness.

"It only needs a pair of handcuffs to make the thing complete," said May to herself. Then she finally gave up all attempts to be conversational, and so they arrived at Jessamine Cottage in solemn silence.

As they walked up the little garden-path in the gathering dusk, they were overtaken by Mr. and Mrs. Simpson. The latter, as soon as she recognized them, began to pour forth a fluent stream of talk, which did not cease when Martha opened the door; and then, in some confused way which neither May nor Owen could afterwards account for, they all found themselves crowding into the little parlour together. As for Theodore, he had from the first resolved to go in if Rivers went in, and to remain as long as Rivers remained.

Mrs. Dobbs looked up astonished at sight of Theodore. She glanced inquiringly at May, who had a queer look on her face, half-distressed, half-amused. Jo Weatherhead rose, staring glumly at the new arrivals, of whom Sebastian brought up the rear, with an expression of countenance which showed that his temper was bristling like his hair. But Mrs. Simpson's sprightly eloquence spread itself impartially over all these shades of feeling, as water makes a smooth and level surface above the roughest bottom.

"So astonished, dear Mrs. Dobbs, to find Mr. Bransby, junior! Having not the slightest idea that he was in Oldchester, you know; and what a singular coincidence our coming upon them all three just at your very door, was it not?"

"Well," observed Sebastian in his rasping voice, "considering that we were coming to sup with Mrs. Dobbs, and that Miss May was on her way home, it would have been stranger if we had met at any one else's door."

"Now, Bassy, I will not be overwhelmed by your stern logic. Ladies are privileged to indulge in some little play of the imagination. Besides"—with an arch smile of triumph—"it really was the fact in this case. Oh! thank you, Mr. Weatherhead; any chair will do for me. Don't let me disturb—! I suppose I may venture to make a shrewd guess, Mr. Bransby, that you have come down to attend Miss Piper's musical party? A great compliment, indeed, when one considers your professional occupations. But the bow cannot always be bent. Even Homer, I believe, is said sometimes—Oh, no; he nods, I fancy: which, of course, is different. I really believe that Miss Hadlow will be the only star of our Oldchester firmament absent from the festive scene. Now acknowledge, dear Mrs. Dobbs, that you were surprised as I was. You did not expect this addition of 'youth at the prow'—if I may venture on the expression—to our little circle this evening. At the same time I must confess that three such sober young persons I never beheld. They were all as silent as—It put me in mind of those beautiful lines: 'Not a drum was heard; not a funeral note, As his—' Not, of course, that there was anything of a funereal nature. Far from it."

This last touch overcame May's self-command. She burst into a fit of uncontrollable laughter; breaking out afresh every time she glanced at Owen's face, provoked and frowning (though with a twitch at the corner of the mouth which showed he had to make an effort not to laugh, too); or at Theodore's, solemnly bewildered. She laughed until the tears poured down her cheeks; and her grandmother exclaimed, "May, May! Don't be so silly, child! You'll get hysterical if you go on that way." But the outburst relieved the nervous tension from which the girl had been suffering; and as she wiped her eyes she was conscious that the laughter had saved her from shedding tears of a different sort.

"I beg your pardon, Mrs. Simpson," she said. "I don't know what possessed me."

"Don't think of apologizing, my dear Miranda. Indeed, why should you? Nothing is more delightful than the unaffected hilarity of youth. I'm sure I always enjoy it," returned the good Amelia, with a beaming glance around her.

"It's lucky Amelia doesn't mind being laughed at," said Sebastian bitterly.

"Oh fie, Bassy! We must distinguish, love. That all depends on who laughs, and how they laugh," observed his wife, with unexpected perspicuity.

"No doubt," said Theodore, "Miss Cheffington's nerves have been agitated by the sad news which I brought her this evening." He spoke in a low mysterious tone, addressing himself apparently to Mrs. Dobbs, although he did not do so by name. At these words Mr. Weatherhead pricked up his ears; and, although he had previously made up his mind not to say a word to this "young spark" until the "young spark" should speak to him, his curiosity so far overcame his dignity that he could not help ejaculating—

"Sad news, ha! What news? What sad news,—eh?"

Theodore turned to Mrs. Dobbs, and pointedly ignored poor Jo, as he said, "Miss Cheffington will doubtless take a fitting opportunity of speaking with you about this event in her family."

"It's nothing that deeply concerns us, Uncle Jo!" broke in May, flushing indignantly, and speaking with impetuosity. "A certain Mr. George Cheffington has been accidentally killed out in Africa. But since neither you, nor I, nor Granny ever saw him—nor even heard of him until quite lately—we cannot pretend to be overwhelmed with grief."

"Nay! George Cheffington killed?" exclaimed Mrs. Dobbs.

Theodore had turned very pale, as he always did when angered. (May had certainly meant to hit him, but she had no idea that the unkindest cut of all had been her publicly addressing Mr. Weatherhead as "Uncle Jo.") He answered slowly, "I should not have chosen this moment when you are—er—entertaining these—ahem!—your friends, to impart the intelligence. But Miss Cheffington has taken the matter out of my hands."

"George Cheffington," repeated Mrs. Dobbs, pondering. "Why, let me see, now; he'll be Lord Castlecombe's eldest son. Poor old man! Oh, I'm sorry to hear it: very sorry. It's hard for the old to see their hopes die before them."

"I'm sorry for him, too, Granny," whispered May, somewhat penitent and ashamed of her vehemence. She had certainly betrayed a touch of the Cheffington imperiousness, and had spoken in a manner quite inconsistent with meek amiability. She had also made Theodore Bransby feel considerable resentment. Nevertheless, he had never been less inclined than at that moment to relinquish the hope of making her his wife. Our passions have various methods of special pleading. But if reason presses them too hard, they will boldly substitute an "in spite of" for a "because," and pursue their aim as though, like Beauty, they were "their own excuse for being."

"Don't let us intrude on a scene of family affliction," said Mr. Simpson dryly. "Now, Amelia! We had better withdraw, I think."

"Don't you talk nonsense, Sebastian Simpson," returned Mrs. Dobbs, without ceremony. "Sit down, Amelia. I'm sorry I can't ask you young gentlemen to stay and share our plain supper, for the truth is I don't know that there's enough of it. But my friends, Mr. and Mrs. Simpson, would break an old charter if they didn't remain."

After that the two young men had, of course, nothing to do but to take their leave. Owen's good humour had quite returned. Wisdom and virtue should, no doubt, have made him disapprove of Miss May's little outbreak of hot temper. But the truth is, that this fallible young man had enjoyed her attack on Bransby. When the latter approached May to say "Good night," he murmured reproachfully, "You were rather severe on me, Miss Cheffington. I had no idea of displeasing you by what I said."

She was conscience-stricken in a moment, and answered quite humbly, "I beg your pardon if I offended you. But I thought you were not civil to Mr. Weatherhead, and that vexed me. Please forgive me." And she endured the tender pressure of her hand which immediately followed, as some expiation of her offence.

Mrs. Dobbs detained Jo Weatherhead that night for a moment, after Mr. and Mrs. Simpson had gone away, and May was in bed.

"I say, Jo, the death of yon poor man in Africa may bring about strange changes," said Mrs. Dobbs, looking at him gravely.

"Changes! How? What changes?"

"Well, not changes for me and you, except through other folks. But do you know that after Lucius Cheffington—who, they say, is but sickly—Lord Castlecombe's next heir is my precious son-in-law?"

"No!" exclaimed Mr. Weatherhead, making his mouth into a perfect round O of astonishment.

"Ay; but he is, though."

"Next heir! Viscount Castlecombe, of Combe Park, and all the property!" gasped Jo.

"I don't know about the property. Only what's entailed, I suppose. But if Lucius was to die, Augustus would be next heir to the title, as sure as you stand there, Jo Weatherhead."

CHAPTER IV.

Probably of all the persons in Oldchester who knew or cared anything about the death of George Cheffington, May was the only one who did not immediately begin to make some calculations based on that event. The contingency of her father's succeeding to the family honours had not occurred to her. And her thoughts and feelings were now occupied with other things. But Oldchester gossips discussed it with gusto; or, at least, that small minority of them who interested themselves in the fortunes of the Castlecombe family. The old lord was little personally known in Oldchester, and the city had long outgrown any sense of the overweening importance of a Viscount Castlecombe of Combe Park, which it might have had a century earlier. To most of the rich manufacturers of the place (whether they really thought themselves "as good as a lord" or not) a lord whom they never beheld, and into whose house neither they nor their children had the remotest chance of being admitted, was, at any rate, genuinely uninteresting.

In the rural parts of the county it was otherwise. People there could not be indifferent to the domestic history of a large land-owner who resided during the greater part of the year on his estate. In many a country dwelling, from luxurious mansions down to mere labourers' cottages, George Cheffington's untimely death was canvassed. From a matrimonial point of view he had been considered the best match in the county, and dowagers with daughters to marry had looked forward to the time (often spoken of, but always postponed) when he should give up his colonial appointment, settle down on his inheritance, and choose a wife. And there was a large number of persons (tenants and dependents) to whom the heir's character and conduct were matters of deep importance. To these, Mr. Lucius Cheffington suddenly became an interesting personage. Lucius had been very little at Combe Park since his boyhood, and the report which gradually spread in the neighbourhood that he was a chronic invalid, was received with many head-shakings and long faces. It seemed impossible that a Cheffington should be delicate or weakly. "Look at the old lord," people said; "why, he was sound and tough as a yew-tree!" And the last time Mr. George was at home he had proved himself a true chip of the old block by out-riding, out-walking, and out-cricketing all his contemporaries.

But that was years ago. Now George was stricken down in his strength, Lucius lay ill of a low fever in London, and Lord Castlecombe sat lonely and sorrow-laden in the home of his fathers.

The old man was not one to seek for sympathy, nor even to tolerate much manifestation of it. The only being to whom for many weeks he mentioned his dead son's name was a superannuated stable-helper, who had set "Master George" on his first pony, and in whose mind that somewhat selfish and hardhearted individual had never outgrown the engaging period of boyhood. "Master George" was the old man's idol, and "Master George" had, to a great extent, reciprocated the man's liking, partly, perhaps, from the sort of gratified vanity which makes us all prize the exclusive attachment of any generally unamiable creature, biped or quadruped. Old Dick was characterized by his fellow-servants as a crusty old curmudgeon, and was notorious for a formidable power of swearing, which he wielded freely, without much respect of persons.

The first day after receiving the news of his son's death, Lord Castlecombe towards evening walked out in a very unfrequented part of the grounds, a path between two high holly hedges, leading by a back way to the stable-yard; and there, with his hat pulled low on his brow, his head bent, and his hands clasped behind him, he paced slowly, plunged in bitter meditation. When he came to the corner whence the stables were visible, he caught sight of old Dick seated on an ancient horse-block, and busily rubbing at something in his hand. Lord Castlecombe stopped short, and looked at the man, who evidently saw him, but made no sign, neither ceased a moment from his occupation. After a minute or so Lord Castlecombe called to him to ask what he was doing, and received no answer. He repeated his question. Still no reply. A third time he spoke, in a harsh, angry tone. And then Dick turned round upon him, and, with a tremendous volley of oaths, answered furiously, "What am I doing of? I'm a rubbing up Master George's little silver spurs as you gave him first time he ever rode to hounds. I've allus kep' 'em bright from that day to this. And I arn't a-going to leave off now, because some d—d blundering fool as didn't ought never to have been trusted with a gun—I wish I'd the rewarding of him, curse him!—has been and put an end to the boy. That's what I'm a doing of, if ye must know!"

A tear fell on the little burnished spur; and then another, and another. But old Dick rubbed on. And his master, after a short silence, came and laid his hand upon his shoulder, and then walked away without a word.

After that Dick was privileged to do what the boldest parson's wife in the county dared not attempt:—talk to Lord Castlecombe about his son George.

Most of the letters of condolence which he received Lord Castlecombe tossed aside contemptuously after glancing at the first line. But one letter he read through, with a heavy frown on his face, and an occasional drawing down of the corners of his mouth into a bitter smile, far more sinister than the frown. It was from his niece Pauline; and its composition had cost her much thought and anxiety. She flattered herself that she had avoided saying a word which could jar on her uncle's irascible temper. And the letter in itself was a good letter enough; but it was a letter which should not have been written at all, if her object were to soothe and conciliate Lord Castlecombe. Pauline did not allude directly to her brother Augustus; but the very fact of her writing seemed to bring his existence offensively into notice. She refrained from expressing any special anxiety about the health of her cousin Lucius. Yet the few words in which she "hoped to hear of his speedy recovery," made the old man writhe as he read them. Pauline had tried to combine duty with policy. It was, of course, her duty to condole with her uncle in his bereavement, and it was clearly desirable not to irritate the dislike with which, as she more than surmised, he regarded Augustus. But the whole calculation was based on a misapprehension of Lord Castlecombe's feeling towards her brother. It was neither more nor less than hatred. And now jealousy was added to it:—a strange, savage jealousy, on behalf of his sons. George—his strong, healthy, hardy eldest-born—was gone. And Lucius—Lucius was not dying! No, no; not so bad as that. But he was very weakly. And to think for one instant of the possibility that Augustus Cheffington might some day reign in their stead—might lord it over the heritage which he had so carefully garnered for his own sons—was maddening. Any one but Augustus, he said to himself. Any distant scion, the son of some impoverished far-away cousin, parson, lawyer, apothecary. Any one, any one, but Augustus!

But of the passionate intensity of this hatred Pauline had no suspicion. A cleverer and more acute woman than she might not have guessed it. No one, in fact, ever guessed it; unless it were Lucius, and he only in part. His own sensitive antipathy to Augustus was an incomparably feebler sentiment. Lucius had no strain of his father's vigour, whether for good or ill.

Mrs. Dormer-Smith had also written by the same post to May. This epistle was more hastily dashed off, and faithfully reflected the wavering mood of the writer. One of her first preoccupations was whether, under the circumstances, it would or would not be desirable for May to pay the promised visit to Glengowrie at this juncture. She did not disguise from herself that George Cheffington's death opened up the possibility of a very different future for May from any which could hitherto have been contemplated. It became a question whether it would be prudent to accept Mr. Bragg. At all events it would be well to avoid precipitation. Mr. Bragg was a fine match for a dowerless girl:—even for a (dowerless) Miss Cheffington. But what if May's father were destined to become a wealthy Peer of the realm? That might be still but a distant possibility. Lucius was not thought to be in any present danger, and certainly might recover. Of course he might recover. And he might marry, and transmit the title and estates in the direct line. But—Pauline felt that there was a "but" of vast import.

And then there were minor cares connected with that great duty towards "society" which she so diligently endeavoured to perform.

"I am most anxious about your mourning," she wrote to May. "It is positively preying on my mind. Of course, nothing could be in worse taste than any assumption of woe in this case. You never saw poor George, and the kinship is not a very close one. In fact, had it been one of the Buckinghamshire Cheffingtons, to whom you are related in exactly the same degree, I do not know that any mourning at all would have been necessary for you. But, of course, the heir to the head of our family occupies a different position. At any rate, do not err on the side of exaggeration. White, with noeuds of pale heliotrope, and jet ornaments; or some black fabric of light texture, with a little jet beading, would probably meet the case. But it is impossible for me to give you precise directions. I am too far away to know what is bien porté at this moment. Would that I could be near you! But I cannot break my 'cure' at this point. Carlsbad has done me good, on the whole; although, of course, the anxiety on your account, connected with this painful news, has to some extent thrown me back. Mrs. Griffin's taste might be thoroughly trusted; and, if she would undertake to order your mourning from Amélie—. But now I think of it, Mrs. Griffin will not return to England until she leaves the Engadine for Glengowrie. And here, again, I am greatly perplexed what to advise in your best interests. All things considered, it might be well for you to put off going to the Duchess. There will be the excuse of this terrible news about poor George, you know.

"I fear that I have written in a sadly décousu fashion; but I cannot help it, and my poor head warns me to leave off. As usual, I have to pay for intense mental effort. Carlsbad has not altered that." And the letter concluded with a postscript: "Pearl-gray gloves."

The only clear idea which May gathered from this letter was that her aunt virtually held her released from her promise to go to Glengowrie, and left her free to do as she pleased. She carried the letter to her grandmother, saying, "Granny, I shall not go to Scotland after all. I shall stay with you, whether you like it or not. Oh, don't ask me to explain. I often feel with regard to Aunt Pauline like a deaf person watching dancers. There is something which regulates her movements, no doubt. But it is generally mysterious to me."

Mrs. Dobbs privately thought that in this case she held a clue to the mystery. "Ay," she said to herself, "Mrs. Dormer-Smith sees, just as I saw from the first hearing of it, that great changes may come to pass from this poor man's death. And she don't want May to commit herself too soon. Lord save us! 'tis a sad, low, worldly way of looking at such a matter." At this point some scarcely-articulate whisper of conscience made Mrs. Dobbs's brow redden; and she added mentally, "Well, but if May likes him? If the man's in earnest, and she likes him, it'll all come right in the end." Nevertheless, Mrs. Dobbs had begun to entertain shrewd doubts as to May's caring one straw for the unknown gentleman of princely fortune.

May, meanwhile, made haste to put her escape beyond the danger of Aunt Pauline's changing her mind. She wrote to Mrs. Griffin, saying that she should not be able to accept the Duchess's kind invitation to Glengowrie. She gave no reason. The excuse which Aunt Pauline had suggested she could not find it in her conscience to put forward. "If I had wished very much to go, that would not have stood in my way," she said to herself. "And it would be base and shocking to play the hypocrite about such a tragedy."

Neither did she think for a moment of refusing Miss Piper's invitation. There had not been wanting a hint that she ought to do so. Mrs. Bransby asked her if she meant to go to the musical party at Garnet Lodge; and, being answered in the affirmative, said, "Well, it seemed to me that it would be quite overstrained to refuse. But Theodore persisted that you would not go; said it would be inconvenable. He almost quarrelled with me about it. You know Theodore's infallible way of laying down the law."

It need scarcely be said that if anything could have strengthened the young lady's determination to attend Miss Piper's party, it would have been hearing that Theodore Bransby took upon himself to object to her doing so.

CHAPTER V.

Like the fairy Pari-Banou's magic tent, which could shelter an army of ten thousand men, and yet was capable of being folded into the smallness of a handkerchief, what one calls "the world" shrinks and stretches to suit the individual case. Into the world of Polly and Patty Piper Lord Castlecombe and his family sorrows entered not at all. They might occasionally be viewed afar from the tent door; but even that distant recognition was not vouchsafed to them now, when the great event of the musical party absorbed the attention of the two sisters.

In addition to Miss Clara Bertram and Mr. Cleveland Turner, the occasion was to be graced by the presence of Signor Vincenzo Valli. He was on a visit to a noble family in Mr. Sweeting's neighbourhood, and had volunteered to accompany that gentleman and his protégé to Miss Piper's party. This honour, like other honours, was somewhat of a burthen as well as a distinction. The programme of the evening's performance, so carefully and anxiously arranged beforehand, must be modified to suit Signor Valli; who, if he condescended to sing at all, would do so only in accordance with his own caprice. And this would probably occasion difficulties; since, although Miss Bertram's amiability might be reckoned on, Mr. Cleveland Turner took a more stiff-necked view of his own importance, and would not be disposed to yield the pas to Valli. Still Miss Piper had no cowardly regrets on hearing of the distinction which was to befall her. She rose to the occasion, and was prepared to undergo almost any impertinence from the popular singing master with a Spartan smile.

"I ought to understand how to manage artists, if anybody does," said she, remembering the many cups of tea she had poured out for that irritable genus in old times.

But the crowning interest and glory of the evening to her would be the performance of an air from "Esther," which Miss Bertram had promised to sing. The Misses Piper had invited her to visit them at first from disinterested kindness; the young singer being tired with the work of the season, and in need of rest and change of air. Under these circumstances, both the sisters were too thoroughly gentlewomen to hint at her singing for them. But Clara Bertram, casting about in her mind for some way to show her gratitude to the kindly old maids, had herself proposed to sing "something from 'Esther.'" And the offer was too tempting to be refused.

The composition selected was of the most infantile simplicity, and could have been learned by heart in ten minutes. But a copy of it had been sent to town a fortnight ago for Miss Bertram to "study." And Mr. Simpson had been supposed to be "studying" the accompaniment for an equal length of time. In fact, the performance of the air from "Esther" was the original germ out of which the musical party at Garnet Lodge had been developed.

Clara Bertram arrived in Oldchester the morning before the great day: partly in order that she might not be over-tired, and partly to give the opportunity for a rehearsal of the air with Mr. Simpson. "Oh, I'm sure we need not trouble Mr. Simpson," Clara began thoughtlessly. "It is certain to go all right." But Miss Polly would not allow such a lax view of responsibility.

"Excuse me, my dear," she said, "but the music of 'Esther' is not quite a drawing-room ballad. Not that you will not sing it charmingly—perfectly! There is no doubt about that. But there is a certain breadth—a certain style of phrasing, necessary for sacred music. It is most important that the accompanist should understand your reading of the air. Indeed, I am anxious to hear it myself. I have my own idea as to the proper rendering of the opening phrase, 'Hear, O King, and grant me my petition!' But I shan't say a word until I have heard you. Your idea may be better than mine; Ha, ha, ha! Who knows? 'Hear, O King, and grant—?' My own notion would be to begin softly—almost sotto voce—in a timid manner: 'Hear, O King;' and then to rise into a crescendo as the strain proceeds 'and grant me my PETITION!' But I won't say a word. You must sing it as you feel it."

May was, by special favour, admitted to the rehearsal. She had called to see Clara Bertram on the afternoon of her arrival, and was ushered into the long, low, old-fashioned drawing-room, where she found Miss Piper seated at one end of it, amid a wilderness of rout-seats, and Mr. Sebastian Bach Simpson at the piano, near to which Miss Bertram was standing.

"Oh, it's dear May Cheffington!" said Miss Piper, who had turned round sharply at the opening of the door. "Yes, yes; come in, my dear. Not at home to anybody else, Rachel! Not to anybody, do you hear? Now come and sit down by me, my dear. She is going to try 'Hear, O King.' Very glad to see you; you are so sympathetic, and such a favourite with Clara! There now, don't make her talk! Nothing worse for the voice than talking. Come and sit down."

May was, indeed, scarcely allowed to exchange greetings with her friend, who whispered smilingly, "We'll have our chat by-and-by."

Then Mr. Simpson struck up the first chords of the symphony, and there was breathless silence. He had not played three bars, however, before Miss Piper jumped up and ran to the piano.

"Oh, I beg pardon, Mr. Simpson, for offering a suggestion to so sound a musician as yourself, but don't you think a little more stress might be laid on that chord of the diminished seventh? It prepares the way, you see, for the pleading tone of the composition. Le-da, de-da—like that! Oh, thank you! Quite my meaning. Please go on."

But Mr. Simpson did not proceed far without receiving another "suggestion."

"A little more force and fulness, don't you think, in that resolution of the discord? I should like a richer effect."

"I don't know how to make it richer," rasped out Mr. Simpson. "It is the simple common chord, just four notes—C, E, G, C. I sounded 'em all. I can play the bass as an octave, if you think that'll be any richer."

"Oh, thank you! Yes, I really think it will. You see 'Esther' was scored for full orchestra, and the composer's ear hankers after the instrumental effects. But that octave in the bass is a great improvement. Many thanks!"

And in this fashion the symphony was at length got through.

Then Clara uplifted her pure, clear voice, and sang. May listened in delight. Surely Miss Polly must be enchanted! Even Mr. Simpson's hard visage relaxed, as the thrilling notes rose in sweet pathetic pleading. When they ceased, he wheeled round on the music-stool, and exclaimed with the most unwonted fervour, "It's the loveliest soprano voice I've heard since your great namesake, Clara Novello. Some of your notes remind me of her altogether. Not that I expect to hear anything quite like her 'Let the Bright Seraphim,' on this side of paradise."

May turned to Miss Piper. But, to her astonishment, Miss Piper's face did not express unmingled delight. There was some slight and indefinable shade on it.

"Well, I do think that is most beautiful," said May.

"Do you, my dear? Do you really?"

"Why, how is it possible to think otherwise, Miss Piper? No one could, surely!"

"Well, it is very kind of you to say so, my dear; and, to be frank, it shows a power of appreciation not quite common at your age. Of course it would be affectation on my part, at this time of day, and with my reputation behind me, to say I am surprised. But I am gratified, very much gratified. And don't you think Miss Bertram did her part delightfully?"

May looked at her blankly, unable to say a word in reply. Fortunately, no reply was needed, for Miss Piper bustled up to Clara and thanked her, and praised her. But still her manner fell decidedly short of its usual cordial heartiness. At length, with many apologies and flowery speeches, she begged that the air might be repeated, if Clara were sure it would not tire her; and, this being at once conceded, she asked, hesitatingly, "And would you mind if I offered a little suggestion? Just a hint!"

"Certainly not, dear Miss Piper! I will do my best to carry out your idea."

"Oh, that is so sweet of you! Thank you a thousand times! If Mr. Simpson will kindly oblige us once more—? Now, you see, it is just here, on that G in alt, where the voice rises on the words, 'Grant, oh, grant me my petition!' The sound 'grant,' according to my original conception, should be given with a sort of wail—not, of course, an unmusical sound, but just with a tinge of sadness expressive of the then miserable and depressed condition of the Jewish nation, and at the same time with a tone—an underlying tone, as it were—conveying the latent hope (which really was in Queen Esther's mind all along, you know) that by her efforts brighter days might yet be in store for them. You feel what I mean?"

"I will try my best," answered Clara gently. And then she sang the air again—precisely as she had sung it before.

"Now," cried Miss Piper, jumping up and clapping her hands in an ecstasy of triumph, "it is perfect—absolutely perfect!"

She poured out unstinted thanks and compliments to both singer and accompanist, observing to the latter that this recalled the great days of the public performance of "Esther," and that she considered Miss Bertram's rendering of "Hear, O King," far superior to that of the well-known vocalist who had sung it originally. "But then, you see, she could not, or would not, take a hint. Consequently—although, of course, she sang the notes perfectly—she never fully mastered my conception. Now a word has been enough to show Miss Bertram the inner meaning of my music; and she interprets it in the most exquisite manner."

Before going away May contrived to have a few words with Clara Bertram in her room.

"It is such a pleasure to hear you sing again," said May. "How I wish Granny could hear you!"

"Will not your grandmother be here to-morrow evening?"

"Oh no," answered May, colouring. "She does not go out to parties. Granny does not belong to the class of the ladies and gentlemen who come here. Her husband was a tradesman in this town. But she is the finest creature in the world. And she has more real dignity than any one I know."

"Your grandmother lives here? But then—how is it—your mother is not a foreigner?"

"A foreigner? Good gracious! No. My mother was Miss Susan Dobbs. She died years ago, when I was a little child. Why do you ask?"

"Oh, nothing. I fancied—Valli said something about having known Madame Cheffington abroad."

"That was possible. My parents lived abroad for years. My father is on the Continent now. I and the two little brothers before me were born in Belgium."

"Oh! I suppose that must be it," said Clara slowly. "Valli talks at random sometimes."

"Signor Valli talks very much at random if he ever said my mother was a foreigner. By the way, do you know he is to be here to-morrow evening?"

"Yes; so I hear."

"You do not hear it with rapture, apparently."

"No; I do not like him very much."

"He likes you very much, if appearances may be trusted," said May laughingly.

"He is always making love to me after his fashion. That is why I do not like him."

Clara spoke gravely, but with her habitual serenity. There was something in her manner which seemed to be akin to her voice; something clear, but not cold: a crystal with the sun in it.

"Oh, that is hideous, isn't it?" cried May, with eager fellow-feeling. "When people want to marry you, and you shudder at the bare idea of marrying them."

"I don't think Valli wants to marry me," answered Clara calmly. "Indeed, I believe he feels a great deal of hostility towards me at times. He is never satisfied unless his pupils will, more or less, flirt with him—a kind of philandering which I object to. Besides, it wastes one's time. But he has been spoiled more than you would believe by fashionable ladies. I suppose you never read much of George Sands' writings?"

"No," answered May, opening great eyes of wonder.

"Nor I, except 'Consuelo,' and the sequel to it. I read them for the musical part, which is wonderfully good. Well, in the 'Comtesse de Rudolstadt' there is a certain Monsieur de Poelnitz, of whom it is said that en qualité d'ex-roué il n'aimait pas les filles vertueuses. It always seems to me that Valli, in his quality of philanderer, dislikes women who won't flirt, whether he wants to flirt with them himself or not."

"How odious! How despicable!"

"And yet he has his good qualities. He is very faithful and generous to his family, and sends a great part of his earnings to them in their little Sicilian village."

Then, seeing that May still looked very much shocked and astonished, Clara added, in a lighter tone, "But let us talk of something more pleasant. You were speaking of your grandmamma. If you think she would like it, I should be so glad to go and sing to her at her own home."

"Like it! Of course she would like it! And I scarcely know how to thank you as you ought to be thanked, for fear of sounding like Miss Piper!"

Clara smiled. "Miss Piper and her sister are both very kind to me," she said.

"Yes; but I wish Miss Polly wasn't so ridiculous. Of course, her music is poor and silly. It is only your beautiful singing that makes it sound well. But then you could make 'Baa, baa, blacksheep,' sound well! And then to hear the outrageous, conceited nonsense she talks—! I wonder that you can endure it so meekly. I couldn't!" answered May, with the trenchant intolerance of her eighteen years.

"Oh yes, you could, under the circumstances. I am only too glad to give the kind old lady any pleasure. And she is not so outrageously conceited—for an amateur. But now I fear I must turn you out, much as I should like you to stay; for Miss Piper sent me upstairs to lie down; and if she finds I am not doing so, I shall have to drink another cupful of Miss Patty's excellent beef-tea, which is so strong, it makes me feel quite tipsy!"

CHAPTER VI.

On the following evening Garnet Lodge wore a brilliantly festive appearance. Miss Polly was dressed betimes. An unprecedented variety of geological specimens adorned her wrists and fingers, and hung over the bosom of her lavender satin gown. She was walking up and down the drawing-room, surveying the rows of empty rout-seats, fully three-quarters of an hour before the earliest guest could be expected to arrive. She was strung up for the great occasion; but, although excited, she was not apprehensive. Miss Patty, on the other hand, was very nervous.

"I am a little anxious about the jellies, Polly; and about that new waiter from Winnick's. But I could face all that, if it wasn't for 'Hear, O King!' To think of hearing it again after all these years! I'm afraid it will upset me. I'll take a back place near the door for I'm sure to cry; and then I can slip out if necessary."

"You need not be ashamed of your tears, my dear Patty. Very probably you will not be the only person powerfully affected."

"Well, I don't know. I don't remember that anybody cried when 'Esther' was brought out at Mercers' Hall," returned Miss Patty thoughtfully.

The first persons to arrive were Mr. and Mrs. Simpson. Amelia was resplendent in a new pink silk gown, which seemed to magnify her florid proportions, and made her a conspicuous object from every part of the room. She was beaming with delight; and her gratification at finding herself in Garnet Lodge under the present circumstances was so frankly and exuberantly expressed, as to cause some mortification to her husband.

"This is, indeed, a memorable evening, dear Misses Piper," she began; for Patty had by this time joined her sister in the drawing-room. "I was telling Bassy that he ought to feel himself honoured by being selected to officiate—if I may so express it—at the pianoforte on this extremely interesting and auspicious occasion."

"The honour is to me, Mrs. Simpson," answered Polly Piper politely.

"There!" turning suddenly round with such vehemence as to sweep down a rout-seat with her pink silk skirts. "What did I tell you, Bassy? Whatever may be the opinion of certain persons enriched by manufactures—and yet, after all, what should we do without manufactures? How many of us would be capable of dealing with the raw material? Blankets, for instance: take a sheep! But still I always say to Bassy, 'Believe me, the real gentry acknowledge and revere the position of the Fine Arts!'"

"Now, Amelia; hadn't you better mind what you're doing?" said Mr. Simpson, setting the fallen rout-seat on its legs again. She irritated him occasionally, but he admired her smart gown very much nevertheless, and thought she looked remarkably well in it, and "quite the lady."

Other guests arriving now claimed the hostess's attention. And presently Clara Bertram, in her simple black evening dress, came into the room. Then appeared Mrs. Martin Bransby on the arm of her stepson, and bearing excuses from her husband, who was not feeling well enough to come out that evening. Her appearance called forth ejaculations of admiration from Mrs. Simpson, which, however exaggerated they might sound, were quite sincere. Mrs. Simpson gave utterance to a kind of prose rhapsody on the subject of Mrs. Bransby's dress; and then, bowing graciously to Theodore, said, "And Mr. Bransby Junior, too. When I had the pleasure of unexpectedly, and, indeed, fortuitously, meeting him the other evening at the house of a mutual friend, I remarked that he was paying Miss Piper a high compliment in abandoning Thetis" (the good lady probably meant Themis) "for the seductions of Apollo. But we are told, on the poet's authority, that 'music hath charms to soothe the savage—' Not, of course, that the epithet is applicable in this case. Quite the contrary." Then, turning her glistening spectacles on the young man, she playfully added, "But, in addition to the magic of the lyre, we have what Hamlet—if I mistake not—so eloquently characterizes as 'metal more attractive:' a collection of youth and beauty which might really, without hyperbole, be termed a bevy."

"That is an intolerable woman," muttered Theodore between his teeth, as he conducted his step-mother to a seat.

"Oh, poor Simmy!" remonstrated Mrs. Bransby. "She is a good creature. But to-night she is in what Bobby and Billy call one of her 'dictionary moods.'"

Rapidly the room filled up. Besides many other Oldchester notabilities with whom this chronicle is not concerned, there were present Major Mitton, Canon and Mrs. Hadlow (the latter bringing May under her wing), Owen Rivers, who came alone, Dr. Hatch, and Mr. Bragg.

Mr. Bragg, after paying his respects to the ladies of the house, and standing for a few minutes in his silent, forlorn-looking way, went up to May, and said, "Will you come and have a cup of tea, Miss Cheffington? They say hot tea cools you. That seems strange, don't it? But I believe it's true. Rule of contraries, I suppose."

May did not wish for any tea; but she saw Theodore Bransby hovering in the distance, and she accepted Mr. Bragg's proffered arm almost eagerly. She rather liked Mr. Bragg. His slow, quiet, common-sensible manner was soothing. And she knew enough of his unostentatious good works in Oldchester to have a considerable esteem for him.

He piloted May into the dining-room, where tea and coffee were being served, and where the new waiter from Winnick's was, so far, conducting himself in an exemplary manner.

"Have one of those little cakes, Miss Cheffington? They look very good."

"No, thank you."

Mr. Bragg provided May with a cup of tea, and then took one of the little cakes himself. "They eat uncommonly short," said he with strong, though quiet, approbation. "All the eatables seem good."

"Not a doubt of it. Miss Patty is a wonderful housekeeper."

"Now, do you suppose she made those little cakes herself?"

"I cannot tell; but I am sure she could if she chose. She makes excellent cakes."

"Ah! I remember her giving me some very good ideas about a beefsteak pudding. I tried to make my cook do one according to her receipt; but it didn't answer," said Mr. Bragg with a sigh. Presently he remarked, as he slowly stirred his tea round and round, "This is a bad job about Mr. George Cheffington."

"Yes; I am very sorry for Lord Castlecombe."

"Ah, your uncle—or great-uncle is he?—I'm not much of a hand at remembering the ins and outs of families—is hard hit. But he bears up wonderfully, to outward appearance."

"Have you seen him, Mr. Bragg?"

"Yes; saw him o' Monday about some business. He's a keen hand at a bargain, is Lord Castlecombe. I don't know that I ever met with a keener."

"Poor old man!"

"Ay, that's what I say, Miss Cheffington. Keenness and all that is very well, so long as you've got somebody to be keen for. But it's a dreary thing to be alone in advancing years. I feel it myself, though I'm—well, I dare say nigh upon twenty years younger than his Lordship."

There was a little pause, during which Mr. Bragg sipped his tea and ate another cake. Then he repeated, "It's a dreary thing to be alone."

"Are you alone, Mr. Bragg?" asked May, feeling that she was expected to say something. "I thought you had sons and daughters."

"Only one son, and he's away in South America—settled in Buenos Ayres years ago. He's a rich man already, is Joshua. I started him well, though I hadn't so much money in those days as I have now, not by a deal, and he's done well. And he married a lady with money—a Spanish merchant's daughter. No; there's no likelihood of Josh coming home to England to keep me company, even supposing I wanted him to."

Then ensued another pause. Then Mr. Bragg said, "I'm to have the pleasure of meeting you at Glengowrie this autumn, I understand."

"No; I have decided not to go. I have written to Mrs. Griffin to say so."

"Oh! What—on account of this death in your family?"

"No, I cannot say that. It would be mere pretence. I never saw George Cheffington in my life; and he was not a very close relation." Mr. Bragg nodded approvingly. "That's a straightforward way of looking at it," he said. "But I'm disappointed you ain't to be at Glengowrie."

"Thank you. But my absence will not make much difference, I should say."

"I don't know. It might make a deal of difference," returned Mr. Bragg, speaking even more slowly than was his wont. "But where shall you be then?"

"Where I like best to be; here, with Granny."

"Granny?"

"My grandmother, Mrs. Dobbs. You must know her by name, at all events, for you are her tenant."

"What! old Dobbs the ironmonger's widow?—begging your pardon."

May drew herself up with a proud movement of the head, which might have satisfied even the deceased dowager that there was a strong strain of the Cheffington nature in her. "There is nothing to beg pardon for, Mr. Bragg," she said haughtily. "You cannot suppose that I am ashamed of my grandparents."

"You've no call to be ashamed of them; but people don't always see things in the right light," answered Mr. Bragg composedly. "Yes; to be sure, now I come to think of it, Mrs. Dobbs's daughter did marry—Ah! Of course, Susan Dobbs was your mother! I never knew her to speak to; but I remember her. Uncommonly pretty she was, too. Why I might ha' known—But, you see, your aunt, Mrs. Dormer-Smith, never mentioned your mother's family."

At this moment Owen Rivers approached them. He said he had been sent by Mrs. Bransby to look for May; and, thereupon, carried her off to the drawing-room. Mr. Bragg remained behind, pondering for a minute or so. "To think of this girl being Lord Castlecombe's grand-niece and old Dobbs's grand-daughter! Well, things do turn out queer in this world!" Then Mr. Bragg also repaired to the drawing-room.

The musical portion of the evening went off brilliantly. But the great success was undoubtedly Clara Bertram's performance of "Hear, O King!" She sang poor Polly Piper's bald and jejeune phrases in a way which made such of the elder auditors as remembered its first performance ask themselves, wonderingly, if this were indeed the music they had listened to long ago. And she concluded with a cadenza, so expressive and beautiful that Mr. Simpson, raptly listening, very nearly omitted to play the final chords.

When the song was over, there was a burst of applause, and an unusually loud clapping together of kid-gloved palms. But, from the doorway, where he had stood to listen, Valli precipitated himself through the crowd like some swift missile; clearing his way, utterly regardless of intervening backs and shoulders, male or female, and rushing up to Miss Bertram, he exclaimed, "Divinamente!"

"I am glad you are content," she answered in English.

But Valli went on volubly in his own tongue, "Content? No; 'content' is not the word. I am enchanted. You sang divinely! Demon of a girl, never in all your life did you sing a song of mine like that! What possessed you?"

"Gratitude," answered Clara quietly.

Miss Piper now came up and kissed her effusively. Composer and singer were soon surrounded by a little crowd, to whose polite exclamations of "Charming!" "Immense treat!" "Really delicious!" and so forth, Miss Polly kept replying, with lofty magnanimity, "Oh, but you must not attribute all the honour to me! I assure you that more depends upon the execution than you are, perhaps, aware of."

This first triumph had a subtle effect on Mr. Cleveland Turner. He was moved by it to play a dashing valse de concert in place of a composition of his own, modelled on a great original, which he entitled "Twilight in the Gardens of Walhalla." It had been much praised in esoteric circles. But it was somewhat trying to the unregenerate ear; so much so, that a profane and flippant outsider had rechristened it "Feeding Time in the Gardens of the Royal Zoological Society." Mr. Sweeting afterwards mildly reproached his young friend for not having performed it, and thus doing something towards improving and elevating the taste of Oldchester.

"It's no answer, my dear boy, to say they wouldn't have liked it," said Mr. Sweeting. "No answer at all!"

But it is to be feared that Cleveland Turner had some depraved enjoyment of the applause which resulted from his lapse into heresy.

Signor Valli, determined not to be eclipsed in popularity, and utterly indifferent to the improvement of Oldchester's musical taste, made himself unprecedentedly amiable. He sang vivacious Neapolitan street songs, quaint Tuscan stornelli, pathetic Sicilian airs. And these tuneful productions were greatly relished by that vast majority of the listeners, who had not progressed so far as to connect ugliness with righteousness—in music.

When Valli at length rose from the piano, Mrs. Simpson made a sudden plunge across the room, and presented herself breathlessly before him. He was in a group of persons, among whom were Mr. Sweeting, Cleveland Turner, and Miss Piper. Amelia's round, plump face was flushed by heat and excitement to a rose-pink hue, several shades deeper than that of her gown; and her spectacles glittered with a blank and baffling brightness.

"I cannot," she said, "quit this elegant scene of the Muses without offering my poor tribute to you, Signor" (which she pronounced "senior"), "for the delightful addition your performances have contributed to refined enjoyment."

Valli looked up rather bewildered, and, not knowing what else to do, made her a profound bow.

"I trust," continued the lady, "that I may be allowed to congratulate you, signor, in the harmonious words of our great poet, upon your 'linked sweetness, long drawn out'—not, I'm sure, that any one present considered for a moment that you were drawing it out at all too long!" And with a sweeping curtsey, in the performance of which she overwhelmed Mr. Sweeting's legs in a flood of pink silk skirt, and backed heavily on to Mr. Cleveland Turner's toes, Amelia withdrew, beaming.

At supper Valli was in high good humour. He had been presented to Mrs. Bransby, and was gratified to find himself placed beside her at the supper-table, she being incontestably the most beautiful woman in the room. Major Mitton sat near them, and pleased Valli by praises of his singing—a pleasure not at all diminished by his quick perception that the good major had no knowledge whatever of the subject.

"It's a real treat, I assure you," said Major Mitton, "to hear a toon. I don't pretend to be a great connoisseur, but I can enjoy a toon. Ah, they may say what they please, but there's no music like Italian music, and nobody can sing it like Italians."

This led to some reminiscences of the major's garrison life in Malta; and to the mention of the prima donna Bianca Moretti. Mrs. Bransby recognized this name as that of the heroine of Miss Piper's story, told at her dinner-party several months ago.

"Oh, you have heard the Moretti?" said Valli. "Yes; she could sing. By the way, I hear she is a kind of marâtre—how do you call it?—to that pretty Miss Cheffington."

"Miss Cheffington? Oh, impossible!"

"Pardon! Not at all impossible! I mean the young lady opposite, at the other end of the table, sitting between those two young men. I know one of them—the one with the blonde smooth head. I meet him in society. He is tremendously annoying—nojoso—what you call a bore."

"That is Miss Cheffington, certainly. But you don't mean to say that Signora Moretti has married her father?"

"Oh, married!" answered Valli, with a shrug. "She has been living with him for years; that is what I mean. I hear la Bianca has grown steady now. But she had a jeunesse pas mal orageuse."

Major Mitton tried to change the subject, glancing uneasily at Mrs. Bransby. But Valli was impervious to the hint. Not that he had any intention of outraging the proprieties, or any suspicion that he was doing so. Mrs. Bransby was not a jeune meess. He had heard of English cant and hypocrisy long before he came to England. But he had been agreeably surprised to find them conspicuous by their absence in the section of London fashionable society which he chiefly frequented. So he went on narrating anecdotes of la Bianca and her adventures, until Mrs. Bransby rose, and quietly left the table. Upon this, Major Mitton and several other men drew closer to Valli. And the consequence was that, not only the mess-table, but other circles in Oldchester, were regaled the next day with some choice morsels of scandal, in which the name of Gus Cheffington figured conspicuously.

But whatever might be the subsequent results of that talk, Miss Piper's musical party had undoubtedly turned out a great success.

That night, when the sisters were alone together, they sat up for an hour discussing the events of the evening in a glow of pleasurable excitement. Every point was remembered and dwelt upon, but of course their interest centred in the song from "Esther."

"It was a real triumph, Polly," said Miss Patty. "There can't be two opinions about that. But—there, I thought I wouldn't tell you; but I can't help it—I overheard Signor Valli and that Cleveland Turner, whom I never did like, and never shall, speaking of 'Hear, O King,' in a sneering, slighting manner."

Quoth Miss Polly with a lofty smile, and laying her hand on her sister's shoulder, "My dear Patty, I am not at all surprised to hear it. I have experience of artists, if anybody has, and in the best of them I have always observed one defect in judging my music—professional jealousy!"

CHAPTER VII.

The day after the party at Garnet Lodge Mrs. Dobbs was surprised by the announcement from her old servant, Martha, that Mr. Bragg was at the gate, and would be glad to speak with her if she was at liberty.

"Quite at liberty, Martha, and very happy to see Mr. Bragg. Now what can he want?" said Mrs. Dobbs to the faithful Jo Weatherhead, who was in his usual place by the hearth.

"Something about the house in Friar's Row?" suggested Jo.

"Ah! I suppose so. Though I don't know what there can be to say. However, it's no use guessing. It's like staring at the outside of a letter instead of reading it. He'll speak for himself."

Meanwhile Mr. Bragg had alighted from the plain brougham which had brought him from his country house; and, walking up the garden path, and in at the open door, presented himself in the little parlour.

"I hope you'll excuse my calling, Mrs. Dobbs. You and me have met years ago."

"No excuse needed, Mr. Bragg. I remember you very well. This is my brother-in-law, Mr. Weatherhead. Please to sit down."

Mr. Bragg sat down; and he and his hostess looked at each other for a moment attentively.

Mr. Bragg was a large, solidly built man, with an impression on his face of perplexity and resolution subtly mingled together. It is a look which may be often seen on the countenance of an intelligent workman, whose employment brings him into conflict with physical phenomena—at once so docile and so intractable; so simply and so eternally mysterious. The expression had long survived the days of Mr. Bragg's personal struggle with facts of a metallic nature. In his present position, as a man of large wealth and influence, he had to deal chiefly with the more complex phenomena of humanity, and very seldom found it so trustworthy in the manipulation as the iron and lead and tin and steel of his younger days.

Mrs. Dobbs marked the changes wrought by time and circumstances in Joshua Bragg. She remembered him—he had even been temporarily in her husband's employment, at one time—in a well-worn suit of working clothes, and with chronically black finger-nails. She saw him now, dressed with quiet good taste (for he left that matter to his London tailor), with irreproachably clean hands—on which, however, toil had left ineffaceable traces—and a massive watch chain worth half a year's earnings of his former days.

"You're very little changed in the main, Mr. Bragg. And the years haven't been hard on you," said Mrs. Dobbs, summing up the result of her observations.

"No; I believe I don't feel the burthen of years much; not bodily, that is. In the mind, I think I do. You see, I've come to a time of life when a man can't keep putting off his own comfort and happiness to the day after to-morrow. Which," added Mr. Bragg thoughtfully, "is exactly where young folks have the pull, I think."

"That's queer, too, Mr. Bragg!" remarked Jo Weatherhead. "Putting off your own comfort and happiness seems a poor way to enjoy yourself, sir."

"Ah, but what you only mean to do, always comes up to your expectations; and what you do do, doesn't!" rejoined Mr. Bragg, with a slow, emphatic nod of the head.

"Well, but as to 'feeling the burthen of years,' that's putting it too strong," said Mrs. Dobbs. "You have no right to feel that burthen yet awhile. Why, you must be—let me see!—under fifty-three."

"Fifty-three last birthday."

"Ay; I wasn't far out. Lord, that's no age! I might be your mother, Mr. Bragg."

"I'm glad to hear you say so!—I mean, I'm glad you don't think me too old—not quite an old fellow, in short."

"No; to be sure not!"

Mr. Bragg was silent for fully a minute. Then he said, "Well, whether I'm quite an old fellow or not, I'm too old to trust much to the day after to-morrow. So, if not inconvenient to you, Mrs. Dobbs, I should like to say a few words to you about a matter that has been on my mind for some little time."

"Certainly, Mr. Bragg. I'm quite at your service."

Mr. Bragg looked slowly round the little parlour; looked out of the window at the tiny garden; looked at Mr. Weatherhead; finally looked at Mrs. Dobbs again, and said, "It's a private matter."

"I had better go, Sarah," said Jo. "I shall look round again at tea-time;" and he made a show of rising from his chair, very slowly and reluctantly.

"Oh, perhaps you've no call to go away, Jo. I have no business secrets from my brother-in-law, Mr. Bragg. He is my oldest and best friend in the world."

Mr. Bragg rubbed his chin slowly with his hand, and answered with a certain embarrassment, but quite straightforwardly, "It's a matter private to me."

After this Jo Weatherhead had nothing for it but to take his departure, and to endeavour to calm the fever of his curiosity with tobacco.

Mrs. Dobbs remained alone with her visitor, wondering more and more what could be the subject of his proposed communication. Her thoughts, in connection with Mr. Bragg, persistently hovered about the house in Friar's Row. But his first words scattered them in widespread confusion.

"Your grand-daughter, Miss Cheffington, tells me that she is not going to Glengowrie Castle this autumn, Mrs. Dobbs."

"Why—no—I believe not," answered Mrs. Dobbs, looking at him curiously.

"In that case I don't think I shall go there myself. I'm no sportsman. I always feel lonely in a house full of strangers. And, besides—I was invited partic'larly to meet Miss Cheffington."

Mrs. Dobbs preserved her outward composure; but something seemed to whirl and spin in her brain; and, although she kept her eyes fixed on Mr. Bragg, she saw neither him nor anything else in the room for several seconds.

"I was asked through Mrs. Griffin. You may have heard speak of her?"

Mrs. Dobbs made an affirmative movement of the head. She could not have articulated a word at that moment to save her life.

"Mrs. Griffin is a well-meaning lady. But she's a lady who now and then gets out of her depth, along of not—what you might call minding her own business. But she always means to be kind. And the best of us make mistakes."

"Ah, that we do!" assented Mrs. Dobbs huskily.

"Well, Mrs. Griffin is always telling me that my money—'a princely fortune' she calls it: but it's a good deal more than that, by what I can hear about princes—lays me under an obligation to marry again."

At the words "princely fortune" Mrs. Dobbs winced, and a deep red flush came into her face; but she answered quietly, "Wealth has its responsibilities, of course, Mr. Bragg."

"Yes, it has; and its troubles. But when all's said and done, it's pleasanter to be rich than poor. I've tried both."

"No doubt. Only—one may pay too dear even for being rich."

"Well, I should be sorry for any lady I married to consider that she paid too dear for being rich."

"Oh, I meant no offence, Mr. Bragg."

"There's nothing you may not pay too dear for, I suppose; except a quiet conscience. You may pay too dear for a wife. And there's two sides to every"—he was about to say "bargain," but he substituted the word "arrangement."

Mrs. Dobbs had taken up her knitting, and was twisting and pulling it with her fingers in a restless, nervous way. When Mr. Bragg made a pause, and looked at her, she said, "Of course, that's quite true."

He went on, "I make bold to hope, Mrs. Dobbs, that you'll give me credit in what I'm going to say, for having some serious reason, and not talking idly, out of pride and vanity; in short, for not being what you might call a fool."

"Yes, I will, Mr. Bragg."

"Thank ye. On that understanding I may say, between ourselves, that Mrs. Griffin has mentioned to me several quarters where I shouldn't meet with a refusal in case I went to look for a wife. I couldn't have supposed it myself—at least, not to the extent it really does run to. But the fact has been brought to my knowledge, so that there's no possibility of making any mistake about it. More than one young lady—some of 'em titled, too," said Mr. Bragg, with an odd glimmer of complacency flitting for a moment like a will-o'-the-wisp above the solid terra firma of his native good sense. "More than one, and more than two, have been what you might call trotted out for me."

Mrs. Dobbs's fingers twitched and pulled at the wool on her knitting-needles, and the muscles round her mouth seemed to tighten. But she said not a word.

Mr. Bragg continued, "Now, perhaps you think I have no business to take up your time with all this, when it's no concern of yours?"

Still Mrs. Dobbs did not speak; so he added—

"But it does concern you in a way."

She made a visible effort to say, quietly, "Ah, indeed! How's that?"

But this time she was perfectly sure beforehand of what he was going to say.

"I'm coming to that in one moment." Here Mr. Bragg paused, took out his handkerchief, and passed it over his face before proceeding. "I mentioned that Mrs. Griffin sometimes gets out of her depth (with the best of intentions) when minding other people's business. She got a little out of her depth when attending to mine. She somehow took it for granted that I should be quite content to marry any lady of high family, who would look handsome in my diamonds and spend my money in the fashionablest style. She was consequently a good deal taken aback when I offered some objections to one or two parties of her recommendation. But I managed to make her understand at last. Said I, 'Mrs. Griffin, I don't undervalue the honour; but I'm too old to wear a tight shoe for the sake of appearances.' The fact was, I did not feel myself what you might call drawn towards any of these young ladies. I couldn't fancy them sitting opposite to me at my own fireside with a kind look on their faces. Now, the reason I say all this to you," continued Mr. Bragg, laying his massive hand on the elbow of Mrs. Dobbs's chair, "is because there is a young lady that I do feel drawn towards—a young lady I've had opportunities of observing at home and abroad. And it was talking of this young lady that I said one day to Mrs. Griffin, 'Now, if you could find some one like Miss May Cheffington who'd condescend to have me, I should think myself a very fortunate man.' She quite jumped at the idea."

"Jumped, indeed!" burst out Mrs. Dobbs, indignantly. "Then she took a most unwarrantable liberty. She could know nothing about Miss May Cheffington's feeling in the matter. What business had she to jump?"

"Nay, nay, my good lady! My good lady! You don't understand. She jumped at the idea on my account. Why, Lord bless me, you couldn't suppose—! She told me at once that May Cheffington was the purest-minded and most unworldly girl she ever knew. I remember her very words; for I couldn't help thinking at the time how queer it was that Mrs. Griffin should admire unworldliness so much."

There was a long pause. Mrs. Dobbs was greatly moved from her usual self-possession. She could not trust herself to speak, while Mr. Bragg was surprised, and somewhat offended, by her reception of what he had to say.

He had really, all things considered, very little purse pride. But he had been accustomed for many years to be dumbly conscious of the power of his wealth, as an elephant is dumbly conscious of the power of his weight; and for a few moments he felt as the elephant might feel if he were subjected to the mysterious process which we hear of as "levitation," and suddenly found himself brushed aside like a fly. Mr. Bragg did not wish to bear down his fellow-creatures unduly by force of wealth. But wealth had come to be a large factor in his social specific gravity.

After a while, Mrs. Dobbs said tremulously, and by no means graciously, "Well, I don't see what I can do for you in the matter."

"I am not asking you to do anything for me, Mrs. Dobbs. I was not aware till last night that you were any relation to Miss Cheffington, or, leastways, I had forgotten it, for I believe I did hear of your daughter's marriage years ago. When I became aware of it, I thought you would take it as a mark of respect and goodwill if I came and spoke to you confidentially. But you don't appear to see it in that light."

Mrs. Dobbs turned round and offered him her hand, saying, "I ask your pardon if I have said anything to offend you. You don't deserve it; you are very far from deserving it. But I'm shaken; my nerve isn't what it was. I haven't been so upset since my poor dear daughter Susy ran away and got married." She was trembling, and her restless fingers were making sad work with the knitting.

"Well, well, there's no occasion for you to put yourself about, you know. I should like you to tell me just this—under the circumstances I think there's no objection to my putting the question—is there anybody else in the field before me?"

"N-no; I think not. I can't say."

"If the young lady has no other attachment," said Mr. Bragg, in his slow, pondering way, "I don't see why I should not be able to make her happy. What do you think?"

"You're a deal older than the child: there's a great disparity, Joshua!" answered Mrs. Dobbs, reverting, in her agitation, to the familiar form in which she had addressed him thirty years back.

"So there is, but that can't be helped; we must just reckon with it as so much alloy. There wouldn't be much romance—couldn't be; but a vast number of people get on very well without romance, and are useful and happy. I have some reason to believe," added Mr. Bragg, looking at her a little askance—for there was no knowing whether this fiery old woman might not take offence again—"that certain members of Miss C.'s family would approve."

Mrs. Dobbs answered with unexpected meekness. "There's no need to tell me that. And you mustn't suppose, Mr. Bragg, that I don't appreciate—that I don't know how the world in general would look upon your offer."

"Why, you see, it doesn't amount exactly to an offer. I thought I would talk matters over with you, and, what you might call, put the case. You see," said Mr. Bragg, placing the forefinger of his right hand upon the thumb of his left, "for my part I could undertake that any lady who did me the honour to marry me should have steady kindness and respect. I wouldn't marry a woman I didn't respect, not if she was the handsomest one in the world and a duke's daughter. Then," placing his two forefingers together, "I ain't a bad temper, nor a jealous temper. Lastly," here he shifted the forefinger of his right hand to the middle finger of his left, "though I don't want to lay too much stress upon money, yet it's a fact that my wife, and, in the course of nature, my widow, would be a very rich woman."

"I suppose you know," said Mrs. Dobbs, leaning her forehead on her hand, and letting the knitting slide from her knees to the floor, "that May's father is alive?"

"Yes; I do know it. And I've got something to say to you on that score. And I'm sure you will agree with me that it is very desirable for Miss C. to have protection and guidance. I'm not speaking for myself now, you understand. Her aunt, Mrs. Dormer-Smith, is a very genteel lady, with very high connections. But—quite between ourselves, you know—I wouldn't give much for her headpiece."

Mrs. Dobbs was looking at him eagerly, and scarcely allowed him to finish his sentence before she said, "But you have something to say about Captain Cheffington?"

"Well, perhaps you know it. If you don't, you ought to. He has been travelling about for years with an Italian opera-singer. She is with him now in Brussels. And people say he has married her."

Mrs. Dobbs clasped her hands together, and ejaculated, almost in a whisper, "Oh, my poor child!"

Mr. Bragg could not tell whether she were thinking of her daughter, or her grand-daughter. Perhaps the images of both were in her mind.

"You had not heard of it, then? Ah! It's a bad prospect for Miss C."

"But is it true? So many stories get about. It seems incredible to me that Augustus, so selfish as he is, should have bound himself in that way."

"I hear it confirmed on all hands. It's an old story now, and pretty widely known. But, look at it which way you will, it's an ugly, disreputable kind of business, Mrs. Dobbs."

She was silent for a while, sitting with her head sunk on her breast, and her hands clasped before her. Then she said, almost as if speaking to herself, "God knows! The woman may not be bad or wicked. How are we to judge?"

Mr. Bragg drew his hand away from the elbow of Mrs. Dobbs's chair, where it had been resting, and said, in a tone of solemn disapprobation, "I don't think there can be much doubt as to the character of the—person, Mrs. Dobbs. I understand she became so notorious in Brussels through keeping a gaming-house, or something of that kind, as to call for the interference of the police."

"May I ask how this information reached you?" said Mrs. Dobbs, turning round and looking full at him.

Mr. Bragg hesitated for a few moments before answering. "It has come to me from various quarters; but the latest is an Italian singer, who has been chattering a good deal. He was at Miss Piper's. There's always a certain amount of risk in having public performers in your house. I don't encourage 'em myself—never did from a boy; and I think it a pity that Miss Piper does. Her sister and me are quite agreed on that point." Mr. Bragg here pushed back his chair and stood up. "I should wish you to understand," he said, "that I should have thought it my duty to tell you this, feeling the interest I do in Miss C., quite independent of our previous conversation."

"I understand. Thank you."

"With regard to that conversation, you can, if you think it advisable, what you might call sound your grand-daughter. I think that might avoid disagreeables for both parties. It can't be pleasant for a sensitive young lady to refuse an offer. And I don't mind saying that it would be extremely unpleasant to me to be refused. A man of my age and—well, I may say my position, don't like to look ridic'lous. Of course you don't care much for my feelings: can't be expected to; but I think, on reflection, you'll see that by coming to you first in this way, I've also done the best I could to spare the feelings of Miss C."

With that Mr. Bragg shook hands with his hostess, and, quietly letting himself out of the house, walked to his brougham, and was driven away to the office in Friar's Row.

CHAPTER VIII.

To one so habitually resolute, sagacious, and self-reliant as Mrs. Dobbs, the shock of discovering that she has been living under a delusion is severe. It is not merely mortifying—it is alarming. After her conversation with Mr. Bragg, Mrs. Dobbs felt like a person who, walking along what seems to be like a solid path, suddenly finds his foot sink into a quagmire. The firmer and bolder the tread, the greater the danger.

She had not been conscious, until the disenchantment came, how much hope and pride she had lavished on the image conjured up in her fancy by Pauline's "gentleman of princely fortune." The image had been vague, it is true, but brilliant. All that she knew of Mrs. Dormer-Smith's pride of birth, her contemptuous rejection of young Bransby's suit, the importance she attached to introducing her niece into the "best set," and so forth, served to strengthen Mrs. Dobbs in all kinds of delusions. She had taken it for granted that the sort of person whom Pauline could approve of as May's husband must possess certain qualifications. She no more thought, for instance, of doubting that he would be a gentleman, than that he would be a white man. The "princely fortune" added something chivalrous to the idea of him in her mind, since he was ready to share it with portionless May. And now these airy visions had been rolled aside like glittering clouds; and the solid, prosaic, ugly fact presented itself in the form of Joshua Bragg!

Mrs. Dobbs sat for more than an hour after he had left her, with bowed head and hands clasped, scarcely stirring. For a while she could not order her thoughts. Her mind was confused. Images came and went without her will. Under all was a bitter sense of disappointment, and a vague disquietude for the future. At first she had dismissed the notion of May's marrying Mr. Bragg, as one too preposterous to be entertained for a moment; but by degrees she began to ask herself whether she might not be as mistaken here as she had been in other undoubting judgments. Mr. Bragg was a man of probity, and—so she had hitherto thought him—of excellent sense. Oldchester held many substantial proofs of his benevolence. Could it be possible that girlish May was willing to think of this man for a husband? Mrs. Dobbs tried to look at the matter judicially.

There were many instances of happy marriages where the disparity in years was as great as in this case. Who could be happier than Martin Bransby and his beautiful young wife? But this example had not the effect of reconciling Mrs. Dobbs to the possibility of May's accepting the great tin-tack maker. Martin Bransby was a man whom any woman might love—well educated, clever, genial, of a handsome presence, and with manners of fine old-fashioned courtesy. There could be no comparison between Martin Bransby and Joshua Bragg.

No, no, no! Such a match would be a mere coarse bargain. The very thought of it was an outrage to May. And yet—the pendulum of her thoughts swinging suddenly in the opposite direction—she remembered that neither Mrs. Dormer-Smith nor Mrs. Griffin had so considered it. And was it not true what Mr. Bragg had said—that many people did very well without romance, and were useful and happy? Self-distrust, once aroused, became wild and uncontrollable. She fought against her better instincts; telling herself that she was a fool, and that the world was no place for story-book sentimentality. If May married this man she would be safe from the gusts of fortune; she would be honoured and caressed (for it was clear that society accepted Mr. Bragg without qualm or question), and she would have boundless possibilities of doing good. This, surely, at all events, was a worthy aim!

At this point—just as after a conflict between winds and waves there sometimes comes a sudden calm and the serenity of sunshine—the turmoil of her mind was stilled all at once, and she saw clearly. She lifted up her head and said aloud—

"'What shall it profit a man, if he shall gain the whole world, and lose his own soul?' Lord, forgive me! I was arguing on the devil's side every bit as much as that poor creature, Mrs. Dormer-Smith. And without her excuse of knowing no better! The whole thing is plain enough. If May could bring herself to care for the man—and such unlikely things happen in that line that one daren't say it's downright impossible!—she'd do right to marry him; if not, she'd do wrong. And that's all about it."

Here, at least, was a firm foothold. And having struggled out of the quagmire, Mrs. Dobbs was able to consider the other subject of Mr. Bragg's talk with her—the rumour that Captain Cheffington had married again. If it were true, and, above all, if his new wife were such a one as Mr. Bragg had described, there was a new source of anxiety as to May's future.

As she was meditating on this point, Jo Weatherhead returned, eager to hear all about her interview with Bragg, and to impart to her something he had just heard himself. Mrs. Dobbs was glad to be able to feed Jo's hungry curiosity by telling him the reports about her son-in-law, since she could not betray Mr. Bragg's confidence respecting May. She found that he had been hearing a version of them from Mr. Simpson, whom he had met in the road. Valli's utterances at Miss Piper's supper-table had already revived all kinds of obsolete gossip about Captain Cheffington.

"It'll be terrible for my poor lamb if half the bad things they say are true," said Mrs. Dobbs, shaking her head.

Jo's private opinion was that Captain Cheffington's conduct under any given circumstances was pretty sure to be the worst possible; but he tried to comfort his old friend, as he had succeeded in comforting himself, by setting forth that her father's behaviour, be it what it might, could scarcely affect May's happiness very deeply, seeing that she had been entirely separated from him for so long.

"And as to her position in the world, that you think so much of"—Mrs. Dobbs winced at this, and turned her head away—"why, I shrewdly suspect, Sarah, that a deal worse things than ever reached you and me have been known about Captain Cheffington in aristocratic circles this long time back. And yet Miranda has been received among the tip-toppest people as if she belonged to 'em. And there's her own great-uncle, the Lord Viscount Castlecombe of Combe Park, a nobleman notorious for his heighth" (Jo did not mean his stature), "has quite taken to her, by all accounts."

After some consultation, they agreed together that it would be well for Mrs. Dobbs to tell her grand-daughter something of the reports which were flying about, lest they might reach her accidentally, or, in a still more painful way, through malice, and find her unprepared. Moreover, Jo urged his old friend to write boldly to Augustus demanding an answer as to the truth of the statement that he had married a second wife. Mrs. Dobbs at length consented to do so, although she had little hope of eliciting the truth by those means. But Jo was strongly of opinion that if Captain Cheffington were not married he would be desirous, for many reasons, of repudiating the statement; and if he were married he might not be displeased at this opportunity of saying so, although pride, or indolence, or a hundred other motives, might prevent him from making the opportunity for himself.

The communication was made to May when she came home from College Quad that afternoon. And, although greatly surprised at first, it did not produce so much effect as her grandmother had anticipated.

May had enough of the healthy, unquestioning veneration of a child for its parent to take her father on trust; and Mrs. Dobbs had always been careful not to lower Captain Cheffington in his daughter's esteem. But May did not—naturally could not—feel for him any of that strong personal attachment which is apt to look jealously on interlopers. She regarded him with a somewhat hazy affection, largely compounded of imagination and dim childish traditions. Some added tenderness sprang, perhaps, from the notion that "poor papa" had been unfortunate, and that the world had treated him below his deserts.

After the first surprise was over, she said, "But why should he keep it secret? Wouldn't he have told you, granny?"

"Perhaps not, May; I hear from him very seldom, as you know."

"Very seldom! Yes; but in such a case as this! Perhaps, though, papa thought it might hurt your feelings, on account of mamma."

"Perhaps," returned Mrs. Dobbs drily.

"People are unreasonably sensitive sometimes, are they not? As for me, it never entered into my head to think of my father's marrying again; but now I do think of it, it seems to me that it would be a very good thing."

"Its goodness or badness would depend, of course, on—circumstances."

"I do really think more and more that it would be a good thing, granny. Papa must have many lonely hours, you know. He likes Continental life best, to be sure; but still he is far away from his own country and his own people. It seems almost selfish in us not to have thought of it for him. Oh, I hope she is a nice, kind woman, who will be good to him and take care of him. I think I ought to write at once and assure him that I have no grudge in my heart about it. And I'm sure you have none either; have you, granny dear?"

Mrs. Dobbs found it at once more painful and more difficult than she had foreseen to breathe degrading suspicions into this frank, pure mind. But it was necessary not to allow May to cherish what might prove to be disastrous illusions.

"It isn't all such plain sailing, May," she answered slowly. "I will write to your father, and you had better wait for his reply. We don't know that he is married at all. And if he is, we don't know that there's much to be glad about. They do say that the lady is not a fit match for your father."

"He is the best judge of that, I should think," returned May. Then she added, her young face flushing with a generous impulse, "I dare say people may have said the same of my own dear mother."

"No, May. No one ever said of your own dear mother what is said of this woman."

There was a sternness in her grandmother's voice and face which startled the girl.

"What do they say, granny?" she asked quickly.

Mrs. Dobbs checked herself. "Oh, I cannot tell you exactly. There are lots of stories about. Some will have it that—her character is not quite blameless."

"Who dares to say so of my father's wife?"

"Hush! May. There's no need to call her your father's wife yet. Signor Valli says the person in question—"

"Signor Valli? Then I don't believe a word of it. Not one word. I know he talks wildly, and jumps at things. Why, he told Clara Bertram that my mother was a foreigner, and that he had met her. So you see how accurate and trustworthy Signor Valli is." Then, after a moment, as if struck by a sudden thought, she asked, "Is—she a foreigner?"

"I believe so."

"Then that is what he meant, I suppose."

"It's right to tell you, May, that Signor Valli is not the only one who has heard disagreeable things."

"Oh, of course, they all baa' one after the other! You have no idea, granny, what foolish back-biting talk goes on among the people whom Aunt Pauline calls 'society.' I've seen them roll a morsel of gossip over and over, while it kept growing all the time like a snow-ball—or a mud-ball. And no doubt many people whom Aunt Pauline doesn't call 'society' are as bad. A sheep is a sheep, whichever side of the hedge it is on," said this young censor with fine scorn.

Mrs. Dobbs in her heart did not put implicit faith in the stories which reached her. The young and the old—when they are sound-hearted—are both prone to disbelieve slander—the young from innocence, the old from experience; for there is no lesson more surely taught by life than the evil lightness with which evil is attributed.

But with regard to these particular stories, unwelcome corroboration was given to Mrs. Dobbs by Clara Bertram. Clara carried out her proposal of going to sing at Jessamine Cottage. She went there one afternoon when May was absent at the Hadlows', and introduced herself. There were only Mrs. Dobbs and Mr. Weatherhead to listen to her; but she sat down at the old square piano—feebly tinkling now, but tinkling always in tune, like the conscientious ghost of a defunct instrument—and sang her best. Her audience, though limited, was highly appreciative; and she soon found that their applause was not given ignorantly.

Apart from the charm of her singing, Clara won their sympathies by her kindly, unaffected simplicity. She inspired trustfulness. One must have been blindly false one's self to doubt her truth. Mrs. Dobbs was moved to question her a little about Valli.

"Of course, you have heard this gossip about May's father?" she said.

"Yes. To say the truth, I almost hoped you might speak on this subject; and so I purposely came when I thought May would not be here. I hinted to her something that Valli had said to me; but I saw she knew nothing."

"I have told her. At least I have told her enough to prevent her being taken by surprise."

"I am glad of that. I think you have done very wisely."

"This Signor Valli, now," said Mrs. Dobbs musingly. "I suppose he tells lies sometimes, eh?"

Clara reflected for a moment before she answered. "In one way—yes. That is to say, if he hated you, and saw you give a penny to a beggar, he would impute some nefarious motive for the action, and say so without scruple; but I don't believe he would be likely to invent circumstances."

Then she went on to tell how Miss Polly Piper remembered a dreadful story about some gambling transactions; and how Major Mitton had furbished up his Maltese reminiscences; and how everybody found something to say, and not one good thing among them all.

Jo Weatherhead listened with a kind of dread enjoyment. So much curious gossip could not but be interesting; yet he wished with all his heart, for May's sake, that it were not true.

"I speak openly to you," said Clara; "but I am reticent about all this with other people. Pray believe that."

Mrs. Dobbs did believe it. Clara seemed to have become intimate with them all at once.

"May I come again?" asked the young singer as she took her leave.

"May you come! Will you come? I didn't ask you, because, when a person generously gives me one pearl of price, it is not my way to snatch at the whole string. Your time is precious; your voice is precious."

"Dear Mrs. Dobbs, your kindness is precious. Not that I am ungrateful for the kindness bestowed on me by—other people; but there is such a delightful feeling of homeliness here. And then, although you have praised me too much, I must say that you and Mr. Weatherhead are good judges of music."

"Well, I won't go so far as to deny that you might strew your pearls before certain animals who would value them less," replied Mrs. Dobbs.

As for Jo Weatherhead, he became so enthusiastic in Miss Bertram's praises behind her back, that Mrs. Dobbs laughingly declared he was in love with her. And perhaps he was, a little. Many more such humble innocent "loves" spring up and die around us every day than we reck of. They do not ripen into fruit, but simply blossom like the wayside flowers; and the world is all the sweeter for them.

When May came home that evening, she was delighted to hear of the favourable impression her friend had made; although she declared it was shabby of Clara to have come in her absence. May brought the news from College Quad that Constance had written home for a prolonged leave of absence, having been invited by the duchess to accompany Mrs. Griffin to Glengowrie.

"Canon Hadlow grumbles a little," said May; "but he will let her go. And I am so glad; I hated the idea of going; but Conny will enjoy it, and everybody else will soon find out that she is the right girl in the right place—which, I am sure, I should not have been."

"Mr. Bragg is not going to Glengowrie either, I understand," said Mrs. Dobbs, growing very red, and coughing to hide her embarrassment.

"No; Mr. Bragg and I are quite agreed in not liking that sort of thing. He says he feels lonely in a strange house; and so do I. If the duke and duchess were my friends, it would be different."

"Mr. Bragg has a good deal of sense, I think."

"Plenty of common sense."

"And—ahem!—and good feeling—don't you think?"

"What's the matter with your throat, granny? Shall I get you a glass of water?—Oh yes; he does a great deal of good with his wealth. Canon Hadlow was saying only this afternoon that Mr. Bragg gives away very large sums in private, besides the public subscriptions, where every one sees his name."

"Mr. Bragg was here the other day to speak to me—on business—No, no; I don't want any water! Sit still, child. And I think you are a great favourite of his."

"It's quite mutual, granny. Often and often, in London, I used to prefer a quiet talk with Mr. Bragg to the foolish chatter of smart people."

"Ay, ay! But 'smart people' need not be foolish, May."

"N—no; they need not. Only so many of them—especially the young men—seem to think it part of their smartness to put on a kind of foolishness."

Mrs. Dobbs looked wistfully at her grand-daughter. In that process of "sounding" May, which Mr. Bragg had recommended, and which Mrs. Dobbs was endeavouring to carry out, there arose this difficulty: the chords gave forth a full response to every touch; but who should interpret the meaning of the notes? Mrs. Dobbs had been accustomed to read May's feelings by swift intuition. She was now afraid to trust to that. Her interview with Mr. Bragg had upset so many of her preconceived ideas as to what could be considered probable, or even possible, in the matter of her grandchild's marriage, that her judgment seemed paralyzed. And then to risk a mistake which should involve May's life-long unhappiness, would be too tremendous a responsibility!

Measured by Mrs. Dobbs's unquiet thoughts it seemed a long time, but in reality less than a minute elapsed between May's last words and her saying—

"Talking of smart people, granny, don't you think Aunt Pauline is sure to know the truth about papa?"

"I cannot tell. There might be reasons why she should not have heard it, May."

"Well, at all events, I have been thinking that I will write to her and ask. If she does know, and is keeping her knowledge back from me for any reason—some of Aunt Pauline's mysterious dancing before deaf people, you know—that will make her speak out."

"I don't see why you should not write to her, if you choose, May."

Mrs. Dobbs had little doubt that Mrs. Dormer-Smith would be annoyed and perturbed by May's writing to her on the subject, whether the story of the marriage were true or false, and whether she herself had or had not heard of it. But Mrs. Dobbs was in no mood to shield Pauline from annoyance or perturbation.

"She and her 'gentleman of princely fortune,' indeed!" said Mrs. Dobbs to herself. "Why couldn't she say old Joshua Bragg? and then one would have known where one was."

So it was settled that May should write to her aunt.

CHAPTER IX.

Theodore Bransby at first indignantly repudiated Valli's scandals about Captain Cheffington. He was quite unprepared for them, having, it may be remembered, heard nothing of Miss Piper's story, told at the dinner-party in his father's house; and having, moreover, loftily snubbed every one in Oldchester who ventured to hint anything to the disparagement of his distinguished friend. What could Oldchester know about such persons as the Cheffingtons?

But general testimony and public opinion were too strong for him, and he was forced to give up his distinguished friend. He fell back on mysterious hints of sympathy and intimacy with "the family," and allusions to what "poor dear Lucius" had said to him on the last occasion of their dining together at Mrs. Dormer-Smith's.

In his heart, Theodore was deeply annoyed. He considered that Captain Cheffington (supposing report to speak truly) had not only derogated from his proper place in the world, but had, in some sense, personally injured him (Theodore) by forming a connection so far beneath him. Nevertheless, it was very possible that Captain Cheffington might some day come to be Viscount Castlecombe, and much would be forgiven to a wealthy peer of the realm. Theodore was conscious that he himself could forgive much to such a one. He was not prone to indulge in idle fancies, yet he caught himself once or twice writing on a corner of his blotting-pad the words "Hon. Mrs. Theodore Bransby," with pensive sentiment. But let her father's fate and fortunes be what they might, Theodore felt that he must still desire to marry May Cheffington. The recognition of this feeling in himself gave him an agreeable sense of his own elevation of soul. That fellow Rivers talked a vast deal of flashy nonsense, which dazzled people; but it was possible to take a serious and sensible view of life without being commonplace. Theodore did not by any means wish to be, or to be thought, commonplace.

He had just been called to the Bar, and ought by this time to have begun his professional career on the Midland Circuit. But he lingered in Oldchester on the plea of delicate health. It was not so much the presence of May Cheffington as that of Owen Rivers which chained him there. If Rivers would but have left Oldchester, Theodore would have turned his back on it also with small reluctance. The dull, vague jealousy of Rivers, which he began to feel long ago, had become acute. Rivers would have been a distasteful personage to him under any circumstances; but viewed as a rival, he inspired something like loathing. And yet the desire to watch him—not to lose sight of him so long as May should be in Oldchester—was irresistible. Theodore had never come so near quarrelling with his step-mother as on the subject of Owen Rivers; but he had failed in causing the latter to be excluded, or even coldly received, by Mrs. Bransby.

There was a painful scene one day at luncheon, when Martin, Mrs. Bransby's eldest boy, vehemently took up the cudgels in defence of his absent friend, Owen, of whom Theodore had been speaking with sneering contempt. Martin was ordered away from the table for being impertinent to his half-brother. But general sympathy was with the culprit; and Mr. Bransby said when the boy had left the room—

"Of course, it would not do to allow Martin to be saucy; but you are too hard upon Rivers, Theodore. He may have his faults; but, if he be idle, he is not self-indulgent. Rivers has a Spartan disdain of personal luxuries; and although he doesn't work, no one suffers by that but himself. He is incapable of a mean thought, has a most noble truthfulness of nature, and is a gentleman to the core."

Theodore turned deadly white, and answered, "I am sorry not to be able to agree with you, sir. To be a lounging hanger-on, as Rivers is at the Hadlows', is not compatible with my conception of a gentleman."

He rose as he spoke, and left the room, so as to cut off any possibility of a reply.

Mrs. Bransby had sat by with downcast eyes, parted lips, and beating heart. She was divided between delight at hearing her husband assert his own opinion against Theodore and her constitutional timidity and dread of a quarrel. When Theodore was gone, she put her hand on her husband's shoulder, and said—

"It is like you, dear Martin, to stand up for the absent. We are all—the children and I—so fond of young Rivers."

"I hate priggishness, and I hate spitefulness," rejoined Martin Bransby, with a sparkle in his fine dark eyes.

The old man's face had flushed when he uttered his protest. It was an unusual outburst; for of late—whether from failing health, or from whatever cause—Mr. Bransby had more and more shrunk from opposing or contradicting Theodore. He seemed almost timidly anxious to conciliate him; and was evidently distressed by any symptom of ill-will between his eldest son and the rest of the family. After a while the flush died from his cheek, and the fire from his eye. He sat with bowed head, softly caressing the white jewelled hand which had slidden down from his shoulder. Presently he said—

"Don't let us cherish feuds, or blow up resentment, Loui. If there are subjects on which Theodore thinks differently from you—and me; and me, too, my dear—let us avoid them. He has his good points, though he has weak ones—as we all have. Let us spare them. Theodore may be very helpful to the boys when I am gone. And I have it very much at heart that there should be peace and goodwill between them."

In Theodore's mind, however, the little incident rankled. He was silent about it. But that was no indication that he had either forgiven or forgotten it.

He was also annoyed and disappointed at seeing May Cheffington so seldom during this sojourn at home. He had formerly met her constantly at College Quad; but he could not now frequent Canon Hadlow's house as he had done in old days, even had he wished it. And although it appeared that Mrs. Bransby had struck up a great friendship with May during his absence, May's visits to her were very brief and rare. Theodore half suspected that his step-mother perversely stinted her invitations to the girl, for the express purpose of vexing him, and at length he plainly asked her how it was that Miss Cheffington came to their house so seldom. Mrs. Bransby was tempted to give him her real opinion as to the reason, but she refrained. She would not vex Martin by saying sharp things to his son. So she answered vaguely that Miss Cheffington now passed a good deal of her time at Garnet Lodge with her friend, Clara Bertram.

"Excuse me," said Theodore, tilting his chair, and looking down as from the summit of Mont Blanc upon his step-mother. "The Dormer-Smiths were very kind to that little Bertram girl in town, and Mrs. Dormer-Smith launched her in some of the best houses; but—pardon me for setting you right—she is not quite on such a footing as to be a friend of Miss Cheffington's."

However, he acted on the hint accidentally given, and began to honour the Miss Pipers with frequent visits.

The good-natured old maids received him very kindly; but it may be doubted whether he were particularly welcome to any of the persons who had taken the habit of dropping in nearly every evening at Garnet Lodge.

Major Mitton and Dr. Hatch were old habitués; but the circle now included some new ones. Mr. Bragg was often there. (Theodore considered it a striking proof of the incurable commonness of Mr. Bragg's tastes—already illustrated, to Theodore's apprehension, by a memorable instance—that he, to whom some of the best county society was accessible, and who had even been invited to Glengowrie, should prefer the middle-class sitting-room, and the middle-class gossip of Polly and Patty Piper.) There was, too, the inevitable Owen Rivers, and occasionally Mr. Sweeting and Cleveland Turner would drive over from the country-house which the former had hired in the neighbourhood. Miss Bertram's visit was prolonged; in Theodore's opinion very unduly. It might be all very well to invite her for professional purposes; but, once the musical party was over, it was absurd to keep the girl as a visitor in the house. Altogether, there was much that Theodore disapproved of at Garnet Lodge; but, as he told himself, he went there for a purpose totally disconnected with its owners. And if he did some violence to his social principles by condescending to frequent such an undistinguished and bourgeois set of people, he was resolved to make amends by totally dropping their acquaintance in the, not distant, future.

As to May, although he genuinely believed that the Dormer-Smiths had influenced her against him, he was not so foolish as to think that she had been coerced, or that she was at all in love with him. Nevertheless, a vast deal might depend on the influence of those around her, in the case of a girl so young, so fresh-hearted, and so inexperienced. He had faith in his own perseverance and constancy. The main point—the only vital point—was to prevent any rival from succeeding. So long as May were free he had good hope. It was quite certain that the Cheffington family would never sanction her marrying Owen Rivers. That must be taken as absolutely sure. And, indeed, Miss Cheffington herself would probably scout the idea. But with regard to what Rivers hoped and intended Theodore could not be mistaken. There, at least, he was clear-sighted. It was disgraceful on the part of a fellow like Rivers, subsisting in idleness on a beggarly pittance, and without prospects for the future, or advantages in the present, to aspire to such a girl as May Cheffington. Of course, Rivers knew very well that it would prove a good speculation. May might prove to be the sole heiress of a rich nobleman. At any rate, she would certainly inherit her grandmother's money. Mrs. Dobbs's savings, however paltry, would be a sufficient bait for Rivers, who had none of that ambition for fine tailoring, upholstery, and the paraphernalia of fashionable life which becomes a gentleman. Jealousy apart, perhaps that which made Owen peculiarly offensive to him was to see a man at once so poor, so contented, and so free from any misgivings as to his right to be generally respected.

On his side, it must be owned that Owen wasted no cordiality on Theodore. To see May speaking civilly to that correctly dressed and dignified young man caused Mr. Rivers a certain irritation which occasionally manifested itself in the most unreasonable ill-humour towards her.

"I really believe you like his empty arrogance," he said to her once. "Why else you should sit and listen to him with that complacent air, I cannot conceive."

"Oh, I enjoy it of all things," answered May mischievously; "otherwise I should, of course, cut him short by remarking, in a loud voice, and with a ferocious glare, 'Mr. Bransby, I look upon you as a tedious prig.' How delightful social intercourse would become if we had all reached that fine point of sincerity!"

But there were other causes of dislike between the young men unconnected with May Cheffington. Owen felt not only admiration, but regard, for Mrs. Bransby, and resented her stepson's demeanour towards her, while Theodore was embittered by hearing Owen's praises in his own family.

The perception of this lurking enmity between them made May anxious to smoothe asperities and prevent a rupture. In her heart, although she admitted he had done nothing to startle or offend her of late, she intensely disliked Theodore Bransby; yet she found herself in a position of taking his part against Owen. Owen was too absolute, too inflexible, too implacable, she said. After all, Theodore had always conducted himself irreproachably. He might not be agreeable to them (May had innocently come to join herself with Owen in this kind of partnership in sentiment), but probably they were not always agreeable to other people; they ought to be tolerant if they wished to be tolerated—and the like sage reflections. All which pretty lectures, though they made Owen no whit less obdurate towards Theodore, melted his heart into ever softer tenderness for May.

She had not gone to Glengowrie. The reprieve he had allowed himself, after which she was to depart, and he must steel himself to endure her absence for, probably, the remainder of his life, had expired. But May was still there. And there, too, was he. He was free to go away at any moment. But he lingered. He began to suffer sharp pangs of regret when he thought of the lost opportunities which lay behind him; for now sometimes it seemed to him as if this sweet, pure girl might come to love him. And what had he to offer her? How could he ask her to share such a life as his? Owen had held certain uncompromising theories: such as that a woman who hesitated to partake poverty with the man she professed to love was not worth winning; and that a man must be but a poor creature who should weigh a woman's fortune against himself, and fear to woo a well-dowered girl lest he might be thought to love her money bags and not her. And he had long ago decided that with his marriage, at least (supposing that unlikely event ever took place), considerations of money should have nothing to do on either side. But theories—even true theories—are apt to find themselves a little out of breath when suddenly confronted with the fact.

The advice so vigorously given by Mrs. Dobbs to do some honest work, if it were but breaking stones upon the road, took a new significance when he thought of May. That on this point May agreed with her grandmother's view he had ascertained, although a shy consciousness restrained her from urging him to change his course of life. He began to cast about in his mind for some possible employment; but he found, as so many others had found before him, how difficult it is to turn "general acquirements" into a definite channel.

A chance word of Mr. Bragg's at length suddenly suggested a hope to him.

Mr. Bragg mentioned one evening at Garnet Lodge that he purposed making a journey into Spain, partly on matters connected with his son's business; and said that he should like to find some trustworthy person to accompany him as secretary and interpreter.

"I don't speak any foreign language myself," said Mr. Bragg. "Of course, there's always somebody that knows English; and pounds sterling are a pretty universal language, I find, and make themselves understood everywhere. But still, you're at a disadvantage with people who can talk your tongue while you can't talk theirs."

"But you could send somebody, couldn't you?" suggested Miss Patty. "Spain, I've heard, is such a horrid country."

"Horrid!" cried Major Mitton indignantly. (He was strong in recollections of sundry youthful escapades and excursions from "Gib.") "Most delightful country! Most picturesque, poetical, and—"

"Oh yes; but I meant the cooking," explained Miss Patty.

Mr. Bragg, however, valorously declared himself ready to face the perils of Spanish cookery. His son was not satisfied with his correspondent at Barcelona. Mr. Bragg wanted change of air; and since he had given up the idea of visiting the Highlands this autumn, he would take this opportunity of seeing foreign parts, and at the same time looking into matters at Barcelona for his son.

Owen's heart beat fast as the thought occurred to him of offering himself to Mr. Bragg as secretary for this journey. He hurried after Mr. Bragg when the latter's carriage was announced, and stopped him in the hall to ask when and where he could have a private interview with him. Mr. Bragg answered in his slow, ruminating way, as he took his coat from the servant—

"An interview with me? Oh, well, why not come over to lunch? My house ain't beyond a pleasant walk for your young legs."

"No, thank you; I won't come to luncheon. But I want an appointment—I shall not take up much of your time—on business."

"Oh, on business, is it?" said Mr. Bragg. It was curious to note how evidently the sound of the word made him bring his mind to bear on what was said to him, with a new and keener attention. "On business! It's nothing you could write, I suppose."

"Yes; I could write it. Shall I?"

"I think it would be the best plan, if you don't mind. You see I find, in a general way, that talk—what you might call, branches out so. Now a letter limits a man. I don't mean this for your partic'lar case, you know, but speaking in a general way. Perhaps, if we find afterwards that there is anything to talk over, you might look me up at my office in Friar's Row. It'll be easier to settle all that when I know what the business is. Good night. My respects to your aunt."

Owen hastened to his lodgings, and set himself at once to compose a letter to Mr. Bragg. Seeing that it was then past eleven o'clock at night, and that Mr. Bragg had set out for his country-house, it was scarcely probable that he should have found a secretary between that hour and the following morning. But Owen felt as if every moment's delay might be fatal. Oldchester persons, who had seen him lounging on Canon Hadlow's lawn, and merely knew him as a young man fond of smoking, and reading, and such unprofitable employments, would have been amazed at the impetuous energy he threw into the writing of this letter. But the same weight of character which gives massiveness to repose adds a formidable momentum to action.

The main difficulty, he soon found, was to make his letter short. This, after several failures, and the tearing up of three copies, he accomplished to a fair extent, if not wholly to his own satisfaction. When he had finished the letter, he put it into a cover, stamped and addressed it, and went out to post it with his own hand. By that time it was considerably past midnight. The letter could have been delivered by hand in Friar's Row next morning, and would probably have reached Mr. Bragg equally soon. But it was a relief to Owen in his restless, impetuous mood to have done something irrevocable. And there are few actions in life so obviously irrevocable as posting a letter. This is what he had written—

"DEAR SIR,

"I venture to offer myself for the post of your secretary during the journey you propose making to Spain.

"My qualifications are—Honesty; a fair knowledge of the Spanish language; and considerable experience of travelling in Spain, where I have made two long tours on foot. Perhaps I ought to add to these good health, and willingness to be useful. My disadvantages are—Ignorance of the forms of mercantile correspondence, and inexperience of the duties of a secretary. I believe I could learn both very quickly.

"I have hitherto been a man without occupation. I am now anxious to have one by which I can earn money. Should you, on inquiry and consideration, think I could honestly earn some as your secretary, I should be grateful if you would give me a trial.

"I am ready to wait on you at your office, or elsewhere, in case you wish for an interview, and remain,

"Dear Sir,"

Yours truly,
"OWEN RIVERS."

The following afternoon Owen was summoned to see Mr. Bragg at his office. The old house in Friar's Row had been painted and varnished inside and out. Plate glass glittered in the window panes, and elaborate brass handles shone on the doors. Owen had never been in the house during the days of Mrs. Dobbs's occupation. But he knew that May had spent much of her childhood there; and he looked round the private room into which he was shown with a tender glance such as probably never before rested on those mahogany office fittings, morocco-covered chairs, and neatly ranged account-books.

Mr. Bragg was sitting at a writing-table, and held out his hand without rising, when Owen entered.

"Sit down, Mr. Rivers," he said, pointing to a chair opposite to his own, on the other side of the table.

Owen sat down, and remained waiting in silence.

"Well, so you think you'd like to go to Spain with me?" said Mr. Bragg, slowly rubbing his chin, and looking thoughtfully at the young man.

"I should like to get work to do, Mr. Bragg. I don't care much where it is. But it struck me that I might be useful to you in Spain."

"Ah! Well, I was surprised at your letter."

"Nothing in it that you object to, I hope?"

"Oh no. Oh dear, no. Only I didn't know you was in want of employment. And I should have thought—"

"Yes?"

"I should have thought you'd ha' liked some more—what you might call professional employment."

"A man can't step into a profession from one day to another. And besides, the professions are overstocked. There's no elbow-room in any of them—especially for a poor man."

"Ah! Yes; I hear that sort of thing is said a great deal; but it seems to me that might be a reason for giving up living altogether. There's a good many of us in all classes, one way and another; but a man has got to make room for himself."

"You have a right to say so, Mr. Bragg, and I have no right to dispute it: for you have tried and succeeded, and I have not even tried."

"Ah! That seems a pity—with your education, and all. However, I didn't intend to branch out, as I said to you last night. With regard to the point in hand, I would just say at once that this situation would be strictly tempor'y, you understand. It couldn't be looked on in the light of what you might call an opening."

"I understand."

"At the same time it might—I don't say it would—lead to an opening," continued Mr. Bragg, indenting the paper before him by drawing his thumb-nail along it with a strong, steady movement, as though he mentally saw the opening in question, and were mapping out the way to it.

"I quite understand that if you engaged me as secretary for this journey, you would not bind yourself to anything beyond. Whether anything further came of it, or not, would depend, first, on my suitableness; and next, on circumstances."

"That's it," said Mr. Bragg, leaning back in his chair, and nodding slowly.

"Well, Mr. Bragg, I can only say I would do my best. As to my knowledge of Spanish, I'm not afraid. I began to learn the language first for the sake of reading Cervantes, as so many people have done before me; but since then I have acquired a colloquial knowledge of it by talking with all sorts of Spaniards when I was tramping about their country."

"I have heard," said Mr. Bragg, not displeased to show himself acquainted with the literary aspect of the matter, "of a man that learned Spanish in order to read a book called 'Don Quixote.'"

"Just as I did."

"Oh! Did you? I thought you mentioned a different name. And can you write it?"

"Fairly well; but I should have to learn the commercial style."

"There'd be more need, perhaps, for you to understand it than to write it yourself. All communications with my son in Buenos Ayres could, of course, be written in English."

Mr. Bragg here made a long, thoughtful pause. It was so long a pause that Owen at length broke it by saying with a smile, though the colour rose to his brow—

"As to my character, I can't give you one from my last place, because I never had a place; but my uncle, Canon Hadlow, will, I believe, guarantee my trustworthiness."

He felt a queer little shock when Mr. Bragg, instead of protesting himself fully satisfied on that score, answered in a matter-of-fact tone—

"Ah! yes, I dare say he will. I make no doubt but what that'll be all right." Then, after a second, shorter pause, he continued, "There's one point, Mr. Rivers, that I must put quite plain. I expect everybody in my employment to obey orders. Now, you see, you, having been what you might call brought up a gentleman, might not—"

"Oh, I hope you don't think that insubordination is part of a gentleman's bringing up?"

"It hadn't ought to be; but it's best to be clear."

"Clearly, then, I can undertake to obey your orders; and I would only warn you to give them carefully, because I shall carry them out to the letter. If you ordered me to make a bonfire of your bank-notes, I should burn 'em all without mercy."

Mr. Bragg laughed his quiet, inward laugh. There was something in the conception of himself ordering bank-notes to be burned, which keenly touched his not very lively sense of the ludicrous.

"All right," said he. "I'll take that risk."

"Then am I to conclude—may I hope that you will engage me?" asked Owen, with nervous eagerness.

"Why, I shall ask leave to turn it over in my mind a little longer. But I'll undertake not to keep you waiting beyond to-morrow morning. You see, if I do make an offer, it's best you should have it in writing. And sim'larly, if you accept it, I ought to have that in writing."

"Thank you. Then I need not intrude longer on your time."

"No intrusion at all, Mr. Rivers. Good morning to you."

Owen turned round at the door, and coming back to the writing-table, said, "May I ask you to keep my application to yourself for the present?"

"Certainly," answered Mr. Bragg. But he looked slightly surprised.

"Of course, I don't mean the thing to be secret so far as I am concerned."

"Why, no; we couldn't hardly keep it secret," said Mr. Bragg gravely.

"Of course not. But if your answer should be favourable, I should like to be the first to tell—a—a person—the one or two persons who take any interest in me."

"But I shall have to say a word to your uncle; and that's pretty well the same thing as saying it to your aunt, I take it."

"Oh yes; to be sure. I didn't mean you not to mention it to them."

"All right. I certainly shall not mention it to anybody else," returned Mr. Bragg.

And when the young man was gone, he said to himself, "I wonder who else there is I could mention it to that would care two straws one way or the other. I like his way. He don't jaw like that young Bransby. And he didn't try to soap me."

The next day Owen Rivers was formally engaged as travelling secretary to Mr. Bragg for three months, beginning from October, which was now near at hand.

CHAPTER X.

Mrs. Dobbs had judged rightly as to the effect of May's letter on her Aunt Pauline. That sorely tried lady was overwhelmed at this time by various troubles. She did not write to May, but addressed a very long and somewhat rambling letter to Mrs. Dobbs. After the strongest expressions of dismay and horror at the rumour of her brother's marriage, Pauline proceeded—

"I really cannot answer May's letter—at all events, not at present. I am deeply distressed that she should have addressed me on the subject at all. It is such terribly bad form in a girl of her age to appear cognisant of anything not brought to her knowledge by the proper channels. I had heard a vague report of the connection—which was bad enough. But who could have supposed that Augustus would have degraded himself to the point of marrying such a person! But I ought not to trouble you with my feelings on this matter, for I am very sure you cannot imagine one tithe of the various distressing results to the family which will flow from it. It is much to be regretted that May so precipitately decided not to go to Glengowrie; particularly under recent untoward circumstances. I learn from a friend in town that my cousin, Mr. Lucius Cheffington, is much better. I do not mean, of course, that this is an untoward circumstance; but it alters the position of affairs. I scarcely know what I write. You may not be aware—few persons are aware—of the delicate state of my nervous system. I suffer keenly from any mental pressure. And of late I seem to have had nothing else! My cure at this place has been sadly interfered with by anxiety for others. But, really whether poor dear Lucius recover or not, if this story from Belgium is true, my niece's position will be a most painful one. From the tone of her letter to me, I can see that she does not at all take in the situation. You can tell her one thing from me: If my brother were to succeed to the title to-morrow, he would have nothing but what the entail gives him. So if she imagines otherwise it would be well to undeceive her. You won't mind my saying that in this respect the circumstances of my brother's first marriage were peculiarly unfortunate, since they prevented any settlement being made for the children."

"Ay," said Mrs. Dobbs, interrupting her reading at this point, "not to mention that by that time Augustus had nothing left to settle!"

Then she resumed the letter—

"You and I, my dear Mrs. Dobbs, must join our forces in face of these new and trying circumstances. The more I think of it the more I regret that my niece has missed the opportunity of going to Glengowrie, especially since I have learned that Mrs. Griffin is going to chaperon another young lady in her stead. In society it is fatal to drop out of sight—you are forgotten immediately—and I cannot expect Mrs. Griffin to do more than she has done. Indeed, both she and the dear duchess have been extraordinarily kind—I fear May scarcely appreciates how kind; but the truth is that she is singularly—I scarcely know what word to use—not dull, but indifferent on certain points. There is an apathy about her sometimes which has caused her uncle and myself a great deal of distress. But really she must rouse herself from it now. It is a great comfort to us to know that you, my dear Mrs. Dobbs, take a sound view of my niece's position, and have her best interests at heart.

"Believe me,

"Very truly yours,

"P. DORMER-SMITH.

"P.S.—I have this moment received a letter from Miss Hadlow, in which she mentions, amongst other items of news, that the gentleman whom I wrote of as being interested in May has declined his invitation to Glengowrie, and is now in Oldchester! There appears to be something absolutely providential in this. I know you have great influence over May. Pray exert it to make her see what is right. I have never been able to get her to look on her social position as involving certain duties. But, indeed, in her case, the duty immediately before her of obtaining a splendid settlement and a fine position is an easy one. I have seen cases of real sacrifice to this social obligation endured without murmur. Since they are both in Oldchester, it must surely be easy to give the gentleman every opportunity of presenting his suit. Indeed, there may be better opportunities than at Glengowrie. The longer we live the more we realize how everything is overruled for good.

"P. D. S."

"I reopen this to write an essential word:—The name of the gentleman I have alluded to! You may form some conception of the pressure on my brain from my having omitted to do so before. He is a Mr. Bragg—a man of very large wealth, and received everywhere. I know that my uncle has more than once received him at Combe Park. And he would, I dare say, have got some chaperon there, and had May down for a time; but, of course, under the bereavement we have all just suffered in the death of my cousin George, this cannot be at present. But there surely must be, among the better families in Oldchester, some whom Mr. Bragg visits? Possibly the bishop, if he is there; or, perhaps the dean? I know Lady Mary slightly. Pray lose no time, my dear Mrs. Dobbs, in ascertaining this."

Mrs. Dobbs pondered long after reading this epistle. In May's absence she often turned over in her mind the advantages of an alliance with Mr. Bragg; remembered favourable precedents; and taught herself to think that it might be. The sight of the girl's face, and the sound of her voice, were apt to scatter these fancies as sunrise scatters the mists. But they returned when May disappeared again, and haunted all the old woman's lonely hours.

One morning, after an evening spent at Garnet Lodge, when Mrs. Dobbs was alone with her grandchild, and was meditating how she should approach the subject chiefly in her thoughts, May unexpectedly began—

"Granny, do you know I have something to say that will surprise you."

"Have you, May? Nothing ought to surprise me at seventy odd. But, somehow, things do surprise me still."

"Of course they do, granny! I think it is only blockheads who are never astonished, because one thing is much the same to them as another."

"Well, I'm glad I can prove myself no blockhead at such an easy rate. What is your surprise about, May?"

"It's about—Mr. Bragg."

The colour came into May's cheeks as she looked up with a bright, shy glance from her favourite low seat beside granny's knee. But it was nothing to the deep, sudden flush which dyed Mrs. Dobbs's face. She looked at her grandchild almost vacantly for a moment, and then grew paler than before. But May did not observe all this. She sat smiling to herself, with the colour varying in her face, as it so easily did on the very slightest emotion, her hands clasped round her knees, and her bright head bent down, as she continued—

"I have had my suspicions for some time past; but I said nothing until last night. Then, when I went into Clara's room to put my hat on, I just gave her a tiny hint; and she said very likely I was right, and did not laugh at me a bit. But I dare say you will laugh at me, granny."

"Let us hear, my lass," said Mrs. Dobbs, moistening her lips, which felt parched.

"Well—I think that Mr. Bragg has a motive in coming so often to Garnet Lodge."

"I suppose he has."

"Ah, but a very special motive—a matrimonial motive. There, granny!"

Mrs. Dobbs looked down with a singular expression at the shining brown hair so near to her hand which rested on the elbow of her easy-chair. But she did not caress it as she habitually did when within reach. She sat quite still, and merely said—

"So you think it surprising that Mr. Bragg should have matrimonial intentions, do you?"

"Oh no. It isn't that. Mr. Bragg is a very kind-hearted man, and would be sure to make a good husband. And, do you know, he is very far from stupid, granny."

"I dare say. Joshua Bragg always had his head screwed on the right way."

"His manner is against him. Of course, he is uneducated; and rather slow. But, after all, that doesn't matter so very much."

"And he's rich," added Mrs. Dobbs in a dry tone.

"Ever so rich! I am sure he must have heaps and heaps of money, or else Aunt Pauline would not approve of him so highly."

"And not quite decrepit."

"Decrepit! What a word to use, granny! No; I should think not, indeed!"

"H'm! Neither a brute, nor in his dotage; and immensely rich—I don't know what a woman can wish for more!" said Mrs. Dobbs, with increasing bitterness.

"Why, granny!" exclaimed May, looking up. "I thought you rather liked Mr. Bragg! I have always heard you speak well of him."

The hand on the chair-arm clenched and unclenched itself nervously, as Mrs. Dobbs answered in short, jerky sentences, and as though she were forcing herself with an effort to utter them, "Oh, so I do. Joshua Bragg is an honest kind of man. I've nothing against him. Don't think that, my lass."

"Well, granny, but now for the surprise. I wonder you have not guessed it by this time. Who do you think is the lady?"

"I can't guess. Tell it out, May, and have done with it."

"To be sure there is not much choice. If it were not one, it must be the other! But I have made up my mind that Mr. Bragg and Miss Patty will make a match of it! What do you say to that, granny?"

Mrs. Dobbs said nothing; but gasped, and laid her head back on the cushion of her chair.

"I thought you would be surprised! But when one comes to think of it, it seems very suitable, doesn't it? Mr. Bragg admires Miss Patty's cookery above everything. And she is such a kind, charitable soul, she would do worlds of good with riches. And they agree on so many points—even their crotchets. And, do you know, Miss Patty would look ten years younger if she would leave off that yellow wig. She has such nice soft grey hair that she brushes back! I have settled that she is to leave off the wig when she marries Mr. Bragg, and take to picturesque mob caps. I have been arranging all sorts of things in my own mind. I'm quite coming out in the character of a matchmaker, granny!"

In the midst of her chatter the girl looked up, and uttered an exclamation of dismay. Her grandmother's head still lay back against the cushion of the chair; her eyes were closed, and she seemed to be laughing to herself. But the tears were pouring down her cheeks. At May's exclamation she opened her arms wide, and then pressed the girl's bright brown head against her breast, saying brokenly—

"Don't be feared, child! I'm all right. I couldn't help laughing a bit. It's so—so funny to think of old Joshua and—and Miss Patty!"

"But you are crying, too, granny! Is anything the matter? Do tell me."

"Nothing, child; I'm all right. Poor Joshua! He was a good lad when he worked for your grandfather. And—and—I remember her a little miss in a white frock and blue sash. It brings up old times, that's all, May. Lord, what fools we are when we try to be cunning!" and Mrs. Dobbs went off again into a fit of laughter, interspersed with sobs.

"I didn't try to be cunning!" said May indignantly.

"You, my lamb! Whoever thought you did?" returned her grandmother, wiping her eyes and kissing May's forehead.

By and by she resumed her usual solid self-possession. She told May that she did not agree in her view of the state of the case, and advised her not to hint her matchmaking project to any one. "You have said a word to Miss Bertram, and that can't be taken back; but she is wise beyond her years, and will not chatter."

"But there's nothing wrong in the idea, granny," protested May, who was considerably puzzled by her grandmother's unusual demeanour.

"No, no, nothing wrong; only Mr. Bragg might not like it—he might be looking after a young wife, who knows? Anyway, we will keep our ideas to ourselves."

As she spoke, the latch of the garden-gate clicked, and, following May's glance, Mrs. Dobbs saw from the open window Owen Rivers advancing up the path towards the house.

The "gentleman of princely fortune," whose image had interposed between her shrewd apprehension and the facts before her, having melted away like a phantom, she perceived that here was a new influence to be reckoned with—a new force which, whether for good or ill, might help to shape her grandchild's future.

"May I come in?" asked Owen.

"Come in, Mr. Rivers."

Mrs. Dobbs felt as though she had invited embodied Destiny to cross her threshold—Destiny, in the prosaic guise of a blue-eyed, square-built young man, in a shooting-jacket and a wide-awake hat. But that Power does not often appear to mortals with much outward pomp and circumstance. We are like children who think a king must needs go about in royal robes, crowned and sceptred. But the decree which changes our lives is mostly signed by some plain figure in everyday clothes, whom we should not turn our heads to look upon.

Owen entered the little parlour, and came and stood opposite to Mrs. Dobbs's chair, without any of the customary salutations. "Well," said he eagerly; "I have some news for you."

"Lord, ha' mercy! This is a day of news," muttered Mrs. Dobbs under her breath. Then she said aloud, "I hope it's good news?"

"I have found some work to do. Is that good?"

Mrs. Dobbs clapped her hands softly. "Very good," she said. Half an hour ago her approbation would have been more heartily expressed; but she was looking at him now with different eyes, and considering his prospects with a new and serious interest.

"You haven't asked me what the work is," said Owen, just a little disappointed by her quietude.

"I suppose it is not stone-breaking? But if it is, I stick to my colours. Better that than nothing."

"You will say, Mrs. Dobbs, that I am luckier than I deserve to be. I am engaged as secretary to a man who is about to travel in Spain. I happen to know Spanish. Luck again; for I learnt it merely to amuse myself."

"Yes; I do think that isn't bad for a beginning, and I hope it will lead to something more. Who is the gentleman, if I may ask?"

Before Owen could answer, May, who had perched herself on the elbow of Jo Weatherhead's vacant chair, said, "I think I can guess. It's Mr. Bragg."

"Mr. Bragg!" echoed her grandmother, as if doubtful of having heard aright.

"I remember hearing him talk of a journey into Spain, and of wanting to find a gentleman to go with him. Am I not right?"

"Quite right," answered Owen.

"Mr. Bragg! Well, that is strange!" whispered Mrs. Dobbs to herself.

Owen had taken a chair, and sat bending forward, with his elbows on his knees, pleating and puckering in his fingers the brim of his soft felt hat. He had not hitherto so much as looked towards May; now he straightened himself in his chair, and, fixing his eyes on her earnestly, asked—

"And what do you say to my news, Miss Cheffington?"

"I say, as granny says, that I am very glad," she answered, smiling, but speaking in a subdued tone.

"It's more to the purpose to ask what Canon and Mrs. Hadlow say to it," put in Mrs. Dobbs. "I hope they are pleased?"

"I dare say—I have no doubt—I—I have not seen Aunt Jane yet. The fact is, I am on my way to College Quad; but I thought I would look in here as I passed, and tell you that I have followed your advice, Mrs. Dobbs."

The direct road from Owen's lodgings to College Quad was a short, and nearly straight, line. To visit Jessamine Cottage "on the way" from one to the other was analogous to going round by Edinburgh on a journey from London to Leeds.

"I wanted a little patting on the back and cheering up, you see," continued Owen.

"Cheering up!" cried May. "Oh! but I remember that Mrs. Hadlow said you always liked to be pitied for having your own way. You must require a great deal of consolation, truly, for the prospect of travelling in that delightful country!"

Owen nodded, and carefully fitted one pleat of his hat-brim into another, as he answered, "I dare say my appetite for consolation is bigger than you imagine."

"I think it is Mr. Bragg who needs cheering up. Poor man, he little knows what a peremptory, protestant, and positive secretary he will have!" retorted May, with a half shy, half saucy, wholly mischievous, glance.

"Not at all! Now, that is just the kind of mistake which Aunt Jane so often makes. But if I serve, I mean to serve honestly, and to be thoroughly obedient; I have told Mr. Bragg so." And Owen proceeded to justify himself, and to develop his views as to the duties of a secretary, with superfluous energy and earnestness.

The old woman sat watching them, and, as she looked, she was amazed at her own previous blindness. How could she—how could any one—have seen them together without perceiving that they were falling over head and ears in love with each other? These two young creatures seemed, in her old eyes, like a couple of children playing in a pleasure-boat. But she knew that the river was running towards the sea—widening and deepening with an irrevocable current. There was room for anxiety about the future, no doubt. Yet a sense of relief in her mind—as if she had escaped out of some oppressive atmosphere—revealed more and more distinctly how repugnant the idea of May's marrying Mr. Bragg had really been to her.

"Sarah Dobbs," said she to herself severely, "you're a worldly, false old woman! You're a nice one to find fault with that poor creature Pauline! What were you doing, pray, but sacrificing your conscience to the mammon of unrighteousness? The Lord be praised, the dear child is better, and purer, and honester than either of us old harridans!"

Then she broke into the conversation between May and Owen, which by this time had sunk into a low murmur, and asked abruptly whether the engagement with Mr. Bragg was to lead to any further employment.

Owen repeated what Mr. Bragg had said to him, as nearly as he could remember it; and Mrs. Dobbs thought it hopeful.

"Joshua Bragg is an honest man—a man to be relied on: one of the few who generally means what he says, all that he says, and nothing but what he says," said she, nodding thoughtfully.

May was glad to find granny doing justice to Mr. Bragg; and remarked to herself that, if it were possible to conceive granny's ever being capricious, she would have called her capricious to-day in her varying tone about that worthy man.

"I shouldn't wonder," pursued Mrs. Dobbs, "if he put you in the way of getting permanent employment—supposing you please him. He might get you a place out in South America with his son. Young Joshua is in a great way of business there, I'm told. Would you go if you had the chance?" she asked suddenly, looking at Owen with a searching gaze.

"Undoubtedly," he replied at once.

"And you wouldn't mind being—being banished like from England?"

"Mind? Oh, well, of course I should prefer a thousand a year and a villa on the Thames; but a fellow who has been an idler up to four and twenty must take any chance of earning something, and be thankful for it."

"That's right." Mrs. Dobbs drew a long breath of relief.

"It would only be for a year or two; I should come back," added Owen wistfully.

Then he shook hands and went away, and Mrs. Dobbs and her grand-daughter were left to discuss the news he had told them. May chatted away cheerfully, even gaily. When Mr. Weatherhead arrived the subject was talked over again. Jo's pleasure in the prospect opening before Mr. Rivers was somewhat tempered by his sense of the incongruity involved in "a gentleman like that, brimful of learning, and belonging to the old landed gentry," being under the orders of Joshua Bragg!

"There's no contradiction at all, Jo, if you look at it fairly," said Mrs. Dobbs. "Mr. Bragg will command where he has a right to—that is, in matters that he knows better than Mr. Rivers, for all his book-learning. It isn't as if Joshua wanted to teach the young man how to be a gentleman. I don't say it's not a good thing to be a gentleman, but it ain't exactly a paying business nowadays, if ever it was, which I doubt."

"Ah, more's the pity!" said Jo, shaking his head.

"Why, if I was a gentleman—or a lady—I shouldn't agree with you there, Jo. If gentlehood don't mean something above and beyond what can be paid for, 'tis a poor business. It seems to me just as pitiful for gentry to expect money's worth for their old family, high breeding, and fine manners, as it is for the grand workers of the world to grumble because they can't have power over the past, as well as the present and the future. Mr. Bragg ain't one of that sort. You'll never catch him inventing a family crest, or painting wild beasts on his carriage."

Jo took his pipe out of his mouth, and looked with solemn approbation at his old friend. "Sarah," said he, "you're right; and I believe you're a better Conservative than me, when all's said and done."

May had been silent during this discussion. She held some needlework in her hands; but they were lying idly on her lap, and she was gazing out of the window as intently as though the small suburban garden offered a prospect of inexhaustible interest. The cessation of the voices roused her. She looked round, and said softly—

"It's a good climate, isn't it, granny? Where Mr. Bragg's son lives, I mean."

CHAPTER XI.

Before going to bed that night Mrs. Dobbs sat down and wrote a letter, marked "private and confidential," to Mr. Bragg.

"DEAR MR. BRAGG" (she wrote),

"I think it my duty to let you know at once that the idea mentioned in your conversation with me must be given up. I have made quite sure in my own mind that there is no chance of its coming to anything. I feel very much how right you were to speak to me first. You have spared other people's feelings as well as your own. When you asked me the question, I answered you truly, to the best of my belief, that there was nobody else in the field. But since our talk together I have found out that I was wrong there. There is another attachment. It may come to something, or it may not. And you will understand that I am putting a great confidence in you. But I know I can trust to your honour as you trusted to mine. Not a word has passed my lips of what you said to me, and never will. Of course, you may think me mistaken, and choose to find out the state of the case for yourself at first-hand. If you do so I shall not have a word to say against it. Anyway, I know you will act upright according to your conscience, as I have tried to act according to mine. I want to tell you that I appreciate how generous your intentions were, though I'm afraid I did not show it at the time, being surprised and upset.

"Believe me,
"With sincere respect,

"Yours truly,
"SARAH DOBBS."

Shortly after that, Mr. Bragg came and called upon her. He thanked her for her letter, and spoke in a friendly tone. But he seemed indisposed to consider the matter as finished.

"Young people sometimes don't know their own minds," he said. He further declared that he had no present intention of speaking to May; but that, as he was going abroad, he might—if nothing were settled meanwhile—resume the subject on his return to England.

"I'm quite sure in my own mind that it's no use," said Mrs. Dobbs firmly. "And it's only fair to tell you so as strong as possible. However, of course, you must act according to your own judgment."

"There is one question I should like to ask if I might," said Mr. Bragg, lingering at the door on his way out. "You and me can trust each other. And, if you feel at liberty to tell me, I should like to know whether the—the party you alluded to in your letter is Mr. Theodore Bransby."

"Certainly not!"

"Well, I'm glad of it. There was a talk of his paying Miss C. a great deal of attention in town. In fact, I did hear she had refused him. Understand, I'm not fishing as to that. It's no matter to me one way or the other, so long as he is not the party. I can't say that I know any harm of the young man; but he's what you might call a poor sort of metal: not pleasant to handle, and, I should fear, brittle in the working. I really am relieved in my mind to know that he is not the party. Thank ye."

The news of Owen's engagement to Mr. Bragg was variously received by his various acquaintances in Oldchester. Some laughed good-naturedly, some ill-naturedly; some said it was a good thing the young man had at last seen the necessity for exerting himself; some wondered why on earth he had accepted such a position; and some—a good many those—wondered why Mr. Bragg had accepted him. Mrs. Hadlow did not feel unmixed satisfaction by any means.

"It's just like Owen," she said to her husband. "There is such a singular perversity about him! He has thrown away one straight stick after the other, and now all of a sudden he clutches at this crooked one, as eagerly as though his life depended on getting hold of it."

Canon Hadlow, for his part, was well pleased enough. The sentiment at the bottom of his wife's heart was that to employ a Rivers in any such base mechanic business as writing commercial letters was like harnessing a thoroughbred Arab to the dust-cart. But the canon could not, in the nature of things, fully share that feeling. Nevertheless, he had a strong regard for Owen, and spoke of him in high terms to Mr. Bragg.

But the testimony in Owen's favour which chiefly impressed Mr. Bragg was the testimony which Owen gave himself—by deeds, not words.

Being moved by a certain energetic simplicity which belonged to him, to perform the duties he had undertaken with the most complete thoroughness he could command, he got a clerk who conducted the foreign correspondence of a great Oldchester manufacturer to give him lessons after business hours. He worked away evening after evening at the composition of mercantile letters in Spanish until he succeeded in producing epistles so surprisingly technical that his instructor declared he went far beyond what was necessary in that line, and would do well to mitigate his business style with a little good Spanish! He studied, also, to improve his handwriting. It was a legible hand already, since he wrote with the single-minded aim of being read. But he strove to make it distinctly commercial in character, and succeeded.

All this became known to Mr. Bragg, who said nothing. But, when it got wind among the little circle of persons who frequented Garnet Lodge, it was the subject of some raillery from Owen's friends. So long as the raillery proceeded from such persons as Dr. Hatch or Major Mitten, there was no offence in it; but with Theodore Bransby the case was different.

Theodore was, in truth, delighted: first of all, because Rivers had, as he phrased it, "entered Mr. Bragg's service" (a step which must for ever disqualify him for aspiring to ally himself with the Cheffingtons, supposing he were not disqualified already); and, secondly, because his engagement would take him out of England for three months. So delighted was Theodore, that his spirits rose to the unwonted pitch of attempting some pleasantries. Now, there is nothing which more surely reveals the quality, if not the quantity, of a man's mind than his notion of a joke. Laughter, like wine, is a great betrayer of secrets; and for incurable coarseness of feeling a stout cloak of gravity is "your only wear."

Theodore would tilt his head, and say with a sneering smile, "Burton's clerk declares that Rivers is as thorough-going as the man who blacked himself all over to play Othello! Do you write a page of round-hand copies every morning before breakfast, Rivers?" or, "I hear that Rivers has taken to frequent the commercial 'gents'' ordinary at the Bull in order to pick up the correct phraseology."

Owen paid very little attention to these sparkling sallies; but Mr. Bragg, after listening for some time, broke silence one evening by saying, in his quiet, ponderous way—

"You're rather hard on me, I think, Mr. Bransby."

Theodore looked at him with sudden gravity and unfeigned surprise. "Hard on you?" he exclaimed.

"Oh, when a young gentleman is what you might call satirical, he's apt to be harder than he means. You needn't look so serious. I'm not offended."

The moment Mr. Bragg declared he was not offended, Theodore began to fear that he was; and, whatever might be his private opinion of the millionaire, he had no intention of affronting him. So he protested that Mr. Bragg must be under some misapprehension, and that he (Theodore) could not even guess what he meant.

"Oh, come, Mr. Bransby! It's pretty clear. I am but a plain business man, but it isn't necessary to copy the company at the Bull in order to come down to my level."

"Good heavens, my dear sir! You can't suppose—! I was—ahem!—merely—" Theodore paused an instant, and then went on with a little disconcerted laugh. "Ha, ha, ha! I was merely paying my humble tribute of admiration to Rivers's energy!"

"Oh yes; I quite understand that. You appreciate seeing how a honourable gentleman sets to work to keep his part of a bargain; whereas a half-and-half chap, like that little clerk of Burton's, don't see the highmindedness of it."

Theodore was so entirely taken by surprise, and so uncertain how far Mr. Bragg was in earnest, that he could but stammer out renewed assurances that he had been misunderstood. And after that, he subsided into a glum and dignified silence for the rest of the evening.

He would probably have cut short his visit and gone away early but for his persistent resolution never to leave Owen in possession of the field when May was present. There was no question of seeing her home now; for either old Martha was sent to fetch her, or one of Miss Piper's servants walked with her to Jessamine Cottage. But, nevertheless, Theodore made a point of outstaying Owen; or, at the very least, going away simultaneously with him. On this particular evening, however, Dr. Hatch interfered with this practice by requesting Theodore to accompany him when his carriage was announced.

"I want to have a word with you quietly," whispered the doctor, "and it is almost impossible to do so in your father's house without alarming Mrs. Bransby. Come along with me, and I'll give you a lift home."

There was no refusing this invitation. But Theodore withdrew, comforted by the conviction that his rival would have no chance of profiting by his absence.

Here, however, he reckoned without his hostess; for, Martha failing to appear at her accustomed hour, and the maid who usually supplied her place being ill, Miss Piper bustled into the drawing-room, after a brief absence, demanding which of the gentlemen present would volunteer to escort Miss Cheffington home.

Mr. Bragg, who kept early hours, had already departed; and only Mr. Sweeting, Major Mitton, and Owen remained. Mr. Sweeting begged to be allowed the honour of lending Miss Cheffington his carriage. But May declined the offer, saying that Mr. Sweeting's horses had a long enough journey before them, and that, moreover, it being a lovely moonlight night, she would prefer to walk. Upon this, Owen offered his services, and Miss Piper at once accepted them.

"It is a good deal out of your way," she said; "but I am sure you will not mind for once, Mr. Rivers. I am responsible to Mrs. Dobbs for sending her grand-daughter safely home."

Owen assured Miss Piper that he should not mind at all.

While May was putting on her wraps, Miss Polly and Miss Patty jocosely reproached Major Mitton for not having displayed his usual gallantry in offering to escort the young lady.

"Major, Major, you are growing terribly lazy!" said Miss Polly.

"You will lose your reputation for being the most devoted Squire of Dames in Oldchester," added Miss Patty.

"I'm getting to be an old fellow," returned the Major quietly. Then, as they all three stood for a moment in the porch, watching the two young figures pass down the garden in a glory of moonlight, the good Major whispered to Miss Patty, "Do you think I was going to spoil that? Lord bless me, one has been young one's self!"

As soon as May and her companion had got clear of Garnet Lodge, the girl said, "I find that I had never thoroughly done justice to Mr. Bragg. The more I know of him, the more highly I think of him."

"Lucky Mr. Bragg!"

"But, now, did he not administer an admirable rebuke to Theodore Bransby?"

"Never mind Theodore. Let us talk about more interesting things."

"What can be more interesting?" asked May, laughing.

"Ourselves." As she remained silent, he went on, "Do you know that we have not had one opportunity for a quiet talk together since I got this engagement?"

"Haven't we?"

"Ah! you don't remember so accurately as I do. But that was not to be expected. Take my arm."

She obeyed as simply as a child. She had been drawing on her gloves when they left Garnet Lodge, but the operation had not been completed, and it chanced that the hand next to Owen was ungloved. She laid her fingers, which gleamed snow-white in the moonlight, on his sleeve.

"You think I have done right in taking this employment?" he said.

"Quite right." She turned her young face, and looked at him with a sweet fervour of sympathy and approval.

Owen raised the white, slender fingers to his lips, and then, replacing them on his arm, laid his own warm, strong hand over them with a gentle pressure. "You know why I did so, don't you, darling?" he said.

"Yes, Owen," was the answer, given in a shy whisper, but with innocent frankness.

"My own dear love!" he exclaimed, pressing her arm strongly and suddenly to his side. "There is no one like you in the world. Look at me, May. Let me see your sweet, honest eyes."

He caught her two hands in both his, and they stood for a moment at arm's length, facing each other, and holding hands like two children. The moonlight shone full on the young girl's fair face, and glittered on the bright tear-drops in her eyes, as she raised them to Owen's.

"What can I do to deserve you?" he said. "But why do I talk of desert? You are God's gift, May, and no more to be earned than the blessed sunshine."

He put her arm under his once more, and they paced on again without speaking. But to them the silence was full of voices. It was the silence of a dream. They might have wandered Heaven knows whither had not their feet instinctively carried them along the right path, and they found themselves, almost with a start, arrived at the white palings in front of Jessamine Cottage.

"We must tell granny, mustn't we?" said May, looking up at Owen, with a delicious sense of implicit reliance on him.

"Yes; but I am terribly afraid. I hope she will not be angry."

"Angry! How can you think so? Granny is fond of you."

"But she is fonder of you, and she knows your value, although, thank God, you don't! If you did, what chance should I have had? You know how poor I am—not quite penniless, but very poor."

"Not so poor as I, since I am really and truly quite penniless; but I don't mind that, if you don't."

Owen felt a desperate temptation to fold her in his arms and beseech her to marry him to-morrow, throwing prudence and pounds sterling to the winds. But the ardour of a genuine passion purifies the nobler soul, as fire purifies the nobler metal, and burns away the dross of self. He answered gravely—

"Our positions are very different, darling. I hope I have not done wrong to tell you how dear you are to me?"

"I think it would have been unkind and cruel to go away without telling me," she answered bravely, though the sound of the words as she said them brought the hot colour into her cheeks.

"Thank you, dearest; that is the best comfort I could have, if I may dare to believe it. But it does seem so wonderful that you should care for me!"

The contemplation of this wonder might have occupied them both for an indefinite time but that they saw a light begin to shine through the fanlight of the little entrance-hall of Jessamine Cottage. In the stillness of the night the sound of their voices, subdued though they were, had reached the ears of Mrs. Dobbs. She presently opened the door, and stood looking at them as they hurried up the garden path.

"Oh, granny dear, I'm afraid I'm late!" said May. "I did not guess that you were sitting up for me."

"Martha had a touch of her rheumatism, so I sent her to bed. I did not mind waiting. I suppose Miss Piper's maid couldn't come with you? Was that it?" asked Mrs. Dobbs.

She lingered at the open door, expecting Owen to say "Good-night." But May took her grandmother's hand and pulled her into the house, while he followed them. When they reached the lamp-lighted parlour, May, still holding her grandmother's hand with her left hand, stretched out her right to Owen, and gently drew him forward. Then she flung her left arm round the old woman's neck, and kissed her. There was no need for words. Mrs. Dobbs sank down, white and tremulous, in her great chair, while May nestled beside her on her knees, and tried to place Owen's hand, which she still clasped, in that of her grandmother. But the old woman brusquely drew her hand away.

"You have done wrong," she said, turning to Owen, and scarcely able to control the trembling of her lips. "I didn't think it of you. But men are all alike; selfish, selfish, selfish!"

"Why, granny!" exclaimed the girl, breathless with dismay. Then she started up with a flash of impetuous indignation, and stood beside her lover. "He is not selfish!" she said vehemently.

"Hush, May! Granny is right," said Owen in a low voice. "I told you that I feared I had done wrong."

Mrs. Dobbs still trembled, but she was struggling to regain her self-command. "You might have waited yet awhile," she said brokenly. "The child is young! You ought not to have bound her until you see your way more clear."

"Oh, believe me, I will not hold her bound," answered Owen. "I never meant that. I ought not to have spoken yet. I feared so before, and now that you say so, I know it. But I am not wholly selfish."

May had stood listening silently, looking, with wide eyes and parted lips, from one to the other. She now fell on her knees again beside her grandmother, and, clasping the old woman's hands in both her own, cried eagerly—

"But listen! If there was any fault, it was mine. I love him so much! And he's going away. Think of that, granny! Come here and kneel down beside me, Owen, and let her look you in the face. Think, if he had gone away and never told me! And I so fond of him! You didn't guess how I cried that night when I heard he was to leave England. He has made me so happy—so happy! And we can wait. We don't mind being poor. You said you were fond of him. And he is so good—and I love him so—and you to speak to him so cruelly! Oh, granny, granny!" The tears were pouring down her face, and dropping warm upon the wrinkled hands she held.

Suddenly Mrs. Dobbs opened her arms, and folding May in one of them, laid the other round Owen's shoulder as he knelt before her, and drew them both into her embrace.

"Come along, you two!" she said, sobbing and smiling. "I've got a precious pair of babies to look after in my old age. No more common sense between you than would lie on the point of a needle! No prudence, no worldly wisdom, no regard for society—nothing but love and truth; and what do you suppose they'll fetch in the market?"

After a few minutes she ordered Owen away. "I'm tired," she said. "And we have all had our feelings worked up enough for one while. Go home now, Mr. Rivers—well, well, Owen, then, if it must be!—go home, Owen, and sleep, and dream. And to-morrow, when you're quite awake—broad, staring, work-a-day-world awake, which you're not now, either of you,—come here, and we will talk rationally."

Owen obeyed heroically, and marched off without a word of remonstrance. But May kept her grandmother listening and talking, long after he had gone. She made Mrs. Dobbs go to bed, and sat by her bedside, pouring out her young heart, joyfully secure of granny's understanding and sympathy, until at length Mrs. Dobbs inexorably commanded her to go to rest.

"Good night, dear, dearest, good, goodest granny!" said May, leaning down to kiss her grandmother's broad, furrowed brow. "Only this one last—very last—word! Do you know, I am very hopeful about Owen's future, because I am sure that Mr. Bragg has taken a great fancy to him, and appreciates him. And Mr. Bragg can make Owen's fortune if he likes."

"Mr. Bragg," murmured Mrs. Dobbs, turning her head on her pillow. "Ah, there's a nice kettle of fish! I'm as big a baby as the children, for up to this very instant I'd clean forgotten all about Mr. Bragg!"

CHAPTER XII.

Before they parted Mrs. Dobbs had arranged with Owen that he should come and have an interview with her at ten o'clock the following morning. But as she desired to speak with him privately, she resolved to go to his lodgings early enough to catch him before he should leave home.

She found Owen already at his writing-desk, and, as he turned a startled face on her, briefly assured him that all was well with May.

"But I must have a private talk with you," she said. "And I can't get that in my own house, without fussing and making mysteries."

Owen was already acquainted with the main incidents in May's young life; but Mrs. Dobbs proceeded to give him the history of her own daughter's marriage, and a sketch of her son-in-law Augustus.

"I'm not speaking in malice," she said; "but the real truth about Captain Cheffington must always sound severe. As a general rule, I never mention his name. But it is right and necessary that you should know what manner of man May's father really is; because only by knowing that can you understand how it is that the responsibility of guiding her rests wholly and solely on my shoulders."

"It could not rest on worthier ones," said Owen.

"Ah! There we differ. It's a shame that the darling girl—such a lady as she is in all her ways and words and innermost thoughts—should have no better guidance than that of an ignorant old body like me. However, 'tis as vain to cry for the moon to play ball with, as to get honour or duty, or even honesty, out of Augustus. There's the naked truth."

"Mrs. Dobbs, I can say from the bottom of my heart, that if ever good came out of evil it has come to May. She has been thrown out of the hands of a worthless father into those of the best of grandmothers. But I suppose I ought to write to Captain Cheffington under the present circumstances?"

Mrs. Dobbs shook her head. "I wouldn't if I was you," she said.

"I only thought that, since with all his faults he is fond of his daughter—"

"Is he?" interrupted Mrs. Dobbs, opening her eyes very wide. "Oh! Well, that's news to me."

"Of course, his fondness is not judicious. But still, as he has not much money, he must make some sacrifice to pay a handsome sum to Mrs. Dormer-Smith for having May with her in London."

"He pay! Lord bless your innocent heart!"

"Does he not? May told me he did."

"Ah! May thinks so. You see I have thought it right to keep some respect for her father in her mind—for her sake."

"Then if Captain Cheffington did not furnish the money, who did?" asked Owen.

Had May been present, one glimpse of "granny's" face, blushing like a girl's to the roots of her hair, would have betrayed the truth to her. But Owen did not guess it so quickly. After a minute or so, however, as Mrs. Dobbs remained silent, he added rather awkwardly—

"Did you pay the money?"

"Look here, young man," answered Mrs. Dobbs. "You must give me your word of honour that you'll never let out a syllable of this to May, without I give you leave;—else you and me will quarrel."

Owen took her broad, wrinkled hand in his, and kissed it as respectfully as if he had been saluting a queen. "I promise to obey you," he said. "But you make us all look very small and selfish beside you!"

"We old folks, that have but a slack hold on life, must lay up our stores of selfishness in other people's happiness. It's a paying investment, my lad. I'm Oldchester born and bred, and you don't catch me making many bad speculations." The old woman laughed as she spoke, but a tear was trembling in her eye. "Come," said she. "We needn't go into all that. There isn't much time to spare. I want to be back to breakfast before May misses me."

Then she proceeded to impress on Owen that she could not at present sanction an engagement between him and her grand-daughter. Each must be held to be free, at least until Owen should return from Spain, and be able to see his future course a little more distinctly. This he promised without difficulty. Next, Mrs. Dobbs insisted that May should go back to her aunt's house, when the Dormer-Smiths returned to London for the winter. May had shown great reluctance to do this; but Mrs. Dobbs believed she would yield, if Owen backed up the proposal. With regard to Captain Cheffington, Mrs. Dobbs recommended that secrecy should, for the present, be preserved towards him, as well as towards the rest of the world.

"He cares not a straw for his daughter. Of that I can assure you. Indeed, lately, since the dear child has taken her proper place in the world, he has shown a strange kind of jealousy of her. He wrote me a regular blowing-up letter, demanding money, and saying that since I was so rich—Lord help me!—as to keep May in London in luxury, I ought at least to assist May's father in his unmerited distress. And he made a kind of a half-threat that he would come to England, and drag her away, if he was not paid off."

"The scoundrel! But you didn't—"

"Didn't send him any money? No, my lad, I did not. First, because I wouldn't; next, because I couldn't. But 'wouldn't' came first. There's no use trying to put a wasp on a reasonable allowance of honey; you must either let him gorge himself, or else keep him out of the hive altogether. So now you know my conditions:—Firstly, no binding engagement for three months at least; secondly, we three to keep our own counsel for that time, and say no word of our secret to man, woman, or child; thirdly, you to urge May to go back to London, and see a little more of the world from under her aunt's wing. I make a great point of that," added Mrs. Dobbs, looking at him searchingly; "but I see you're rather glum over it. Are you afraid of May's being tempted to change her mind?"

"It isn't that," answered Owen, with unmistakable sincerity. "If she is capable of changing her mind, I should be the first to leave her free to do so. I don't say that it wouldn't go near to break my heart, but I need not be ashamed as well as wretched; whereas, if I took advantage of her innocence, and generosity, and inexperience to bind her to me, and found out afterwards that she repented when it was too late—! But that won't bear thinking of! No, I see nothing to object to in your conditions; only I was thinking that it will be hard on you to part from her again this winter."

Mrs. Dobbs suddenly stretched out her hand towards him, with the palm outward. "Stop!" she said. "I can go on all right enough if you don't pity me." She set her lips tight, and stood for a few seconds breathing hard through her nostrils, like a tired swimmer. Then the tension of her face relaxed; she patted Owen's head, as if he had been six years old, saying, "You're a good lad, and a gentleman; I know one when I see him."

Before Mrs. Dobbs went away, Owen said a word to her on two points—the probability that Augustus Cheffington might eventually be his uncle's heir, and the rumour of his second marriage.

As to the first point, although she allowed it seemed likely that Augustus might inherit the title, yet Mrs. Dobbs assured Owen (speaking on Mrs. Dormer-Smith's authority) that he would certainly get no penny which it was in Lord Castlecombe's power to bequeath.

"If you're afraid of May being too rich," said Mrs. Dobbs, with a shrewd smile, "I think I can reassure you."

"Thank you," said Owen simply. He was struck by her delicacy of feeling, and thought within himself, "That well-bred woman, Mrs. Dormer-Smith, would have suspected me, not of fearing, but of hoping, that May would be rich; and she would have hinted her suspicions in terms full of tact, and a voice of exquisite refinement."

With regard to the question of Captain Cheffington's second marriage, Mrs. Dobbs declared herself utterly in the dark.

"But," said she, "if I was obliged to make a bet, I should bet on no marriage. Augustus is too selfish."

When, later, Owen went to Jessamine Cottage, he found May very unwilling to return to London for the winter. But she yielded at length. The other conditions she acceded to willingly. But she made one stipulation; namely, that "Uncle Jo" should be admitted to share their secret.

"You know you can trust him implicitly, granny," said May. "He likes news and gossip, but he will be true as steel when he once has given his word to be silent."

So it was agreed that Mr. Weatherhead should be taken into their confidence.

When May and Owen were alone together afterwards, he asked why she had so specially insisted on this point.

"Don't you see, Owen," she answered, "that it will be an immense comfort to granny, when she is left alone, to have some one whom she can talk with about—us?"

Meanwhile no answer arrived from Captain Cheffington to the letter which Mrs. Dobbs had written about the report of his marriage. May might have been uneasy at his silence but for the new and absorbing interest in her life, which confused chronology, and made time fly so rapidly that she did not realize how long it was since her grandmother had written to Belgium.

The gossip set afloat by Valli at Miss Piper's party gradually died away, being superseded in public attention by fresher topics. One of these was the disquieting condition of Mr. Martin Bransby's health. The old man had seemed to recover from the serious illness of last year. But it must have shaken him more profoundly than was generally supposed at the time; for after the first brief rally he seemed to be failing more and more day by day. Dr. Hatch kept his own counsel. He was not a man to interpret the code of professional etiquette too loosely on such a point; but besides professional etiquette old friendship moved him to be cautious and reticent in this case. He had some reasons for uneasiness about Martin Bransby's circumstances, as well as his bodily health. This uneasiness was vague truly; but it sufficed to make the good physician keep a watch over his words. So all those who listened curiously to Dr. Hatch's voluble, and apparently unguarded, talk about the Bransbys went away no wiser than they came as to old Martin's real condition.

To Martin Bransby's eldest son, however, Dr. Hatch did not think it right to practise any concealment. On the evening when he invited Theodore to drive home with him from Garnet Lodge, the doctor plainly told the young man that he had grave fears for his father's life.

Theodore seemed more moved than the doctor had expected. He was not demonstrative indeed; but his voice betrayed considerable emotion as he said, "But you do not give him up, Dr. Hatch? There surely is still hope?"

"There is hope. Yes; I cannot say there is no hope. But, my dear fellow"—and the good doctor laid his hand kindly on Theodore's shoulder—"we must be prepared for the worst."

"You have not, I gather, mentioned your fears to Mrs. Bransby," said Theodore, after a pause, during which he had been leaning back in the corner of the carriage.

"No, no, poor dear! No need to alarm her yet."

"She must know, however, sooner or later," observed Theodore coldly.

"I'm afraid she must. But why protract her misery? She is very sensitive, devotedly attached to your father, and not too strong."

"Mrs. Bransby always appears to me to enjoy good health enough to take any exertion she feels inclined for."

"I was not alluding to muscles, but nerves," returned the doctor drily. "There is a little hysterical tendency. And her health is too valuable to her children to be trifled with."

They drove on in silence to Mr. Bransby's garden gates. Theodore alighted, and stood at the carriage door.

"Does my father know?" he asked in a low voice.

"There, I confess, I am puzzled," said Dr. Hatch. "I have never told him his danger in plain words; but he is too clever a man to be hoodwinked. My own impression is, that your father suspects his state to be critical, but shrinks from admitting it even to himself. I think there must be some private reason for this," added the doctor, leaning forward and peering into Theodore's face as he stood in the moonlight: the moonlight which at that same moment was shining in May's eyes, looking at her young lover. "It certainly does not arise from cowardice. Your father is one of the manliest men I have ever known."

If Theodore knew, or guessed, that his father had any secret reason for anxiety, he did not betray it.

"I have observed increasing weakness of character in him lately," he said.

The words might have been uttered so as to convey perfect filial tenderness. But there was a subtle something in the tone suggestive of contempt; or at least of remoteness from sympathy, which jarred painfully on Dr. Hatch. He said "Good night" abruptly, and gave his coachman the order to drive on.

After this conversation, it somewhat surprised the doctor to learn that Theodore meant to leave home at the beginning of October, although he was not to enter on his practical career as a barrister until the winter. He had accepted one or two invitations to country houses during the pheasant shooting; and gave, as his reason for going at that time, that his health required change of air.

"His health!" growled Dr. Hatch, when Mrs. Bransby gave him this piece of news. "I should have thought he might stay and be of some use to his father in business."

"Oh, we are rather glad he is going," exclaimed Mrs. Bransby impulsively. Then she said apologetically, "Martin does not want him at home. Theodore has never taken any interest in office matters; and Tuckey manages capitally. Tuckey is Martin's right hand."

Mr. Tuckey was the confidential head clerk in the office which still retained the name of the firm, "Cadell and Bransby," although Cadell had departed this life twenty years ago, and the business had been, ever since that time, wholly in the hands of Martin Bransby.

Mrs. Bransby did not hint at one motive for Theodore's departure which her woman's wit had revealed to her; namely, that Miss Cheffington would be leaving Oldchester about the same time. It was true that Theodore had calculated on this; and also on the fact that Owen Rivers would be safely out of the way across the Pyrenees. But there was another motive which lay deeper; and, indeed, formed a part of the very texture of Theodore's temperament:—he shrank from the idea of being present during his father's last illness.

It has already been stated that he was subject to the dread of having inherited his mother's consumptive tendency, and he shunned all suggestions of sickness and death with the sort of instinct which makes an animal select its food. The very mention of death produced the effect of a physical chill on his nervous system. He was not without affection for his father; although it had been much weakened by Mr. Bransby's second marriage. Many persons who knew Theodore's tastes for gentility, assumed that Miss Louisa Lutyer's descent from a good old family would be gratifying to him, and help to make him accept the marriage good-humouredly. But the fact was quite otherwise. Theodore constantly suspected his step-mother of vaunting the superiority of her birth over that of her predecessor. He had never seen either of his maternal grandparents, and did not know all the details which Mrs. Dobbs could have given him about the history of "Old Rabbitt." But he knew enough to be aware that his mother had been a person of humble extraction. And he could more easily have forgiven his father had the latter chosen a person still humbler for his second wife. It was chiefly his ever-present consciousness that Louisa was a gentlewoman by birth and breeding, which made him jealously resent the luxuries with which his father surrounded her, and even the fastidious elegance of her dress. And, apart from all other considerations, it would have given him sincere satisfaction to marry a wife who should have the undoubted right to walk out of a drawing-room before Mrs. Martin Bransby.

One of the many points of antagonism between Owen and Theodore was the opposite feeling with which each regarded Mrs. Bransby. Owen had a chivalrous devotion for her; Theodore was nothing less than chivalrous. Owen's admiration was made tender and protecting by a large infusion of pity; Theodore held that in marrying his father Miss Louisa Lutyer had met with good fortune beyond her merits. As to his step-brothers and sisters, Theodore's feeling towards them was one of cool repulsion, with the single exception of little Enid, the youngest, whom he would have petted, could he have separated her in all things from the rest.

As soon as Owen's engagement with Mr. Bragg was assured, Owen called at the Bransbys' to tell his news in person. On inquiring for Mrs. Bransby, he was told that she was with her husband in the garden, and, being a familiar visitor, the servant left him to find his way to them unannounced.

It was a warm September afternoon; everything in the old garden—the lichen-tinted brick walls, the autumnal flowers, the deep velvet of the turf, the foliage slightly touched with red and gold—looked mellow and peaceful. Under the shadow of a tall elm-tree, whose topmost boughs were swaying with the movement, and resounding with the caw of rooks, Martin Bransby reclined on a long chair, and his wife sat on a garden bench a yard or two away. When she saw Owen approaching, Mrs. Bransby laid her finger on her lips, and then Owen saw that Mr. Bransby was asleep.

The old man lay with his head supported on a crimson cushion, against which his abundant silver hair was strongly relieved. The brows above the closed eyelids were still dark. The placidity of repose enhanced the beauty of his finely moulded features; but he was very pale, and his cheeks and temples looked worn and thin. Mrs. Bransby welcomed Owen with a smile and an outstretched hand. At the first glance he had thought that she, too, looked pale and suffering, but the little glow of animation in her face when she spoke effaced this impression.

"Am I disturbing you?" asked Owen in a whisper.

"No, no; sit down. You need not whisper, it is enough to speak low; he sleeps heavily. I am so glad to see him sleep, for his nights have been restless lately." As Mrs. Bransby spoke, she pushed aside a heap of gay-coloured silks with which she was embroidering a rich velvet cushion, and made room for Owen on the garden-seat beside her. "I know your news already," she continued, "and I must congratulate you, although you will be sadly missed. My boys will be in despair; we shall all miss you."

"I am glad, at all events, that you seem to approve of the step I have taken."

"Of course. All your friends must approve it."

"Well, they are not so numerous as to make their unanimity absolutely impossible."

Then, after a short silence, during which Mrs. Bransby resumed her embroidery, and Owen thoughtfully raked together some fallen leaves with his stick, he said—

"But you don't know the extent of my good fortune. There is a chance—rather a remote one, but still a chance—that this employment may lead to more, and that I may get some work to do in South America."

She started, and the gay embroidery fell from her hands on to the grass, as she exclaimed with plaintive, down-drawn lips, like those of a child, "Oh, not to South America! Don't go so far away!"

He merely shook his head.

"Oh, that is terrible!" she said. "I never thought of that! But, perhaps, you will not go."

"Very much, 'perhaps.' It would be better luck than I could expect."

"And you really could have the heart to leave us all, and go off to the other side of the globe? Oh, I can't bear to think of it!"

"Don't speak so kindly! You will take away all my courage," he said, looking for a moment at the beautiful eyes fixed on his face.

"Ah, I am very selfish. Of course you ought to go, if going will lead to a career for you. Although one can't help feeling that you will be, somehow wasted in mere commercial pursuits. Yes, yes, of course, I am wrong!" she added, hastily anticipating his rejoinder. "It is all very proper and Spartan, no doubt. But I am not in the least Spartan, you know."

"People usually find it easy to be Spartan for their friends. Very few keep their stoicism for themselves, and their soft-heartedness for others—as you do!"

He glanced involuntarily at Martin Bransby, as he spoke; and she followed his glance with instant quickness of understanding.

"How do you think he is looking? You do not think he seems worse, do you?" she said.

"No, indeed, no!"

"I was afraid, when you talked about stoicism—"

"No, I only meant that you always show great courage when Mr. Bransby is ill."

"I don't think I am naturally courageous. But love gives courage."

"Yes,—the genuine sort of love."

"Although it makes one frightened, too, in one way. I am sometimes very uneasy about him." She turned a gaze of profound tenderness on her husband's sleeping face.

"I trust your uneasiness is needless," said Owen. "Mr. Bransby seems to be going on well, does he not?"

"Oh yes, I hope so. But he does not gain strength. His rest is very troubled, and he talks in his sleep. And I think his spirits are much less cheerful than they were. He has a great regard for you. He will approve of what you are doing, I know. But he will be as sorry as the rest of us to think of your going so far away."

She said all this in her usual sweet voice, and with her usual soft grace of manner. Then all at once she broke down in a sudden passion of tears, and burying her face in her handkerchief, she sobbed out, "If you go to South America he will never see you again;—never, never! I know his days are numbered. They think they keep me in ignorance; but I know it, I know it!"

Owen was melted by her grief. In the eyes of sound-hearted manhood, beauty, while it attracts, adds a sort of sacredness to a pure woman. To see that lovely face convulsed with weeping made an impression on his senses, such as he might have felt at seeing an exquisite work of art defaced or mutilated. And beyond that, there was the warm human sympathy, and the feeling of compassionate protection due to her sex.

"Dearest Mrs. Bransby," he said, looking at her piteously, "pray, pray take comfort. Oh, how I wish that I could give you any help or comfort!"

She continued to weep softly and silently for a little while longer. Then she wiped away her tears, and spoke with calmness. "Forgive me! It was selfish to distress you," she said. "But it has relieved my heart to cry a little. And you have always been so friendly. I have as great reliance on you as if I had known you all my life."

"As far as the will goes, you cannot over-rate my friendship. But the power, alas! is small; or rather none."

"No; don't say that. Whenever I have forced myself to look forward to the great sorrow which may soon come upon me, I have said to myself, 'I know Mr. Rivers would be good to me and the children, and would help us with honest advice.' I have no one belonging to me—of my own family—left to rely on. The boys and I would be very desolate and forlorn, if we were left to guide ourselves by our own wisdom."

"There is Theodore," said Owen. But he said it with dry awkwardness, as though there were something in the words to be ashamed of.

"Theodore does not love us," returned Mrs. Bransby quickly. "You were praising me just now for caring about my friends. But you see how selfish my thoughts were all the time! It does seem so dreary to imagine you far away out of our reach!"

She wore on her wrist a bracelet consisting of a broad gold band, in which was set the portrait of her youngest child. Now, little Enid had a special affection for Owen. She caressed him and tyrannized over him. And whenever Bobby and Billy desired to coax Mr. Rivers into playing with them, they conspired to make Enid prefer the request, secretly agreeing that Mr. Rivers spoiled Enid, and would never resist her. In short, Mr. Rivers was Enid's sworn knight, and did her suit and service. The sweet, baby face looked out of its gold frame, with large, grave eyes, and faintly smiling mouth, and soft yellow hair like the down on a nestling bird. Owen took Mrs. Bransby's hand, and bent over it until his lips touched little Enid's portrait. "Near or far," he said, "you and your children may always count on my faithful affection."

When he raised his head again, Theodore was standing in front of them.

He had come noiselessly along the grass, and halted a little behind his father's chair. Mrs. Bransby's head was turned in the opposite direction, and she did not see him immediately. But Owen saw him, and caught a singular expression on young Bransby's face which made his own blood run swiftly with a confused sense of furious anger. It was an expression of mingled surprise, suspicion, and an indescribable touch of exultation. But even as Owen fixed his eyes on him sternly, the look was gone; and Theodore's smooth face was as coolly supercilious as usual.

"Your father has been having a good sleep, Theodore," said his step-mother, when she saw him.

"So I see," he answered. And, again, something singular in his tone made Owen long to seize him and hurl him away out of Mrs. Bransby's presence.

"Mr. Rivers has been telling me his news," said Mrs. Bransby. "We ought to rejoice, I suppose. But I can't help feeling selfishly sorry."

"We must hope that our loss will be his gain," replied Theodore. He felt instinctively that Owen's eyes were still fastened on him. And Owen's eyes, like many light-blue eyes, had the power of expressing an intensity of fierceness when he was thoroughly incensed which few persons would have found it easy to support. But Theodore had averted his own gaze, and was looking down on his father with ostentatious solicitude.

The old man slightly moved his head, and Mrs. Bransby was by his side instantly. "Are you refreshed by your sleep, dear Martin?" she asked as he opened his eyes.

"Yes, Loui, yes. Oh, there's Rivers! How are you, Rivers?" He rose from his chair and shook hands with Owen, asking him to come to the house and have tea. Mrs. Bransby offered her husband her arm, but he took her hand and laid it tenderly upon his sleeve. "Not yet, Loui; not yet!" he said, smiling down upon her. "I needn't lean upon you yet." Then the two walked slowly side by side towards the house, leaving the young men to follow.

As they did so, crossing the wide lawn side by side, it suddenly occurred to Theodore, with a shock of surprise, that he and Owen had not exchanged any sort of greeting or salutation whatever.

CHAPTER XIII.

The Dormer-Smiths arrived in London early in November, and May joined them almost immediately. Her aunt was delighted to find May looking remarkably well.

"Some good has come of her vegetating in Oldchester," said Pauline to her husband. "Her complexion is radiant. Also I think her figure has improved. If she would but consent to have her stays taken in! Smithson could manage it half an inch at a time; and might easily get her waist down to eighteen inches. But there is that lamentable touch of self-indulgent apathy about May! However, she has really a great deal of charm; and, in spite of all the drawbacks connected with poor Augustus's unfortunate marriage, she looks thoroughbred."

The two little boys, Harold and Wilfred, had returned from their sojourn in a farm-house so much strengthened that their father seriously talked of sending them into the country altogether for a couple of years. Even Mrs. Dormer-Smith, although unwilling to relinquish her character of chronic invalid, confessed that Carlsbad had done her good. In fact, the whole family returned to London in improved health and spirits. A great many "nice people" were to be in town for the winter; and the excuse of May's presence, and the assistance of May's allowance, would enable Pauline to enjoy society, and at the same time to satisfy that singular worldly conscience of hers with the sense of duty fulfilled.

There was a little disappointment at Mr. Bragg's absence from England. But even here Mrs. Dormer-Smith had the not inconsiderable consolation of knowing that if he were far from May's attractions, he was also far from those of Constance Hadlow. And she more than ever rejoiced at that providential interposition in the interests of the Cheffington family which had kept Mr. Bragg away from Glengowrie. Another symptom which filled Aunt Pauline with complacent hopes, was May's newly developed interest in Mr. Bragg, and her eager willingness to talk about his Spanish tour. Pauline was inclined to attribute something of this improved state of mind to Mrs. Dobbs's influence; and confessed to herself that the old woman was doing all she could to compensate the House of Cheffington for the injury done to it by the disastrous mésalliance.

Mrs. Dormer-Smith's cheerfulness at this time would have been absolutely unclouded but for the dread hanging over her about her brother. She had given May to understand that the rumours spread by Valli and others were based on error. And she even conveyed the idea to her niece (although scrupulously abstaining from explicit falsehood) that Captain Cheffington himself had denied those rumours in private communications to her and Frederick. But the fact was that

Augustus had remained inflexibly silent. The Dormer-Smiths knew nothing of him. And so completely had he dropped out of the society of all with whom they were likely to consort, that a doubt sometimes crossed Pauline's mind as to whether her brother were still living or not.

Meanwhile, every week May received a letter from Owen, forwarded by Mrs. Dobbs. The latter had restricted the correspondence to one letter a week on each side. Owen wrote very joyously. His work was easy—too easy, he said; and he was constantly seeking opportunities to be useful to his employer. Mr. Bragg he pronounced to be an excellent master: clearheaded in his commands, and reasonable in his exactions. He seemed to approve of his secretary so far; and although he was rather taciturn, and not prone to encourage sanguine expectations, yet Owen began to have good hope that Mr. Bragg would not turn him adrift when the three months' engagement should be at an end.

May now became decidedly more popular in society than she had been during the height of the season. Happiness, like sunshine, beautifies common things; and the new brightness of her outlook on it was reflected by the world around her. That feeling which she had expressed in writing to her grandmother—the forlorn feeling of a child who, in the midst of some gay spectacle, wearily cries to go home—had disappeared. She knew that when the curtain should fall on the puppet-show in Vanity Fair, her own true love was waiting to welcome her.

Sometimes she speculated on how Aunt Pauline would take the revelation of her attachment to Owen Rivers. That she should have had any doubt on the subject proved her ignorance of Aunt Pauline's views. Mrs. Dormer-Smith would not for the world have expressed to May any gross or sordid sentiments about marriage. She had not the slightest idea that she entertained any such herself! But, as she had long ago said, there are many things—never put into words—which "girls brought up in a certain monde learn by instinct." Now in that kind of instinct May was greatly deficient.

May reflected that her aunt had spurned Theodore Bransby's proposal on the avowed ground of his being "nobody." And she understood—or thought she understood—that Aunt Pauline accorded a tangible existence only to such persons as could be proved by genealogical records to have had a certain number of great-grandfathers. Now, thus considered, Owen was very undeniably and solidly "somebody." He was poor, certainly; but how often had Aunt Pauline mingled her plaintive regrets with Mrs. Griffin's about the increasing worship of Mammon which vulgarized London society! And although Aunt Pauline sometimes showed a deference for wealth which was rather puzzling in the face of these utterances, yet May observed that her personal liking and admiration were given on very different grounds. Witness her regard for Constance Hadlow!

Mrs. Dormer-Smith even kept up an intermittent correspondence with that young lady. Constance's letters were precisely of the kind which Mrs. Dormer-Smith delighted in—budgets of social gossip selected with unerring tact. Constance had returned to Oldchester, but she did not spend many consecutive weeks in her parents' house, being invited to visit among "the élite of the county aristocracy," as Mrs. Simpson phrased it. Miss Hadlow had, in fact, achieved what might be called, all things considered, a brilliant social position. Her visit to Glengowrie had been a great success. She had made a conquest of the duchess; and also—though that was comparatively of small consequence—of the duke. Mrs. Griffin was charmed that her protégée had done her so much honour; and promised to take her into society the following season, if Canon and Mrs. Hadlow would give her leave to come to town. Indeed, Mrs. Griffin began seriously to revolve in her mind whether she could not contrive to marry Charley Rivers's grand-daughter, and secure her a fine establishment. Mrs. Griffin was proud of her achievements in that line, which, though few, were brilliant. Like a certain famous Italian singing-master, who was wont in his old age to decline unpromising pupils on the ground that it was not worth his while to make seconde donne, Mrs. Griffin practised only the higher branches of matchmaking; and refused to fly her falcons at anything under twenty thousand a year—or a peerage.

What made Miss Hadlow's letters particularly interesting to Mrs. Dormer-Smith at this time, was that the former was frequently staying in the neighbourhood of Combe Park, and occasionally met Lord Castlecombe and Lucius, whom she reported to be constantly ailing—as, indeed, he had been since before his brother's death. But his state did not seem to inspire any immediate apprehension. And Constance even said a word now and then about "creaking wheels," and intimated her belief that Mr. Lucius Cheffington would probably outlive many more robust-looking persons.

But it was not only these polite chronicles which kept the Dormer-Smith household informed as to the doings of Oldchester people. Mrs. Dobbs, of course, wrote frequently to her grandchild. The saddest news which she had to give May was the continuous and rapid decline of Mr. Bransby's health. Theodore was still away from home, Mrs. Dobbs wrote, and she commented severely on his heartless neglect of his father. She had learned through Mrs. Simpson that old Martin Bransby showed great anxiety for his son's return; and it was reported that he had caused a letter to be written, telling Theodore that he desired to speak with him, and urging him to come home without delay.

In the first days of December the end came. Martin Bransby died—rather suddenly at the last—and his eldest son was not with him. On being telegraphed to he arrived in Oldchester with the utmost possible despatch—but too late to see his father alive.

"People are very sorry for the widow and her children," wrote Mrs. Dobbs; "for it's beginning to be said now that they're left rather badly off, and that the bulk of everything will go to Theodore. I don't know any facts, one way or the other; but I do know that foolish folk cackle louder over a grave than almost anywhere else. So we may hope things are not so bad with that pretty, gentle woman as Oldchester gossip makes out."

One of May's first thoughts on reading this letter was, "How grieved Owen will be!" She grieved herself for the kindly old man who had always been good to her, and for the grief of those who loved him. And she incurred a mild rebuke from her aunt by appearing at a dinner party that evening with pale cheeks and red eyelids.

Contrary to Mrs. Dobbs's hope, it turned out that the gossip had for once been correct. Martin Bransby's affairs were left in a strange entanglement. There were many debts, and, as it seemed, very little money to meet them. People inquired how he had got rid of the handsome property left him by his father. He had not got rid of it in the ordinary sense of the words; but the bulk of it was as far beyond his control as though he had thrown it into the sea.

At the time of Martin Bransby's first marriage, old Rabbitt had made most stringent arrangements in his daughter's interest. Not only her own dowry (which was a handsome one), but nearly the whole of Martin's property was strictly settled on her and her children. Mr. Rabbitt was enabled to drive a hard bargain by his command of ready money. He advanced a large sum to his son-in-law for the purchase of Cadell's share in the firm. Mr. Cadell was old, and wished to retire; the opportunity was favourable, and promised brilliant results. Nor were these promises belied by experience. The old-established solicitor's business was a very flourishing and lucrative one. Martin Bransby was soon able to pay back the loan to his father-in-law with interest. Old Rabbitt observed that this was only taking from one hand to give to the other, for it would all come back to him and his in the end. As a matter of fact, old Rabbitt left every penny he had in the world to his daughter and her children after her; but the money was strictly tied up out of her husband's reach.

This seemed a trifling matter in those days to Martin Bransby. Whom should he desire to enrich but his own children? and things were going so well in the office that it seemed probable he might amass another fortune. But when, after his second marriage, a young family began to gather round him, he could not help regretting the terms of his original marriage settlement. As soon as Theodore came of age Mr. Bransby made an attempt to induce him to relinquish some part of the property in favour of his younger brothers and sisters; but the attempt failed, and was never repeated. Mr. Bransby was deeply wounded by Theodore's attitude, and, on his side, Theodore considered his father's request unreasonable and unfair.

"If I might venture on a suggestion, I would advise your retrenching a little, sir," he had said with icy politeness; "in that way you would soon save enough to provide for Mrs. Bransby and her children in a style fully equal to what they have any right to expect from you."

The remembrance of that interview was a thorn in the flesh of Martin Bransby, and it left in Theodore's mind increased resentment against his father's second marriage.

But Theodore's advice, however unfilially proffered, was sound enough. Retrenchment in the daily expenses of that easy-going and lavish household would have been judicious; but then to retrench would have been to deprive Louisa of the luxuries and elegancies which so became her, and which gave her so much pleasure. Instead of taking this disagreeable method, Mr. Bransby tried speculation. He made one or two lucky strokes, but at the first loss became panic-stricken, and threw good money after bad in a kind of desperation.

After his death something of all this leaked out in a confused way, to the public astonishment. "To think of Martin Bransby's money matters being in a bad way!" people said. "There must be more in this than meets the eye, for he was acknowledged to be a first-rate man of business."

In brief, as much amazement was expressed as though "men of business" were commonly infallible, and the world had never heard of a man of business whose conduct was not ruled by self-restraining prudence. At the same time many persons declared they had long ago prophesied disaster, and had even warned Martin to put some check on his wife's extravagance. But such little inconsistencies as these are but pebbles in the stream of general gossip; diversifying it with an agreeable ripple, but never checking its flow.

May wrote an affectionate letter of condolence to Mrs. Bransby. She received no answer to it; and presently she learned that Mrs. Bransby and her children had left Oldchester, and gone to London. Constance Hadlow did not mention the family at all in writing to Mrs. Dormer-Smith. They had fallen out of the sphere of her observation; and no one can be expected to turn away his telescope from contemplating the fixed stars in order to stare at common terrestrial phenomena—especially phenomena of a non-metallic and unproductive nature.

About Christmas time Theodore Bransby called unexpectedly at Mrs. Dormer-Smith's house in London. He came early in the forenoon—so early, indeed, that Mrs. Dormer-Smith was not yet visible. On asking to see Miss Cheffington, he was shown into a room where May was sitting with the children. (Harold and Wilfred were now permitted to spend part of the morning with their cousin, at her particular request. And it was found that this arrangement answered the double purpose of delighting the boys, and leaving Cecile more leisure for needlework.)

May started and flushed on hearing Mr. Theodore Bransby's name announced. But the first glimpse of Theodore disarmed her wrath. He was paler than ever—or seemed to be so, in his deep mourning, and there was unmistakable sorrow in his face. May rose quickly, and gave him her hand in silence. There were tears in her eyes, and the unexpected sight of tears in his, made her forgive him for pressing her hand harder, and holding it longer than mere politeness warranted.

"I have been so sorry!" said May.

"Thank you," he answered. "You are always kind and good."

"So sorry for you all—the widow—the poor children—!" added May, as a bright drop brimmed over, and rolled down her cheek.

Theodore relinquished her hand, and rapidly passing his handkerchief across his eyes, gave a dry, husky, little cough in his throat. It was a sound which curiously repelled sympathy.

"You were not in Oldchester when your dear father died," said May. She did not intend any covert reproach. Her words were prompted by a pitying thought of the undying regret which must haunt Theodore on this score.

"No; I was not there. I know I have been blamed for that."

"Oh, indeed I had no such meaning!"

"I well believe it. But I have been blamed—most unjustly. I went away with my father's full consent; indeed, he thought I needed the change. He wrote to me when he found himself growing worse, to ask me to come back. Of course I meant to comply with that request. You cannot doubt it?"

"I have no right to doubt it," answered May gently.

"No, but pray listen! I wish to justify myself in your eyes. The truth is, I was in the act of packing my valise to return to Oldchester when a telegram reached me, saying that my father's danger was imminent. I was in Yorkshire, in a country house, where there was but one postal delivery a day. Letters were often delayed, and, in fact, my father's letter had preceded the telegram only by a few hours."

"Oh, how sad! I am so sorry for you!" cried May, clasping her hands. She felt some generous compunction for having done him injustice.

"Yes; I have lost a good father," said Theodore.

"You have, indeed. And what a loss is Mrs. Bransby's!"

A subtle change came over his face, although he did not seem to move a muscle, and he made no answer.

"How is she?" asked May, leaning forward eagerly.

Theodore's eyebrows took their old supercilious curve, as he replied, "Mrs. Bransby? Oh, she's quite well, I believe."

"Believe! Have you not seen her lately?"

"Oh yes; I have seen her. She appeared perfectly well. I did not at first quite take in the sense of your question; but I see now what you meant. Every one has not such keen sensibilities as you, May."

Even this familiar use of her name she let pass, although it jarred upon her.

"I am sure Mrs. Bransby is not insensible," she answered. "And she loved your father dearly."

"I am not disputing it. But she was, and is, a doating mother, and her feelings are greatly engrossed by her children. In one way this is happy for her. She does not feel the void, the loneliness, which oppresses me."

It seemed to May that there might be some truth in this. Theodore was not generally beloved. Cold as he seemed, he doubtless missed his father's affection. He would feel isolated and forlorn. This might be in great part his own fault; but May pitied him. She softened towards him still more when he went on to speak of his plans for assisting his young step-brothers. He had already offered to send Martin to school at his own expense. He was endeavouring to be of use to Mrs. Bransby. She was, unfortunately, very unpractical, and rather impracticable; but he hoped that, when her grief calmed down, she would listen to reason and take advice.

"Is she not well off?" asked May, moved by genuine interest in the widow and her family.

Theodore shook his head. "I may tell you," he said, "that she is in very straitened circumstances. I do not proclaim this generally, because people who know how indefatigably my poor father worked, and what a large income he earned, are apt to blame her, and accuse her of extravagance."

While he was still speaking, a message came from Mrs. Dormer-Smith asking Mr. Bransby to go to her in the drawing-room. She, too, was touched by his mourning garb and pale face, and received him with sympathetic gentleness. May's report of his behaviour in Oldchester had been favourable, in so far that he had not attempted to renew his suit. But what most of all conciliated Mrs. Dormer-Smith was the thought of Mr. Bragg. Now that her niece was so near making a splendid marriage, it was easier to forgive Theodore's presumption. Doubtless the young man had already seen his error; and really, putting aside that one aberration, he was very nice!

Her good opinion was increased in the course of their private conversation, which turned on matters very interesting to Pauline. Theodore had seen her uncle lately; he had, moreover, had a good deal of talk with him about matters political. A vacancy was likely to occur shortly in the representation of that division of the county where Lord Castlecombe's landed property was situated. The Castlecombes were anxious to oppose a threatened Radical candidate, and Theodore had offered to stand.

On his elder brother's death, Lucius Cheffington had resigned his post in the Civil Service, and, under normal circumstances, his father would have desired that he should return to the House of Commons; but his health was at present too feeble to warrant his attempting any exertion. Then old Lord Castlecombe thought it would be well to put some one into the vacant seat who might be willing to resign it whenever Lucius should be able and willing to come forward again as a candidate. This was not expressed, but understood; and Lord Castlecombe had approved of Theodore's ready comprehension of the state of the case, and his clear view of the advantages such an arrangement would afford to himself. Election expenses, even in these days of purity and the ballot, retain as mysterious a rapidity of growth as Jack's beanstalk, and the assistance of Lord Castlecombe would be very solidly valuable. On the other hand, Theodore considered that, ambition apart, it would be useful to him in his career as a barrister to write M.P. after his name, and was willing to assume some share of the cost of the canvass. The old lord discovered in this sententious young gentleman two merits—the possession of money, and the knowledge how to spend it advantageously.

Lucius acquiesced passively in all his father's arrangements; but he could not be induced to thaw half a degree in his personal relations with Theodore.

"The fellow is an intolerable prig," he said to his father; "and his vulgarity is of a particularly objectionable kind—the fine pretentious kind."

"Oh, of course, he's a damned snob," answered my lord, with cheerful candour. "But what the deuce does that matter? We are not going to take him to our arms; only to throw him into the arms of the voters! And I can tell you, it will be a vast deal better to have him for our member than Mr. Butter, the Radical button-maker. At any rate, this young Bransby won't go in for abolishing the Peers, or starting a Separatist crusade in the Scilly Islands."

In the course of his talk with Mrs. Dormer-Smith, Theodore hinted to her as much of his political outlook as seemed good to him. The account of his relations with Lord Castlecombe greatly impressed her; for she was very sure her uncle would not waste any of his time and attention on an entirely insignificant person. And Theodore's tone in speaking of the political position of the Castlecombe family was such as to win her complete approval and sympathy.

When Pauline talked over his visit with her husband, after narrating that part of it which concerned Lord Castlecombe, she added, "And the young man has a great deal of proper feeling. I really begin to think that mistake he made must have been in some way May's fault:—oh, not intentionally, Frederick; but she is so—so unformed in her ideas! However, we need not discuss all that; for I am convinced Mr. Bransby is quite safe now. I was going to say that he told me confidentially that he would not advise us to encourage any intimacy between May and his step-mother. She is in London, I believe; letting lodgings, or some dreadful thing of that sort. It is just the kind of thing May would delight in, if I would let her—visiting and championing people who are in impossible positions, and talking all kinds of Quixotic nonsense about them! However, this Mrs. Bransby is not the kind of person who can be encouraged. She is very handsome, I understand, and tant soit peu, coquette. There was some not too creditable flirtation with young Rivers before her husband's death; and Mr. Bransby evidently thinks she is the kind of woman always to have some one dangling after her. He spoke really very nicely, and said he hoped she might soon marry again, as she is scarcely fit to be trusted with the responsibility of bringing up a young family. You are so apt to indulge May in her whims, that I thought it necessary to repeat all this with distinctness. You must see, as I do, that it would be quite disastrous for May to keep up any intimacy with such a person as this Mrs. Bransby—a handsome, flirting, needy widow! If she were even in society—!"

CHAPTER XIV.

The sale of Martin Bransby's handsome furniture, books, plate, carriage, and horses realized a considerable sum; but only a small portion of that sum remained when all debts were paid. Theodore made all the arrangements, and Mrs. Bransby passively acquiesced in them. She was crushed by grief, and timidly acknowledged herself to be sadly helpless and ignorant of business matters.

It was Theodore who had decided that the family should leave Oldchester. It was Theodore who had taken a house for them in a northern suburb of London. It was Theodore who suggested that Mrs. Bransby might eke out her income by receiving one or two lodgers. For Martin's schooling he promised to be responsible; and he would also guarantee the rent of the London house for one twelvemonth. But he could promise no further assistance, giving as a sufficient reason for not doing more the heavy claims on his purse which would result from his forthcoming political candidature.

A tiny annual sum was secured to the widow—a sum smaller than that which she had been in the habit of spending on her dress; and this was all she had to rely on to keep herself and her five children. It was clear that an effort must be made to earn some money.

Some articles of furniture remaining from the Oldchester sale nearly sufficed to furnish the small London dwelling. The house, fortunately, was clean, freshly painted, and in good repair; but the vulgar wall-papers were an affliction to Mrs. Bransby's eyes, and the dimensions of the rooms seemed to her painfully cramped. When she ventured to hint as much to her stepson he gave her a severe lecture, and begged her to understand that the days when her whims could be lavishly indulged were over.

"But it can scarcely be called a whim to want air for my children to breathe!" returned Mrs. Bransby, with a flash of indignation which she repented the next moment. And when Theodore pointed out that the house was a remarkably airy one for the rent; and that he, in his kind consideration, had taken a great deal of trouble to find a dwelling for them in a healthy locality, she meekly apologized for having been betrayed into any expression of impatience, and promised to make the best of her new circumstances.

They were such as might have depressed a stronger and less sensitive person. When Theodore had gone away, and the children were in bed, and the widow sat alone in the mean little room which, small as it was, was but dimly illuminated by one candle, the sense of her forlorn position weighed her down, and seemed to make the atmosphere thick with misery. It was not the loss of material luxuries which afflicted her. A month ago she would have felt that keenly; but now her great sorrow had absorbed all minor troubles. Poverty! What was poverty, compared with desolation of spirit? How willingly would she have faced severer bodily hardships than any which threatened her if her lost husband could be restored to her!

She dropped her head on her folded arms resting on the table. The widow's cap slipped aside, and a veil of bright, brown, waving hair fell over her bowed face. She had been forced to restrain her tears all day. There were the children to be thought of. There were Theodore's cold, clear questions and suggestions to be answered. But now, in solitude, her tears gushed out. She wept with long, deep-drawn sobs. The words of the Litany seemed to be repeated over and over again, as by a voice whispering in her ear, "The fatherless children, and widows, and all who are desolate and oppressed." She rocked herself from side to side, and moaned out, "Oh, come back to us! Come back, Martin—Martin!"

A hand was gently laid on her shoulder. With a great start she raised her head, and saw her eldest boy standing by her side.

He was a handsome boy, very like his father. But now his naturally ruddy face was pale, and his eyes had a depth of yearning tenderness in them which went to his mother's heart.

"Don't cry so, mother dear!" he said. "Father couldn't bear to see it, if he knew."

She clasped the boy in her arms; and, although she still wept, her sobs were less convulsive, and she gradually grew calmer. Martin stood beside her very quietly, occasionally stroking back the pretty soft hair which strayed over her face, and was damp with tears.

Presently Mrs. Bransby said, "I thought you were in bed, Martin. How silently you came downstairs!"

"I took off my shoes, mother," he answered, showing his feet. "I didn't want to disturb the others. The children are asleep, and Phoebe is snoring away."

Phoebe was their one servant, a housemaid from their Oldchester home—who had volunteered to remain with them and follow their fortunes.

"Poor Phoebe! I dare say she is tired," said Mrs. Bransby.

"I should think she was rather. She has been working like a brick all day," returned Martin.

There was a little silence, during which Mrs. Bransby dried her eyes, put up her dishevelled hair, and replaced her cap.

"Ought you not to go to bed, my boy?" she said, looking wistfully at him.

"I want to stay and talk to you quietly a little, mother."

Mrs. Bransby hesitated. "I should dearly like you to stay awhile, Martin," she answered; "but I'm afraid it would not be right. You look pale and worn out. You and I must help each other now to do what is right;—and what—what he would have wished," she added with quivering lips.

"Yes, mother," answered the boy eagerly. "That's just what I want; and I know he would have wished me to spare you all the bother I can. So now just listen, mother; indeed, indeed I couldn't sleep if I went to bed now—and it's far wearier work to lie awake than to sit up and talk. Look here, mother; Theodore has offered to send me to school, hasn't he?"

"Yes, Martin. I am very thankful for that. I don't see how I could have afforded it."

"Well, but now, I've been thinking that it would be better if Theodore would give you that money, instead of paying for my schooling, and for me to get a situation and earn something."

"Earn! My darling boy, how could you earn anything?"

"Why, mother, I could do all that the office boy did at Oldchester. Old Tuckey told me once that he earned fifteen shillings a-week. Just fancy, mother! That's a good lot, isn't it?"

It looked a very childish face that he turned towards his mother: a face with frank, sparkling eyes and rounded cheeks, to which the excitement of making this proposition had brought back the roses.

"Oh, Martin, my dearest boy, it is sweet of you to think of this! But you are too young, darling."

"I'm going on for thirteen, mother!" interrupted Martin.

"Yes, dear; but still even that is very, very young," answered his mother gravely, although the phantom of a smile flitted across her pale face.

Martin looked disappointed, and, for a moment, almost angry. He had a naturally hot temper. But he battled down the temptation, and merely said, "Well, mother, you need not decide anything to-night. You can think it over. I believe I could earn something; and I'm sure that if I can, I ought."

"But your education, Martin!"

"I might, perhaps, go on learning a little at home—in the evenings," he rejoined, but more slowly, and less confidently than he had spoken before.

"You know, Martin, he wished you to study. He was so proud of your abilities—so fond of you—" Her voice broke, and she turned away her head.

"Yes, mother; but he was fonder of you," answered Martin simply. "I know quite well that if father could speak to me now, this minute, he would say, 'Martin, take care of your mother.' That's what he did say one day when I was alone with him, only a week before—" The boy paused, made a violent struggle to master his emotion, and then went on bravely, though his young face grew white to the lips, "And I'm going to do it, please God!"

The tears that poured down his mother's cheeks as she embraced him and kissed his forehead were not all bitter. "Not desolate—not wholly desolate," she murmered, "while I have you, my precious, precious son!"

They sat awhile, talking of their means, and their plans, and their prospects. Mrs. Bransby felt that although many of Martin's notions were, of course, crude and childish, yet there was a strain of firm manliness in him on which she could rely; and the boy had a quick intelligence. Before parting from his mother for the night, he proposed that she should write to Owen Rivers and ask his advice. "You'll believe what Mr. Rivers says, mother, if you don't believe me. And I think you'll find that he will consider it my duty to earn something if I can; anyway, he's such a good fellow, and has such a thundering lot of sense, he's sure to give us good advice."

The widow caught at the suggestion; she had almost as implicit faith in Owen as her children had. She promised that Martin should enclose a letter of his own in hers to Mr. Rivers; and when she bade the boy "good night" at the door of his poor little chamber, she was surprised to find her heart somewhat lightened of its load.

"I say, look here, mother!" whispered Martin, beckoning her in from the open door. "Don't those young shavers sleep like one o'clock?" He pointed to Bobby and Billy, who occupied one large bed—a relic from the Oldchester nursery—while Martin's little camp-bedstead was squeezed into a corner of the same room. The two little fellows were sleeping the profound sleep of healthy childhood. Bobby had a smile on his parted lips, and Billy lay with one fat hand doubled up under his cheek, and the other buried in the thick masses of his brother's curly hair.

"This isn't half a bad room when the window's wide open," went on Martin cheerfully. "I can see a tree—quite a good-sized elm—from my bed. Good night, mother dear; I hope you'll sleep. I think this'll turn out an awfully nice little house, when we get used to it."

The two letters to Owen Rivers—Martin's and his mother's—were written the next morning. Mrs. Bransby sent them under cover to Mr. Bragg, addressed to Oldchester, to be forwarded, and with a line from herself to Mr. Bragg, begging that he would let Mr. Rivers have them without delay. She had written very fully and frankly to Owen, telling him, without reserve, what her means were. Only on one point had she been reticent—Theodore's conduct. In her heart she thought Theodore cruelly cold and hard towards her and the children. But she would not complain of him; he was her dear husband's son, and she felt as if it would be disloyal to that honoured husband's memory to paint Theodore to others as she saw him.

Theodore's recommendation to his step-mother, to "take good, steady, paying lodgers," was in the nature of those vague counsels we are all apt to proffer freely to our neighbours; such as, to "cheer up;" not to "yield to weakness;" to "look on the bright side;" to "dismiss disagreeable thoughts;" to "set to work briskly and earn money," and the like. That is to say, it was easier said than done. When, after the family had been somewhat over a week in town, Theodore came again to see them, and found that no steps had been taken to carry out this suggestion, he showed considerable displeasure, and said a sharp word or two about the difficulty of helping unpractical people.

This word, "unpractical," was, in fact, a favourite reproach to apply to poor Mrs. Bransby on the part of a great many persons. Mrs. Dormer-Smith caught it up from Theodore. Constance Hadlow echoed the same phrase when, at length, in answer to some private inquiries of Mrs. Dormer-Smith's, she wrote about the Bransby family.

May's first eager proposal to go and see Mrs. Bransby was met by her aunt with an absolute refusal; but she was so urgent, and appealed so strongly to her uncle, that Mrs. Dormer-Smith, making a virtue of necessity (for she feared that if leave were refused May might go without it), graciously consented that her niece should pay one visit to Mrs. Bransby.

"One visit will be enough, May," said Aunt Pauline. "Quite enough to show that you feel kindly towards her, and that sort of thing. It is really stretching a point. However, if it must be, it must be. I only implore you not to talk about these people in society. Pray, pray do not poser as a district visitor, or whatever it is called."

May shrugged her shoulders, and was silent. She knew how vain it was to reason with Aunt Pauline on a point of this kind; but she comforted herself by looking forward to the time—very near now—when Owen would return, and when, in some mysterious way, not explicable to her head, but quite sufficing to her heart, all her difficulties would vanish before his presence. And that same afternoon she set off to Collingwood Place, Barnsbury Road, in a cab, attended by Smithson.

Mrs. Bransby received her affectionately, and thanked her for her visit; but she did not ask her to repeat it. She perceived, far more quickly than May had perceived it, that Mrs. Dormer-Smith would not like her niece to keep up any intimacy with a family who lived in Barnsbury, and were served by one maid-of-all-work. When the children clung round May, and clamoured to know when she was coming to see them again, Mrs. Bransby interposed. She told them that May could not be running in and out of their house in London as she had done in Oldchester; and they must understand she could not take up the time of her aunt's maid in making long journeys to Barnsbury. And she said privately to May—

"Don't get into trouble with your aunt by coming here, my dear. I know you would help us if you could; but you cannot. But I ought not to say that! It is helpful to know you are unchanged, and warm-hearted as ever. Some day, please God, we may be able to see each freely."

"Yes; some day!" cried May joyfully, thinking of him who would help to make that and all the other good things possible. And then she coloured vividly, as though she had betrayed a secret.

Mrs. Bransby, however, did not notice this. She went on pensively, "And yet I am almost afraid to look forward to any pleasant thing lest it should be snatched away from me. Misfortune makes one a sad coward. I have had a disappointment just lately—about Mr. Rivers. He is not coming back so soon as was expected."

"He is coming back at the end of this month," said May in a quick, almost breathless way.

"No. He was to have returned to England at the end of December, but that is altered. His present engagement is prolonged for some weeks. I had a letter from him last evening from Barcelona, and he does not expect to be in England before the latter part of January at the soonest."

May drove homeward much depressed and out of spirits. It was not only that Owen's return was postponed, but that she had not been the first to hear of it! To be sure, his weekly letter was not yet due, and he was rigidly scrupulous in keeping his promise to Mrs. Dobbs about corresponding with May. But need he have volunteered to give this news to Mrs. Bransby before writing it to her? A dull feeling of discontent seemed to oppress her; but on reaching home she tried to shake it off, and to forget it in fighting her friend's battle against Aunt Pauline.

Aunt Pauline had constructed for herself an image of Mrs. Bransby founded on Theodore's hints. She had decided in her own mind that Mrs. Bransby was a weak-minded, lounging, lazy woman, who, no longer able to adorn herself with fine clothes, would sink into slattern-hood, and throw herself and her family as a dead weight on to any shoulders who would carry them.

"A woman belonging to the provincial middle-class, who thinks of nothing but dress," said Mrs. Dormer-Smith, shaking her head mournfully. "One knows what that must come to!"

"But Mrs. Bransby thought of a great many things besides dress!" cried May. "She thought of her household, and her children, and, above all, of her husband."

Mrs. Dormer-Smith merely shook her head again, with an air of mild martyrdom, as though some one were unjustly accusing her.

"And I assure you, Aunt Pauline," May continued, "that the little house she is living in—poor and humble, of course, in comparison with her old home—is a pattern of neatness."

"You say 'poor and humble,' May; but do you not think that a house at forty-five pounds a year is quite as good as she has any right to expect, under the circumstances? I do. And that poor young Bransby has to be responsible for the rent."

"I am sure Mrs. Bransby won't let him be out of pocket, if she can possibly help it."

"I dare say. But she is a sadly unpractical person."

"It was most touching to see her with all those children about her, trying to be cheerful and composed; and looking so lovely in her melancholy mourning dress."

"I presume she wears crape? Ah! There's no more extravagant wear. She might have one dress trimmed with crape for occasions; but her ordinary everyday frocks ought to be of plain black stuff. Hemstitched muslin collars and cuffs, perhaps," added Mrs. Dormer-Smith, relenting at the image of uncompromising ugliness she had herself conjured up. "But they can be made at home, and need not cost much. Has she any lodgers?"

"No, not yet. But there has been very little time. And it is difficult, she says, to find suitable persons."

"Yes, that is precisely the kind of thing one would expect her to say. That is the speech of a thoroughly unpractical person."

"The fact is," burst out May hotly, "it is unpractical to be poor! It is unpractical to be left a widow, with five children, and only a miserable pittance to keep them on!"

It was intolerable to hear Aunt Pauline sitting in judgment on this poor lady, of whom she really knew nothing whatever save her misfortunes. And May was greatly astonished at the glib way in which her aunt, usually so prosaically matter-of-fact, discoursed about Mrs. Bransby, putting in visionary details with a lavish fancy. The girl had yet to learn that the most narrow and commonplace minds are capable of wild exaggeration within their own sphere, and that to be unimaginative is no guarantee for truthfulness of perception.

Mrs. Dormer-Smith, whatever her defects might be, possessed almost perfect gentleness of temper. She merely said softly, "May, May, when will you understand that nothing can be worse form than that habit of raving about people? You are so dreadfully emphatic!"

"I don't care a straw about what you call 'good form'! I prefer good substance," answered May, still in a glow of indignation.

"My dear child, what does this woman matter to you?"

"Matter! She is my friend. She has always been kind to me; and even if she were not my friend, I would defend her against unfair accusations."

Mrs. Dormer-Smith was silent for a few minutes. Then she said, in her slow, somewhat muffled tones, "May, you compel me to say what I would rather leave unsaid. Mrs. Bransby is not the kind of person your uncle and I wish you to associate with. I do not assert that there has been anything positively wrong in her conduct. Now oblige me by listening quietly! If you start up in that melodramatic way, you will bring on one of my nervous headaches. I was merely going to remark that a woman so handsome as I am told she is, and so very much younger than her husband, ought, in the most ordinary view of what is convenable, to avoid anything like—like seeking to attract men's admiration, and that sort of thing. But instead of that, Mrs. Bransby carried on a very flagrant flirtation during her husband's lifetime with a young man considerably her junior. It was noticed, of course, and commented on. If she was so led away by foolish vanity when she had a sensible husband to guide her, what will it be now that she is left to her own devices?"

May stood staring at her aunt like one suddenly awakened out of sleep. "This is all false," she said, after a moment; "false, and very cruel. Who told you such things, Aunt Pauline?"

"I decline to tell you, May. Some one who has had the means of knowing what went on in this Bransby household, and some one whose judgment I can trust. It must suffice to assure you that I am quite certain of my facts." And, strange, as it may seem, Mrs. Dormer-Smith really thought she was certain of them.

May turned away contemptuously. "Mrs. Bransby is really very much to blame," she said. "It is bad enough to be poor and unprotected, but to be the most beautiful woman in all her circle of acquaintance as well, is not to be forgiven!"

Then May left her aunt's presence, and betook herself to her own room, where she locked the door and burst out crying. These calumnies were bewildering. She sat on the side of her bed for more than an hour, in a drooping posture, depressed and miserable. As she thought over her aunt's words, the belief flashed into her mind that Mrs. Dormer-Smith's informant must have been Constance Hadlow. She did not suspect Constance of having deliberately invented stories to the poor widow's discredit; but she did think that Constance had repeated them, and that they had lost none of their venom in her repetition. It chanced that on that very morning her aunt had spoken of a letter just received from Miss Hadlow; and May knew very well the sort of gossip which made up the staple of that correspondence. Not for one moment did her suspicions point to Theodore. The idea that he could have originated odious insinuations against his father's wife was inconceivable to her. But Conny—She had observed latterly a tendency in Conny to bitterness and detraction when speaking of Mrs. Bransby. Was she jealous? And why? When they talked of Mrs. Bransby's flirtations with a man younger than herself, whom did they allude to?

All at once May drew herself sharply into an upright attitude, while a burning flush covered her face and throat. She dashed away some stray tears with her handkerchief, and exclaimed, speaking out loud in her excitement, "I will not think of such mean, malicious, despicable folly! I will turn my mind away from it. It is shameful even to be conscious of anything so base-minded!"

CHAPTER XV.

Two days after May's interview with Mrs. Bransby, Owen's weekly letter arrived. In it he informed her of the unexpected postponement of his return; and he mentioned having written this news to Mrs. Bransby in answer to a letter from her appealing to him for help and advice. But he did not expend many words on the Bransby family. He had to keep May minutely informed of his own doings, and of his prospects, so far as he could judge of them. And whatsoever time and space remained at his disposal when this was accomplished was devoted to a theme which touched him more nearly than the fortunes of gentle Louisa Bransby—although his regard for her was very real. Owen was deeply in love, and wrote love-letters. And that species of composition does not deal with circumstantial and connected narrative—at any rate, about third persons.

But although Owen did not return to England at the end of December, Mr. Bragg did. He appeared one day in Mrs. Dormer-Smith's drawing-room, when he was received by that lady with marked graciousness, and by May with a changing colour and shy eagerness which he might have been excused for misinterpreting.

Mrs. Dormer-Smith was delighted. May's behaviour appeared to her to be just what it ought to be. Uncle Frederick, too, who happened to be at home—for Mr. Bragg called at so unfashionably an early hour that the master of the house had not yet gone out to his club—had reason to be gratified. He took the opportunity of consulting Mr. Bragg as to a little investment he purposed making. And Mr. Bragg, while dissuading him from that particular investment, spontaneously offered to put his money into "a good thing" for him.

"I make it a rule not to advise people in general about such matters," said Mr. Bragg. "The responsibility's too great; not to mention that if it once, what you might call got wind that I did give such advice, I should have my time took up altogether with other people's business. And I don't see the force of that."

"Of course not! Most inconsiderate!" murmured Mr. Dormer-Smith.

"But I reserve the right to make exceptions now and then," continued Mr. Bragg. "And I shall be happy to be of use to you."

All this while no word had been said about Owen. May's secret consciousness made her too bashful to introduce his name. But at length Mr. Bragg mentioned it of his own accord. It was in speaking of Mr. Bransby's death. Mr. Bragg expressed kindly sympathy with the widow, and added—

"She has one good friend, poor soul, anyway. My secretary takes the greatest interest in her. You know him, Miss Cheffington—Mr. Owen Rivers."

"Yes," answered May, in as constrained a tone as though the subject were distasteful to her. Yet the poor child was longing with all her heart to speak of Owen, and to hear him spoken of.

"To be sure you do. We used to meet him at the Miss Pipers' pretty well every evening, didn't we? Besides, he's a cousin of your great friend, Miss Hadlow."

"Oh, of course!" exclaimed Mrs. Dormer-Smith, with a sudden remembrance of that relationship, and a consequent increase of interest in Owen, whom personally she knew but very slightly. "A cousin of Constance Hadlow's! Yes, yes; I recall it now. Mrs. Griffin told me that his grandfather, who married a Lespoony—" She stopped, remembering that family genealogy was a subject not likely to be specially agreeable to Mr. Bragg, and asked that gentleman sweetly, "How do you like him? Does he do well?"

"First rate!" answered Mr. Bragg emphatically.

May coloured with pleasure, and turned aside her face, to hide a broad, childlike smile which stole over it.

"First rate," repeated Mr. Bragg. "He gives full satisfaction. Not but what there are little what you may call twists in him here and there. He's peculiar in some ways. But I never did expect angels from heaven to come down and do office-work for me. I consider myself lucky if I get honesty and fair industry. Now, Mr. Rivers is more than honest—he's honourable."

"Isn't that a distinction without a difference in this case?" asked Mr. Dormer-Smith lightly.

"Well, no; I don't think so," answered Mr. Bragg in his slow, pondering way. "You see, honesty makes a capital slow-combustion kind of fire, but if you want a white heat you must have honour. I can't express myself quite clear, but I have it in my mind."

"And so Mr. Rivers takes a great interest in this Mrs. Bransby," said Pauline. Her thoughts had been busy with this point ever since Mr. Bragg had uttered the words. And she was pleased that May should hear something like corroboration of the charge against Mrs. Bransby.

"Uncommon. He's quite what you might call devoted to her."

"She's a deuced pretty woman, isn't she?" put in Mr. Dormer-Smith, with a little knowing laugh.

Mr. Bragg replied, with perfect seriousness, "Mrs. Bransby is a lady of great personal attractions, and, so far as I know of her, most amiable. I'm sorry to hear she's left in poor circumstances. Martin

Bransby seems to have made most imprudent speculations. If he'd have come to me, poor man, I could have given him some useful warnings; and would have done it, too. I'd have made one of my exceptions in his favour."

Mrs. Dormer-Smith's interest in the deceased Martin Bransby was too slight to enchain her attention. When the widow was no longer being spoken of, Pauline's thoughts flew off rapidly to the fashion and texture of May's wedding-dress (which had already haunted her solitary musings), and to the question whether Mr. Bragg would be likely to do anything for her boy Cyril, who was just about to be entered at the University. But her eyes remained fixed with a politely attentive look on Mr. Bragg, and, when he ceased speaking, she murmured plaintively, as being a safe thing to say, "That is so good of you!"

As soon as Mr. Bragg was gone, May sat down to write an account of his visit to Owen. Her heart swelled with pride as she repeated to him Mr. Bragg's words about himself. Indeed, she was so enthusiastic about Mr. Bragg, that Owen jestingly told her in his next letter that he was growing jealous of his "master"—so he always termed Mr. Bragg.

It was out of the question that May should hint to Owen a word of the unkind things which were said of Mrs. Bransby. She could not bring her pen to write them. It seemed to her as if she could never even speak them to him. But she said all the most sympathetic and affectionate things she could think of about the poor widow and her children, being inspired by the malicious gossip only to a more chivalrous warmth on her friend's behalf. But yet—that gossip was like a barbed seed that clings where it alights, and could not wholly be shaken out of her memory. If she could but have spoken with granny! She could not write all the confused feelings that were in her mind. To have tried to do so would have seemed almost like hinting something which might be construed into a doubt of Owen! But if she could speak, with her living voice, granny—who loved her so much, and would listen with such understanding ears—would surely find the right words to conjure away the oppression which weighed on her spirits! She was ashamed of not feeling so happy as she had felt three weeks ago. And yet it was impossible to deny that a cloud—light and filmy, but still a cloud—had come between her and the sun. She was very lonely. Sometimes she was startled by the sudden recognition of how completely aloof she was in spirit from the beings around her.

Next to Owen's letters, her little cousins were her chief comfort. She had them with her as much as possible, helping them with their lessons, and joining in their play. Their brother Cyril being now at home from Harrow, the younger children received even less than the scanty share of her attention which their mother had ever vouchsafed to them. Mr. Dormer-Smith was a good deal engrossed by his eldest son; and Harold and Wilfred would have been forlorn indeed, at this time, but for Cousin May. Yes, the children were a great comfort to her; and, after them, she liked Mr. Bragg's society better than that of most people! He was so closely associated with Owen.

Mr. Bragg had become a frequent and familiar guest at the Dormer-Smiths' house. Uncle Frederick highly valued his advice and assistance in financial matters, while Aunt Pauline was never tired of repeating his praises. Only—as she privately complained to her husband—he "hung fire" a little.

"Why in the world he shouldn't speak out, I cannot conjecture," said she, with that soft, suffering expression of countenance, which Mr. Bragg's assiduous visits had recently banished for as much as two or three days together. "It really is not May's fault this time. Nothing could be nicer than she is to him. I should be uneasy about the Hautenvilles, but that they are spending the winter at Rome. And besides, Mrs. Griffin assured me that he wouldn't look at Felicia. In fact, he told her in plain terms that Miss Cheffington was the one young lady he admired. Dear Mrs. Griffin! I shall never forget what a friend she has been all through the affair. And the dear duchess! But really, Mr. Bragg does hang fire most unaccountably! I think it is beginning to tell on May herself a little. She mopes. Now, that is a very serious matter, for her complexion is of the delicate kind which will not stand worry."

The new year opened dark and damp in London. But the external gloom did not quench social gaiety, of which there was a good deal going on at this time. Mrs. Dormer-Smith entered into it, and insisted on May's entering into it, as much as possible. She reflected that this would be the last year during which she would have the assistance of May's allowance, and that it would be well to profit by it to the utmost while it lasted. The allowance was never expended in any way by which May could not benefit. For example, if Mrs. Dormer-Smith were going to a dinner-party without her niece, she would not spend May's money on the hire of a carriage to save her own hard-worked brougham horse; but when May accompanied her she would do so. And on such occasions she would indulge in some little extra elegance of dress, on the plea (quite genuinely preferred) that she must be decently dressed in the girl's interests.

In spite of Theodore Bransby's recent mourning they frequently met in society.

"It is my duty to keep up my social connections," he would say to Mrs. Dormer-Smith, with a grave, resigned air. And no one could have more fully appreciated and approved the sentiment than she did.

Theodore travelled rather frequently backwards and forwards between London and Oldchester in these days. He was busy in the neighbourhood of his native city, preparing the ground for his political campaign; while he was constantly attracted to London by the hope of seeing May. He had discovered that Mrs. Bransby wrote sometimes to Owen Rivers, and he frequently volunteered to give her items of news about May, which he thought and hoped she might transmit to Spain. Miss Cheffington had sat near him at Lady A.'s dinner-party; he had escorted Miss Cheffington and her aunt to Mrs. B.'s soirée musicale; Mrs. C. had given him a seat in her box at the theatre—where he met Miss Cheffington; and so forth.

"Miss Cheffington appears to be very gay!" said Mrs. Bransby once, with a sigh, not envious, but regretful; her own life was so dull and dark.

"Miss Cheffington is very much in the world, of course. Her birth and her beauty entitle her to a good deal of attention, and she gets it. I see no objection to that. On the contrary, it delights me that she should be admired."

His step-mother stared at him in sudden surprise.

"Theodore!" she exclaimed impulsively. "There is nothing between you and May, is there?"

He drew himself up, and answered in as coldly offended a tone as though he had not desired, and even angled for, that very question. "Excuse me, Mrs. Bransby, but I do not think it well to use a young lady's name in that way. It is too delicate a matter to be handled at all in its present stage."

"Don't you believe him, mother," said Martin when Theodore had gone away. "May Cheffington isn't likely to think of him."

"I don't know, Martin. It may not seem likely to us, because—"

"Because we know what Theodore is," interposed Martin boldly.

His mother let that suggestion lie, but she said, "You must remember, my boy, that Theodore has many qualities which—which—He is very well educated, and clever, and gentlemanlike."

"No; that he is not!" put in the irrepressible Martin.

"And he probably has a distinguished career before him. Besides, he is rich now, you know."

"As if May would care for that!" exclaimed Martin, with innocently lofty disdain.

"Her friends might care for it for her," answered Mrs. Bransby thoughtfully.

She had fallen into the habit of consulting with Martin on all kinds of subjects. Sometimes she reproached herself for harassing the boy with cares and questions beyond his years. But, in truth, it would have been impossible at that time to keep Martin from sharing her cares; and the pride of being allowed to share her counsels also, more than made him amends.

Mrs. Bransby had a lodger now—a lodger who was the incubus of her life. He was an elderly German, engaged in the City; and, besides occupying the chamber which Theodore had ordained must be let if possible, he breakfasted with the family every day, and dined with them on Sundays. The man was vulgar, greedy, and sullen in his manners. His habits at table, without being absolutely gross, were revolting to Mrs. Bransby's refinement. And his exigencies on the score of the Sunday dinner were such as to keep her in constant anxiety, and to excite boundless indignation in Phoebe. Phoebe, indeed, so detested Mr. Bucher, that Mrs. Bransby was occasionally reduced to beg for a cessation of hostilities; and (very much against the grain) to plead Mr. Bucher's cause even with tears in her eyes.

Such being the state of things, it can well be imagined with what an ebullition of joy Mrs. Bransby hailed a letter from Owen Rivers, announcing his approaching arrival in London, and proposing himself to her as a lodger. He would like, he said, to board entirely with the family, and offered terms which Mrs. Bransby feared were almost too generous. Martin, it is needless to say, enthusiastically welcomed the idea of having Owen Rivers to live with them. And Phoebe's delight in the prospect of Mr. Bucher's being speedily superseded, made her volunteer to prepare his favourite pudding on the very next Sunday, although hitherto she had obstinately professed the blankest ignorance of its composition.

Before, however, giving the unpopular Mr. Bucher notice to quit her house, Mrs. Bransby thought herself bound to consult Theodore. Her mind misgave her lest Theodore, who, as she knew, detested Owen Rivers, should strongly set his face against receiving him; and she wrote her letter to her stepson in considerable trepidation. But, to her surprise, she speedily received an answer entirely approving the plan. It was not gracious; Theodore was never gracious to her. But that was a small matter in comparison with obtaining his consent to the arrangement, and this consent was unmistakably given.

"I believe," he wrote, "that you will be justified in taking Rivers for a lodger, if you wish it. I meet his employer, Mr. Bragg, very frequently at the house of Mrs. Dormer-Smith, and he apparently intends to retain Rivers in his service—at all events, for the present. You will, therefore, I should say, be quite sure of regular payments."

So Owen's offer was joyfully and gratefully accepted.

He had, of course, written to tell May as nearly as possible the time of his arrival in England, but he had not mentioned his scheme of living at the Bransbys, fearing lest it might not be practicable. He did not, in fact, receive Mrs. Bransby's reply to his proposal until he was on his way home. He found it addressed, as he had directed Mrs. Bransby, to the "Poste Restante" in Paris, where he spent one day on business for Mr. Bragg. And thus it chanced that the first intimation which May received of the matter came from Theodore Bransby.

He was dining at the Dormer-Smiths'. Mr. Bragg was there also. It was what Mrs. Dormer-Smith called "a very quiet little dinner—just one or two people, quite cosily," and had been given simply and solely for Mr. Bragg. There was but one other guest, Lady Moppett. Mrs. Dormer-Smith did not consider Lady Moppett to be worth cultivating. She was rich, but not "in the best set." Moreover, she had a craze for music. Mrs. Dormer-Smith's private sentiment about all the Arts was akin to that of the Turkish potentate who inquired at a ball why they did not make their slaves dance for them, instead of taking all that trouble themselves! She considered, in fact, that the Muses ought to be kept in their places. But she would never have uttered any word approaching to such a Boeotian phrase. She had an almost perfect taste in phrases. There, however, sat Lady Moppett at her dinner-table. Mr. Dormer-Smith had stipulated for "some human being to speak to." Mr. Bragg must, of course, be left to May, and Mr. Dormer-Smith could not endure young Bransby. Theodore was not generally popular with his own sex, but Pauline had quite reinstated him in her good graces. And, indeed, how was it possible not to feel agreeably towards a young man whom Lord Castlecombe himself delighted to honour?

Lady Moppett was an old acquaintance of her host's, as has been stated. And, except on the subject of music, she was a good-humoured woman enough; making amends for the inflexible rigidity of her dogma as to the divine art by a rather broad indulgence towards the merely moral shortcomings of her fellow-creatures. Mr. Dormer-Smith led her out to dinner. Mr. Bragg, of course, conducted his hostess; and Theodore, therefore, had to give May his arm to the dining-room. There was no help for that. But the party was small and the table was round, and Mr. Bragg would not be far sundered from May. And once in the drawing-room, Aunt Pauline would take care that he should have abundant opportunities for private conversation with her niece.

May endured Theodore's proximity far more graciously than would have been the case three months ago. He was not naturally quick at discerning the effect he produced on others, nor careful to spare their feelings. But Love stimulates the perceptions in a wonderful way. Prosaic though his subjects may be, the Arch-Magician has lost nothing of his cunning; and under his potent influence Theodore Bransby developed some little sympathetic insight into May's feelings. He even divined that part of her new, soft kindliness of manner towards himself was due to pity for his bereavement. And he had learned in a more unmistakeable way—for she had told him so—that she approved his care of his step-mother and young brothers and sisters. Theodore was pretty safe in vaunting his disinterested efforts on their behalf. Mrs. Bransby and May were effectually kept apart, and neither of them suspected that this was chiefly his doing.

He now, as he sat by May's side, had something in his mind which he greatly desired she should hear. But some feeling, unaccountable to himself—or, at least, which he did not choose to account for—made him hesitate to utter it to her directly. At length, in a little pause of the conversation, he bent slightly forward towards Mr. Bragg, who sat opposite to him, and said—

"I suppose you do not propose returning to Spain, Mr. Bragg?"

"Me? Oh no. I don't think I've any call to do so. And there's plenty for me to look after elsewhere."

"Of course! Transactions on such a colossal scale! When I heard that Rivers was coming back to London, I concluded that you had wound up the business which took you to Spain."

"Mr. Rivers has been very helpful to me, indeed. I feel myself under an obligation to him."

To say the truth, Mr. Bragg was impelled to offer this testimony—even at the cost of dragging it in somewhat inopportunely—by his lively remembrance of sundry spiteful speeches made by young Bransby in former times; but rather to his surprise, Theodore did not now seek to divert the conversation from Owen's praises.

"Yes; Rivers has come out wonderfully well, I understand," said Theodore. "I hear a good deal about him. He is in constant correspondence with Mrs. Bransby; as, perhaps, you know?"

"Oh!" said Mr. Bragg quietly. "No; I can't say I know it. By the way, I do call to mind Mrs. Bransby sending me a letter for him some time ago. Well, he may be in correspondence with her."

"Oh, he is. I have reason to know it, for I think he is the sole topic of conversation at my step-mother's house just now. The whole family are in a fever of excitement about his coming to live with them."

Without turning his head, or even glancing at May, he felt that she was listening with a new and suddenly concentrated attention; and he said to himself, with a glow of elation, "She did not know it."

"Ah! Really?" said Mr. Bragg, addressing himself to his dinner. The matter did not seem to him one of any very special interest. If young Rivers went to lodge at Mrs. Bransby's, it would probably be a good arrangement for both.

"Who's that? Anybody I know?" asked Lady Moppett from her place at the host's right hand.

Theodore answered, "I was merely speaking of a man named Rivers, who—"

"Owen Rivers? Oh, of course I know him. A dreadful heretic! He enunciates the most intolerable, old-fashioned stuff! And he's so frightfully obstinate; battles, and argues one down, positively! I really have no patience. But what about him? Is he going to be married?"

"Not that I know of," replied Theodore, with his correct air, and an odd effect, as though his white cravat and shirt-front had been suddenly petrified.

"Oh, I beg your pardon. I thought you said something of the sort."

"By Jove, more unlikely things have happened," put in Mr. Dormer-Smith jocosely. "He's exposing himself to a tremendous fire. Dangerous work for a fellow to live under the roof of a lovely and captivating woman who sets him up as a kind of 'guide, philosopher, and friend,'—eh?"

"Dangerous! I should think the end of that arrangement is a foregone conclusion!" exclaimed Lady Moppett. "Mr. Rivers is a very agreeable young fellow—when he isn't talking about music. But who's your 'lovely and captivating woman?' Does anybody know her?"

There was an instant's pause, during which Pauline cast an expressive glance of the most poignant reproach at her husband. Then Theodore answered very gravely, "Mr. Dormer-Smith was merely jesting. The lady is Mrs. Martin Bransby—my father's widow."

VOLUME III.

CHAPTER I.

The following morning Mrs. Dormer-Smith was in a flutter of excitement. She left her bedroom fully an hour earlier than was her wont. But before she did so she sent a message begging May not to absent herself from the house. For even in this wintry season May was in the habit of walking out every morning with the children whenever there came a gleam of good weather. Smithson, Mrs. Dormer-Smith's maid, who was charged with the message, volunteered to add, with a glance at May's plain morning frock—

"Mr. Bragg is expected, I believe, Miss."

"Very well, Smithson. Tell my aunt I will not go out without her permission."

Smithson still lingered. "Shall I—would you like me to lay out your grey merino, Miss?" she asked.

"Oh no, thank you!" answered May, opening her eyes in surprise. "If I do go out, it will only be to take a turn in the square with the children. This frock will do quite well."

Smithson retired. And then Harold, who was engaged in a somewhat languid struggle with a French verb, looked up savagely, and said—

"I hate Mr. Bragg."

Wilfred, seated at the table with a big book before him, which was supposed to convey useful knowledge by means of coloured illustrations, immediately echoed—

"I hate Mr. Bragg."

"Hush, hush! That will never do!" said May. "Little boys musn't hate anybody. Besides, Mr. Bragg is a very good, kind man. Why should you dislike him?"

"Because he's going to take you away," answered Harold slowly.

"Nonsense! I dare say Mr. Bragg will not ask to see me at all. And if he does, I shall not be away above a few minutes."

"Shan't you?" asked Harold doubtfully.

"Of course not! What have you got into your head?"

"Yesterday, when they didn't think I was listening, I heard Smithson say to Cécile—"

May stopped the child decisively. "Hush, Harold! You know I never allow you to repeat the tittle-tattle of the nursery. And I am shocked to hear that you listened to what was not intended for your ears. That is not like a gentleman. You know we agreed that you are to be a real gentleman when you grow up—that is, a man of honour."

"I didn't listen!" cried Wilfred eagerly.

"I am glad you did not."

"No, I didn't listen, Cousin May. I was in Cyril's room. Cyril gave me a long, long piece of string;—ever so long!"

May laughed. "Your virtue is not of a difficult kind, Master Willy! You never do any mischief that is quite out of your reach." Then, seeing that Harold looked still crest-fallen, she kissed his forehead, and said kindly, "And Harold will not listen again. He did not remember that it is dishonourable."

The child was silent, with his eyes cast down on his lesson-book, for a while. Then he raised them, and looking searchingly at May, said, "I say, Cousin May, I mean to marry you when I grow up."

"And so do I!" said Wilfred, determined not to be outdone.

"Very well. But I couldn't think of marrying any one who did not know his French verbs. So you had better learn that one at once."

Harold's naturally rather dull and heavy face grew suddenly bright; and he settled himself to his lesson with a little shrug, and a shake like a puppy. "No; you wouldn't marry any one who didn't know French, would you?" said he emphatically.

"And I know F'ench!" pleaded Wilfred.

"There now, be quiet, both of you, and let me finish my letter," said May. And there was nearly unbroken silence among them.

Meantime Mr. Bragg was having an interview with Mrs. Dormer-Smith. He had gradually made up his mind to put the same question to her that he had put to Mrs. Dobbs: namely, whether May were free to receive his proposals. He could not help being uneasy about young Bransby's relations with May. Mrs. Dobbs, it was true, had denied that her granddaughter thought of him at all; and Mr. Bragg did not doubt Mrs. Dobbs's veracity. But he underrated her sagacity; or, rather, her opportunities for knowing the truth. She lived very much outside of May's world. She might divine the state of May's feelings, and yet be mistaken as to their object. The story he had heard of young Bransby's having been rejected by Miss Cheffington could not be true; for was not young Bransby a constant visitor at her aunt's house—frequenting it on a footing of familiarity—talking to May herself with a certain air of confidential understanding? He had observed this particularly during last night's dinner.

But if, on the other hand, the possibility of Mrs. Dobbs being mistaken on this question were once admitted, all sorts of other possibilities poured in after it as by a sluice-gate, and lifted Mr. Bragg's hopes to a higher level. At any rate, he resolved to take some decisive step. Time had been lost already. He had told Mrs. Dobbs that he was too old to trust to the day after to-morrow; and that was now three months ago! Hence his visit to Mrs. Dormer-Smith by appointment—an appointment made verbally the preceding evening, with the request that she would mention it to no one; least of all to Miss Cheffington.

Aunt Pauline was, of course, quite sure beforehand what was to be the subject of their conversation; and was not in the least surprised (although inwardly much elated) when Mr. Bragg broached it.

"Understand me, ma'am," said Mr. Bragg. "I only wish you to tell me truly whether, according to the best of your belief, Miss C.'s affections are engaged. I ask no questions beyond that. I don't want to pry."

"Engaged! Oh dear, no; I assure you—"

"Excuse me, ma'am. But I mean a little more than that," said Mr. Bragg, slightly hastening the steady stride of his speech, lest she should interrupt him again. "Of course, I don't expect you to be inside of your niece's heart. A deal of uncertainty must prevail in what you may call assaying any human being's feelings. You may use the wrong test for one thing. But ladies are keen observers; specially where they like—or, for the matter of that, dislike—any one very much. And what I want to know is this: Have you any reason to think Miss C. is in love with any one?"

Mrs. Dormer-Smith, who was listening with a bland smile, almost started at this crude inquiry. She felt the need of all her self-command to preserve that repose of manner which she considered essential to good-breeding. But she answered gently, though firmly—

"My dear Mr. Bragg, that is out of the question. My niece is entirely disengaged. A girl of her birth and breeding is not likely to entertain any vulgar kind of romance in secret!"

"Thank you, ma'am," said Mr. Bragg. Then he added ponderingly, "It might not be vulgar, though!"

Mrs. Dormer-Smith privately thought Mr. Bragg no competent judge of what might, or might not, be vulgar in a Cheffington. She merely replied, with a certain suave dignity, referring to a former speech of his—

"Do I understand rightly that you desire to speak with Miss Cheffington yourself?"

"If you please, ma'am. Yes; I think I should like to go through with it."

"I will send for her to come here, Mr. Bragg."

She rang the bell and gave her orders; and during the pause which ensued, neither she nor Mr. Bragg spoke a word. He was absorbed in his own thoughts, and by no means as fully master of himself as usual. She was plaintively regretting that May had refused to change her morning frock for something more becoming. "Not that it can be of vital importance now," thought Mrs. Dormer-Smith, faintly smiling to herself, with half-closed eyes.

Presently the door opened, and May stood on the threshold.

"Come in, darling," said her aunt. "Mr. Bragg wishes to speak with you. And I will only assure you that he does so with my and your uncle's full knowledge and approbation." With that, Aunt Pauline glided into the back drawing-room, and withdrew by a door opening on to the staircase, which she shut behind her, immensely to May's surprise.

All at once a nameless dread came over the girl, chilling her like a cold wind. They had some bad news to give her of Owen! She turned suddenly so deadly pale as to startle Mr. Bragg; and looking up at him with piteous, frightened eyes, stammered faintly, "What is the matter?"

"Nothing at all! Nothing is the matter that need frighten you, my dear young lady. Lord bless me, you look quite scared!"

His genuine tone reassured her. And the colour began to return to lips and cheeks. But the wilful blood now rushed too hotly into her face. Her second thought was, "They have found out my engagement to Owen!" And although this contingency could be confronted with a very different feeling, and with sufficient courage, yet she could not control the tell-tale blush.

"Just you sit down there, and don't worrit yourself, Miss Cheffington," said Mr. Bragg. In his earnestness he reverted to the phraseology of his early days. "There's no hurry in the world. If you was startled, just you take your own time to come round."

"Thank you," answered May, dropping into the armchair he pushed forward.

"I am very sorry to have alarmed you," she said. "I'm afraid I must be growing nervous! I never thought I should be able to lay claim to that interesting malady."

Although she smiled, and tried to speak playfully, she had really been shaken, and she profited by the advice, which Mr. Bragg repeated, to "sit still, and take her own time about coming round."

By-and-by she said, almost in her usual voice, "Will you not sit down, Mr. Bragg? I am quite ready to listen to you."

Mr. Bragg hesitated a moment. He would have preferred to stand. He would have felt more at his ease, so. But, looking down on the slight young figure before him, it occurred to him that it would be—in some vaguely-felt way—taking an unfair advantage of the girl to dominate her by his tall stature. So he brought himself nearer to her level by sitting down on an ottoman opposite, and not very near to her.

"I suppose," said he, after a little silence, during which he looked down with an intent and anxious frown at the floor, "I suppose you can't give a guess at what I'm going to say?"

May believed she had guessed it already. But she answered, "I would rather not guess, please. I would rather that you told me."

"Well, perhaps it may simplify matters if I mention that I have had some conversation on the subject with Mrs. Dobbs."

"With Granny?" exclaimed May, looking full at him in profound astonishment.

"Yes; it's some little while ago, now. Mrs. Dobbs spoke very straightforward, and very kind, too; but I'm bound to say she did not give me any encouragement."

May stared at him in a kind of fascination. She could not remove her eyes from his face. And she began to perceive a dreadful clear-sightedness dawning above the confusion of her thoughts.

Mr. Bragg was not looking at her. He was leaning a little forward, with his arms resting on his knees, and his hands loosely clasped together. He went on speaking in a ruminating way; sometimes emphasizing his phrase by a slight movement from the wrist of his clasped hands, and as if he were, with some difficulty, reading off the words he was uttering from the Oriental rug at his feet.

"You see, Miss Cheffington, of course I'm aware there's a great difference in years. But that's not the biggest difference in reality. I don't believe myself that I'm so very much older in some ways than I was at five-and-twenty. I was always a steady kind of a chap, and I never had much to say for myself—never was what you might call lively, you know."

May sat spell-bound; looking at him fixedly, and with that dawn of clear-sightedness rapidly illumining many things, to her unspeakable consternation.

"No; it isn't the years that make the biggest difference. I'm below you in education, of course, Miss Cheffington, and in a deal besides, no doubt. But I can be trusted to mean all I say—though I'm not able to say all I mean, by a long chalk."

As he said this he raised his eyes for the first time, and looked at her. She was still regarding him with the same fascinated, almost helpless, gaze. But when she met his clear, honest, grey eyes, with a wistful expression in them which was pathetically contrasted with the massive strength of his head and face, she was suddenly inspired to say—

"Please, Mr. Bragg, will you hear me? I want to tell you something before you—before you say any more. I think you are my friend, and if you don't mind, I should like to tell you a secret. May I?"

He nodded, keeping his eyes on her now steadily.

"Well, I—I hope you will forgive me for troubling you with my confidence. I know you will respect it. If I had not such a high esteem and regard for you I—I could not say it." She stopped an instant, there was a choking feeling in her throat. She paused, mastered it, and went on. "I have promised to marry some one whom I love very much, and no one knows about it but Granny."

When she had spoken, she hid her hot face in her hands, and cried silently.

There was absolute stillness in the room for some minutes. At length she looked up and saw Mr. Bragg still sitting as before, with loosely clasped hands and downcast eyes. May rose to her feet, and said timidly, "I hope you are not angry with me for—for telling you?"

Mr. Bragg stood up also, and placing one broad, powerful hand on her head, as a father might have done, looked down gravely at her upturned face.

"Angry! Lord bless you, my child, what must I be made of to be angry with you?"

"Oh, thank you, Mr. Bragg! And will you promise—but I know you will—not to betray me?"

He did not notice this question. His mind was working uneasily. He thrust his hands into his pockets, and walked to the other side of the room and back, before saying—

"This person that you've promised to marry, is he one that your people here"—he jerked his head over his shoulder in the direction in which Mrs. Dormer-Smith had disappeared—"would approve of?"

"Oh, yes!" answered May. Then she added, not quite so confidently, "I think so. At any rate, I am very proud to be loved by him."

"And Mrs. Dobbs—"

"Oh, of course, dear Granny thinks no one could be too good for me," said May apologetically. "But she knows his worth."

"Will you please tell me how long Mrs. Dobbs has known of this?" asked Mr. Bragg, with a touch of sternness.

"Known? She knew, of course, as soon as I knew myself—on the twenty-seventh of last September," answered poor May, with damask-rose cheeks.

Mr. Bragg made a mental calculation of dates. His face relaxed; and he now replied to May's previous question.

"Yes, of course, I'll promise not to say a word till you give me leave. Especially since Mrs. Dobbs knows all about it. Otherwise, you're young to guide yourself entirely in a matter so serious as this is."

She thanked him again, and dried some stray tear-drops that hung on her pretty eyelashes.

He stood for a moment looking at her intently. But there was nothing in his gaze to startle her maiden innocence, or make her shrink from him; it was an honest, earnest, kindly, though melancholy look.

"Well," said he at last, "you're not so curious as some young ladies. You haven't asked me what it was I was going to say to you."

"I dare say it was nothing serious," she answered quickly. "In any case I am quite sure you will say, and leave unsaid, all that is right."

"That's a—what you might call a pretty large order, Miss Cheffington. I'm an awkward brute sometimes, I dare say, but I'll tell you this much: If I don't say what I was going to say, it isn't from pride. I have had that feeling, but I haven't it now, in talking to you. No, it isn't from pride, but because I want you and me to be friends—downright good friends, you know. And, perhaps, it would be more agreeable for you not to have anything concerning me in your memory that you'd wish to be what you might call sponged out of the record. I appreciate your behaviour, Miss Cheffington. You acted generous, and like the noble-hearted young lady I've always thought you, when you told me that secret of yours. Why now—Come, come, don't you fret yourself!" he exclaimed softly, for the tears were again trickling down her cheeks.

"You are so—so very kind and good to me!" she said brokenly.

"Lord bless me, what else could I be? There, there, don't you vex yourself by fancying me cast down or disappointed about—anything in particular. A man doesn't come to my age without getting used to disappointments, big and little."

He took up his hat and stopped her by a gesture as she moved towards the bell.

"No; don't ring, please! I've got an appointment in the City, and not much time to spare if I walk it. So I'll just let myself out quietly, without disturbing anybody. You can mention to your aunt that I shall have the honour of calling on her again very soon. Good-bye, Miss Cheffington."

May held out her hand. He touched it very lightly with his fingers, and then relinquished it silently.

"You are sure," she said pleadingly, "you are quite sure you are not angry with me?"

"There ain't a many things I'm so sure of as I am of that," answered Mr. Bragg, in his ordinary quiet tones. And then he opened the door and was gone.

He went down the stairs, and through the hall, and into the street without being challenged. He shut the street door softly behind him, with a kind of instinct of escape; and marched away rather quickly, but square and steady as ever.

After a while he looked at his watch, hesitated, and finally hailed a hansom cab.

"Poultry! You can take it easy. I'm not in a hurry," he said to the driver, as he got into the vehicle.

Then Mr. Bragg leaned back, and began to think. He had a habit of frequently closing his eyes when meditating, and this habit it was which had impelled him to get into a cab, since a pedestrian in the streets of London could only indulge in it at the risk of his life; and Mr. Bragg had no—not even the most passing—temptation to suicide. He shut his eyes tight now, tilted his hat backward from his forehead, and reviewed the situation.

He had behaved very well to May, and was conscious of having behaved well to her; she deserved the best and most considerate treatment; but Mr. Bragg was no angel, and he was extremely angry with Mrs. Dormer-Smith. He felt some irritation—very unreasonably, as he would by-and-by acknowledge—against Mrs. Dobbs—she had been rather exasperatingly in the right. But Mrs. Dormer-Smith had been most exasperatingly in the wrong, and he was very angry with her. Why had she not confessed that she knew nothing at all about her niece's feelings? It was clear she was quite ignorant of them. She had only to say that she could not undertake to answer for May; that would at least have been honest!

"I dare say I might have spoken, all the same," Mr. Bragg admitted to himself. "I think p'r'aps I should. I'd got to that point where a man must know for himself what the answer is to that question, and when 'likely' or 'unlikely' won't serve his turn. But I could ha' managed different. I needn't have looked like a Tomnoddy. Trotted out there—making a reg'lar show of a man; not a doubt but what that flunkey knew all about it. Woman's a fool!"

Mr. Bragg's indignation rolled off like thunder in these broken growlings. And beneath it all—deeper than all—there lay an aching sorrow. It would not break his heart, as he knew; it might not even spoil his dinner; but it was a real sorrow, nevertheless. In the moment of assuring him that he must not hope to win her, May had seemed to him better worth winning than ever; her soft touch had opened a long sealed-up spring of tenderness. There was some rough poetry within him, none the less pathetic because he knew thoroughly, sensitively, how unable he was to give it expression, and how ridiculous the mere suggestion of his trying to do so would seem to most people. He resolutely refrained as much as possible from letting his mind busy itself with these hidden feelings; his very thoughts seemed to hurt them at that moment.

He preferred to nurse his wrath against Mrs. Dormer-Smith, and to resent her having betrayed him into an undignified position. Mr. Bragg had been prosperous and powerful for many years, and the sense of being balked was very irksome to him; more irksome than in the days of his poverty, when youth and hope were elastic, and battle seemed a not unwelcome condition of existence.

But before he reached the end of his eastward journey Mr. Bragg began to speculate about the man whom May loved. In spite of Mrs. Dobbs's emphatic denial, he could not dismiss the idea that Theodore Bransby was the man. He had gathered the impression that Mrs. Dobbs did not like Theodore, and he remembered May's deprecating words, "Granny would not think any one too good for me!" which seemed to indicate that Mrs. Dobbs had not hailed the engagement with rapture. Thinking over the dates, he concluded—quite correctly—that May's lover, whoever he might be, had declared himself not long after his (Bragg's) interview with Mrs. Dobbs. Now, Theodore Bransby had been in Oldchester at that time, as he well remembered.

Why Theodore, if it were he, should keep his engagement secret from the Dormer-Smiths, was not easily explicable. But Mr. Bragg knew the young man's political projects; and it might be that Theodore would wish to approach May's family armed with all the importance which a successful electoral campaign would give him. One thing Mr. Bragg felt tolerably sure of—that Aunt Pauline would regret acutely the declension from a nephew-in-law with fifty thousand a year, to one whose income did not count as many hundreds! It was, perhaps, rather agreeable to Mr. Bragg to think of this. It was certainly a comfort to him to be able to dislike May's lover on independent grounds. He had always entertained an antipathy towards the young man; and, however sincere and tender his interest in May Cheffington might be, it did not modify, by a hair's breadth, his opinion of young Bransby.

"And, after all, it may not be him!" said Mr. Bragg, reflectively and ungrammatically. "But if it isn't him, it can't be anybody I know."

The person he had appointed to meet in the City was an Oldchester man; and when the business part of their interview was concluded, he said to Mr. Bragg—

"There's bad news from Combe Park. Haven't you heard? Oh! why they say Mr. Lucius Cheffington can't live many days. So that scamp, What's-his-name, the nephew, will come in for it all. The old lord's awfully savage, I'm told. Shouldn't wonder if it balks young Bransby's hopes of getting his seat. Old Castlecombe won't like paying election expenses for him now. Great pity! He's a very rising young man, and a credit to Oldchester."

CHAPTER II.

When Mr. Bragg was gone, May felt a cowardly temptation to run away to her own room, and there recover her composure in solitude. But she reflected that that would be scarcely fair to her aunt, who, no doubt, was waiting with some impatience to hear the result of the interview. So she dried her eyes, and resolutely ascended the stairs to her aunt's room.

The gentle, refined voice which had once so charmed her (but which, as she had long since learned, could utter sentiments singularly at variance with its own sweetness) answered her tap at the door by saying, "Is that dear May? Come in." May entered, and saw her aunt reclining in a lounging chair by the fireside. A book lay open beside her; but she evidently had not been reading recently. She looked up at May's flushed face and tear-swollen eyes, and these traces of emotion seemed to her satisfactory indications of what had passed. "He has spoken! It's all right!" she said to herself. Then aloud, with a tender smile, holding out both her hands, "Well, darling?"

The softness of her tone had a perversely hardening effect on May. If her aunt had expected her to accept Mr. Bragg—and May was not dull enough to doubt this, now that her eyes were illumined by that dawn of clear-sightedness which had been so amazing to her—the least she could do was to be quiet and common-sensible about it. Any assumption of sentiment seemed to May to be sickening under the circumstances. So she answered dryly—

"Mr. Bragg desired me to tell you that he will have the honour of calling on you again before long."

"Is he gone?" asked Mrs. Dormer-Smith, with a momentary twinge of anxiety.

"Yes; he is gone. He had an appointment in the City, and was rather pressed for time; so he could not stay to take leave of you."

"Oh!" exclaimed her aunt, sinking back among her cushions with a smile, "I forgive him." Then seeing May turn away as if to leave the room, she suddenly sat up again, and said with an air of gentle reproach, "And have you nothing to say to me, dear May?"

"Nothing particular, Aunt Pauline."

"Nothing particular! I do not think that is very kindly said, May."

May's conscience told her the same thing. She had yielded to a movement of temper. The most sensitive chords in her own nature had been jarred, and were still quivering. But that was no reason why she should be unkind or uncivil to her aunt; she repented, and, with her usual impulsive candour, said—

"I beg your pardon, Aunt Pauline. I ought not to have answered you so."

"You have been agitated, dear child. Come here, and sit down by me. Now tell me, May—you surely will tell me—Mr. Bragg has proposed to you, has he not?"

"No, Aunt Pauline."

"What?"

Mrs. Dormer-Smith would have been shocked if she could have seen her own face in the glass at that moment. The vulgarest market-woman's countenance could not have expressed surprise and consternation more unrestrainedly.

"I think he, perhaps, would have asked me to marry him: but I stopped him."

"You stopped him?" echoed her aunt, with clasped hands. But a little gleam of hope revived her. The matter had been mismanaged in some way. May was so deplorably devoid of tact! All might yet be well. "And why, for pity's sake, May, did you stop him?"

"Because, as I could not accept him, Aunt Pauline, I wished to spare him as much as possible."

"Could not accept him! Good heavens, May, this is frightful! Have you lost your senses? Do you know who and what Mr. Bragg is?"

"He is a good, honest man; and I esteem him and like him."

"And is not that enough? Do you know that there are girls of—I won't say better family, but—higher rank than yours, who would give their ears to be—But it can't be! You are a foolish, inexperienced child, who don't understand your own good fortune. You cannot be allowed to throw away this splendid opportunity. I will write to Mr. Bragg myself, and—"

"Stay, Aunt Pauline. Please to understand that I will never, under any circumstances, dream of marrying Mr. Bragg. He is quite persuaded of this. He and I understand each other very well, and we mean to continue good friends; but pray do not lower your own dignity by writing to him on this subject!"

Mrs. Dormer-Smith burst into tears. "Go away, you ungrateful child," she said, from behind her pocket-handkerchief. "I could not have believed you would have behaved in this manner after all I have done for you!"

May would have been more distressed than she was had the spectacle of her aunt's tears been rarer. But she had seen Mrs. Dormer-Smith weep from, what seemed to her, very inadequate motives:—even once at the misfit of a new gown. Nevertheless, she tried to soothe her aunt.

"Please don't cry, Aunt Pauline. I can't bear you to think me ungrateful. But, after all, what have I done? I dare say—I am sure, indeed, that you are only anxious for my welfare. And what sort of a life could I expect if I married a man I could not love?"

"I beg you will not talk such nursery-maid's nonsense to me, May," returned her aunt, sprinkling some rose-water on her pocket-handkerchief, and dabbing her wet cheeks with it. "Could not love, indeed! Why could you not love him? Do you expect to rant through a grande passion like a heroine on the stage? I am shocked at you, May! Girls in your position owe a duty to society."

May knew that her aunt was unanswerable when she broached these mysterious dogmas about "society"—unanswerable, at all events, by her. She could as soon have attempted a theological argument with a devotee of Mumbo Jumbo. So she held her peace, and stood still, anxious to escape, and yet fearful of seeming to be unfeeling by going away at that moment. One idea at length suggested itself to her as a possible consolation for her aunt, and she proceeded to offer it with unreflecting rashness.

"But, Aunt Pauline," she said, "after all, you know, Mr. Bragg is a very low-born man. He was once a common artisan in Oldchester. And you remember you even thought Theodore Bransby presumptuous—"

The immediate reply to this well-meant suggestion was a fresh burst of tears. "You are too insupportable, May. One might suppose you to be an idiot! What has been the use of all my care, and my endeavours to make you look at things as a girl of your condition ought to look at them? Mr. Bragg could have placed you in a brilliant position. Now, I dare say, he will marry Felicia Hautenville. I have no doubt he will, and it will serve you right if he does. You think of no one but yourself. What do you suppose that worthy woman, Mrs. Dobbs, will say when she hears of your behaviour? After all the money she has spent on sending you to London!"

May turned round suddenly. "What do you say, Aunt Pauline?" she asked, almost breathlessly. "Granny has spent money to send me to London?"

Mrs. Dormer-Smith caught at a forlorn hope. Might it not be possible, even now, to influence May through her affection for her grandmother?

"Of course, May," she replied, with an injured air. "Where do you suppose the money came from? Your uncle and I, as you must be well aware, find it difficult enough to keep up our position in society, with Cyril to place in the world, and those two little boys to provide for!"

"But papa!" gasped May. "I thought my father was paying—"

"You chose to assume it. I never told you so. Mrs. Dobbs particularly wished us to keep the arrangement secret, and we did so. I appreciate her wisdom now in keeping it secret from you, May; for your conduct to-day shows you to be destitute of the most ordinary tact and prudence."

"And Granny—dear old Granny—has been depriving herself of money to keep me in town!" exclaimed the girl, still entirely possessed with this new revelation.

Mrs. Dormer-Smith gallantly tried to improve her opportunity. She raised herself into an upright posture in her chair, and said solemnly, "Yes, May; and a nice return you make for it! The good old creature, no doubt, has been pinching herself for years on your account. She has paid for your schooling, your dress, and everything; she even contrives, I dare say, by enduring some privations" (Mrs. Dormer-Smith did not in the least suppose this to be the case, but she felt it was a rhetorical "point," and likely to affect her niece), "she even contrives to give you a season in town, with charming toilettes from Amélie, and a presentation dress that a duke's daughter might have worn, and everything which a right-minded girl ought to appreciate—and this is her reward! You refuse one of the finest matches in England! I cannot believe you will persist in such wicked perversity, May," continued Pauline, rising to new heights of moral elevation. "No, I cannot believe you will be so ungrateful to that good old soul, and, indeed, I may say, to Providence! Really, there is something almost impious in it. Mrs. Dobbs does all she can to counteract the results of your father's unfortunate marriage—we all do all we can; circumstances are so ordered by a Superior Power as to give you the chance of catching—of attracting the regard of a man of princely fortune—you, rather than a dozen other girls whose people have been looking after him for the last three seasons, and all this you reject! Toss it away, like a baby with a toy! No, May; you are a Cheffington—you are my poor unfortunate brother's own flesh and blood, and I will not believe it of you." Then, sinking back in her chair, she added in a faint voice, "Go away now, if you please, and send Smithson to me. I shall have to speak to your uncle when he comes in, and I really dread it. He will be so shocked—so astonished! As for me, I am utterly hors de combat for the day, of course."

May willingly escaped to her own room, and locked herself in. Her thoughts were in a strange tumult, busied chiefly with this news about Mrs. Dobbs. Why had she not guessed it before? Was there any one in the world like that staunch, generous, unselfish woman? This explained her giving up her old, comfortable home in Friar's Row. This explained a hundred other circumstances. May thought, between laughing and crying, of Jo Weatherhead's eccentric eulogy on her grandmother as compared with classical heroines, and she longed to tell him that he was right. The full tide of love and sympathy and gratitude towards "Granny" rose in her breast above all other emotions, and, for the moment, even Mr. Bragg's wonderful proposals, and her aunt's still more wonderful reception of them, were forgotten. It even overflowed and temporarily obliterated impressions and feelings far keener than any which poor Mr. Bragg had power to awake in her heart.

What a fool's paradise had she been living in! And what a mistaken image of her father she had been cherishing all this time! He had contributed nothing to her support; he had coolly left the whole care of her to others; he had been thoroughly selfish and indifferent. Every one seemed selfish but Granny! One thing she hastily resolved on: not to remain another week in London at her grandmother's expense.

When Mr. Dormer-Smith came home, and was duly informed by his wife of May's incredible conduct, his dismay was nearly as great as Pauline's. Perhaps his surprise was even greater; for he had accepted his wife's assurances that May was quite prepared to give Mr. Bragg a favourable answer. He could not bring himself to regard May's behaviour with such lofty moral reprobation as his wife did, but he certainly thought the girl had acted foolishly, and even blameably.

Mr. Dormer-Smith was extremely anxious not to offend or disgust Mr. Bragg. To have a man of that wealth in the family might be the making of all their fortunes. Already Mr. Bragg's advice and assistance had profited him. He and his wife had even privately reckoned on Mr. Bragg's doing something handsome (in a testamentary way) for their younger children. May was very fond of her cousins, and what would a few thousands be to Mr. Bragg? Now the unexpected news which met him broke up all these glittering hopes, as a thaw melts the frost-diamonds.

"You must speak with her, Frederick. I have said all I can, and I really am not equal to another scene," said Pauline.

She had subsided into an attitude of calm despondency, and seemed to be supported chiefly by the sense of her own unappreciated merits. She did not mention that she had already written a private and confidential letter to Mr. Bragg, and despatched it by special messenger to the hotel where he usually stayed when in London.

Mr. Bragg had no town house, and the choosing and furnishing of a suitable mansion for him and his bride had been one of the rewards of virtue which Mrs. Dormer-Smith had, for some time past, been anticipating for herself. May was so young and inexperienced, and Mr. Bragg—dear, good, rich man!—had so little knowledge of the fashionable world, that Pauline confidently expected to be for some years to come the presiding genius of the elegant entertainments to which they would invite only the very best society. For—giving the rein to her fancy—Pauline had resolved that Mr. and Mrs. Bragg were to be extremely exclusive. A well-born girl who, without fortune or title, had succeeded in marrying a millionaire, might surely—if there were any poetical justice at all in the world—indulge herself in the refined pleasure of social selection, and quietly decline to receive those doubtful "Borderers" who made society, as Mrs. Griffin often complained, so sadly mixed!

All this was not to be relinquished without a struggle. Mrs. Dormer-Smith would do her duty to the last. Duty had commanded her to make an immediate appeal to Mr. Bragg not to take May's answer as final; but duty did not, she considered, require her to tell her husband anything about it until she saw how it turned out.

"You must see her, Frederick," repeated Mrs. Dormer-Smith. And Frederick accordingly sent for May to come and speak with him.

He awaited her in the drawing-room; and when May entered the room her eye fell on the easy-chair which Mr. Bragg had placed for her, standing out just where she had left it. The whole scene came back to her mind as vividly as if she saw it in a picture before her bodily eyes; and the colour rose to her forehead.

Her uncle went to her, and took her hand kindly. "Well, May," said he, "what is all this I hear?" He was leading her towards the armchair; but May avoided it, and took another seat, and Mr. Dormer-Smith dropped into the armchair opposite to her, himself.

In considering what could have been the motives which had induced her to reject Mr. Bragg, he had prepared himself to listen to some—perhaps foolishly—romantic talk on May's part. Mr. Bragg certainly could not, by any stretch of friendship, be considered romantic. But Uncle Frederick would try to show his niece how much sounder and solider a foundation for domestic happiness Mr. Bragg was able to offer her than any amount of the qualities which go to make up a young lady's hero of romance.

What he was not at all prepared for was May's saying earnestly, as she leant forward with clasped hands, "Oh, Uncle Frederick what is all this I hear? My dear, good grandmother has been impoverishing herself to pay for keeping me in London! Why did you not tell me the truth? Nothing should have induced me to accept such a sacrifice!"

Mr. Dormer-Smith was not a ready or flexible man by nature; and it took him a minute or so to alter the sight, so to speak, of the big gun he had been getting into position to mow down May's resistance against making a splendid marriage.

"Why—eh? Oh, Mrs. Dobbs's allowance! Oh yes. Well, my dear, you have pretty well answered your own question. If you had known, you would not have consented to come to town, and take your proper place in society. Your aunt considered it most important that you should do so. And I'm sure, May, you must allow that she has done her very best for you in every way."

"Her very best!" thought May; "yes, perhaps!" Then she said aloud, "Aunt Pauline has been very kind to me. But how could there be any 'proper place' for me in society, unless I could honestly afford to take it? To get it by imposing privations on my grandmother, who is not bound, except by her own abundant goodness, to do anything for me at all—this surely could not be right or just, could it?"

Mr. Dormer-Smith was not prepared with a cogent answer on the spur of the moment. So he fell back on murmuring some faint echoes of his wife's maxims about "duty to society." But he had not Pauline's sincere convictions on the subject, and did it but feebly.

"And, oh, Uncle Frederick," proceeded May; "what a mean impostor I have been all this time!"

"Impostor, my dear? No, no; that's nonsense, you know."

He was rather relieved to find May talking nonsense. That seemed much more normal and natural in a girl of her age than being so deuced logical and high-strung, and that sort of thing.

"That," he repeated firmly, "is really nonsense."

"But, Uncle Frederick, I was appearing before everybody under false pretences. People thought—I thought myself—that my father supplied all my expenses."

Mr. Dormer-Smith pursed up his mouth and puffed out his breath with a little contemptuous sound. Then he answered—

"Your father! My dear May, your father hasn't paid a penny piece for you since you were seven years old."

May was silent for a minute or so. She could not help some bitter thoughts of her father, but it was not for her to utter them. At length she said—

"I cannot go on accepting my grandmother's sacrifice, Uncle Frederick. I will not."

It occurred to Mr. Dormer-Smith, as it had occurred to his wife, that May's affection for Mrs. Dobbs might supply the fulcrum they wanted for their lever. He answered—

"Well, my dear, I don't blame your feeling, though it is a little overstrained, perhaps. But you have it in your own power to more than pay back all Mrs. Dobbs has done for you."

"How?" asked May innocently.

"Why, I am sure Mr. Bragg would be only too delighted—"

"Oh, Mr. Bragg! I was not thinking of Mr. Bragg, and I would rather not talk of him just now."

This was a little too much. Mr. Dormer-Smith's face assumed a very serious, not to say severe, expression as he looked at his niece and said—

"Excuse me, May, but you must think of him, and talk of him also. That was the subject I sent for you to speak about. I don't know how we have drifted away from it. Your aunt tells me that you have not actually refused Mr. Bragg, but merely stopped him from proposing to you. Now, if that is the case, the matter is not past mending. No doubt Mr. Bragg may feel a little offended."

"He is not in the least offended," interposed May.

"Ah! Well, so much the better. But you can hardly expect me to believe that he particularly enjoyed the interview! Mr. Bragg is a person of a great deal of importance in the world, and not accustomed to be treated as if he were of no consequence. However," proceeded Mr. Dormer-Smith, relaxing into a milder tone, "I dare say he can make allowances for a young lady taken by surprise—it seems you did not expect his proposal?"

"Expect it! How on earth could I have expected it?"

"Some girls would. However, let us stick to the point. I don't think it is too late for you to make everything well again."

"Uncle Frederick, I am bound to assure you most positively that I can never marry Mr. Bragg."

"Now, don't be obstinate, May. What is your objection to him?"

The girl hesitated. Then she replied, looking up with pleading eyes, "How can I say, Uncle Frederick? One does not marry a man simply because one has no particular objection to him. Mr. Bragg is old enough to be my grandfather!"

"No; scarcely that. Look here, May, I have a great affection for you. You have been very good and kind to my little boys, and they doat on you. I am not ungrateful for all you have done for the children, although I may not have said much about it."

May was melted in an instant by these words of kindness, and said warmly, "And I am not ungrateful, Uncle Frederick. I know you mean well by me, and Aunt Pauline, too."

"Certainly we do. Naturally so! Well now, just listen to me, my dear. If you were my own daughter I should give you just the same advice. I should be very glad and thankful for a daughter of mine to marry Mr. Bragg. I know a great deal more of the world than you do—or ever will, please God!—for it isn't a very pleasant kind of knowledge—and I tell you honestly, there are very few men, young or old, in the society we frequent, whom I'd choose for your husband rather than Mr. Bragg. He is a little uneducated, and unpolished, of course. We needn't pretend not to know that. But he is a man of sound heart and sound principles—a man whose private life will bear looking into. I'm talking to you as if I really were your father, May; and I do assure you that I would not urge you to marry a man twice as rich as he is, if I knew him to be—to be what some men are, and what you in your innocence have no idea of. I want you to believe that, May."

"I do believe it, Uncle Frederick," sobbed May, taking his hand, and kissing it.

"There, there, my dear, don't cry! I couldn't talk in this way to many girls of your age; but you have so much sense and right feeling! I wanted you to understand that I'm not an altogether hard, worldly kind of man, ready to offer you up to Mammon—eh? Look here, May; I would stand by you against—against every one, if I thought you were going to be sacrificed. But you must trust a little to the experience of those older than yourself, my dear. Come, come, there now, don't distress yourself! You are not to be pressed and hurried, you know. You will think it all over quietly. Go to your own room and lie down a while. I will take care that you are not disturbed or worried in any way."

He led her gently to the door. She was now sobbing uncontrollably. She longed to tell her uncle the truth about her engagement, but she thought that loyalty to Owen and to her grandmother forbade her to speak out fully without their leave. As she was quitting the room, she turned round, and, making a strong effort to speak firmly, said—

"Uncle Frederick, I shall never, as long as I live, forget the kind words you have said to me. And, whatever happens, don't believe I am ungrateful."

"Well, Frederick?" said Mrs. Dormer-Smith, when her husband re-appeared in her room.

Frederick walked to the window, took out his pocket-handkerchief, and answered from behind it, rather huskily—

"Well, I don't know. I almost hope it may come right."

"Do you? Do you really? Well, that is a feeble ray of comfort. But it is rather too bad to have to undergo all this wear and tear of feeling, in order to secure that perverse child's fortune in spite of herself!"

There was a long pause, during which Mr. Dormer-Smith continued to look out of the window, and to blow his nose in a furtive kind of way. "I wonder—" he began slowly, and then stopped himself.

"You wonder—Frederick? Pray speak out! I assure you I am not able to stand much more suspense and anxiety."

"I was merely going to say, I wonder if there can be any one else."

"Any one else?"

"Any man she cares for."

"Good Heavens, Frederick, who should there be? Really, you are not very considerate to startle me with such extraordinary suppositions without the least preparation. There is no one, of course."

"You are sure?"

"I am sure there is no one possible. I know, of course, every man she has danced with, or who has paid her the smallest attention, and there is not one who could be thought of for a moment, even if Mr. Bragg did not exist. I should not hesitate to speak very strongly if I suspected her of any culpable folly of that kind. A girl without a farthing in the world! And her father, my poor unfortunate brother Augustus, in Heaven knows what dreadful position! That May, under all the circumstances, can behave in this way, is too intolerable. The more one thinks of it the more flagrant it seems. No sense of duty! No consideration for her family! I shall be compelled to say to her—"

Suddenly, in the midst of these fluent, softly uttered sentences, Mr. Dormer-Smith turned round, wiped his eyes, blew his nose defiantly, and said, with an explosion of feeling—

"The girl's a fine creature, and, by God, I won't have her baited!"

CHAPTER III.

Each mortal's private feelings are the measure of the importance of events to him. And it often happens that while our neighbours are pitying or envying us, on account of some circumstance which, all the world agrees, must have a weighty bearing on our fate, we are mainly indifferent to it, and are occupied with some inner grief or joy, which would seem to them very trivial.

To have received and rejected an offer of marriage from a man worth fifty thousand a year would have been deemed by most of May Cheffington's acquaintance about as important an event as could have happened to her—short of death! But to her it was absolutely as nothing, compared with the facts that Owen was on the point of returning to England, and that he was to live in Mrs. Bransby's house.

Why did this second fact seem to embitter the sweetness of the first?

No, it was not the fact, she told herself, that was bitter; the bitterness lay in the manner of its coming to her knowledge. Why had not Owen written to her? There could be no reason to conceal it! Of course, none! Owen was doing all that was right, no doubt. But to allow her to hear of this step for the first time from Theodore Bransby at a dinner-table conversation—this it was which irked her. So, at least, she had declared to herself last night. Then the tone in which her uncle and all of them had spoken of Mrs. Bransby and Owen had jarred upon her painfully. Theodore had not joined in the tasteless banter; but then Theodore's way of receiving it—with a partly stiff, partly deprecatory air, as though there could possibly be anything serious in it—was almost worse!

The pathway of life which had stretched so clear and fair before her but a short while ago, seemed now to have contracted into a tangled maze, in which she lost herself. The events of the morning had made May resolve that all secrecy as to her engagement must come to an end. She must see Owen immediately on his arrival in London. But how to do so? She did not know whether he was or was not in England at that very moment! Well, at all events she knew Mrs. Bransby's address, and could write to him there.

This thought gave her a pang. And the pang was intensified by the sudden and vivid perception—as one sees a whole landscape by a lightning-flash out of a black sky—that it was caused by jealousy!

Jealousy! She, May Cheffington, jealous—and of Owen? Yes; it might be painful, humiliating, incredible, but it was true. The flash had been inexorably sharp and clear.

To young creatures, every revelation that they—even they—are subject to the common woes, pains, and passions of humanity about which they may have talked glibly enough, is an amazement and a shock. Still earlier in our earthly course we doubt that Death himself can touch us. What child ever realizes that it must die? It is only after many lessons that we begin to accept our share of mortal frailties and afflictions as a matter of course.

Poor May felt sick at heart. Oh, if she could but see Granny! She longed for the motherly affection which had never failed her since the day her father left her—a rather forlorn little waif, whom no one seemed ready to love or welcome—in the old house in Friar's Row. She thought that to sit quite still and silent by Granny's knee, while Granny's kind old hand softly stroked her hair, would charm away all her troubles, or at least lull them to sleep.

But for the present she could not rest. When she left her uncle, and felt secure from interruption in her own room, she sat down and wrote two letters. The first was to Owen, begging him to come and see her without delay, and at the same time telling him that circumstances had arisen which made it desirable to declare their engagement. The second letter was to Granny.

To Granny she poured out her gratitude. She thanked her and scolded her in a breath. Who had ever been so generous, and so careful to conceal their generosity? And yet Granny had done very wrong to make such a sacrifice as was involved in giving up the old home in Friar's Row.

"Had I known this a week ago," wrote May, "I do believe I should have tried to coax Mr. Bragg into breaking the lease, and making you go back to the old house which you loved. But I cannot ask any favour of Mr. Bragg now!" Then she told her grandmother all about her interview with Mr. Bragg, and her aunt's bitter disappointment, and her uncle's kind behaviour, although she could see that he was disappointed too. "I wonder," she added, "if you will be as astonished as I was? Perhaps not. I remember some things you said when I told you my grand scheme for marrying Miss Patty! Oh, dear me, I feel like some one who has been walking in his sleep—calmly and unconsciously tripping over the most insecure places. But now I have been suddenly awakened, and I feel chilly, and frightened, and all astray."

When she had written them, she resolved to post the letters herself. Since she had volunteered to take her little cousins out for a walk occasionally, the stringent rule which forbade her to leave the house unattended by a servant had been relaxed—it was so very convenient to get rid of the little boys for an hour or two at a time! It left Cécile free to do a great deal of needlework, a large proportion of it expended on the alteration and re-trimming, and so forth, of May's own toilettes. Mrs. Dormer-Smith was strictly conscientious as to that; and since May never went beyond the limits of the neighbouring square, there could be no objection to the arrangement. One point, however, Aunt Pauline had insisted on—that these walks should always take place in the morning, or, at all events, during that portion of the day which did duty for the morning in her vocabulary. The proprieties greatly depend, as we know, on chronology; and many things which are permissible before luncheon become taboo immediately after it.

By the time May had finished her letters, however, it was well on in the afternoon. Carriages were rolling through the fashionable quarters of the town, and the footman's rat-tat-tat sounded monotonously like a gigantic tam-tam, sacred to the worship of society.

May went downstairs, and, opening the hall-door, found herself in the street alone, for the first time since she had lived under her aunt's roof. There was a pillar letter-box, she knew, not far distant. To this she proceeded, and dropped her letters into it. It had been a fine day for a London winter; but the last faint glimmer of daylight had almost disappeared as she turned to go back home.

There was an assemblage of vehicles waiting before a house which she had passed on her way to the post-box. Now, as she returned, there was a stir among them. Servants were calling up the coachmen, and opening and shutting carriage doors. A number of fashionably dressed persons, mostly women, came down the steps of the house and drove away. May paused a moment to let a couple of ladies sweep past her on their way to their carriage. As she did so, she heard her name called; and, looking round, she saw Clara Bertram's face at the window of a cab drawn up near the kerbstone.

"Is it really you?" exclaimed Clara, as they shook hands. "I could scarcely believe my eyes! What are you doing here alone?"

"I have been posting some letters." Then, reading an expression of surprise in the other girl's eyes, she added quickly, "You wonder why I should have done so myself. For a simple reason: I did not wish the address of one of them to be seen. But Granny knows all about it."

"I am quite sure, dear, you have some good reason for what you have done," answered Clara, in her quiet, sincere tones.

"And you?" asked May. "What are you doing here?"

"I have been singing at a matinée in that house. I was just about to drive off, when I caught a glimpse of you. I was not sure that it was not your ghost in the dusk!"

"I suppose you are constantly engaged now?"

"Yes; I have a great deal to do."

"Oh, I hear of you. Your praises are in every one's mouth. Lady Moppett declares you are rapidly becoming the first concert singer of the day. She is as proud of you as if she had invented you! Indeed, she does say you are her 'discovery': as if you were a Polynesian island! I could find it in my heart to envy you, Clara. It must be so glorious to be independent, and earn one's own living!"

Clara smiled a faint little smile. "I am thankful to be able to earn something," she said. "But I don't think I should care so much about it if it were only for myself."

"No, of course, dear! I know," rejoined May quickly. She had been told that the young singer entirely supported an invalid father and sister. Then she added, "Your voice is a great gift. There are so few things a woman can do to earn money."

"Why, one would suppose that you wanted to earn money!" said Clara, smiling.

"Perhaps."

Clara looked more closely at her friend. The street lamps were now lighted, and she could see May's face distinctly. "You are not looking well, dear," she exclaimed. "You seem fagged."

"I am sick of London. I want to go home to Granny and be at peace," answered May wearily. Then she went on quickly, to stave off any possible questionings as to her state of mind. "But I must return for the present to my aunt's house. Good-bye."

"Stay!" cried Clara. "Will you not get into the cab, and let me drive you home?"

"Drive! It is an affair of some two or three minutes at most."

"Well, then, if you have half an hour to spare, let me drive you round the square, and then drop you at home. I have been wanting for three or four days past to speak to you quietly. I can't bear to lose this rare opportunity. We do not meet very often." Then seeing that her friend hesitated, she asked, "Are you thinking about the cost of the cab for me?"

"Yes," answered May frankly.

"I thought so! That is just like you. But, indeed, you need have no scruples. The cab is engaged for the afternoon. When I sing at people's houses, unless they send a carriage for me, the cab-fare is 'considered in my wages.' Do come in!"

May complied, and the cab moved away slowly.

When they had proceeded a few yards, Clara said, "I wanted to tell you—I think it right to tell you—something I have learned on good authority. Your father—I hope it won't distress you—is really married."

May's first thought was that here again her Aunt Pauline had deceived her!

"Are you sure?" she asked.

"Yes, I think I may say so."

"And how did you learn it?"

"From Valli."

"Oh, from Signor Valli! But you told me he was not to be trusted."

"In some ways not. But I do not doubt what he says on this subject. He has no motive to invent the information. He cares nothing about the matter—except that I think he rather likes La—Mrs. Cheffington than not."

"Is she a foreigner?" asked May, with a little more interest than she had hitherto shown. Her listless way of receiving the news had surprised her friend.

"Yes, an Italian. At least, she is Italian by language, if not by law; for she comes from Trieste. But she is almost Cosmopolitan; for she has travelled about the world a great deal. She is—or was—an opera-singer. Her name in the theatre is Bianca Moretti. She was rather celebrated at one time." Clara paused a moment, and then added, "I hope this news does not grieve you, dear?"

"No," answered May dreamily, "it does not grieve me. If my father is content, why should I grieve? He and I have been parted—in spirit as well as body—for so many years, that his marriage can make but little difference to me."

"I was afraid you might feel—Of course, Captain Cheffington's family will look on it as a dreadful mésalliance."

May was silent for a few minutes. Then she said a very unexpected thing—

"Poor woman! I hope he is good to her!"

"I suppose," said Clara, rather hesitatingly, "that the reason why Captain Cheffington has not announced his marriage to his relations is that he thinks they would object to receive an opera-singer."

"Possibly," answered May. (In her heart she thought, "The reason is that he cares nothing for any of us.")

"It must be that," proceeded Clara. "For as far as I can make out there seems to be no concealment about it in Brussels."

Then they arrived at Mrs. Dormer-Smith's house, and May alighted and bade her friend farewell.

"Thank you, Clara," she said, "for telling me the truth. I loathe mysteries and concealments. When one thinks of it, they are despicable."

"Unless when one conceals something to shield others," suggested Clara gently.

She had told her friend what she believed to be the truth so far as the fact of her father's marriage was concerned. But she had not given her all the details and comments which Signor Valli had imparted to her on the subject. His view of the matter was not flattering to Captain Cheffington. Valli declared, with cynical plainness of speech, that Captain Cheffington had married La Bianca merely to have the right to confiscate her professional earnings. Latterly these had become very scanty. La Bianca did not grow younger, and her voice was rapidly failing her. A good deal of gambling had gone on in her house at one time. But it had been put a stop to—or, at least, shorn of its former proportions by the ugly incident of which Miss Polly Piper had brought back a version to Oldchester. Since that, things had not gone well with the Cheffington ménage. Captain Cheffington had become insupportable, irritable, impossible! He was, moreover, a malade imaginaire; a querulous, selfish, tyrannous fellow; always bewailing his hard fate, and the sacrifice he had made in so far derogating from his rank as to marry an opera-singer. La Bianca was a slave to his caprices. To be sure she was not precisely a lamb. There were occasions when she flamed up, and made quarrels and scenes.

"But," said Signor Valli, "he is an enormous egoist, and, with a woman, the bigger egoist you are, the surer to subjugate her. La Bianca would have stabbed a man who loved her devotedly, for half the ill-treatment she endures from that cold, stiff ramrod of an Englishman."

Such was Vincenzo Valli's version of the case; and Clara Bertram, in listening to him, believed that, in the main, it was a true one. Valli had recently been in Brussels, where he had seen the Cheffingtons; and one or two other foreign musicians whom she knew had come upon them from time to time, and had given substantially the same account of them. As to persons in the rank of life to which Captain Cheffington still claimed to belong, they were no more likely to come across him now than if he were living on the top of the Andes.

May went into the house wearily. In the hall she met her uncle Frederick, who had just come in, and had seen the cab drive away.

"Who was that with you, May?" he asked, in some surprise.

"It was Miss Bertram," she answered. Then she asked her uncle to step for a moment into the dining-room. When he had done so, and closed the door, she said quietly, "My father is married to a foreign opera-singer; they are living in Brussels. Did you and Aunt Pauline know this?"

"Know it? Certainly not!"

May was relieved to hear this, and drew a long breath. The sensation of living in an atmosphere of deception had oppressed her almost with a feeling of physical suffocation. She then told her uncle all that Clara Bertram had said.

Mr. Dormer-Smith puckered his brows, and looked more disturbed than she had expected. "This will be another blow for your aunt," he said gloomily.

"I don't see why Aunt Pauline should distress herself," she answered coldly; "my father is not likely to trouble her. Married or unmarried, my father seems determined to keep aloof from us all." Then she went to her own room.

Mr. Dormer-Smith shrank from communicating this news to his wife, and as he went upstairs he anticipated a disagreeable scene. He did not very greatly care about the matter himself, for he agreed with May that it was unlikely Augustus would trouble any of the family with his presence; and to keep away was all that he required of his brother-in-law. On entering his wife's room, he found her still in a morning wrapper, reclining on her long chair; but her hair had been dressed, and she announced her intention of coming down to dinner. Her countenance, too, wore an unexpected expression of placidity, almost cheerfulness. The country post had arrived, and there were several letters scattered on a little table by Mrs. Dormer-Smith's elbow.

Her husband went and placed himself with his back to the fire, which was burning with a pleasant glow in the grate. "Well," he said, in a sympathizing tone, to his wife, "how are you feeling now, Pauline?"

They had not met since his outburst about May, and he had been rather nervously uncertain of his reception. Pauline never sulked, never stormed, and rarely scolded. But when she felt herself to be injured, she would be overpoweringly plaintive. Her plaintiveness seemed to wrap you round, and damp you, and chill you to the bone, like a Scotch mist, and when used retributively was felt—by her husband, at all events—to be very terrible. But on this occasion, as has been said, there was a certain mild serenity in her face which was reassuring.

"Thanks, Frederick," she answered. "There seems to be a little less pressure on the brain. Smithson bathed my forehead for three-quarters of an hour after you were gone."

Mr. Dormer-Smith hastened to change the subject. "Post in, I see," he said. "Any news?"

"I have a very nice letter from Constance Hadlow," answered Pauline, with her eyes absently fixed on the fire. "How thoughtful that girl is! What tact! What proper feeling! Ah! the contrast between her and May is painful at times."

Mr. Dormer-Smith made a little inarticulate sound, which might mean anything. Despite her beauty, which he admired, Miss Hadlow was no great favourite of his. But he would not imperil the present calm in his domestic atmosphere by saying so.

"Misfortunes," pursued Pauline, still gazing at the fire, "never come singly, they say; and really I believe it."

"Does Miss Hadlow announce any misfortune?"

"Oh no!—at least, we are bound not to look on it as a misfortune. Who could wish him to linger, poor fellow? She is staying near Combe Park, and she says Lucius has been quite given up by the doctors. It is a question of days—perhaps of hours."

"No? By George! Poor old Lucius!" returned Mr. Dormer-Smith, with a touch of real feeling in his tone.

"Of course, this will make an immense difference in May's prospects. I don't mean to say that she will easily find another millionaire, with such extraordinarily liberal ideas about settlements as Mr. Bragg hinted to me this morning; that is, humanly speaking, not possible," said Mrs. Dormer-Smith solemnly. "Still, the affair may not be such an irretrievable disaster as we feared."

"How do you mean?" asked Frederick, whose mind, as we know, moved rather slowly.

"It must make a difference to her," repeated his wife in a musing tone. "The only child and heiress of the future Viscount Castlecombe, of course—"

"By George! I didn't think of that at the moment. Yes, Gus is the next. I suppose that's quite certain?"

Mrs. Dormer-Smith did not even condescend to answer this query, but merely raised her eyebrows with a superior and melancholy smile.

Frederick pondered a minute or so; then he said, "You say 'heiress,' but I don't think your uncle would leave Gus a pound more than he couldn't help leaving him."

"I fear that is likely. Still, there is much of the land that must come to Augustus, and Uncle George has enormously improved the estate. Do you know I begin to hope that I may see my poor unfortunate brother come back and take his proper place in the world? When I remember what he was five-and-twenty years ago, it does seem cruel that he should have been absolutely eclipsed during all this time. I recollect so well the day he first appeared in his uniform. He was brilliant. Poor Augustus!"

Mr. Dormer-Smith felt that the difficulty of telling his wife what he had just heard assumed a new shape. He had feared to add to the load of what Pauline considered family misfortunes; now it seemed as if his news would dash her rising spirits, and darken roseate hopes. He passed his large hand over his mouth and chin, and said, with his eyes fixed uneasily on his wife, who was still contemplating the fire with an air of abstraction—

"Ah! Yes. But—there may be a Lady Castlecombe to find a place in the world for."

"Not improbable. I hope there may be. Augustus is little past the prime of life. It would compensate for much if—"

"I'm sorry to say, Pauline, that there's no chance of that—I mean of such a marriage as you are thinking of. I came upstairs on purpose to tell you. In one way it won't make any difference to us. And I'm sure your brother has never deserved much affection or consideration from you. But still, I know it will worry you."

Mrs. Dormer-Smith sat upright, with her hands grasping the two arms of her chair, and said, with a sort of despairing calm, "Be good enough to go on, Frederick. I entreat you to be explicit. I dare say you mean well, but I do not think I can endure much more suspense."

"Well, you know the rumours we've heard from time to time about that disreputable Italian woman in Brussels—opera-singer, or something of the kind? Well—I'm afraid there's no use deluding ourselves; I think it comes on good authority—your brother has married her."

CHAPTER IV.

Although the little house in Collingwood Terrace had not, perhaps, fully justified Martin's cheery prophecy that it would turn out an "awfully jolly little place when once they got used to it," yet there, as elsewhere, peace, goodwill, order, and cleanliness mitigated what was mean and unpleasant. Mrs. Bransby's love of personal adornment rested on a better basis than vanity, although she was, doubtless, no more free from vanity than many a plainer woman. She had an artistic pleasure in beauty and elegance, and an objection to sluttishness in all its Protean forms, which might almost be described as the moral sense applied to material things. Her delicate taste suffered, of course, from much that surrounded her in the squeezed little suburban house. But, far from sinking into a helpless slattern, according to the picture of her painted by Mrs. Dormer-Smith's commonplace fancy, she exerted herself to the utmost to make a pleasant and cheerful home for her children. Her life was one of real toil, although many well-meaning ladies of the Dormer-Smith type would have looked with suspicion on the care Mrs. Bransby took of her hands, and would have been able to sympathize more thoroughly with her troubles if her collars and cuffs had occasionally shown a crease or a stain.

Mr. Rivers's room had been prepared with the most solicitous care. It was a labour of love with all the family. Martin and his sister Ethel did good work, and even the younger children insisted on "helping," to the irreparable damage of their pinafores, and temporary eclipse of their rosy faces by dust and blacklead. The young ones were elated by the prospect of seeing their playfellow Owen once again; Martin relied on his assistance to persuade Mrs. Bransby that he (Martin) should and could earn something; and even Mrs. Bransby could not help building on Owen's arrival to bring some amelioration into her life beyond the substantial assistance of his weekly payments.

He arrived in the evening, and was received by the children with enthusiasm, and by Mrs. Bransby with an effort to be calm and cheerful, and to suppress her tears, which touched him greatly, seeing her, as he did for the first time, in her widow's garb. He was touched, too, by her almost humble anxiety that he should be content with the accommodation provided for him, and earnestly assured her that he considered himself luxuriously lodged.

And, indeed, for himself he was more than satisfied; but he could not help contrasting this mean little house with Mrs. Bransby's beautiful home in Oldchester, and he found it singularly painful to see her in these altered circumstances. In this respect, as in so many others, his feeling differed as widely as possible from Theodore's. For Theodore, although fastidious and exacting as to all that regarded his own comfort, sincerely considered his step-mother's home to be in all respects quite good enough for her, and had privately taxed her with insensibility and ingratitude for showing so little satisfaction in it.

All the family, including Phoebe, who grinned a recognition from the top of the kitchen stairs, agreed in declaring Owen to be looking remarkably well. He was somewhat browned by the Spanish sunshine, and he had an indefinable air of bright hopefulness. In Oldchester he used to look more dreamy.

"It is business which is grinding my faculties to a fine edge," he answered laughingly, when Mrs. Bransby made some remark to the above effect. "I shall become quite dangerously sharp if I go on at this rate."

"I don't think you look at all sharp," replied Mrs. Bransby gently.

Whereupon Martin told his mother that she was not polite; and Bobby and Billy giggled; and they all sat down to their evening meal very cheerfully.

When the table was cleared, and the younger children had gone away to bed under Ethel's superintendence, Mrs. Bransby said, "You smoke, do you not, Mr. Rivers?"

"Not here, in your sitting-room."

"Oh, pray do! It does not annoy me in the least."

Owen hesitated, and Martin thereupon put in his word. "Mother does not mind it, really. Not decent, human kind of tobacco such as gentlemen use. That beast, old Bucher, used to smoke a great pipe that smelt like double-distilled essence of public-house tap-rooms."

"Well, a cigarette, if I may," said Owen, pulling out his case. Then, drawing the only comfortable easy-chair in the room towards the fireside, he asked, "Is that where you like to have it?"

"That is your chair," said Mrs. Bransby timidly.

"Good Heavens!" exclaimed Owen, genuinely shocked, "what have I done to make you suppose I could possibly be capable of taking your seat?"

He gently took her hand and led her to the chair. Then, looking round the little parlour, he spied a footstool, which he placed beneath her feet. As he looked up from doing so, he saw her sweet pale face, with the delicate curves of the mouth twitching nervously in an endeavour to smile, and the soft dark eyes full of tears. "You must not spoil me in this fashion," she began. But the attempt to speak was too much for her. She broke down, and covered her face with her trembling hands.

Martin instantly crossed the room, and stood close beside her, placing one arm round her shoulders, and turning away from Owen, so as to fence his mother in. The boy's protecting attitude was pathetically eloquent. And so was the way in which his mother presently laid her head down upon his shoulder. They remained thus for a little while. Owen stood by the fire with his elbow on the mantelpiece, and his forehead resting on his hand. And all three were silent.

At length, when Martin felt that his mother was no longer trembling, and that her sobs were subsiding, he looked round and said, "Mother's upset by being treated properly. No wonder! It's like meeting with a white man after living among cannibals. If you had ever seen that beast Bucher, you'd understand it."

"Shall I go away?" asked Owen.

Mrs. Bransby quickly held out one hand entreatingly, while she dried her eyes with the other. "Please stay!" she said. "And please light your cigarette! And please draw your chair near the fire, and make yourself as comfortable—or as little uncomfortable—as you can! Forgive me. I do not often break down in this way; do I, Martin?"

"No," answered Martin, moving the lamp so as to throw his mother's tear-stained face into shadow, and then squeezing his own chair into the corner beside hers, "no; you were cheerful enough with Bucher. Well, of course one had either to take Bucher from the ludicrous side, or else shoot him through the head, and have done with him!"

"I see," said Owen, nodding, and not sorry to hide his own emotion under cover of a joke. "And Mrs. Bransby was unable to make up her mind to justifiably homicide him?"

"Yes. He was a beast, though, and no mistake! Phoebe was in such a rage with him once, that she threatened to throw a hot batter-pudding at his head. I'm sorry now she didn't," added Martin, with pensive regret.

Then they talked quietly. Mrs. Bransby, with womanly tact, led Owen to speak about himself and his prospects. There was little to tell in the way of incident. He had been working steadily, and did not dislike his work. And he had been well contented with his treatment by Mr. Bragg. Mr. Bragg had made him an offer to send him, in the spring, to Buenos Ayres. It might be an opening to fortune.

"I suppose you will go? Of course, you will go!" said Mrs. Bransby.

She could not help her voice and her face betraying some disappointment. They did not, however, betray all she felt; for the prospect of Owen's going away again so soon sent a desolate chill to her heart. Owen looked at her quickly, and then as quickly looked away and tossed the end of his cigarette into the fire, before lighting another.

"I don't know," he answered, bending down over the flame; "it will require some consideration. I believe the alternative is open to me of remaining in Mr. Bragg's employment in England. Anyway, there is time enough before I need decide—several months, I hope."

Mrs. Bransby breathed a low sigh of relief; then she said, in a perceptibly more cheerful tone, "It seems so odd to think of you writing business letters, and making up accounts, and being altogether turned into a—a—"

"A clerk."

"No; not precisely that. You are Mr. Bragg's secretary, are you not?"

"What I am aiming at—what I hope to be—is a clerk, you know. If I called myself a field marshal or an archbishop it would not alter the fact; but it does seem odd to me, too, when I think of it. Better luck than I deserve, as my shrewd old friend Mrs. Dobbs said to me."

"Talking of Mrs. Dobbs, May Cheffington came to see me here."

Owen had heard regularly from May every week; he carried her last letter in his breast-pocket at that moment (not the note which she had posted herself—that had not yet reached Collingwood Terrace), so that he was not starving for news of her. Nevertheless, he felt a wild temptation to cry out, "Tell me about her! Talk of nothing else!" But he answered composedly, "That was quite right; she ought, of course, to have come to see you."

"She only came once," observed Martin.

"That was not her fault," said his mother. "She could not, as I told you all, make frequent journeys here—she could not command her time or her aunt's servants; she goes out a great deal."

"Her aunt lives for the world, you see," said Owen apologetically.

"Oh, there is no reason why May should not enjoy her youth and all her advantages," answered Mrs. Bransby softly; "she is a very sweet, lovable creature—much too good for—" Mrs. Bransby here checked herself, and stopped abruptly.

"Oh, mother! that's all bosh!" cried Martin, flushing hotly. "I mean that notion of yours. Now, I ask you, Mr. Rivers, is it likely that May Cheffington would think of marrying Theodore? Ah! you may well look flabbergasted! Anybody would who knew them both. You see, mother, Mr. Rivers takes it just as I did. You don't think it likely, do you, Mr. Rivers?"

Owen had recovered from the first startling effect of hearing those two names coupled together; but he was inwardly raging and lavishing a variety of the most unparliamentary epithets on Theodore.

"If you ask my candid opinion, I don't think it likely," he answered curtly.

"Of course not!" exclaimed the boy. "It's only Theodore's bounce; I told mother so."

"Why, you don't mean that Bransby has the confounded impudence to say—"

"No, no," interposed Mrs. Bransby. "Don't let us exaggerate. Theodore has never made any explicit statement on the subject. But he meets May very frequently in society. He is constantly invited by Mrs. Dormer-Smith. They are thrown a great deal together. May has evidently become much more kind and gracious to him of late—for I remember when she used positively to run away from him!—and as for him, he is as much attached to her as he can be to any human being. I do believe that."

"Attached your granny!" cried Martin, apparently unable to find a polite phrase strong enough to convey his deep disdain. "Theodore is much attached to number one, and that's about the beginning and the end of his attachments!"

"Hush, Martin," said his mother severely. "You are talking of what you don't understand. And you know how much I dislike to hear you use that tone about—your brother."

She brought out the word "brother" with an obvious effort. In truth, she had a repugnance to speaking, or even thinking, of Theodore as her children's brother. But it was a repugnance for which she blamed herself.

"I think," she added, "that you had better go to bed, Martin."

The boy rose with an instant obedience, which had not always characterized him in the happy Oldchester days, and bent over his mother to kiss her.

"I'm very sorry. I did not mean to vex you, mother," he whispered. "You're not angry with me, are you?"

"I can't be angry with you, my darling boy. But I must do my duty. You know he would say, I was right to correct you."

Martin lifted up his face cheerfully, with the happy elasticity of boyish spirits. "All right, mother. Good night. Good night, Mr. Rivers."

"Good night, old fellow," responded Owen, grasping the boy's hand heartily. He felt very strongly in sympathy with Martin, just then.

Martin lingered. "May I ask just one thing, mother?" he said wistfully.

"You know we agreed not to tease Mr. Rivers with our affairs immediately on his arrival, Martin," replied his mother. Then, unable to resist his pleading face, she said, "If it really is only one question, perhaps Mr. Rivers would not mind—?"

"What is it you want to know, Martin? Speak out," said Owen.

"It's about the question I asked in my letter," replied Martin, blushing and eager. "Don't you think I ought to try and help mother? And don't you think I might have a chance of earning something?"

"That's two questions," said Owen, with a smile. "But I'll answer them both. To number one, yes, undoubtedly. To number two, perhaps; but we must have patience."

"There, mother!" cried Martin, triumphantly turning his glowing face and sparkling eyes towards her. Then he shut the door, and rushed upstairs: his round young cheeks dimpled with smiles, and his heart so full of joyous hopes, that he was impelled to find some vent for his overflowing spirits by hurling his bolster at Bobby and Billy, who were sitting up in bed, broad awake. Thereupon there ensued smothered sounds of scuffling and laughter, mingled with the occasional thud of a bolster against the wall; until Phoebe, sharply rapping at the door, announced that unless Mr. Martin was in bed in two minutes, she would take away the light, and leave him to undress in the dark.

When the widow was alone with Owen she began to pour forth the praises of her eldest boy. She hoped Mr. Rivers did not think her selfish in letting the boy share so much of her cares and anxieties. But although only a child in years he was so helpful, so loving, so sensible—had such a manly desire to shield her and spare her! And then, after asking Owen's advice about the boy, she added, naïvely—

"Only, please, don't advise me to make a drudge of him. He is so clever, he ought to be educated. His dear father looked forward to his doing so well at school and college."

"If I am to advise, really," said Owen, "I ought first to understand the state of the case with as much accuracy as possible."

Mrs. Bransby at once told him the details of her circumstances as succinctly as she could. There was a small sum secured to her, but so small as barely to suffice for finding them all in food. Theodore had made himself responsible for the rent during one twelvemonth. He had also (or so she had understood him) promised to send Martin to his old school for a couple of years. But it now appeared that his offer was limited to paying for Martin's being taught at a neighbouring day school of a very inferior kind. And even this seemed precarious.

"I thought at one time," said Mrs. Bransby, "that I might, perhaps, earn, a little money by teaching. But I must do what I can to educate Ethel and Enid and the younger boys until they get beyond me. I fear I could not find time to go out and give lessons, even if I succeeded in getting an engagement. So I am trying to get some sewing to do. I can use my needle, you know, while I hear Ethel say her French lesson, and make Bobby and Billy spell words of two syllables."

Poor Mrs. Bransby spoke with much diffidence of her plans and projects. She had a very humble opinion of her own powers, and was touchingly willing to be ruled and directed. Owen suggested that it might have been better for her to have remained in Oldchester, where she was among friends. But she answered that she had had scarcely any choice in the matter. It was Theodore who had decided that she was to remove to London. It was Theodore who had chosen that house for her. In the first days of her loss she had blindly accepted all Theodore's directions.

"Perhaps I was to blame," she said. "But I was so overwhelmed, and I felt so helpless; and it seemed right to listen to Theodore. But—although I never say a harsh word about him to strangers, nor to the children if I can help it—I cannot pretend to you, who know us all so well, that he is kind to us. Martin resents his behaviour very much. I do my best, but it is impossible to make my boy feel cordially towards his half-brother."

"Of course it is!" said Owen. Then he closed his lips. He would not trust himself to talk of Theodore at that moment.

It was a comfort to Mrs. Bransby to speak openly to a sympathizing listener, and one whom she could thoroughly trust. She talked on for a long time; and at length, looking at her watch, accused herself of selfishness in keeping Owen so long from the rest which he must need after his journey. As she returned the watch to her pocket, she said deprecatingly—

"Perhaps you think I ought not to possess so handsome a watch under the present circumstances? Theodore was quite displeased when he saw it, and said it ought to be sold. But, you see, I need some kind of watch; and this is an excellent time-keeper; and—and my dear husband gave it to me on the last birthday we spent together."

She turned away to hide the tears that brimmed up into her eyes; and, going to a little side table, lit her chamber candle.

Owen rose from his chair. "Look here, Mrs. Bransby," he said. "Of course we must have more talk together, and more time to consider matters; but it seems to me that Martin is right in wishing to earn something. Young as he is, it might be possible to find some employment for him which should bring in a weekly sum worth having. And as to his education—it has occurred to me that I could, at least, keep him from forgetting what he has learnt already; and, perhaps, coach him on a little further. An hour or two every evening, steadily occupied, would do a good deal. It would be a great pleasure to me to be able to do this small service for you. That is to say," he went on quickly, in order to check the outburst of thanks which trembled on her lips, "if you are good enough to allow me the advantage of continuing to occupy a room here. I hope you will be able to put up with me. I don't think that Phoebe will want to throw a hot batter-pudding at my head. But that may be my vanity! Good night. Don't say any more now, please. We will think it over on both sides. I will smoke one more cigarette, if I may, before I turn in."

He opened the door, and held it open for her. As she passed him, she paused an instant, and said in a low, trembling voice, "God bless you!"

CHAPTER V.

The next morning's post brought Owen May's note. She had written it hurriedly—not so much from stress of time as under the influence of that kind of hurry which comes from thronging thoughts and eager emotions. The sight of her handwriting was a joyful surprise to Owen; and he wondered, as he tore open the cover, how she could have learned his arrival so quickly. But he found that she had written simply in the hope that he might get her letter as soon as possible, and without any knowledge of the fact that he was already in London.

The contents of it did not much disquiet him. She had something to say to him: he must come and speak with her as soon as possible after his arrival. She was safe and well, he knew; and, with that knowledge, he thought that he could defy fortune. As to urging him to go to her quickly—that was, he told himself with a smile, a superfluous injunction. What need of persuasion to do that which he ardently longed to do?

He rapidly planned out the hours of his day. At ten o'clock he must be with Mr. Bragg in the City. He had received a telegram in Paris making that appointment. He would probably find duties to detain him there until the afternoon. Between two and three o'clock, however, he thought he could reach Mrs. Dormer-Smith's house at Kensington. From what he knew of the habits of the household, he judged that May would be at home at that hour.

He had much to think of regarding the future. A momentous decision lay with him. Had Mr. Bragg's offer of sending him to Buenos Ayres come a couple of months earlier, he might have accepted it. It was not, of course, a certain road to success; and it had many draw-backs—chief among them being banishment from England. But, as he had told Mrs. Dobbs, he was ready to face that if it were required of him, understanding that he who starts late in a race must needs run hard. But latterly he had come to think that it might not be best for May that he should go; and to do what was best for her was the supreme aim of his life. He discovered from her letters that she was not happy and contented in her aunt's house. The necessity of concealing her engagement was already painful and oppressive. How could she endure it for two years? Truly, she might announce it, and go back to Oldchester to her grandmother's house (for Owen had more than a suspicion that the Dormer-Smiths would be very unwilling to keep her with them as the betrothed bride of Mr. Bragg's clerk!)

But there were other objections. Theodore Bransby, Owen was inwardly convinced, was his rival. He might try to injure him in his absence. The absent are always in the wrong. Or Theodore might annoy

May with persecutions. If he and May were to wait for each other, had they not better wait, at all events, in the same hemisphere? Owen knew very well that some money—a decent competency—was indispensable to his marriage. But that he might now reasonably hope to obtain in England. The balance of his judgment, the more he reflected on the situation, inclined the more decisively towards remaining.

Other considerations than what was due to May could not have inclined the scale one hair's breadth in these deliberations. But when he thought over his last evening's interview with Mrs. Bransby, it pleased him to believe that his stay, if he stayed, would be very welcome to her and hers.

He felt a profound and tender compassion for the widow. He admired her patience, and the simple way in which she tried to do hard duties; accepting them as matters of course. And he was filled with indignation against Theodore Bransby. To these sentiments may be added the sense that Mrs. Bransby relied on him; and the recollection of that day in the Oldchester garden, when he had solemnly promised to be a friend to her and her children at their need. All these were powerful incentives to help her and stand by her.

There was in Owen a somewhat unusual combination of heat and steadfastness. He seldom belied his first impulse—the mark of a rarely sincere character, swayed only by honest motives. The offer he had made last night to teach Martin he was not inclined to repent of in the "dry light" of next morning. It was plain, too, that his contribution to the weekly income was a matter of serious importance to the family;—far more so than he had any idea of when he first proposed to board with them, although the offer had been made in the hope of assisting them. He turned over in his mind various projects on their behalf as he walked down to the City. It occurred to him that he might do well to speak to Mr. Bragg on the subject. It was even possible that Mr. Bragg might find some place for young Martin. Owen had a high opinion of his employer's rectitude and good sense; and he thought him, moreover, a kindly disposed man. But he had no glimpse of the tenderness which was hidden under Mr. Bragg's plain, unattractive exterior, nor of the yearning for some affection in his daily life, which sometimes made the millionaire look back regretfully on the days when he and his comely young wife toiled together; and when he, Joshua Bragg, in his fustian working suit, had been the dearest being on earth to a loving woman.

Mr. Bragg appeared that day at his place of business looking as usual. He was clean shaven, and soberly and appropriately attired. He was attentive to the matter in hand, mindful of details, accurate, deliberate—all as usual. And yet, so subtle is the quality of the spiritual atmosphere which we all carry about with us, there was not a junior clerk in the place who did not feel that there was a cloud on Mr. Bragg's mind, and did not wonder "what was up with the governor."

One wag opined that "Old Grimalkin had caught him at last." By which irreverent phrase the profane fellow meant that the Most Noble the Dowager Marchioness of Hautenville had succeeded in arranging an alliance between Mr. Bragg and her daughter, the Lady Felicia. For it was an open secret in the office, and the theme of infinite jest there, that Lady Hautenville pursued this aim with an indomitable, and even ferocious, perseverance worthy of the Berseker race from which she professed to trace her descent. Her ladyship's hired barouche might often be seen during the season, floating like a high-beaked ship of the Vikings on the busy tide of commercial life, and coasting down towards that plebeian shore of Tom Tiddler, where Mr. Joshua Bragg picked up so much gold and silver. She would willingly have made as clean a sweep of all his treasure as any piratical Scandinavian who ever carried off the peaceful wealth of Kentish villages. Neither craft nor valour were wanting to her. She made ingenious excuses to see him:—sometimes she wanted to consult him as to the investment of non-existent sums of money; sometimes to engage his presence at some fashionable gathering, where he was, of course, peculiarly fitted to shine. She sent in to his office little perfumed notes, directed by the fair hand of Felicia in Brobdingnagian characters. Felicia herself, bright-eyed and crowned with gorgeous bonnets—spoil gallantly wrested from some lily-livered West End milliner, who had not the courage to refuse her credit,—sat by her mother's side, and smiled with haughty fascination on Mr. Bragg, whenever he could be coaxed forth to speak with their ladyships at the carriage door. And every creature in Mr. Bragg's wholesale office, down to the sharp Cockney urchin who sprinkled and swept the floors, perfectly understood why Lady Hautenville did all these things, and watched her proceedings as a spectacle of very high sporting interest.

Thus it was that when the wag before-mentioned opined that "Grimalkin had caught the governor," by way of accounting for Mr. Bragg's low spirits, it was received with the benevolence due to a deserving old jest which has seen service. But when a younger man ventured to suggest—more than half seriously—that, "perhaps the governor was in love," the suggestion was received with genuine hilarity, and the originator of it immediately took credit for having fully intended a capital joke.

Owen Rivers, arriving punctually, was shown into Mr. Bragg's private room. There he was greeted with the invariable grave, "How do you do, Mr. Rivers?" And then, after a moment, Mr. Bragg added, "So you've got over punctual. I thought you might manage without an extra day in Paris. But you must have put your shoulder to the wheel to do it." A speech expressive, in Mr. Bragg's mouth, of very marked approbation.

Then Owen proceeded to report what he had done in Paris, and to lay letters and papers before Mr. Bragg; and for some time they attended to various matters of business. When these were over, Owen said—

"When could I speak to you about some affairs of my own?"

"Well, now, p'raps; if you don't want to be long."

"Half an hour?"

Mr. Bragg looked at his watch, nodded, and, leaning his head on his hand, prepared to listen with quiet attention.

Owen began by saying that he was inclined towards remaining in England rather than accepting the opportunity of going abroad; whereat Mr. Bragg looked thoughtful, but waited to hear him out without interruption. Then Owen went on to speak of Mrs. Bransby and her altered circumstances, and of his wish and intention to assist and stand by her.

When he ceased Mr. Bragg, having heard him with careful attention, said—

"The first point to be considered is your own position. Concerning the situation we spoke of, I think I can promise to keep you on as my—what you might call business secretary. As to a private secretary, I don't have much private correspondence, and what I have, I can pretty well manage myself. I should expect you to take a journey now and then into foreign parts if necessary. Terms as before. But I tell you frankly, I see no immediate prospect of a rise for you. If you went to Buenos Ayres you might have a chance—only a chance, of course—of getting into something on your own account. One 'ud be steady as far as it went; the other 'ud be like what you might call a throw of the dice at backgammon—chance and play. It's for you to choose. With regard to Mrs. Bransby, I—of course—Look here, Mr. Rivers, I'm a deal older than you—old enough to be your father—and I should like to give you a little word of advice, if I could do it without offence."

"I shall take it gratefully, Mr. Bragg, whether I act upon it or not."

"Oh! as to acting upon it," said Mr. Bragg slowly; "it's a great thing to be sure that your advice won't be picked up and pitched back at your head like a stone. Well, you must understand that I don't mean any disrespect to Mrs. Bransby, who is an excellent lady, I've no doubt. I haven't much acquaintance with her, though I have dined at her table. Her husband, Martin Bransby, I knew for years. I was his client, and had reason to be well satisfied with him in all respects. So, you understand, my feeling is quite friendly. But I would just drop a word of warning. You're a young man, and Mrs. Bransby, though she's older than you are, is still a young woman. And what's more, she's a very handsome woman. And—Ah, I see you're making ready to shy back that stone, by-and-by. But just listen one moment. For you, at your age, to get entangled in that sort of engagement, and to undertake the charge of a ready-made family of hungry boys and girls, would be simply ruin. You'd repent it; and then she'd repent it because you did, and you'd all be miserable together; that's all."

Owen's mouth was set, and his eyes sparkling with a rather dangerous look. But he answered quietly, "Thank you, Mr. Bragg. I am sure you mean well, or why should you trouble yourself to speak at all on the matter?"

"Just so; I'm glad you see that."

"But may I ask what put the idea of any—any 'entanglement,' as you call it, between me and Mrs. Bransby into your head?"

"Understand me, Mr. Rivers; I meant all in honour, you know."

Owen winced. The very assurance was almost offensive, but he returned, "I spoke very stupidly and awkwardly; I'll amend my phrase. I should have said, what put it into your head that I was likely to marry Mrs. Bransby?"

"Put it into my head? Well, when a young man feels a soft sort of compassion for a beautiful woman who—who throws herself a good deal on his sympathy, and looks to him for help and advice and all the rest of it, and when the young man and the beautiful woman have opportunities of seeing each other pretty constantly, why then I believe such a thing has been heard of in history as their falling in love with each other. It don't need much 'putting into your head' to see that when you've come to my years."

"Are you quite sure," persisted Owen, "that no suggestion of this kind was made to you by any third person? I have a particular reason for wishing to know."

Mr. Bragg pondered. He had, in fact, heard Theodore's hints and innuendos at the Dormer-Smiths, and although he was not consciously moved by them in what he had now said, there could be no doubt that the idea had been originally suggested to him by young Bransby and Pauline; Owen's words to-day had merely revived those impressions. After a long pause, he answered—

"Well, I think I have heard it spoken of; but, if so, all the more reason for you to be cautious."

"I thought so!" said Owen. "Spoken of by—"

"Why, by Mrs. B.'s step-son for one; so you may suppose there was nothing said against the lady. He'd think it an uncommon good thing, I dare say; it would relieve him of a burthen. He might wash his hands of the family if she was to marry again."

"Relieve him of a burthen!" cried Owen, starting up from his chair. "Have you any idea what he does for his father's widow and children, Mr. Bragg? Theodore Bransby is a liar. I know him. There's nothing too base for him to insinuate against his stepmother, who is, I declare to God, one of the best and most innocent women breathing! Theodore has a grudge against her and her children—a jealous, petty, despicable kind of grudge; and he's a mean-minded scoundrel!" He checked himself in walking furiously about the room, and turned to Mr. Bragg with an apology. "I beg your pardon, but I cannot talk coolly of that fellow."

"I'm inclined to agree with you, and yet I wish I could think better of him; or rather, I wish he was somebody else altogether," said Mr. Bragg enigmatically, thinking of May.

"Mr. Bragg," said Owen, with a sudden inspiration, "will you come to Collingwood Terrace and see Mrs. Bransby? You will learn more about them all with your own eyes and ears in ten minutes than I could convey to you in an hour. You shall take them unprepared. If you would look in this evening about their tea-time you would find them all at home; it would be a kind and natural act on your part, and would need no explanation. Do come."

"Well, yes; I will," answered Mr. Bragg. "Perhaps I ought to have done so before. Any way, I'll come; just put down the address."

"Thank you. Shall I write those Spanish letters now?"

"Ah! you'd better. Mr. Barker, there, will give you a seat for the present in his room."

And so they parted.

Mr. Bragg was by no means reassured as to his secretary being in considerable danger from the widow's fascinations. He remarked to himself that Rivers had not said one word explicitly denying any attachment between them, but he felt a new bond of sympathy with Rivers. It was agreeable to meet with such thorough fellow-feeling about Theodore Bransby. Perhaps a mutual dislike is a stronger tie than a mutual friendship, because our hatreds need more justifying than our affections.

By the time Owen's business was transacted, and he had eaten some food at a neighbouring chop-house, it was past two o'clock, and then he set out for Mrs. Dormer-Smith's house on foot. It was a long way off, but it seemed to him more tolerable to walk than to jog along on the top of an omnibus, or to burrow underground in the crowded railway. In his impatient and excited frame of mind the rapid exercise was a relief.

It was barely three o'clock when he reached the house in Kensington. The servant who opened the door murmured something in a low voice, about the ladies not receiving visitors in consequence of a family affliction. Being further interrogated, he believed that Mrs. Dormer-Smith's cousin, Lord Castlecombe's son, was dead.

"Tell Miss Cheffington that I am here," said Owen. "Give her this card, and say I am waiting to see her."

His manner was so peremptory that, after a brief hesitation, the man took the card, and ushered Owen into the dining-room to wait. The room was dimmer than the dim wintry day without need have made it, by reason of the red blinds being partly drawn down, and filling it with a lurid gloom.

The servant had not been gone many seconds before the door opened, and a rather pale face, not raised very high above the level of the floor, peeped into the room. The eyes belonging to the face soon made out Owen's figure in the dimness, and a childish voice said, in a subdued and stealthy tone, "Hulloa!"

"Hulloa!" returned Owen, in a tone not quite so subdued, but still low; for there was a general hush in the house which would have made ordinary speech seem startling.

"Do you want May?" asked the child.

"Yes; I do."

"I heard you tell James to give her your card. Who are you?"

"I'm Owen. Who are you?" replied Owen, listening all the while for the expected footfall.

"I'm Harold."

Upon this, a second rather pale face, still nearer to the ground, peeped in at the door; and a second childish voice piped out faintly, "And I'm Wilfred." Then the two children marched solemnly into the room, shutting the door behind them, and stared at Owen with judicial gravity.

"May's my cousin," said Harold, after contemplating the stranger for a while in silence.

"And May's my cousin, too," observed Wilfred.

"I'm fond of her," pursued Harold.

"So am I," exclaimed Owen, walking across the room impatiently. "But why doesn't she come? Where is she? Do you know?"

"Yes," replied Harold, with deliberation; "I know."

"What can that man be about? He can't have given her the message!" said Owen, speaking half to himself, his nervous impatience rising with every minute of delay.

Harold looked profoundly astute, as he answered, with a series of emphatic nods, "No; he didn't. He took the card to Smithson; and I know what Smithson will do; she'll read it first herself, and then she'll take it to mamma, and then perhaps mamma will tell May—if you're a—what is it?—a proper person. Are you a proper person?"

"I say," said Owen suddenly, "will you go and fetch May? Tell her Owen is here waiting. Do go, there's a good boy!"

"Is May fond of you?" inquired Harold hesitating.

"May will be pleased with you if you go and fetch her. Run! Be off at once now—quick!"

After one searching look at Owen's face, the child disappeared swiftly and silently. In less than two minutes a light footstep was heard descending the stairs at headlong speed. The door opened, and May, almost breathless with haste and surprise, half stumbled into the dark room, and he caught her in his arms.

"Is it really you?" she exclaimed, looking up at him with one hand on his shoulder, and the other pushing back the hair from her forehead.

Owen took the hand which rested on his shoulder, and pressed it to his lips. "It is very really I," he said, with his eyes fixed on her face in a tender rapture.

"It seems like a dream! So unexpected!"

"Unexpected! Why, you summoned me, and of course I am here!"

"Yes, it really does seem as if my note had been a spell to bring you across the seas."

"'Over seas, over mountains,
Love will find out the way!'

It doesn't alter that truth, that I happened to arrive in England only last night."

"Only last night! How strange it seems! And you never let me know—"

"Darling, by the time it was quite certain what day I should be in England, a letter would not have outstripped me. I got my orders by telegram. Oh, my love, what a long, long time it seems since I looked on your dear face!"

"Tell me all about yourself, Owen. I want to hear everything."

"So you shall. But you must explain first the meaning of your note. Tell me now—sit down here—what has happened?"

"I have so many things to say, I scarcely know where to begin!"

"Begin with what was in your mind when you wrote that note."

May sat down close to him, and began in a low voice, little above a whisper, and with some confusion, to narrate the story of Mr. Bragg's wooing, and its effect on her aunt and uncle. As he listened, Owen's face expressed the most unbounded amazement.

"Oh, it can't be!" he exclaimed. "It's impossible! There must be some mistake!"

May laughed, though the tears were in her eyes. "You are not very civil," she said. "Nobody else seemed to think it impossible."

"But old Bragg!" repeated Owen incredulously.

"Perhaps he was temporarily insane, but I really think he meant it," answered May, blushing so bewitchingly, that Owen could not resist the temptation to kiss the glowing cheek so close to his lips.

At this point, Harold called out in a resolute tone, "You mustn't kiss May."

The lovers started. They had forgotten the children—had forgotten everything in the world except each other. But the two little boys had followed May into the room, and had been witnessing the interview in dumb astonishment. It was characteristic that they now held each other by the hand, as though seeking support from union, in the presence of this stranger, who might, they instinctively felt, turn out to be a common enemy.

"Halloa!" said Owen. "Here's another rival. Their name seems to be Legion."

"It was Harold who told me you were here," said May.

"Yes; I sent him to fetch you," answered Owen. Then he added ungratefully, "They might as well be sent off now, mightn't they?"

"Oh, let them stay. There are no secrets now. At least, I hope you will agree with me that we ought to say out the truth. Come here, Harold and Wilfred. You must love Owen, for my sake."

Harold advanced and stood in front of them.

"I say," he said, with a curious look at Owen, "I'm going to marry May when I grow up."

"Are you? That's a little awkward."

"Why is it a little awkward?" demanded Harold gravely.

"Well, because, to tell the truth, I was rather hoping to marry her myself."

The child had evidently intended to draw forth this explicit statement, for he looked full at Owen, and said doggedly, "I just thought you were!" Then he suddenly turned away and hid his face on May's lap. Upon which Wilfred, conscious of a cloud in the air, began to cry softly.

"Don't be angry with them, poor little fellows!" said May, checking some manifestation of impatience on Owen's part. Then she coaxed the children, and soothed them, and the childish emotion, brief though poignant, soon passed. And at length Harold lifted up his face, and, after a short struggle, said—

"I will shake hands with him, if you like, but I won't love him—not if he kisses you."

"All right, old fellow," said Owen, taking the child's hand. "I sympathize with your feelings."

Wilfred, of course, put out his small paw to be shaken like his brother's, and peace once more reigned.

May then hurriedly—for she knew not how long they might remain uninterrupted—repeated what Clara Bertram had told her of her father's marriage; and, lastly, she spoke in terms of deep affection and gratitude of "Granny's" generosity. But on this point, as we know, Owen was already informed.

All that he now heard strengthened and justified the strong inclination he already felt to abandon the idea of Buenos Ayres and to remain in England at all costs. With her father more completely cut off from his family than ever by this new marriage, her aunt hostile, her uncle, to say the least, dissatisfied, and sure to oppose her engagement when it should be announced, and no one friend in the world to rely upon except her grandmother, May's position would be very desolate if he, too, were far away on the other side of the world. Mrs. Dobbs was the trustiest and most devoted of parents, but she was old; and, moreover, she would have no power to insist on keeping May with her should her father take it into his head to decide otherwise. No; he must and would remain at hand to protect and watch over her. These were the sole considerations which decided him to come to this resolution then and there. But as soon as he had taken his resolution the thought arose pleasantly in his mind that it would bring some cheerfulness into the household at Collingwood Terrace, and he expressed it impulsively by saying all at once—

"I have made up my mind, darling, to stay in London. Poor Mrs. Bransby will be overjoyed. She is in such need of some one to stand by her."

May felt a little chill, like the breath of a cold wind. In the first warm delight of seeing her lover again, all the lurking jealousy, which she hated herself for feeling, but which was alive in spite of her hate, had been forgotten. But his words revived it. "Is she?" she answered.

"Oh yes; I have not had time to tell you—haven't even begun to say the thousand things I want to say to you."

"You could not have written them, I suppose?" said May, withdrawing her chair slightly from its close proximity to his, and thereby allowing Harold, who had been watching for this opportunity, to wedge himself in between them.

"No; I could not have written all about her, because I have only just heard many of the details."

"All about 'her'? You mean about Mrs. Bransby?"

"Of course. Poor soul, she has been so harshly, so cruelly treated! Theodore's conduct is—"

"You know I have no partiality for him," interrupted May. "But I think you are a little unjust, or at least mistaken, in this instance. Theodore Bransby has done a great deal for his stepmother."

"Done a great deal for her! Good Heavens, my dear child, you can't conceive with what meanness he treats her! It's dastardly. A woman who was so idolized, so tended, so petted—And what a sweet creature she is! And as lovely as ever! Her sorrows seem only to have spiritualized her beauty."

"Yes," said May. And the dry monosyllable cost her a painful effort to utter it. Perhaps the constraint of her tone, the deadness of her manner—naturally so warm and cordial—would have aroused Owen's surprise, and led to an explanation. But they were interrupted here by the door being thrown open, not violently, but very wide open, and the appearance of Mrs. Dormer-Smith on the threshold.

CHAPTER VI.

Even in the moment of her first dismay, that admirable woman Pauline Dormer-Smith was true to the great social duty of keeping up appearances. She turned her head over her shoulder to James, who was hovering uneasily in the background, and said softly, "Oh yes; it is Mr. Owen Rivers. That is quite right"—as if Mr. Owen Rivers's presence were the most natural and welcome thing in the world. Then, shutting the door on James and on society, she advanced towards the two young people, who had risen on her entrance, and said, with a kind of reproachful feebleness, conveying the impression that she was reduced to the last stage of debility, and that it was entirely their fault, "I had scarcely credited the footman's statement that you were here having a private interview with my niece, Mr. Rivers. He tells me that he informed you of the family affliction which has befallen us. Under the circumstances, you must allow me to say that I think you have shown some want of delicacy in insisting on being admitted."

May glanced at Owen, but as he did not speak on the instant, she did. She took her aunt's passive fingers in her own, and said, "Aunt Pauline, he had a right to insist on seeing me, because—"

"Excuse me, May," interrupted Mrs. Dormer-Smith, waving the girl off, "I beg you will go to your own room; I will speak with this gentleman."

Her tone would have suited the announcement that she was prepared to undergo martyrdom; and she sank into a chair in an attitude of graceful exhaustion.

"No, Aunt Pauline, I cannot go away until I have spoken," cried May pleadingly. "Please to hear me. I wished to tell you the truth long ago, but I was bound by a promise; now we are both agreed that it is right to speak out, are we not?" she said, looking across at Owen. It seemed to her that he was less eager to claim her, less proud of her affection, less ardently loving, than her imagination had pictured him. There was something in the quietude of his attitude which depressed and mortified her; it was like—almost like indifference. An insidious jealousy was discolouring everything which she looked on with her "mind's eye." It is not always a sufficient defence against a poison of that sort to have a noble, candid nature, any more than it is a sufficient defence against foul air to have sound, healthy lungs; it will fasten sometimes on the worthiest qualities: a humble opinion of ourselves, a high admiration for others. The hinted slanders which May had heard had aroused no baser suspicion in her than that Owen perhaps did not love her so entirely as he at first had fancied—that his sympathy and compassion and admiration for Louisa Bransby were strong enough to compete with his attachment for her. And she knew by her own heart that if this were so his love was not such a love as she had dreamed of—not such a love as she had given to him. And yet all the while she was struggling against the influence of this subtly-penetrating distrust, and trying to shake it off, like an ugly dream.

"I am engaged to marry Owen Rivers," she said abruptly, after a pause which lasted but an instant, but which had seemed long to her.

"No, no; I must beg you to retire. I cannot hear this sort of thing," returned her aunt, waving her hand again, and turning away her head. "You, at least, must understand, Mr. Rivers, that it is entirely out of the question. How you can have entertained so preposterous an idea I cannot imagine. You must have seen something of the world, I presume? You ought to be able to perceive that—but, in short, the thing is preposterous, and cannot be seriously discussed for a moment."

May Cheffington's blood was rising. "I do not intend to discuss it," she said haughtily.

"Dearest, since your aunt addresses me, let me reply to her," said Owen. He spoke in a quiet tone, although inwardly he was excited and indignant enough. "I must tell you, Mrs. Dormer-Smith, that we are neither of us acting on a rash impulse. We have been parted for more than three months, during which time May has been free to give me up without breaking any pledge, or incurring—from me, at least—any reproaches. If she had wavered—if she had found that she had mistaken her own feelings—she was free as air. I should have made no claim, and laid no blame, on her."

"Made no claim on her!" repeated Mrs. Dormer-Smith. Then she laughed the low laugh which, with her, indicated the very extremity of provocation. "Oh, really! Ha, ha, ha! This is too monstrous. The whole thing appears to me like insanity."

"To marry without loving—that appears to me like insanity," said May scornfully.

"May! I beseech you! Really, in the mouth of a young girl of your breeding that sort of thing is inconceivable—I am tempted to use a harsher word. This then, is the reason why you have rejected one of the most brilliant prospects! Are you aware, Mr. Rivers, that this school-girl nonsense has prevented—" She caught herself up hastily, and changed her phrase—"might have prevented Miss Cheffington from obtaining one of the most splendid establishments in England?"

"Aunt Pauline!" cried May with hot indignation. "How can you say so? I would never have thought of marrying Mr. Bragg, even if Owen had not existed!"

"But apart from that," pursued Mrs. Dormer-Smith, ignoring the interruption, "your pretensions would have been quite inadmissible. You have heard of the death of my poor cousin Lucius. You had probably calculated on it. I do not mean to bring any special accusation against you there. Of course, in the case of a person of poor dear Lucius's social importance all sorts of calculations were made by all sorts of people. My brother Augustus is now the next heir to the family title and estates. Under these circumstances I leave it to your own good sense to determine whether he is likely to consent to his daughter's marrying—really I am ashamed to speak of it seriously!—a person who, in however praiseworthy a manner, is filling the position of a hired clerk!"

This shaft fell harmless, since both May and her lover were honestly free from any sense of humiliation in the fact of Owen's being a hired clerk, and sincerely willing to accept that position for him.

Owen answered calmly, "You can probably judge far better than I, as to what your brother is likely to think on that subject." Then turning towards May, he said, "I think, my dearest, that you had better leave your aunt and me to speak quietly together. You have been sufficiently pained and agitated already. You look quite pale! Go, darling, and leave me to speak with Mrs. Dormer-Smith."

"Agitated!" echoed that lady. "We have all been sufficiently agitated. What I have endured from pressure on the brain is unspeakable. Certainly you had better go away, May, I have said so several times already."

May walked slowly to the door. "I will do as you wish," she said to Owen.

"You see I am right, dear, do you not?"

"Yes; I suppose so."

The listlessness of her tone, he interpreted as a sign of her being weary and over-wrought. And, in truth, it was partly due to that cause.

As she moved across the room, two little figures crept out from a dark corner, behind an armchair, and followed her.

"Good gracious!" cried Mrs. Dormer-Smith faintly. "What is that? Have those children been here all the time?" She always spoke of Harold and Wilfred as "those children," in a distant tone as though they were somebody else's intrusive little boys. On this occasion, however, she did not altogether disapprove of their presence. It was certainly less inconvenable that they should have been known by the servants to be present at the interview, than if May had been without even that small amount of chaperonage. She had no idea that it was Harold who had brought about the interview, or he might not have got off so easily!

"Go away, little boys," she said, in her sweet, soft voice. "Go away upstairs. Cannot Cécile find some lessons for you to do? You really must not prowl about this part of the house in the afternoon."

The children trotted after their cousin willingly enough. They never wished to stay with their mother.

"We shall meet again soon, my dear one," whispered Owen, as he opened the door. And then, with Mrs. Dormer-Smith's eyes fixedly regarding him, he took May's cold little hand in his own, and kissed it, before she passed out.

Pauline observed his demeanour with an unbiased judgment. She would, in the cause of duty, willingly have had him kidnapped and sent off to New Caledonia at that moment. But she said to herself, "He has the manner of a gentleman. It is most disastrous!" For she felt that this circumstance increased her own difficulties.

"Now, Mrs. Dormer-Smith," said Owen, when the door was shut, "I can answer you with more perfect frankness than I should have liked to employ in May's presence. You were so kind as to say that you would leave it to my good sense to determine whether Captain Cheffington was likely to consent to my marriage with his daughter. My answer is quite simple. I do not intend to ask his consent."

"You do not intend—to ask—his consent?" ejaculated Pauline, leaning back in her chair, and, in the extremity of her astonishment at this young man's audacity, letting fall a hand-screen which she had been using to shield her face from the fire.

Owen picked it up and restored it to her before repeating, "No; I do not intend to ask his consent."

"And do you hope to persuade my niece to disregard her father's authority?—Not to mention other members of the family who have a right to be heard!"

"There is only one member of the family who has a right to be heard—Mrs. Dobbs. And her consent I hope I have obtained."

Pauline was for the moment stricken speechless by hearing Mrs. Dobbs mentioned as a member of the family. "The family!" Good heavens, what was the world coming to? She pressed her hand to her forehead with a bewildered look.

Owen went on resolutely. "As to parental authority—Mrs. Dormer-Smith, your brother has abdicated all parental authority over May. He abandoned her—pardon me, I must use that word; for it is the only one which expresses what I mean—when she was a young, motherless child. He went away to his own occupations, or pleasures—any way, he went to live his own life in his own way, utterly careless of May's welfare and happiness. You may tell me that he was sure of her finding the tenderest treatment under her grandmother's roof. He was not sure of it; for he never troubled himself to consider the question. But if he had been sure, he had no right to leave his child as he did. At any rate, having done so, it is too late to pretend that she is morally bound to consider his wishes."

Pauline put her handkerchief to her eyes. "My poor brother Augustus is much to be pitied," she murmured. "Allowances must be made for a man in his position. That unfortunate marriage—"

"I have never been told," said Owen, "that Miss Susan Dobbs seized upon Captain Cheffington and compelled him by main force to marry her. And—judging from what I know of her mother and daughter—I should think it unlikely."

"Oh, one understands that sort of thing," returned Pauline, with languid disdain. "A young woman in her class of life is not to be judged by our standards. No doubt she thought herself justified in doing the best she could for herself."

"It strikes me that she did very badly for herself—lamentably badly. I do not wish to say anything needlessly offensive, but we are in the way of plain speaking, and I must point out to you that so far from any consideration being due to your brother, he is—from the point of view of an honest man wishing to marry May—a person to be decidedly ashamed of. There are in the city of Oldchester, his late wife's native place, many tradesmen, and even mechanics, who would strongly object to connect themselves by marriage with Captain Cheffington."

To say that Mrs. Dormer-Smith was astonished by this speech would be but faintly to express her sensations. She was bewildered. She had often heard Augustus severely blamed. She had been compelled to blame him herself. Of course he ought not to have thrown away his career as he had done. They had agreed as to that. But all this blame had assumed that Augustus had chiefly injured—firstly, himself; and in the second place, and more indirectly, the whole Cheffington family.

Persons who live exclusively in any one narrow sphere are apt to have a strange simplicity, or ignorance, as one may choose to call it, as to large sections of their fellow-creatures outside that sphere. And in no class is that kind of naïveté more commonly found than in the class to which Mrs. Dormer-Smith belonged, where it is often intensified by the conviction that they possess what is called "knowledge of the world" in a supreme degree.

It was far too late in the day to bring much enlightenment to Mrs. Dormer-Smith. Owen's words merely struck her mind with a shock of wonder and dismay, and then glanced off again. The impression of having received a shock, however, did remain with her, and made her as resentful as was possible to her placid nature. In speaking of Mr. Rivers afterwards to her husband, she said—

"I believe him, Frederick, to be a Nihilist."

But for the present her mind was concentrated on the aim of breaking off what Owen chose to call his engagement to her niece, and she was not to be turned aside from it. She addressed herself to argue the case with Owen. In argument she possessed the immense advantage—if it be an advantage to reduce one's adversary to silence—of supposing that the statement of any one truth on her part was a sufficient answer to any other truth which might be advanced against her. As, for instance, when Owen insisted on Captain Cheffington's having forfeited all moral claim to May's duty and affection, she replied that it was a dreadful thing to set a child against a parent; and when Owen denied the right of May's relatives to prevent her from making a marriage of affection, she retorted that Mr. Rivers came of undeniably gentle blood himself, and ought to understand her (Mrs. Dormer-Smith's) strong family feeling.

But when even this powerful kind of logic failed to make any impression on Owen's obduracy, she changed her attack, and inquired what he was prepared to offer to her niece, in exchange for the magnificent prospect of being Mrs. Joshua Bragg, with settlements and pin-money such as every duke's daughter would desire, and very few dukes' daughters achieved.

"But, my dear madam," said Owen, "why speak of that alternative when May has assured you, in my presence, that nothing would induce her to marry Mr. Bragg?"

"Oh, Mr. Rivers, I am surprised you know so little of the world! May is a mere child: peculiarly childish for her age. Besides, even supposing she definitively rejected Mr. Bragg, there will be other good matches open to her now. The death of my poor cousin Lucius has made a vast difference in all that, as you must be well aware."

"To me, Mrs. Dormer-Smith, it has made no difference. May is herself. That is why I love her. She is not in the least transfigured, in my imagination, by being the daughter of a man who may, or may not, be Lord Castlecombe at some future day!"

"Oh," said Mrs. Dormer-Smith, shaking her head with the old plaintive air, "you need not entertain any doubts as to my brother's succession. He is the next heir. And the estates—at least the bulk of them—are entailed."

"Good heavens!" cried Owen, in despair, "can you not understand that I care not one straw whether they are entailed or not? That I would proudly and joyfully make May my wife—she being what she is—if her father trundled a barrow through the streets?"

Whether Mrs. Dormer-Smith could, or could not, understand this, at any rate she certainly did not believe it. She merely shook her head once more, and said softly—

"I think you ought to consider her prospects a little, Mr. Rivers. It appears to me that your views are entirely selfish."

This seemed very hopeless. With a last effort to come to an understanding, Owen took refuge in a plain and categorical statement of facts. He had loved May when she was penniless. So far as he knew, she was so still. He hoped to be able to offer her a modest home. She had not been accustomed to luxury or show—the season in London having been a mere episode, and not the main part of her life. Absolute destitution they were quite secure from.

He possessed one hundred and fifty pounds a year of his own. (Pauline gave a little shudder at this. It positively seemed to her worse than nothing at all. With nothing certain in the way of income, a boundless field was left open for possibilities. But a hundred and fifty pounds a year was a hard, hideous, circumscribing fact, like the bars of a cage!) He was receiving about as much again for his services as secretary. Moreover, he had tried his hand at literature, not unsuccessfully. He had earned a few pounds by his pen already, and hoped to earn more. That was the state of the case. If May, God bless her! were content with it, he submitted that no one else could fairly object.

Mrs. Dormer-Smith rose from her chair, to signify that the interview was at an end. Indeed, what use could there be in prolonging it?

"I confess," she said, "you have astonished me, Mr. Rivers. If May—an inexperienced young girl not yet nineteen—is content, you think no one else has a right to interfere! At that rate, if she chose to marry the footman, we must all stand by without raising a finger to prevent it. That is, certainly, very extraordinary doctrine."

Owen drew himself up, and looked full at her with those blue eyes, which could shine so fiercely upon occasion as he answered—

"I have already admitted the right of one person to be consulted about May's future:—the benevolent, unselfish, high-minded woman, who befriended her, and cherished her, and was a mother to her, when she was deserted by every one else. As to her marrying the footman—it is clear, madam, that she might have married the hangman, for all the effort you would have made to prevent it, until Mrs. Dobbs bribed you to take some notice of your niece! But in marrying a Rivers of Riversmead I need not, I suppose, inform you that she will confer on you the honour of a connection with a race of gentlemen compared with whom—if we are to stand on genealogies—half the names in the Peerage are a mere fungus-growth of yesterday."

It was the first word he had said to her which was less than courteously forbearing. And it was the first word which gave her a momentary twinge of regret that his suit was altogether inadmissible. She contrasted his bearing with that of May's two other wooers:—Bransby the smooth, and Bragg the unpolished; and she said to herself with a sigh, that there was no doubt about this young man's pedigree, and that "bon sang ne peut mentir." But not therefore did she flinch from her position. She answered him in the same words she had used years ago to her brother, in that very room.

"It will not do, Mr. Rivers. I assure you, it will not do!"

Then she bent her head with quiet grace, and moved to go away.

"One instant, Mrs. Dormer-Smith!" Owen said, following her to the door of the dining-room. "I wish, if you please, to speak with May again before I go away."

"Impossible. I cannot, compatibly with my duty, consent to your seeing her now, or at any future time."

"Am I to understand that you forbid me your house?"

"If you please. Unless, indeed, you consent to come in any other character than as my niece's suitor. In that case it would give me great pleasure to receive you as I have done before."

He stood looking at her rather blankly. The position was undeniably awkward. It was impossible—for May's sake, if from no other consideration—to make a scene of violence, and insist upon seeing her. And, even if he did so, Mrs. Dormer-Smith might still resist. She was mistress of the situation so far. Even in his vexation and perplexity, the ludicrous side of the affair struck him.

"Well," said he, after a moment, taking up his hat, "I cannot intrude into your house against your will. Our only resource must be to meet elsewhere. I warn you we shall do so. Of course, it is idle to suppose that you have the power to keep us apart."

Mrs. Dormer-Smith shook her head, and repeated with gentle obstinacy, "It will not do, Mr. Rivers. I really am very sorry, but it will not do."

"War, then, is declared between us?"

"Oh, I hope not! I trust you will think better of it," she said in a mildly persuasive tone, as though she were suggesting that he should leave off tea, or take to woollen clothing. "I, at least, have no warlike intentions, Mr. Rivers; for I am going to ask you to do me a favour. Be so very kind as to wait until I ring, and let my servant show you out in a civilized manner. It is quite unnecessary to publish our differences of opinion to the servants' hall."

Accordingly she rang the bell, and, when James appeared, said sweetly, in an audible voice, "Good-bye, Mr. Rivers." Whereupon Owen made her a profound bow, and departed.

As he passed through the hall, he looked about him wistfully in the hope that May might be lingering near—might possibly be looking down from the upper part of the staircase. But she did not appear. The house was profoundly silent. James stood waiting with the door in his hand. There was no help for it. He strode away with various conflicting feelings, thoughts, projects, and hopes struggling in his mind—of which the uppermost at that special moment was a strong inclination to burst out laughing.

CHAPTER VII.

It was not until Owen had nearly reached Collingwood Terrace that the thought struck him, "What if Mr. Bragg should withdraw his countenance from him, and dismiss him from his employment, when he learned that he was betrothed to May?"

The idea of Mr. Bragg in the light of a rival disconcerted and confused all his previous conceptions of his employer. At the first blush it had appeared ludicrous—incredible; but, on reflection, there was, he found, nothing so extravagant in it. Mr. Bragg had a right to seek a wife to please himself; he was but little past middle life, after all; and as to the disparity in years between him and May, that was certainly not unprecedented. He had taken his rejection well, and manfully—even with a touch of chivalry; but he might not, any the more, be disposed to continue his favour towards Owen when he should discover the state of the case. He might even suspect that there had been some kind of plot to deceive him! That was a very uncomfortable thought, and sent the blood tingling through Owen's veins.

There was clearly but one thing to be done—to tell Mr. Bragg the truth at all hazards. As he walked along the pavement within a few hundred yards of Mrs. Bransby's door, he reflected that the revelation would come better and more gracefully from May than from himself, he was not supposed to be aware of what had passed between May and Mr. Bragg—it was best that he should still seem to ignore it. He had a sympathetic sense that Mr. Bragg's wounded feelings might endure May's delicate handling, while they would shrink resentfully from any masculine touch.

Owen regretted now more than ever that he had not seen May again before leaving her aunt's house; they had had no time to consult together, or to form any plan of action for the future. Their interview seemed, in Owen's recollection, to have passed like a swift gleam of light in a sky over which the clouds are flying. (It had, in sober fact, lasted above half an hour before Mrs. Dormer-Smith's appearance on the scene.) And now he was forbidden the house! Forbidden to see her! And yet he told himself over and over again that he could not have acted otherwise than he had acted at the time. Well, it was too absurd to suppose that she could be treated as a prisoner. They must meet soon, and meanwhile there was a penny post in the land, and her letters, at least, would not be tampered with. He would write to her the moment he got home; she would receive his letter the next morning, and by that same afternoon she could put Mr. Bragg in possession of the fact of her engagement.

And after she had done so—

The "afterwards" seemed hazy, certainly. But at least there was no doubt as to the plain duty of both of them not to keep their engagement any longer secret from Mr. Bragg. It was a comfort to see clearly the right course as regarded the steps immediately before them. For the rest—they had youth and hope, and they loved each other!

Owen let himself into the house with his latch-key, and went straight to his own room to write to May. When the note was finished, he took it out and posted it, and then proceeded to the sitting-room.

The table was spread for tea; all the tea equipage bright and glistening as cleanliness could make it. A cheerful fire burned in the grate. Bobby and Billy, seated side by side on a couple of low stools in one corner, were occupied with a big book full of coloured pictures. Ethel was sewing. Martin stood leaning against the mantelpiece close to his mother's armchair. And in a chair at the opposite corner of the hearth sat Mr. Bragg, with Enid on his knee!

When Owen entered, Mr. Bragg said, "Well, Mr. Rivers, you see I've found my way to Mrs. Bransby's. I ought to have come and paid her my respects before now. But you know I've had my hands pretty full since I came back to England."

Something in his tone and his look seemed to convey a hint to be silent as to their conversation of that morning; and accordingly Owen made no allusion to it.

"It is so pleasant to see an Oldchester face, is it not?" said Mrs. Bransby.

"Some Oldchester faces," returned Owen, laughing. Then he said, "Well, Enid, have you not a word to say to me? Won't you come and give me a kiss?"

Miss Enid, who was a born coquette, and who was, moreover, greatly interested in Mr. Bragg's massive watch-chain and seal, replied with imperious brevity, "No; don't want to."

Mr. Bragg looked down gravely on the small creature, and then up at Owen, as he said—half shyly, and yet with a certain tinge of complacency, "Why, she would come and set on my knee, almost the first minute she saw me."

"Perhaps you had better get down, baby," said Mrs. Bransby. "I am afraid she may be troublesome."

"Troublesome? Lord, no! Why, I don't feel she's there, no more than a fly. Let her bide," said Mr. Bragg.

"Ah, I know what she is:—she's fickle," observed Owen, drawing up his chair.

"Not pickle!" declared Miss Enid, with great majesty.

"Yes, you are! False, fleeting, perjured Enid!" said Owen.

He was delighted to perceive that the little home and its inmates had evidently made a favourable impression on Mr. Bragg. Observing that gentleman in the new light of May's revelation, he saw something in his face which he had not seen there before:—a regretful, far-away look, whenever he was not speaking, or being spoken to. It was wonderfully strange, certainly, to think of him as May's wooer! And yet not absurd, as it had appeared at first. In Mr. Bragg's presence, the absurdity, somehow, vanished. The simplicity and reality of the man gave him dignity. Owen even began to feel something like a vague and respectful compassion for Mr. Bragg; and every now and then the peculiarity of their mutual position would come over him with a fresh sense of surprise.

"We have been having a little conversation, Mrs. Bransby and me, about her boy here," said Mr. Bragg, glancing across at Martin, who coloured, and smiled with repressed eagerness. Mr. Bragg continued to observe him thoughtfully. "He tells me he wants to help his mother; and he's not afraid or ashamed of work, it seems."

"Ashamed!" broke out Martin. "No, I hope I ain't such a cad as that!"

"Martin!" cried his mother anxiously. She was nervous lest he should give offence.

But Mr. Bragg answered with a little nod, which certainly did not express disapprobation, "Well, the boy's about right. To be ashamed of the wrong things, does belong to—what you might call a cad. I expect," pursued Mr. Bragg musingly, "that if we could always apply our shame in the right place, we should all of us do better than we do."

"I suppose I dare not offer you any tea at this hour?" said Mrs. Bransby gently. "You have not dined, of course."

"Well, no; not under the name of dinner, I haven't! But I ate a hearty luncheon; and I believe that's about as much dinner as I want; to do me any good, you know. I'll have a cup of tea, please."

Mrs. Bransby certainly felt no misapplied shame as to the humbleness and poverty of her surroundings; and was far too truly a gentlewoman to think of apologizing for them. Ethel, who was growing to be quite a notable little housewife, quietly fetched another cup and saucer from the kitchen; and that was all the difference which Mr. Bragg's presence made in the ordinary arrangements.

Enid insisted on having her high chair placed close to Mr. Bragg at table; and, but for her sister's watchful interposition, she would have demonstrated her sudden affection for him by transferring sundry morsels of bread-and-butter which she had been tightly squeezing in her small fingers from her plate to his, with the patronizing remark, "Oo have dat. I can't eat any more."

While the meal was still in progress there came a knock at the street door. It was a very peculiar knock; consisting of two or three sharp raps, followed by one solemn rap, and then—after an appreciable interval—by several more hurried little raps, as if the hand at the knocker had forgotten all about its previous performances, and were beginning afresh.

"Who can this be?" said Mrs. Bransby, looking up in surprise. Visitors at any time were rare with her now; and at that hour, unprecedented.

"Old Bucher come back to say he can't live without us," suggested Martin.

Whereupon Bobby and Billy, with consternation in their faces, exclaimed simultaneously, "Oh, I say!" And Enid, perceiving the general attention to be diverted from her, took that opportunity to polish the bowl of her spoon, by rubbing it softly against Mr. Bragg's coat sleeve.

The family were not kept long in suspense. As soon as the door was opened, a well-known voice was heard saying volubly, "Ah! at tea, are they? Well, never mind! Take in my card, if you please, and—Dear me! I haven't got one! But if you will kindly say, an old friend from Oldchester begs leave to wait on Mrs. Bransby."

"Why, it's Simmy!" cried the children, starting up, and rushing to the door. "Here's a lark!" exclaimed Bobby. While Billy, tugging at the visitor's skirt, roared out hospitably, "Come along! Mother's in there. Come in! Mother, here's Simmy!"

Mrs. Sebastian Bach Simpson it was. She appeared on the threshold—rubicund visage, glittering spectacles, filmy curls, and girlish giggle, all as usual; and began to apologize for what she called her "unauthorized yet perhaps not wholly inexcusable intrusion," with her old amiability and incoherency. She had come prepared to keep up a cheerful mien, having decided, in her own mind, not to distress the feelings of the family by any lachrymose allusions. But when Mrs. Bransby rose up to welcome her, and not only took her by the hand, but kissed her on the cheek, and led her towards the place of honour in the armchair, this proceeding so overcame the kind-hearted creature that she abruptly turned her back on them all, pulled out her pocket-handkerchief, and burst into tears.

"I really must apol—apologize," she sobbed, still presenting the broad back of a very smart shawl to the company—an attitude which made her elaborate politeness extremely comical; for she addressed her speech point-blank to the wall-paper, with abundance of bows and gestures. "I am ashamed, indeed. Pray excuse me! The suddenness of the emo—emotion, and the sight of the dear children, coupled with—I believe—a slight touch of the prevalent influenza, but nothing in the least infectious, dear Mrs. Bransby! But pray do not allow me to disturb the harmony of this fest—festive meeting with 'most admired disorder,' as our immortal bard puts it! Although what there is to admire in disorder, and who admired it, must probably remain for ever ambiguous."

By the end of this speech—the utterance of which had been interrupted by several interludes of pocket-handkerchief—Mrs. Simpson was sufficiently composed to turn round, and take the chair offered to her. The children were grinning undisguisedly. "Simmy" was associated in their minds with many pleasant and many comical recollections. Mrs. Bransby was smiling too. But perhaps it was only the warning spectacle of Mrs. Simpson's emotion which enabled her to choke down her own inclination to cry.

"This is a most pleasant surprise," she said. "When did you arrive in London?"

"Why, the fact is—" began Amelia. But suddenly interrupting herself, she jumped up from her seat, and made Mr. Bragg a sweeping curtsey. "Pardon me," she exclaimed, "if, in the first moment, I was oblivious of your presence! Although not personally acquainted, Oldchester people claim the privilege of recognizing Mr. Bragg as one of our native products. An unforeseen honour, indeed! And—do my eyes deceive me, or have I the pleasure of greeting Mr. Owen Rivers? What an extraordinary coincidence! I had heard you were residing here in the character of a boarder," she added, as emphatically as though that were an obvious reason for being surprised to see him there. "Really, I seem to be transported back into our ancient city; and should scarcely start to hear the cathedral chimes, or the steam-whistle from the brewery, or any of the dear familiar sounds—although the steam whistle, I must admit, is trying, and, in certain forms of nervous disorder, I believe, excruciating."

It was not easy, at any time, to obtain a clear and collected answer to a question from Mrs. Simpson. But in her present state of excitement the difficulty was immensely increased. Her language—partly in honour of Mr. Bragg—was so flowery, and she kept darting up every discursive cross-alley which opened out of the main line of talk in so bewildering a fashion, as to become at moments unintelligible. And it was a long time before any of the party elicited from her how it was that she came to be in London. At length, however, it appeared that "Bassy" was entrusted with a commission to buy a pianoforte; and having found a substitute to take his organ and attend to his pupils for a week, he and his wife had suddenly resolved to take a holiday in London together.

"I had, of course, intended to seek you out, dear Mrs. Bransby," she said; "ever mindful, as I must be, of the many kind favours I have received from you and"—here she gulped dangerously; but recovered herself and went on—"from all the family. But we came away in such a hurry at the last, a cheap excursion train being, in fact, our immediate motive."

"Locomotive," put in Martin jocosely.

"Quite so," said Amelia, with the utmost suavity. "A very proper correction." Then, seeing his mischievous face dimpling with laughter, she exclaimed, "Oh, of course!—locomotive. Very good, Martin! Ah, I am as absent as ever, you see!" Here she playfully shook her head until sundry metallic bobs upon her bonnet fell off, and had to be hunted for and picked up. "Well, so it was. I was hurried away by Bassy's impetuosity—although, in justice to him, I must state that the time bills were peremptory, and there was no margin for delay or deliberation—almost without a carpet bag! I had no opportunity, therefore, of inquiring of any mutual friend in Oldchester for your address."

"There are scarcely any who know it, or care to know it," said Mrs. Bransby, in a low voice.

"Oh, pardon me, dear Mrs. Bransby! No, no; that must not be said, for the honour of Oldchester! Your memory is affectionately cherished by all the more refined and sympathetic souls among us. Only last week Mr. Crump, the butcher, was respectfully inquiring for news of you. You remember Crump! A worthy man, whose spirit—notwithstanding the dictum of the Swan of Avon—is by no means 'subdued to what it works in,' beyond a transient greasiness, which lies merely on the surface."

"Yes; I remember him very well. But who, then, was it who directed you to this house?" asked Mrs. Bransby, hoping that her guest was not aware why Martin had suddenly retired behind the window curtains in a paroxysm of laughter.

"Ah! That, again, is one of the most extraordinary circumstances! Who do you think it was?"

"I cannot tell at all."

"Guess!"

"Miss Piper, perhaps," suggested Ethel.

"Not exactly Miss Piper," said Mrs. Simpson, with strong emphasis on the qualifying adverb, as though her informant's identity were only barely distinguishable from that of Miss Piper. "But you burn, Ethel! You are very near. However, I will not keep you longer in suspense. It was Miss Clara Bertram."

"Oh! I might have thought of her, for she is a neighbour of ours," said Mrs. Bransby.

"Is she?" asked Owen.

"Yes; she lives in a house with a rather good garden, not far from here. The situation is a little inconvenient for her profession, I fancy. But she has invalid relatives, to whom the garden is a great boon. We met accidentally in the street one day, and she recognized me at once. I was surprised that she did so."

"Nay, I should rather have been surprised had she forgotten you," said Mrs. Simpson, "'For the heart,'" dear Mrs. Bransby, "'that once truly loves, never forgets, but as fondly loves on to the—' Not, of course, that there was anything beyond the very slightest acquaintance between you and Miss Bertram in Oldchester. Bassy is, in fact, at her house now, with a few musical professors, whom she kindly invited us to meet—the artistic element which is so akin to Bassy's soul—combined with the seductions of the Indian weed, of which Miss Bertram's papa is quite a devotee—so that, you see, finding you were so near, I slipped away to see you; and I have promised to return before it is time to go back to the boarding-house where we are staying."

At this point Mr. Bragg got up to take his leave.

"I shall look in again before long, Mrs. Bransby, if you'll allow me," he said; "and we'll have a little more talk about my young friend there. Good night to you, ma'am," turning to shake hands with Mrs. Simpson.

This brought that lady "to her legs" in more senses than one. She favoured Mr. Bragg with a long and enthusiastic address, embracing an extraordinary variety of topics, from the proud pre-eminence of British commerce, to the force of friendship as portrayed in the classical example of Damon and Pythias.

"I will not ask, in the beautiful words of the Caledonian ditty, 'Should auld acquaintance be forgot, and days o' lang syne?' for I am certain that you are entirely incapable of doing anything of the sort, as is proved by your presence beneath this refined roof-tree," said Mrs. Simpson. "But I must bear my humble testimony to the eminent virtues of our exquisite friend—if I may be allowed the privilege of calling her so. I have seen her basking in prosperity, and unspoiled by the smiles of fortune, and now in the cold shade of comparatively untoward circumstances, she beams with the same congenial lustre. In short," cried Amelia, suddenly abandoning what Bobby and Billy called her "dictionary" style for a homelier language which came straight from her heart, "a better wife and mother, a gentler mistress, a kinder friend there never was, or could be, in this world."

Owen offered to accompany Mr. Bragg in order to show him the way to the nearest cabstand, and they left the house together.

"She's a sing'lar character," observed Mr. Bragg, after they had walked a few steps.

"You mean Mrs. Simpson?"

"Ah, yes; Mrs. Simpson. There's too much clack about her; and her talk's puzzling from being—what you might call of a zigzag sort of a nature; and she's cast in a queer kind of a mould altogether. But I think she rings true, and that's the main thing, in mortals or metals."

"I'm quite sure her praise of Mrs. Bransby is true, at any rate," said Owen warmly.

"H'm!" grunted Mr. Bragg, and walked on in silence. When they came within view of a cabstand, he turned round, and said he would not trouble Owen to come any further with him. And just as the latter was about to say "Good-night," Mr. Bragg observed meditatively, "She has that little place beautifully neat, and as clean as a new pin. Seems to be bringing up those children in the right way, too. Poor soul! it's a heavy charge for a delicate lady like her. I think I shall be able to do something for that eldest boy. But p'r'aps you'd better not say anything at present—eh? It's cruel to raise up false hopes; and some folks build such a wonderful high scaffolding of expectations on a word or two; and if there's not bricks enough to do anything adequate to the scaffolding—why, then that's awkward. Good night, Mr. Rivers."

Owen well knew that hopes had already been aroused by the mere presence of the rich man in that poor little home. But he knew, also, that there was no danger of Mrs. Bransby's hopes turning into claims; and that she would be humbly grateful for very small help. He felt almost elated on her behalf as he returned to Collingwood Terrace. "I only hope," he said to himself, "that Mr. Bragg won't visit any of my sins on Mrs. Bransby's head, when he finds them out! But no; to do the old boy justice, I believe he is above that."

Meanwhile, Amelia Simpson had been imparting a budget of Oldchester news. After many discursive sallies she came to the topic of Lucius Cheffington's recent death. He had died since the Simpsons' departure from Oldchester, but his case had been known to be hopeless for several days previous. The old lord was said to be dreadfully cut up; more so, even, than on the death of his eldest son. But Lucius had always been understood to be his father's favourite.

"And they do say," continued Mrs. Simpson, "that to a certain fair young friend of ours the blow will be very severe."

"A young friend of ours! Do you mean May Cheffington?"

"Ah, no! Our dear Miranda knew scarcely anything of her noble relatives at Combe Park. And even the most affectionate disposition—and I'm sure our dear Miranda is imbued with every proper feeling—can scarcely cling with personal devotion to an almost total stranger, although united by the ties of kindred! No; I was speaking of Miss Hadlow."

"Constance!"

"Yes, although I have never been on terms to address her by her baptismal appellation, that, I confess, is the young lady I do mean."

Then Mrs. Simpson went on to tell her astonished listener how that Constance Hadlow had been visiting some county magnates in the near neighbourhood of Combe Park during the latter part of Lucius's illness; how she had been admitted to see and talk with the invalid, when other persons had been excluded with scant courtesy; how she had rapidly come to be on a footing of intimacy at the great house, which astonished the neighbourhood; and how at length that fact was explained by the current report that if Lucius had recovered—which at one time appeared not unlikely—he would have married her, with his father's full approbation.

"I did not venture to allude to the subject before Mr. Rivers—how brown he has become! Quite the southern hue of romance!—because, you know, he was said at one time to be desperately in love with his cousin; and I feared to hurt his feelings."

"Oh, I don't think it would hurt his feelings," said Mrs. Bransby; "I really do not believe he cares at all for his cousin, in that way."

"I'm sure he doesn't!" cried Ethel, who took a thoroughly feminine interest in the subject.

"Ethel! I scarcely think you know anything at all about the matter. And I am sure it is not for a little girl like you to give an opinion."

"No, mother. Only—Martin and I know who we should like him to marry. Don't we, Martin?"

Martin was rather shamefaced at being thus brought publicly into the discussion, and rebuffed his sister with a lofty air.

"Oh, don't talk bosh and silliness," he rejoined. "Girls are always bothering about a fellow's getting married. Leave him alone. He's very well as he is."

"He is certainly most affable, and thoroughly the gentleman," observed Mrs. Simpson, with her universal, beaming benevolence.

"Oh, he is good!" cried the widow, clasping her hands. "So delicately considerate! Such a true, loyal friend!"

In her own mind she was convinced that Mr. Bragg's visit was entirely due to Owen's influence. And her heart was overflowing with gratitude.

A new idea darted into Mrs. Simpson's imagination, always ready to accept a romantic view of things. How charming it would be if young Mr. Rivers were to marry the beautiful widow! They would make a delightful couple. Considerations of ways and means entered no more into Mrs. Simpson's calculations than they would have entered into little Enid's. The building of her castles in the air was entirely independent of money.

But there was, at bottom, a more common sensible reason which made the idea that Owen might marry Mrs. Bransby, agreeable to Amelia Simpson. In spite of the sympathy of Mr. Crump, the butcher, and other congenial spirits, it could not be denied that some rumours of a very unpleasant sort had recently been circulated in Oldchester to the discredit of Mrs. Bransby. When it became known that young Rivers, on his return from Spain, was to live in her house, the rumours began to take a more definite shape. No one could trace them to their source—perhaps no one tried very seriously to do so.

People asked each other if they had not always thought there was something a little odd—not quite becoming and nice—in the way that young Rivers used to be running in and out of Martin Bransby's house, at all times and seasons. Even during poor Mr. Bransby's lifetime, strange things had been said—at least, it now appeared so; for very few of the gossips professed to have heard any whispers of scandal themselves, while Martin lived. There was a strange story of young Rivers being caught kissing Mrs. Bransby's hand in the garden. There might be no harm in kissing a lady's hand. But, under the circumstances, there was something, almost revolting, was there not? And, then, why was Mrs. Bransby in such a hurry to run away from Oldchester?—away from all her friends and all her husband's friends? Surely she would have done better to remain there! At all events Mr. Theodore Bransby had been much annoyed by her doing so; and had replied to old friends, who spoke to him on the subject, that he could not control his step-mother's actions; could only advise her for the best; and should endeavour to assist her and her children, if she would allow him to do so. Of course people understood when he said that, that Mrs. Bransby was acting contrary to his judgment. And now, Mr. Rivers was actually going to reside in her house! It positively was not decent! No wonder Theodore looked distressed, and avoided the subject. It must be altogether a very painful affair for him.

This kind of scandal, with its inevitable crescendo, had been very differently received by Sebastian Simpson and his wife. He could not be said to encourage it; but neither did he repudiate it indignantly. But Amelia was true and devoted to Mrs. Bransby, and incurred some unpopularity by her enthusiastic praises of that absent lady. But there were also people who said what a good creature Mrs. Simpson was, and that—although she was a goose, and had probably been quite taken in—they liked to see her stand up for those who had been kind to her.

Under these circumstances, it was a great triumph for Amelia to find Mr. Bragg—the respectable, the influential, the rich Mr. Bragg—visiting Mrs. Bransby on a friendly footing, and treating her with marked kindness and respect. Simple though she might be, Amelia was not at all too simple to understand that the millionaire's approbation would carry weight with it. But now the idea of a marriage between Owen and the widow seemed still more delightful than the mere clearing of Mrs. Bransby's character from all aspersions. People had said that, as for him, the young man was probably suffering under a temporary infatuation. And that, even supposing the best, and taking the most charitable view of this—flirtation, it was out of the question that he should think of marrying a woman of Mrs. Bransby's age, and with five children to support!

Why should it be out of the question? Amelia said to herself. The few years' difference in their ages was of no consequence at all. And as to the family—Mr. Bragg would probably take Owen into partnership. He was evidently devotedly fond of them both! She had privately arranged the details of the wedding in her own mind before Owen returned from conducting Mr. Bragg to his cab.

When he did so, Mrs. Simpson declared it was time for her to go, and got up from her chair. But between that and her actual departure a great many words had still to intervene. She reverted to the death in the Castlecombe family; made a brief excursion to the report of Captain Cheffington's second marriage, "truly deplorable! But still, or dear Miranda is happily launched among the élite of the beau monde, so, perhaps, it is not so bad after all!" And then suddenly added—

"By the way, dear Mrs. Bransby, it was reported that your step-son, Mr. Theodore, intended to withdraw his candidature at the next election. But I am told on the best authority—Mr. Lowe, the political agent—that that is a mistake. So I hope we may see him among the legislators. Quite the figure for it, I'm sure. However, of course, you must know all that news far better than I. I hope to see our dear Miranda before leaving town."

Owen observed, with indignation, that the mention of Theodore appeared to have suggested May to her mind. Nor did the circumstance escape Mrs. Bransby.

"Do you say you shall see May Cheffington?" she asked.

"Yes; I purpose calling. Although well aware of Mrs. Dormer-Smith's high social position, still I think our dear Miranda's warm heart will welcome one who has so recently seen her beloved grandmamma. Ah, we do not easily relinquish the fond memories of childhood. Thank you, my dear Ethel. Is that my pocket-handkerchief? Really! I wonder how it came there!" (Ethel had picked it up from under the tea-table.) "I believe that even in the princely halls—I think I left my umbrella in the passage. Eh? Oh, Bobby has found it—in the princely halls of Castlecombe her memory will revert to Friar's Row. In the words of the poet, 'though strangers may roam, those hills and those valleys I once called my home'—although, of course, Oldchester is not mountainous. And as to roaming, I presume that hills and valleys are always more or less liable to be roamed over by strangers, whether one calls them one's home or not."

By this time Mrs. Simpson had got herself out of the room into the narrow outer passage; and, seeing Owen put on his great coat again, in order to escort her, she stopped to protest against his taking that trouble.

"Oh, pray! Too kind! It is but a stone's throw from here, and I am not at all afraid. Sure of the way? Well, no; not quite sure. I took two wrong turnings in coming. But I can easily inquire for Marlborough House. Eh? Oh, Blenheim Lodge is it? To be sure! Marlborough House is the august residence—However, historically speaking I was not so far wrong, was I? Well, if you insist, Mr. Rivers, I will accept your polite attention with gratitude. Good-bye, once more, dear children. If I possibly can come again before leaving London, dear Mrs. Bransby—"

At this point Owen perceived that decisive measures were necessary, if the good lady's farewells were not to last until midnight. He took Mrs. Simpson's arm, signed to Phoebe to open the door, and led his fair charge outside it, almost before she knew what was happening.

"Excuse me for hurrying you," he said; "but the night is cold; Mrs. Bransby is not very strong; and I thought it imprudent—for both of you—to stand talking in that draughty passage."

"Oh, quite right. Thank you a thousand times. She is deserving, indeed, of every delicate care and attention."

A slighter circumstance would have sufficed to confirm Mrs. Simpson's romantic fancies. She said to herself that Mr. Rivers's devotion was chivalrous indeed. And she forthwith proceeded to sound Mrs. Bransby's praises, in an unbroken stream of eloquence, all the way to Blenheim Lodge. Owen had intended to ask her one or two questions—about Mrs. Dobbs, and as to when she thought of calling at Mrs. Dormer-Smith's house. He had even held a half-formed intention of entrusting her with a message for May. But it was hopeless to arrest her flow of speech—unless by making his request in a more serious fashion than he thought it prudent to do. Amelia's goodwill might be relied on. But she was absolutely devoid of discretion. And, at all events, if he said nothing, there would be no ground for her to build a blunder on.

He little knew!

CHAPTER VIII.

When Mrs. Dormer-Smith practised any deception—a necessity which unfortunately arose rather frequently in the prosecution of her duty to society—she was wont to call it diplomacy. She called it so to herself, in her most private cogitations. She was not a woman whose conscience could be satisfied by any but the best chosen phraseology.

In speaking to May of her conversation with Owen, she gave a "diplomatic" version of it. It was May herself who innocently suggested the line her aunt took. When she found that Owen had left the house without any further farewell to her, she said not a word, she demanded no explanation; but the disappointed look in her eyes, the drooping curves of her young mouth, were sufficiently eloquent. Had she fired up into indignation against her aunt, assuming as a matter of course that

Owen had been refused permission to see her again, that would have seemed quite in accordance with her character. This was, in fact, what Pauline had prepared herself to meet. But this quietude was strange. It seemed as though May were ready to be wounded. Her aunt thought that it would not have occurred to the girl—who was high-spirited enough in certain directions—to suspect that her lover might be less eager to see her again than she was to see him, unless some previous fact or fancy had put the suspicion into her head. Fact or fancy, Mrs. Dormer-Smith thought it mattered little which, so long as the suspicion were there.

Of course it would not do to pretend that Owen had not asked to see her. That would be a clumsy falsehood, sure of speedy detection; and, besides, Mrs. Dormer-Smith wished to avoid explicit falsehood. She was only diplomatic.

"I was obliged, I need scarcely tell you, May," she said, "to refuse Mr. Rivers's request for some more words with you. It would have been a gross dereliction of duty on my part to permit it."

"He did ask to see me, then?" said May, with a bright eager look in her eyes. It was a look her aunt was well acquainted with, and usually presaged some speech which had to be deplored as being "odd," or "bad form."

"Oh yes," replied Mrs. Dormer-Smith wearily. "Of course, he asked; I had to go through all that. Under the circumstances he could scarcely do less."

The shadow of the eyelashes suddenly drooped down over the bright eyes; and Aunt Pauline saw that her shot had told.

"Has it ever occurred to you, May," Mrs. Dormer-Smith went on, "that you are prejudicing the future of this gentleman?"

May looked up quickly, but made no answer.

"Of course, it cannot be allowed to go on—this engagement, as he absurdly terms it."

"It is an engagement," interrupted May in a low voice.

Her aunt passed over the interruption, and continued. "But I think that in justice to him you ought to reflect that meanwhile you are injuring his prospects. I do not mean," she added with gentle sarcasm, "that you will injure him by preventing him from marrying the Widow Bransby; because I cannot honestly say that I think that a good prospect for any young man."

"All those stories are malicious falsehoods," said May resolutely; but her throat was painfully constricted, and her heart felt like lead in her breast.

"My dear child, one scarcely sees why people should trouble themselves to invent stories about this lady and gentleman, who, after all, are persons of very small importance. But at any rate the stories are circulated, and believed. Under these circumstances it seems to me a—well, to say the least, an indiscreet proceeding, that Mr. Rivers, the moment he returns to England, should rush to Mrs. Bransby's house, and take up his abode there! However, it may be quite a usual sort of thing among persons in their position. Very likely. I only know that in our world it would not do. We are less Arcadian. When I spoke of injuring Mr. Rivers's prospects, I meant as between him and his employer."

"Oh!" cried May, turning round with a pale indignant face. A confused crowd of words seemed to be struggling in her mind; but she was unable, for the moment, to utter one of them.

"Dear May," said her aunt, "do not, I beg and implore you, do not be tragic! I don't think I could stand that sort of thing. It would be the last straw."

"Do you think—do you mean that Mr. Bragg would turn Owen away, out of spite?" asked May in a quiet tone, after a short silence.

"We need not employ such a word as that. But Mr. Bragg made you an offer of marriage, and we can hardly expect him to find it pleasant when he is told 'the young lady refused you in order to marry your clerk.'"

"Not 'in order to—' You know I have assured you that under no circumstances would I have married Mr. Bragg."

"Yes, May; you have assured me so. But you are not yet nineteen; and I—alas!—was nineteen more than nineteen years ago. It struck me that Mr. Rivers was desirous that you should take your full share of responsibility in the matter. And he seemed a little anxious about his place. At all events he brought forward the salary he is earning with Mr. Bragg as an important element in the financial budget with which he favoured me. (How the man could think for a moment that your family would consent!) I gathered that he was decidedly unwilling to lose it."

"He only took it for my sake."

"Ah! That was particularly kind of him. Well, it strikes me that he would now like to keep it for his own. Of course I must write to your father. I presume you will admit that it is proper to inform him of the state of the case?"

"You can write if you choose, Aunt Pauline. It will make no difference, now."

"I think you will find it will make a considerable difference! Circumstances have entirely altered your father's position in the world. You will be daughter and heiress to a peer of the realm."

There was a long pause. May stood with one foot on the fender before a bright fire in her aunt's dressing-room, her elbow on the mantel-shelf, and her cheek resting in her hand.

Then Mrs. Dormer-Smith resumed softly, "Perhaps I deceive myself—the wish may be father to the thought—but I confess I got the impression that it might not be hopeless to induce Mr. Rivers to withdraw, voluntarily, from his false position. Of course he could do no less than stand to it so long as you appeared resolved to stand to it; but—I hope and trust, May, that if it should be as I think, you would not insist on being obstinate?"

"You know, as well as I know it myself, Aunt Pauline, that I would die sooner than hold him bound for one instant, unless—But I won't answer you as if I took your words seriously."

Upon that she managed to walk out of the room with dignity and dry eyes. But the poor child, for all her brave words, did take her aunt's hint so seriously as to throw herself on the bed in her own room, and lie sobbing there for an hour.

To her husband, Mrs. Dormer-Smith had reported the interview with Owen as accurately as she could. She did, indeed, declare her belief that the young man was a Nihilist. But that was said genuinely enough. A man of gentle birth, who deliberately stated—apparently with sympathetic approval—that there were mechanics who would be ashamed to own Captain Cheffington as a father-in-law, was, in her opinion, evidently prepared to demolish the existing bases of human society.

Mr. Dormer-Smith was very sorry for his niece: more sorry than he thought it necessary to express at that moment to Pauline. But still he agreed with his wife that every effort ought to be made to prevent her marrying so disastrously. It might have been supposed, perhaps, that Mr. Dormer-Smith, not having found his own mode of life productive of unalloyed felicity, in spite of a fair income, aristocratic connections, and a wife devoted to keeping up their position in society, would have been not unwilling to let May try her fate in a different fashion. But it is a common experience that, although the possession of certain things gives them not the smallest gleam of happiness, yet, to a large class of minds, the thought of doing without these things suggests misery. The unusual is a terrible scarecrow, and keeps many weak-minded birds from the cherries.

Mr. Dormer-Smith was to go down to Combe Park to attend the funeral of his deceased cousin-in-law. He had some liking for Lucius, and thought, as he sat in the railway carriage speeding down to the little wayside station beyond Oldchester, where he was to alight, that it was a truly inscrutable dispensation which took away Lucius—a man at least harmless, and of honourable principles—and left Augustus alive; and he could not help regretting the death of Lucius on May's account. Lucius had been, in his dry, peculiar manner, very kind towards his young cousin. He had resented her father's neglect of her; and he treated her, when they met, with a certain air of protection, and almost tenderness, such as one might assume towards a child or an animal that one knew to have been hardly used. Frederick thought it not impossible that, had Lucius lived, his influence might have been brought to bear on May for her good. But Lucius was gone; and Augustus remained to disgrace the family and annoy his relations more than ever.

This, however, was not Pauline's idea. Although her brother's second marriage had, apparently, receded into the background, in consequence of these new troubles about May, yet it had really been occupying many of Mrs. Dormer-Smith's thoughts. She certainly considered it to be not quite so terrible a business now that Lucius—poor dear Lucius!—was out of the way, as it would have been had he lived. A Viscountess Castlecombe might be floated, Pauline said to herself, where a Mrs. Augustus Cheffington would stick in the mud. They could live chiefly abroad—not, of course, in a shabby street in Brussels; but on the Riviera, for instance. A warm climate had always suited Augustus. And as for herself, she, Pauline, would never willingly pass an hour in England between the first of November and the last of April. It really would not be at all disagreeable to spend one or two of the winter months with one's brother and sister-in-law—thank Heaven that, at least, she was not English! So many deviations from "good form" might be got over on the plea of foreign manners—at some charming, sunny place, say St. Raphael! That was not so far from Nice as to preclude the enjoyment of some little gaiety and society. They would have a villa of their own, of course. Perhaps, Augustus might build himself one. That sort of life would enable them to catch a good many travellers on the wing. And, with sufficient tact and savoir faire (which Pauline flattered herself she could supply), it might be possible to fill their house with a succession of "nice" people. The "nicest" people were sometimes rather less exigent on the other side of the Channel! At any rate, there would be less difficulty in "floating" Lady Castlecombe on the stream of society abroad than at home. Augustus would be rich; Uncle George could not prevent that, let him do what he would with his savings and his investments. For the estates were strictly entailed; and Uncle George had nursed them into something like treble their value when he succeeded to the property. Mrs. Griffin heard from Lady Mary, the Dean of Oldchester's wife, who had it from the Rector of Combe, that Lord Castlecombe was crushed by the loss of Lucius. Augustus might not have to wait very long for his inheritance. How strangely things turn out! Well, she would write very kindly and gently to her brother. There was the excuse of addressing him about May; and she would take the opportunity of sending a civil word to his wife. It must be done delicately, of course. But Augustus should see that there was no disposition to be hostile, on the part of his sister, at any rate.

It was in the forenoon of the day after Owen's visit that Mrs. Dormer-Smith was thus meditating. Her husband had started for Combe Park. The house was very quiet; the fire in her dressing-room was very warm; several budgets of gossip had arrived by the post from various country houses, and lay unopened within reach of her hand. Mrs. Dormer-Smith felt that there was a certain "luxury of woe" in a family affliction which justified one in saying "not at home," and sitting in a wadded dressing-gown, without causing one either heart-ache or anxiety. And she had been softly rocking herself in the day-dreams recorded above, when they were interrupted as suddenly, if not as fatally, as those of La Fontaine's milkmaid. James stood before her with a visiting card on a salver, and a cloud of depression—which was the utmost revelation of ill-humour his well-trained visage ever allowed itself, above-stairs—on his shaven countenance.

"What is this, James? What do you mean by bringing me cards here—and now?"

"I said 'not at home,' ma'am, but the—the party didn't seem to understand; and, unfortunately, Miss Cheffington happening to pass through the hall at that moment—"

"Who is it? Where is the person?"

Mrs. Dormer-Smith took the card and examined it through her eyeglass with a sinking heart. Could that subversive young man have returned? Or was there, perchance, some other suitor in the field? An anarchical shoemaker, possibly! Pauline's confidence in Mrs. Dobbs had been completely blown into the air by learning that she had approved and encouraged May's engagement to a young man who calmly avowed that he possessed one hundred and fifty pounds a year of his own; and she felt that any dreadful revelation might be made at any moment. But the name on the card was not a masculine one, at any rate. Mrs. Something-or-other Simpson, she read on it.

"Is the—lady with Miss Cheffington now, James?"

"Yes, ma'am. Miss Cheffington took her into the dining-room. I thought that, as last time—I mean as Smithson wasn't in the way—I'd better let you know, ma'am."

"Did the lady ask for me?"

"N-no; I—well, I really hardly know, ma'am."

"You hardly know?"

"Well, ma'am, she talked a great deal, and so—so—It was uncommonly difficult to follow what she said. At first I thought she announced her name as being Oldchester. I did say 'not at home' twice, but it was no use; and then Miss Cheffington happening to pass through the hall—"

"That will do."

James retired with an injured air, and Mrs. Dormer-Smith was left to consider within herself whether duty required her to be present at the interview between May and this unknown Mrs. Simpson, or whether she might indulge herself by sitting still and reading Mrs. Griffin's last letter in comfort and quietude. After a brief deliberation, she resolved to go downstairs. There was no knowing who or what the woman might be. James had said something about Oldchester. No doubt she came from that place. Perhaps she was an emissary of Mr. Rivers! Pauline, as she rose and drew a shawl round her shoulders, before facing the chillier atmosphere of the staircase, breathed a pious hope that her brother Augustus might sooner or later compensate her for all the sacrifices she was making on behalf of May.

Before she reached the dining-room, she heard the sound of a fluent monologue. May was not speaking at all, so far as Mrs. Dormer-Smith could make out. When she entered the room, she found the girl sitting beside a stout, florid woman, dressed in trente-six couleurs—as Pauline phrased it to herself—who was holding forth with a profusion of "nods, and becks, and wreathed smiles."

Mrs. Dormer-Smith made this stranger a bow of such freezing politeness as ought to have petrified her on the spot; and, turning to May, inquired with raised eyebrows, "Who is your friend, May?"

But Amelia Simpson had not the least suspicion that she was being snubbed in the most superior style known to modern science. She rose, with her usual impulsive vehemence, from her chair, and said smilingly—

"Mrs. Dormer-Smith? I thought so! Permit me to apologize for a seeming breach of etiquette. I am well aware that my call ought properly to have been paid to you, the mistress of this elegant mansion; but, being personally unknown—although we are not so 'remote, unfriended, melancholy, or slow'—not that I use the epithet in a slang sense, I assure you!—in Oldchester, as to be unaware that Mrs. Dormer-Smith, the accomplished relative of our dear Miranda, is in all respects 'a glass of fashion and a mould of form.' Only I wish our divine bard had chosen any other word than 'mould,' which somehow is inextricably connected in my mind with short sixes."

"Oh!" ejaculated Pauline, in a faint voice, as she sank into a chair; and she remained gazing at the visitor with a helpless air.

At another time, May would have had a keen and enjoying sense of the comic elements in this little scene; but although she saw them now as distinctly as she ever could have done, she was too unhappy to enjoy them. She said quietly—

"This is Mrs. Simpson, Aunt Pauline. Her husband is professor of music at Oldchester; and they are both very old friends of dear Granny."

Now, Pauline was not prepared to break altogether with Mrs. Dobbs. Mrs. Dobbs had behaved very badly in that matter of young Rivers; but something must be excused to ignorance; and her allowance for May continued to be paid up every quarter with exemplary punctuality. Let matters turn out as well as possible, there must still be a "meantime" during which Mrs. Dobbs's money would be valuable—and, indeed, indispensable—if May were to remain under her aunt's roof. It occurred to Pauline to invite this incredibly attired person to share Cécile's early dinner in the housekeeper's room, and then to withdraw herself and May on the plea of some imaginary engagement. She was just about to carry out this idea when the reiteration of a name in Mrs. Simpson's rapid talk struck her ear, and excited her curiosity: "Mrs. Bransby." Amelia was talking volubly to May about Mrs. Bransby. She had resumed what she was pleased to call her "conversation" with May, having made some sort of incoherent apology to Mrs. Dormer-Smith, to the effect that she had a very short time to remain, and "so many interesting topics of mutual interest to discuss."

She rambled on about her last evening's visit to Collingwood Terrace. Mr. Rivers and dear Mrs. Bransby would make a charming couple; and as to the difference in years—what did years signify? And the difference was not so great, after all. Mr. Rivers was very steady and staid for his age; and Mrs. Bransby looked so wonderfully youthful!—not a line in her forehead, in spite of all her troubles. And then Mr. Bragg's friendship and countenance would be so valuable! He evidently approved it all. And if he gave Mr. Rivers a share in his business—"even a comparatively small share," said Amelia, feeling that she was keeping well within the limits of probability, and even displaying a certain business-like sobriety of conjecture—considering how colossal an affair that was, everything would be made smooth for them. Mrs. Bransby's children evidently adored Mr. Rivers—which was so delightful! And as for Mr. Rivers's devotion to Mrs. Bransby, no one could doubt that who saw them together. (This was said rather to a shadowy audience of Oldchester persons, who had declared that, however ridiculous Mrs. Bransby might make herself, young Rivers was not likely to tie himself for life to a middle-aged woman with a family, than to Amelia's present hearers.) And after all the unkind things which had been reported in Oldchester, it would be a heartfelt joy to Mrs. Bransby's friends to see her widowhood so happily brought to a close.

"What unkind things have been reported in Oldchester? What do you mean?" asked May. She spoke eagerly, but quite firmly. There was no tremor in her voice, no rising of unbidden tears to her eyes. Her whole heart and soul were concentrated on getting at the truth.

Amelia pulled herself up a little. She had been running on rather too heedlessly. Some things had latterly been said of Mrs. Bransby which could scarcely be repeated with propriety to a young lady—at least, according to Amelia's code of what was proper.

"Oh, my dear Miranda," she stammered, "the world is ever censorious; but as the lyric bard so beautifully puts it—

'I'd weep when friends deceive me,
If thou wert like them, untrue.'

Although why it is taken for granted that friends—in any true sense of the word—should be expected to deceive, I must leave to meta-physics to determine!"

Mrs. Dormer-Smith here put in her word. "Oh, we had already heard of these scandals," she said. "My niece was inclined to doubt their existence, I believe. I hope you are convinced now, May!"

"Really!" exclaimed Mrs. Simpson, glancing with growing uneasiness from May to her aunt. Something, she perceived, was wrong—but what?

"Dear Mrs. Simpson," said May, "I am very sure that whoever else was unkind and scandalous, you were not."

"Ever the same sweet nature!" murmured Amelia; "but, perhaps, it was not so much that people were unkind, not exactly unkind, but mistaken. You see, when a person tells you a thing, positively, there is a certain unkindness in not believing it! And yet, on the other hand, one would not willingly accept evil reports of a fellow-creature. There is a difficulty in harmoniously blending the two horns of this dilemma—if I may be allowed to say so—which, to some extent, excuses error."

The good lady's habitual confusion of ideas was increased by the nervous fear that she had said something unfortunate. She brought her visit to an end earlier than she otherwise might have done; and in taking effusive leave of May she whispered—

"I trust I did not commit any solecism against the code of manners which belongs to the élite of the haut ton, in alluding to our fair friend, Mrs. B—?"

"No, no," answered May gently; "don't vex yourself by thinking so."

Mrs. Simpson brightened up a little, and asked aloud, "And what message shall I give to grandmamma?"

May scarcely recognized "Granny" under this appellation, adopted in honour of Mrs. Dormer-Smith's social distinction. But after an instant she said—

"Oh, give her my dear love; I shall write to her to-morrow. And, please, my love to Uncle Jo."

"Ah, I recognize our dear Miranda's affectionate constancy there!" cried Amelia. "Mr. Weatherhead will be much gratified."

"Gratified! I think he would have a right to be disgusted if I forgot him! Dear, good, honest, kind-hearted Uncle Jo!"

"Who is this person?" demanded Pauline, genuinely aghast at the idea that some hitherto unknown brother of Susan Dobbs was in existence. The one extenuating circumstance in that unfortunate marriage had always appeared to her to be the fact that Susan was an only child.

"He is a certain Mr. Joseph Weatherhead," answered May, with great distinctness. "He was originally a bookbinder's apprentice, and then a printer and bookseller in a small way of business at Birmingham. He is my grandmother's brother-in-law, and one of the best men in the world. He used to give me shillings when I went back to school; and once I remember—that was just before my father left me on granny's hands—he noticed that my boots were disgracefully shabby, and took me out and bought me a new pair."

Then Mrs. Simpson went away in a nervous flutter, and with the positive, though puzzled, conviction that there was something very wrong indeed between the aunt and niece.

CHAPTER IX.

Of course Mrs. Dormer-Smith availed herself to the utmost of Mrs. Simpson's revelations. They were most valuable. And they had the effect of confirming her own vague suspicions in an unexpected manner. That which had been merely "diplomatic" colouring in her presentment of the situation to May, turned out to be real, solid, vulgar fact!

The state of things was certainly very singular. But she did not doubt that she had discovered the true explanation of it. Mr. Rivers had probably been infatuated with Mrs. Bransby before her husband's death. Such infatuations were by no means rare at their respective ages. The lady had been willing to coquette after a sentimental fashion: which, also, was not unprecedented! There had probably been no serious intention of evil-doing on either side. "At all events we can give them the benefit of the doubt!" reflected Pauline charitably. Meanwhile, Mr. Rivers had met with May. He had been thrown a great deal into her society, had been encouraged by her stupid old grandmother, had thought her connections and prospects desirable, and had probably admired herself a good deal. Pauline did not see why not. It was very possible for a man to admire more than one woman at a time! Mr. Rivers makes love to May, persuades her to enter into a clandestine engagement, and goes abroad. But then something unforeseen happens: the husband dies; and all the old feeling is revived. Mr. Rivers hastens back to England. The widow is pathetic—helpless—throws herself on his advice and support. He goes to live under her roof, and the mischief is done! A handsome, scheming woman, under these circumstances, might well be irresistible. As to him, of course he had behaved badly in a way. But, after all, one must accept men as they are. And, as Pauline said to herself, the folly of young men in such matters, and their invincible tendency to sacrifice themselves to the wrong woman, are simply unfathomable! At any rate whether her cousin's death had made Rivers more willing to fulfil his engagement to May; or whether he would be glad of a pretext to break with her in order to marry Mrs. Bransby and her five children; May must clearly perceive that she could have nothing more to say to him.

All these considerations, and the conclusion to which they led, Mrs. Dormer-Smith administered to her niece, in larger or smaller doses, during the remainder of the day. Sometimes it was by way of a few drops at a time:—a hint, a word, perhaps merely a sigh, accompanied by an expressive shrug of the shoulders. Sometimes it was a copious pouring forth of the evidence. Sometimes it was an appeal to May's pride: sometimes to her principles.

The girl was worn out with fighting against shadows. And, though they might be shadows, they were gathering darkly.

The worst was that she was, in one sense, as solitary as though she had been alone on a desert island. There was absolutely no communion of spirit between her and her aunt on this subject. Had her uncle been there, she thought that even he would have understood her better. She could write, of course, to granny; and of course granny would answer her. But another whole long day must elapse before she could have the comfort of granny's letter: even supposing it were sent without a post's delay. She could not see Owen. She was not sure, at moments, whether she wished to see him. And then again, with a sudden revulsion of feeling, she would long for his presence.

She had in her pocket the note he had written on the previous evening, begging her to inform Mr. Bragg of their engagement. It had reached her hands only an hour or two before Amelia Simpson's visit; and was, as yet, unanswered. The note had been dashed off quickly, as we know. And to May, disheartened and confused as she was already by her aunt's version of the interview with Owen, it seemed needlessly brief and dry.

He begged May to tell Mr. Bragg of their engagement at once. Under the circumstances he thought Mr. Bragg ought to know it, and the announcement would come best from her. He had not had a moment in which to speak of it during their hurried interview. But he did not doubt that May would feel as he felt on this point. She had better, if possible, send her communication so that Mr. Bragg should receive it that same afternoon; since he certainly ought to know the truth soon, at any cost.

These last words had reference to the possibility that the revelation might affect the fortunes of the Bransby family. But May knew nothing of that; and they jarred on her. Why should Owen speak to her of the "cost"? It was almost like a boast that he was ready to sacrifice himself. In talking to Aunt Pauline he had shown that he was anxious not to lose his situation. For her sake? Oh yes; no doubt for her sake. But the words jarred on her. The lightest touch will jar upon a bruise.

And then the loneliness of spirit was so trying! Solitude may sometimes be a good counsellor for the brain. But it is rarely so for the heart. Nothing so strengthens our best impulses, faiths, and affections as to see them reflected in the soul of a fellow-creature. To the young especially, want of sympathy with their emotions is like want of daylight to a flower. Those who have travelled half way along life's journey are apt to forget how much diffidence is often mingled with a young girl's acceptance of love. The gift seems so unspeakably great! A trembling sense of unreality sometimes comes with the recognition of its preciousness and beauty.

"Can it be? Am I really loved so much? Dare I believe it?" These questions are often asked by sensitive young hearts. Happiness begets humility in the finer sort of nature.

Elder spectators, looking on at the old, ever-new story, find it clear and simple enough. But to the actors it may seem complex and difficult. Lookers on, in any case, see but a small portion of the drama of our lives. The intensest part of it—the most poignant tragedy, the sunniest comedy—is played within ourselves by invisible forces. Truly, and in dread earnest, "we are such stuff as dreams are made of."

All the day May kept Owen's note in her pocket, and when evening came, she had neither answered it, nor written to Mr. Bragg. Owen was right, no doubt, in saying that Mr. Bragg ought to know the truth. But what was the truth? In the whirlpool of her agitated thoughts sometimes one answer would float uppermost, and sometimes another. Could her aunt be right in saying that she would prejudice Owen's future by holding him to his word? Holding him! But it was rather for Owen to hold her. He could not suspect that his claim would be disallowed. He, at least, had no reason to doubt the completeness of her love for him. And then a scarlet blush would burn her cheeks, and hot tears would be forced from her eyes, by a thought which touched her maiden pride to the quick:—was he not leaving it to her to claim him? If she wrote that letter to Mr. Bragg, she would, in fact, be claiming him.

She had told Mr. Bragg, she remembered, when he asked her if her family approved of the man she had promised to marry, that she, at any rate, was proud to be loved by him. Yes; but too proud to accept a love that was not eagerly given. Oh, it was all weariness, and bitterness, and perturbation of spirit!

Sometimes, for a moment, the recollection of Owen's look and Owen's words would pierce the clouds like a ray of sunshine, and her heart would cry out, "Why am I troubled and tormented by lies and foolishness? Owen is loyal, tender, and true—the soul of truth and honour! I need only trust to him, and all will be well." But then Aunt Pauline would repeat some of poor Amelia Simpson's glowing words about "the charming couple" in Collingwood Terrace—made all the more impressive by the fact that Aunt Pauline really believed them; and the fog would gather again, and she would ask herself, "How if he should be loyal against his inclination?"

In the evening she said to her aunt, "Aunt Pauline, I will go away from London; I will go to Granny. I could not, in any case, continue to take her money for keeping me here. I will go down to Oldchester; that will be best. And Owen and I can arrange afterwards what we will do." For not by a word would she betray a doubt of Owen. To her aunt she upheld his faithfulness unwaveringly; she upheld it, indeed, in her own heart, chiding down her doubts as one chides down a snarling dog. But though she could chide, she could not remove them; they were there, crouching. She was conscious of their existence, as pain is felt in a dream.

But it did not at all suit Mrs. Dormer-Smith's views that her niece should go away in that fashion. "I cannot let you leave my house, May," she said; "I am responsible for you to your father."

Then May rebelled. She declared that Granny had been father and mother and friend to her, and that she did not feel she owed any filial duty except to Granny.

Pauline privately thought that she recognized the influence of Mr. Rivers in this speech. She put her handkerchief to her eyes, and observed plaintively that she was sorry May had no touch of affection for her or for her uncle, who had striven to treat her as their own child. She was genuinely hurt, and thought she had reason to complain of the girl's ingratitude. May recognized that her aunt was sincere in this. She, too, felt that Aunt Pauline had meant to do well for her, although it had all turned out amiss. She thought of the day of her first arrival in town, of her aunt's affectionate reception of her, and gentle sweetness ever since, until these last unhappy days. Her thoughts went back farther—to the time when the dowager was alive, and her aunt used to see her in the dreary old house at Richmond, and mourn over her clothes, and kiss her kindly when she went away.

With a sudden impulse she knelt down beside Mrs. Dormer-Smith's chair, and put her arms round her.

"Aunt Pauline," she said, "I know you have meant to be kind. You have been kind. No doubt I have given you trouble and anxiety; partly, perhaps, by my fault, but more by my misfortune. I am not insensible of all that. But, dear Aunt Pauline, I want you to believe—do, pray, believe—that it would be cruel to separate me from Owen. Nothing shall part us, except his own will," she added in a low voice. Then, after an instant, she went on, pressing her soft young face against her aunt's shoulder, "Perhaps you think I don't care so very deeply for him? Of course you cannot know; you have never seen us together; it has all come upon you quite suddenly. But, indeed, indeed, if I had to give him up, I think it would break my heart. Oh, dear Aunt Pauline, do be kind to us, and help us! I have no mother. And I—I love him so!"

Pauline folded the sobbing girl in her arms. Perhaps she had never felt the great duty she owed to society so hard of fulfilment as at that moment. It was really frightful to think of the havoc wrought by the selfish recklessness of that Nihilist with his hundred and fifty pounds a year! The recollection of the cold-blooded effrontery with which he had mentioned the sum made her shudder.

For a little time she held her niece silently in a motherly embrace. Then she said softly, "This is very sad and distressing, dear May." And her own eyes were full of tears. "However much I may disapprove"—(the clinging arms around her shoulders relaxed their hold a little here; but she gently pressed the girl close to her again)—"and—and deplore the state of the case, it is most painful to me to see you suffer. But we must not allow feeling to override all considerations of what is right and proper. We must not forget that we have duties—duties towards society."

May quietly removed one arm from her aunt's neck, and began to dry her eyes.

"I don't say that those duties are easy. Those who have no position in the world to keep up may be enviable in some respects. I'm sure I am often tempted to envy the people one sees riding in omnibuses," said Pauline, with what she felt to be a bold but forcible hyperbole. "But noblesse oblige. You and I are both born Cheffingtons. It may be all very well for the bourgeoisie to indulge in sentiment, and sweet-hearts, and that sort of thing; but from us society expects something different. There are certain opportunities which, it appears to me, it is absolutely flying in the face of Providence to neglect. I know perfectly well that if the Hautenvilles had the slightest inkling of an idea that you had refused Mr. Bragg, Felicia would come flying back from Rome like a whirlwind. However, I will not dwell on that now. You are dreadfully worn out, my poor child, and your eyes will not be fit to be seen for a week. Rose-water the last thing before going to bed. There is nothing so soothing. Poor child! I must steel myself to do my duty, May; but it really is excessively trying. Go to rest now, dear, and sleep off your agitation. To-morrow we will talk more calmly."

May had gently withdrawn herself from her aunt's embrace, and had risen from her knees. "To-morrow I will go to Granny," she said quietly.

"Ah, no, dearest! that cannot be. It is out of the question. But you may write to Mrs. Dobbs and hear what she says."

Pauline had resolved to write herself to Mrs. Dobbs, detailing all she knew (and a great deal more which she thought she knew) about Mr. Rivers's conduct, and setting forth the change in May's position as the daughter of the future Lord Castlecombe. Things were very different from what they had been three or four months ago. Even Mrs. Dobbs—although she had turned out so disappointingly foolish as to this preposterous love affair—must see that.

"Good night, dear child; you will get over this distress; and you will acknowledge hereafter, I am quite confident, that you have had a good escape. As to that odious woman, she is sure to be miserable, whether he marries her or not, that's one comfort!" said Aunt Pauline.

The sight of May's tearful white face exacerbated her virtuous indignation against Mrs. Bransby; nor was this feeling in the slightest degree mitigated by her strong desire that Mrs. Bransby should marry young Rivers, and take him out of their way for ever.

"Good night, Aunt Pauline," answered May, bending down, and slightly touching her aunt's forehead with her lips.

Pauline embraced the girl tenderly. "Poor darling!" she murmured. "Don't forget the rose-water."

CHAPTER X.

When May went up to her room, she neglected her aunt's advice as to the rose-water. She sat down beside the fire, and tried to think of what she had best do.

Help from her aunt was clearly not to be hoped for. She did not feel anger against Aunt Pauline at that moment. She had felt it some time before, but not now. Would it not be like feeling angry with a Chinese for not comprehending English? They simply did not understand one another. There was a barrier between their minds—at least, on the one subject which May had at heart—which, as it seemed, neither of them could pass or penetrate.

She would go to Granny! There she would find love and sympathy, and the sheltering mother-wings she yearned for. And, at the bottom of her heart, there was the half-unconscious feeling that Granny would be a staunch partisan of Owen's, and would be able to justify her trust in him.

But then Aunt Pauline had refused to let her go, and had said she might write. Write! and lose time, and probably fail to convince Granny of the sick longing, the positive need she felt to get away from London. There would be correspondence and discussion, and then her uncle would come back, and there would be more discussion, and she could not see Owen. If she wrote to him and he came, he would not be admitted to the house; and she could not go to him.

Well, then, she would run away. There was nothing for it but to run away to Granny, and she made up her mind to do so. Nothing should prevent her. Nothing! She started up and took her purse out of a drawer. She was but slenderly provided with pocket-money, the bulk of her allowance from Mrs. Dobbs being administered by Aunt Pauline. She counted out the contents of the little smart porte-monnaie with deep anxiety. There was half a sovereign and some silver. Only fifteen shillings! That would not suffice to carry her to Oldchester—and then she must have a cab. She could not find her way to the station on foot: and, besides, it would take such a long time! How much time she did not know exactly; but she remembered that it had seemed a rather long drive from the terminus to Kensington. And even if she could walk the distance, she would not know at what hour to set out in order to catch the express train, which would bring her into Oldchester a little after five o'clock the same evening.

A little thrill ran through her veins as she pictured herself arriving at Jessamine Cottage in one of the station flys, looking from the vehicle at the cheerful firelight which would surely be shining from the parlour window at that hour. And then Martha would come to the door, and not recognize her at first in the darkness; and Granny would cry out in surprise at the sound of her voice; and then there would be the dear motherly arms round her, the dear motherly breast to lay her troubled head upon, the blessed sense of rest, and trust, and comfort!

Feverishly May counted and re-counted her money. The fifteen shillings remained inexorably fifteen, and no more. All sorts of schemes passed through her mind. Cécile might perhaps lend her some money—or Smithson! But to ask for a loan from either of them would excite too much wonder and suspicion; it would at once be reported to her aunt.

Suddenly there darted into her mind the recollection that Harold had some money. Uncle Frederick had given the child half a sovereign on his birthday, a day or two ago. That was an inspiration! She would ask Harold to lend her the money, and to keep the secret until she should be gone. She knew that she could trust him; the child was staunch, and would be proud of being confided in. Poor little Harold! She remembered that it was he who had told her of Owen's presence in the house on that day—when was it? Yesterday? Impossible! It was weeks—months ago, surely! A large part of her life seemed to have passed since then.

May lay down to rest, tired out with the various emotions of the day, but with her brain so beleaguered by shifting thoughts and images that she was certain she should not be able to sleep. But she might at least rest her body, which felt bruised and weary, as though she had been walking with a heavy burthen all day long. She dropped off to sleep, nevertheless, almost immediately, but soon awoke again with a start and a sensation of falling swiftly, and a vague terror. But at length, towards morning, she did sleep continuously and heavily; and when she next awoke her watch, and a dull yellowish glimmer through the window-blind, told her it was day.

It was a dismal London morning, wet and cold. The wind was howling among the chimney-pots, and sending down showers of soot and smoke, mingled with sleet. It was the day appointed for the funeral of Lucius Cheffington. Mr. Dormer-Smith was not expected home that night; the trains did not fit conveniently. It had therefore been arranged that he should stay at Combe Park until the following morning. Her uncle's absence made her opportunity, May thought. The train she wished to travel by started from London, she believed, at about two o'clock; but she resolved to be at the terminus much earlier. The departure might be at some minutes before two; it would be too dreadful to miss the train! She felt an irrational hurry and eagerness to be gone, as if each minute's delay might be fatal. She knew the feeling was groundless, but it mastered her.

Preparations she had none to make, except clothing herself in a warm gown, and putting a few toilet necessaries into a little handbag. Mrs. Dormer-Smith always breakfasted late, and, during the cold weather, in her own room; and May shared the morning meal with her uncle. To-day, at her request, Harold and Wilfred were allowed to come downstairs and breakfast with her. This arrangement suited Cécile, who much preferred breakfasting with Smithson in the housekeeper's room to cutting bread-and-butter and pouring out milk-and-water in the nursery.

As soon as the meal was over, May asked Harold for the loan of his golden half-sovereign. His first reply was a severe blow. "You mean that yellow sixpence papa gave me? I haven't got it, Cousin May."

May felt as though the child had struck her. But the next moment he added—

"Papa put it into that little box with a slit in it. You can't get it out. Nobody can get it out. It belongs to me, you know; only I can't buy anything with it. Papa says it's proper—property."

May coaxed him to bring the box to her room, and found that it was closed by a little cheap lock, which it would be perfectly easy to force open. When she proposed this strong measure to Harold, he demurred at first; but finally yielded, on his cousin's saying that she wanted the money very much, and would be unhappy if she could not get it. A glove-box lined with quilted satin was offered him by way of immediate compensation; and he was promised that his yellow sixpence should be repaid with ample interest in the shape of coin which would not share the inconvenient dignity of being "property," but might be freely spent.

May felt as if she were a criminal as she wrenched open the little money-box, and took out the half-sovereign, which lay glistening amid a small heap of pennies and sixpences. Harold stood watching her intently.

"You do look funny, Cousin May!" he said. "Your cheeks are quite white, and your eyes are queer, and your hand burns. Mine is ever so cold. Feel!" He put his little red, cold hand on May's forehead, and the touch seemed deliciously refreshing to her.

"My head aches a little, Harold. I shall soon be well, though. I am going to see my dear granny. I have often told you about her. She is so good and kind! She makes people well when they are sick or sorry."

Harold's experience of being made well when he was sick was not of such a nature as to make this praise particularly attractive to him.

"I s'pose she gives you powders?" he said, in a disparaging tone, and then added gloomily, "I wouldn't go to her, if I was you."

May kissed him, and assured him that Granny's methods were all pleasant ones.

Wilfred—who had been kept outside the room during the financial transaction, as being too young to be trusted with a secret of such importance—was now admitted in compliance with his reiterated petition; and the two little fellows stood quietly watching their cousin, as in a hurried, feverish way, she put a few articles into her little bag, and took a fur-lined cloak out of the wardrobe, and laid her hat and gloves ready on the bed.

"I say, Cousin May," said Harold, all at once, "you'll come back again, sha'n't you?"

She looked down at the child's upturned face, with a start. It had not occurred to her before, but the thought now struck her that it was very likely she should never return to that house.

"I will see you again, darlings, if I live," she said, bending down to kiss and embrace the children.

Wilfred, always inclined to be tearful, showed symptoms of setting up a sympathetic wail. But Harold said, with a dogged little setting of the lips—

"Well, if you don't come back, I know what I shall do. I've got all those pennies left in the box, and I shall buy a stick and a bundle, and run away, and go along the high road ever so far, till I find you."

"I shall come too," cried Wilfred. "Papa gave me sixpence!"

All three looked, indeed, almost equally childish and innocent: Harold and Wilfred, with their project of running away, derived from a nursery story-book, and May clutching the "yellow sixpence" as a talisman that was to carry her afar from all trouble and persecution!

She did not, of course, mean to leave Aunt Pauline in any anxiety as to what had become of her; but she wanted to get a good start. After some deliberation, she wrote a short note to her aunt, and entrusted it to Harold. His instructions were to keep it until luncheon-time, and then give it to his mother. But, in case he heard them asking for May in the house, and wondering where she was, he might deliver it sooner. In any case, he must not give it to Cécile or Smithson, but place it in his mother's own hand. This latter was a service which Harold felt to be a severe one; but he undertook it, with a feeling akin to that of a knight doing battle with giants and dragons, on behalf of his liege lady. Not that his mother would be harsh or cruel; that was quite out of the question. She would not even scold him much, probably; but she would look at him with that complaining air of disapproval, as if he were an unmerited affliction, and call him and his brother "those dreadful little boys," and send him away to the nursery, all which things the child felt keenly in his heart, although he was entirely unable to analyze them in his brain.

May also wrote to Owen, telling him of her departure, and confessing that she had not written to Mr. Bragg.

"What is the use of my remaining in London, when we cannot meet?" she wrote. "We are as far apart, really, as when you were in Spain. I am worn out, dear Owen, and feel that I need Granny's help. Do not be angry with me for taking this step without consulting you. You will know I am safe and well-cared for with Granny, who is your friend, instead of having to fight against the arguments of those who are hostile to you." Then, in a postscript, she added, "Mrs. Simpson came here yesterday. She said she had seen you. You did not send me any message by her. Perhaps you did not know she meant to see me?" This note she put in her pocket to be posted at the station.

It was now past twelve o'clock; for early hours were not kept in the Dormer-Smith household. May's nervous impatience to be gone was no longer to be resisted. She took the children into the little back room where she had been accustomed to give them their lessons, and on her own responsibility gave them a book full of coloured pictures which Cécile never entrusted to their mischievous little fingers without her personal supervision. And this unusual indulgence delighted them and absorbed their attention. Then she stole back to her own chamber, and looked out of the window. The rain was still falling at intervals in driving showers. All the better! There was the less chance of any one whom she knew in that neighbourhood being abroad to recognize her.

She had told Smithson immediately after breakfast that she was going to her own room, and did not wish to be disturbed until luncheon-time. She now put on her hat and gloves, wrapped herself in the warm cloak, and carrying a tiny umbrella, which looked very unequal to offering much resistance to the wind and rain that were now sweeping along the street, she crept downstairs and let herself out at the hall door.

She had to walk some distance before reaching a cabstand, and by the time she did so her feet were wet. She had no boots fitted to keep out mud and damp. Aunt Pauline considered thick boots superfluous in London. In the country, of course, it was quite "the right thing" to tramp about in all weathers, and proper chaussures must be provided for the purpose. Although, had it been a dogma laid down by "the best people" that one ought to march barefoot through the mire, Aunt Pauline would have desired May to conform to that as well as to all other sacred ordinances of the social creed.

May was driven to the railway station in due course by a cabman who, on being asked what she had to pay, contented himself with only twice his fare. She found she was much too early for the express train. But there was a slow train going within half an hour. It would not reach Oldchester until after the express, although starting before it; but May decided to travel by it. She was frightened at the idea of remaining in the big terminus, where she might be seen and recognized by some passing acquaintance at any moment. And the idea of being actually on the road to granny, safely shut up in a railway carriage out of reach, was tempting. She took her ticket, the purchase of which reduced her funds to the last shilling, and was put into a carriage by herself—first-class passengers by that train not being numerous.

The girl's head was throbbing, and the damp chill to her feet made her shiver. She leaned back in a corner of the carriage, and closed her eyes. The train trundled along, its progress arrested by frequent stoppages. The dim daylight faded. At wayside stations the reflections from the lamps shone with a melancholy gleam in inky pools of rain-water. May began to suffer from want of food. She was not hungry; but she felt the need, although not the desire, for some sustenance. At one place where they stopped a quarter of an hour, she thought of getting some tea; but there was a crowd of men in front of a counter where beer and spirits were being sold, but where she saw no tea; and the steam from damp great coats, mingled with tobacco-smoke and close air, made her feel sick. She tottered back to the carriage, carrying with her a huge fossilized bun, which she tried, not very successfully, to nibble at intervals; and at length she fell into an uneasy doze.

She was awakened by the opening of the carriage-door, and a voice saying, "You'll be all right here, sir." A dark lantern flashed in her eyes. A hat-box and dressing-bag were put into the carriage by an obsequious porter. A gentleman entered and took his seat in the corner farthest away from her. The door was slammed to, and they moved on again.

May put up her hand to her forehead in a dazed manner. She felt confused, and could not, for the moment, understand where she was. Her head ached and throbbed painfully. Then she recollected it all, and wondered what o'clock it was, and whether they were drawing near Oldchester.

"Can you tell me what station that was?" she asked in a faint voice, of her fellow-traveller.

The gentleman turned his head sharply, and peered at her where she sat in the darkness of her corner-seat. He could not distinguish her face; for, before his entrance, she had drawn the movable shade half across the lamp in the roof of the carriage. Thinking he had not heard, or had not understood her, she repeated the question—

"What is the name of that last station, if you please?"

Upon which the gentleman, instead of making any such reply as might have been expected, exclaimed, "Lord bless my soul!" and leaving his place at the other extremity of the carriage, he came and seated himself opposite to her. "It is Miss Cheffington!" he said, in a tone of the utmost wonder. And then May recognized Mr. Bragg.

"My dear young lady, how come you to be travelling alone—by this train? Is anything the matter?"

His tone was so sincere and earnest, his face and manner so gentle and fatherly, that May at once felt she could trust him fully and fearlessly.

"I am so glad it's you, Mr. Bragg, and not a stranger!" she said, putting her hand out to take his.

"Thank you," said Mr. Bragg simply. "I'm glad it is me, if I can be of any use to you." Then he asked again, "Is anything the matter?"

"N—no; nothing very serious. I have run away from Aunt Pauline—"

"Run away!"

"And I'm going to Granny. You won't feel it your duty to give me up as a fugitive from justice, will you?" she said, trying to smile, with very tremulous lips.

"Mrs. Dormer-Smith has never been treating you bad or cruel?" said Mr. Bragg wonderingly. "No, no; she couldn't."

"No, truly, she could not be consciously cruel to me, or to any one; but she has ideas which—she tried to persuade me—We don't understand one another, that's the truth."

Mr. Bragg all at once remembered a certain private note despatched to his hotel in town by Mrs. Dormer-Smith, wherein she had assured him that May was an inexperienced child, who didn't know her own mind, and begged him not to take her too absolutely at her word. He had never replied to that note, having, indeed, nothing to say which it would be agreeable to his correspondent to hear. But he recalled other instances in which ladies of the highest gentility had hunted him (or, rather, not him—he had no illusions of vanity on that point—but his large fortune) with a ruthless unscrupulosity which had amazed him, and a gallant perseverance in the teeth of discouragement which almost extorted admiration. And the question stole into his mind, "Could Mrs. Dormer-Smith have been persecuting May on his account?" The idea was inexpressibly painful to him. But, anyway, he was relieved and thankful to find that the girl did not shrink from him, but was sweet and gracious as ever.

"Well, to be sure," he said in his slow, pondering way, "'tis a strange chance that we should meet just now, isn't it? For I've just come from your family place, you know."

"From where?"

"From the home of your ancestors, as Mr. Theodore Bransby calls it. You asked me the name of that station I got in at. Well, it's Combe St. Mildred's, the station for Combe Park you know."

"Is it? Then we cannot be far from Oldchester."

"Not very far in miles; but this is an uncommon slow train—stops everywhere. Stops just now at Wendhurst Junction; the express runs through. I'm afraid you're very tired, Miss Cheffington." He could not see her at all distinctly, but her voice betrayed great weariness, he thought.

"Not very—yes, rather. It does not matter now; we shall soon be there."

"Yes," went on Mr. Bragg, "I've been attending the funeral."

"Oh yes. Poor Lucius! I had forgotten that it was for to-day," said May, with a self-reproachful feeling. "He was very kind to me, although, at first, he seemed so dry and eccentric. I think he liked me. I know I liked him."

"Yes; no doubt but what he liked you. That can't be disputed. And it does him honour, in my opinion. I suppose I ought to congratulate you, Miss Cheffington—although congratulating may seem out of place with a crape band round your hat. And yet I don't know!"

"Congratulate me! Do you mean because my father is the heir? I think there is more sorrow in Lord Castlecombe's heart than there can be satisfaction in any one else's?" answered May. She was surprised at this manifestation of coarseness of feeling in Mr. Bragg. It was the first she had ever observed in him.

"Your father? Lord bless me, no! Nothing to do with your father. I was alluding to your cousin's last will and testament. I was present when it was read, by Lord Castlecombe's desire, although having no particular claim that I know of. Still, when we came back from the old churchyard, his lordship invited me into the library, and the will was read out then by Wagget, the lawyer, poor Martin Bransby's successor."

"But what has all that to do with me?" asked May, sitting upright, and holding on by the elbows of the seat. As she did so, everything seemed to waver and swim before her eyes. The cushions on which she sat seemed to be sinking down through the earth. The long fast, her broken sleep on the previous night, the tears she had shed, and all the emotions of this journey, which to her was an adventure fraught with all kinds of anxieties, were telling upon her. But she made a desperate effort to listen—not to be ill, not to give trouble. The train was to stop shortly. She would hold up her courage until then. Had not the gloom caused by the lamp-shade baffled Mr. Bragg's observation, he would have been startled by her countenance.

As it was, he merely answered, "Well, because your cousin has left you all the little property he inherited from his mother. It isn't a great fortune—a matter of four hundred and fifty, or five hundred pound a year, as well as I can make out. But it's all in sound investments—mostly Government securities—and it's settled on you every penny of it."

But May, struggling against a sick sensation of faintness, was scarcely able to grasp the meaning of what was said to her. Her eyes grew dim; she half-rose up from her seat, made a vague movement with her hands, such as one makes in falling and clutching at whatever is nearest, and then sank down in a heap on the floor of the carriage, like a wounded bird. She was in a dead swoon, and her young face looked piteously white and wan under the crude glare of the gas, as the train moved slowly, with much resounding clangour, into the big station at Wendhurst Junction.

CHAPTER XI.

With that indescribably dreadful rushing, whirling sensation in the brain, which can never be forgotten by whoever has once experienced it, May Cheffington recovered out of her swoon, and her senses returned to her.

She was lying on a cushioned seat in the ladies' waiting-room at Wendhurst Junction. Her dress had been loosened, her own warm cloak had been spread over her as a coverlet, a woollen shawl was thrown across her feet, and an elderly woman was sprinkling water on her forehead. She opened her eyes, and then shut them again lazily. The glare of the gas made her blink, and the sense of rest was, for the moment, all she wanted.

"She'll do now," said the elderly woman, wiping May's wet forehead with a handkerchief. Then she went to the door of the room, and half opening it, said to some one outside, "Coming round beautiful, sir; she'll be all right now."

"Who's there?" asked May, in a little feeble, drowsy voice.

"Your pa, dear. He has been in a taking about you. But I'm telling him you're as right as right can be. So you are, ain't you? There's a pretty!"

Every second that passed was bringing more clearness to May's mind, more animation to her frame. By the time the elderly woman had finished speaking, May said—

"Oh, ask him to come in. Ask him, pray, to come here and speak to me!"

This message being transmitted, the door was opened, and in walked Mr. Bragg, with a most disturbed and anxious countenance.

May was lying with her head supported on a pillow formed of a great coat hastily rolled up, which the attendant had covered with her own white apron. The pretty soft brown hair, dabbled here and there with water, was hanging in disorder. Her eyes looked very large and bright in her pale face. Mr. Bragg came and stood beside her, and looked at her with a sort of tender, pitying trepidation: as an amiable giant might contemplate Ariel with a broken wing: longing to help, but fearing to hurt, the delicate creature.

May put out her hand and took hold of Mr. Bragg's as innocently as little Enid might have done. "Oh, I am so sorry!" she said.

"Yes," returned Mr. Bragg, in a subdued voice. "And I'm so sorry, too. But you are feeling better now, ain't you?"

"Oh, but I mean I am sorry for you. Sorry to frighten you and to give you so much trouble."

"Trouble! Well, I don't know about that. This good lady here has been taking what trouble there was to take. Not such a vast deal, was it, ma'am?"

The "good lady" who had begun to doubt the correctness of her assumption that these two were father and daughter, smoothed the shawl over May's feet, and murmured that they were not to mention it.

Mr. Bragg pulled out his watch impatiently.

"What! haven't they found anybody yet?" he said. "I sent off a man in a fly ten minutes ago."

The attendant observed apologetically that the first doctor they'd gone to might not have been at home, and then they'd have to go on a goodish bit further.

May started up on her elbow.

"Doctor!" she cried, in dismay. "You haven't sent for a doctor?"

"Yes, I have," answered Mr. Bragg, dismayed in his turn by her evident distress. "I couldn't do less. You might have been dying for anything I knew. You don't know how bad you looked!"

"But I don't want a doctor. I'm quite well. I only want to go on. I want to go on to Granny."

And May's head fell back on the pillow, while a tear forced its way beneath the closed eyelids.

"You came by the slow down, didn't you? Ah, well, there's no passenger train going on that way before eleven-five to-night," observed the elderly female.

At this intelligence the tears poured down May's cheeks, and she turned away her head on the cushion.

"Don't cry! Don't fret!" exclaimed Mr. Bragg. "You shall be in Oldchester within an hour if the medical man says you're able to travel. I'll speak to the station-master at once. Only we must hear what the doctor says, mustn't we? I dursn't run a risk, now durst I? You see that yourself. You're what you might call laid on my conscience to take care of. Good Lord, will this fool of a fellow never come back? I told him to drive as fast as he could pelt."

May was crying now less from vexation than from exhaustion.

"I'm not ill, indeed," she murmured, trying to check her tears.

"But, my dear young lady, people don't faint dead away like that, and look so white and ghastly, without there's something the matter. It wasn't the news I told you upset you like that, surely?"

"No; of course not. I think it was because I—I had had no dinner."

"Lord bless me!" cried Mr. Bragg. "Why, you're starving! That's what it is, then!"

In his anxious solicitude for her Mr. Bragg would have ordered everything eatable to be brought which the refreshment-room afforded. But he yielded to May's entreaty that she might have a cup of tea and a piece of bread. The attendant suggested a teaspoonful of brandy in the tea, but at this May shook her head. Mr. Bragg, however, thought the suggestion a good one, and producing a small flask from his travelling bag, insisted on pouring a few drops of its contents into the cup of tea.

"That's fine old Cognac," he said; "like a cordial. I wouldn't ask you to swallow the stuff they sell here; but this'll do you nothing but good. Dear me, if I'd only thought of giving you some of this before!"

He was quite self-reproachful, and May had some difficulty in persuading him that no blame could possibly attach to him for not having administered a dose of brandy to her as soon as they met in the railway carriage.

By this time the doctor sent for from Wendhurst had arrived. A brief interview with his patient convinced him that she was perfectly well able to travel on as far as Oldchester.

"Rather delicate nervous organization, you see," said the doctor to Mr. Bragg, when he left May. "And there has been some mental distress; family troubles, she tells me; and then the long fast, and the journey, quite sufficient to account—oh, thanks, thanks. She'll be all right after a good night's rest, I haven't the least doubt." And the doctor withdrew with a bow; for Mr. Bragg, apologizing for having disturbed him and brought him so far through the rain, had put a handsome fee into his hand.

Mr. Bragg had also mentioned in the hearing of the waiting-room attendant, who was hovering inquisitively in the background, that the young lady had been put under his charge, and that he had just left the house of her great-uncle, Lord Castlecombe. He was aware that he himself was far too well-known a man in those parts for the adventure not to be talked about. And his experience of life had taught him that, while it is as difficult to check gossip as to bring a runaway horse to a standstill, yet that both may generally be turned to the right or left, by a cool hand.

His sagacity was amply justified. For the waiting-room attendant, for weeks afterwards, would narrate to passing lady travellers how that sweet young lady, Lord Castlecombe's grandniece, was so cut up by the death of her cousin that she fainted right away coming back from the funeral at Combe Park, not having been able to touch food for more than twelve hours in consequence of her grief; and how Mr. Bragg, the great Oldchester manufacturer, who was taking charge of the young lady on her journey home, was so kind and anxious, and quite like a father to her; and how they both repeatedly said, "Mrs. Tupp, if it hadn't been for your care and attention, we don't know whatever we should have done."

Soon after the doctor had departed, Mr. Bragg came back to May, and informed her that arrangements had been made for their starting for Oldchester in three-quarters of an hour, if that would be agreeable to her. And in reply to her wondering inquiry as to how that could have been managed, he said quietly, "Oh, I've got a special train. I'm a director of this line, and they know me here pretty well."

May had always understood that a special train was an immensely costly matter. But in her ignorance she was by no means sure that it might not be part of the privileges of a railway director to have special trains run for his service gratis, whensoever he should require them. Which, probably, was precisely what Mr. Bragg desired her to suppose.

He then called aside the attendant, and held a short colloquy with her in the adjoining room, the result of which was to put the worthy Mrs. Tupp into a great fuss and flutter. She dashed at a cupboard in the wall and plunged her hand into it, drawing it out again with a battered old black bonnet dangling by one string, as though she had been fishing at a venture and brought up that rather unexpectedly. Further, Mrs. Tupp, with many apologies, took the checked shawl which had been laid over May's feet and put it on her own shoulders; and then, assuring Mr. Bragg, in a speech which it took some time to deliver, that she wouldn't be gone not ten minutes, for her house was close by—better than half a mile before you really come into Wendhurst High Street, going the shortest way from the station—she finally disappeared.

"Now, Miss Cheffington," said Mr. Bragg, "I want you to do something to oblige me. Will you?"

"Most gladly, if I can; but I'm afraid it will turn out to be something to oblige me," answered May, looking up at him timidly. "Don't you want some food? I dare say you do."

"Why, no, Miss Cheffington, I can't say I do; I ate a most uncommon hearty luncheon. I wonder why people always eat so much when there's a funeral going on! Besides, it isn't dinner-time yet, you know."

"Isn't it? I have no idea what o'clock it is. If you told me it was the middle of next week, I don't think I should feel surprised," and she smiled with one of her old, bright looks.

"That's right," said Mr. Bragg. "You're picking up. Well, now, I was going to say that I noticed in the refreshment-room a cold roast fowl, which didn't look at all nasty; no, really, not at all nasty," insisted Mr. Bragg, with the air of one who is aware that his statement may not unreasonably be received with incredulity. "And if you'll let them bring it in here on a tray, and try to eat a bit of it, and drink another cup of tea—no! I promise not to put any brandy in it,—I shall esteem it a favour."

Of course there was no refusing this. But May said wistfully, "I was going to ask you—would you mind—I have something to say to you; and if I don't say it soon that woman will be here. She is coming back immediately."

"Why, as to that, Miss Cheffington, I don't think she is. From what I can make out, she's the kind of person that never can realize to themselves that fifteen minutes, one after the other, end to end, make up a quarter of an hour. She lost a lot of time here talking, and I saw her stop to tell the young woman at the bar over yonder what a hurry she was in. No; I make no doubt but what she'll be back before we start, but not just yet awhile."

The roast chicken and some freshly made tea were brought in due course, and Mr. Bragg had the satisfaction of seeing May partake of both. Then he professed his readiness to hear what she wished to say.

"Are you comfortable? Light not too much for you? There! Now—provided you don't overtire yourself, nor yet what you might call overtry yourself—I'm listening."

He sat down in a chair nearly opposite to the fire, so that his profile was turned to May, and looked thoughtfully into the hot coals, folding his arms in an attitude of massive quietude which was characteristic of him.

"First of all, you must let me thank you for all your kindness," said May.

"No, don't do that," he answered, without removing his gaze from the fire. Then he repeated musingly, "No, no; don't do that! Don't ye do that!"

Then ensued a pause. It lasted so long that Mr. Bragg, glancing round at the girl, said—

"That wasn't all you had in your mind to say, was it?"

"No, Mr. Bragg."

"Perhaps you've changed your mind about speaking? Well, don't you worrit yourself. You do just what you feel most agreeable to yourself, you know."

"But I want to speak! I was so anxious to tell you—This chance, which I could never have expected or dreamt of, gives me the opportunity, and now—now I don't know how to begin!"

He was silent for a moment, pondering. Then he said, "Could I help you? I wonder if it is about a certain conversation you and me had together a few days back?"

"Yes—partly."

"Well, now, you remember that on that occasion I said to you that I hoped we might be friends, you and me—real, true friends. You remember, don't you?"

"Gratefully."

"Well, I meant what I said. If you have been—" He was about to say "persecuted," but changed the word. "If you have been any way bothered in consequence of that conversation, I'm truly sorry for it. But don't let it make any difference as between you and me. Your aunt, Mrs. Dormer-Smith, she's a most well-meaning lady, and has beautiful manners. But she's liable to make mistakes like the rest of us. And don't you fret, you know. You're going to your grandmother, Mrs. Dobbs, you tell me. And she's a woman of wonderful good sense. She'll understand some things better than what your aunt can. It'll be all right. Don't you worrit yourself."

He spoke in a gentle, soothing tone, such as one might use to a child, and kept nodding his head slowly as he spoke, still with his eyes fixed on the fire.

"It isn't that! I mean—I wanted to tell you something!"

He turned his head now quickly, and looked at her. Her eyes were cast down, and she was plucking nervously at the fur lining of the cloak which lay on the seat beside her.

"Is it something about that confidence that you made me, and that I look upon as an honour, and always shall? Well, now, if you're going to speak about that, I shall take it as a sign that you really mean to be friends with me, and trust me. And there's nothing in the world would make me so proud as that you should trust me, full and free."

Then she told him all the story of her engagement to Owen. How it had been kept secret for three months by her grandmother's express stipulation. How, when Owen returned to England, they had revealed it to Mrs. Dormer-Smith; how that lady had disapproved and forbidden Owen the house, and had written to Captain Cheffington requesting him to interpose his parental authority; how, finally, May had felt so miserable and lonely, that she had made up her mind to leave her aunt's house and take refuge with her grandmother.

Mr. Bragg sat like a rock while she told her story, hesitatingly and shyly at first, but gathering courage as she went on. When she first mentioned Owen's name, his brows contracted for a moment, in a way which might mean anger, or perplexity, or simply surprise. But he remained otherwise quite unmoved to all appearance, and perfectly silent.

When May had finished her little story, she said timidly, as she had said to him on that memorable day in her aunt's house, "You are not angry, Mr. Bragg?"

He answered nearly as he had answered then, but without looking at her, and keeping his gaze on the fire, "Angry, my child! No; how could I be angry with you? You have never deceived me. You have been true and honest from first to last."

"But I mean, you are not—you are not angry with Owen?"

The answer did not come quite so promptly this time; but after a few seconds, he said, "I don't know that I've the least right to be angry with Mr. Rivers. Only I should have liked it better if he had told me how things were, plain and straightforward, when we were talking about—something else." He brought his speech to an abrupt conclusion.

Upon this May assured him that Owen had never desired secrecy. The engagement had been kept secret in deference to "Granny." And as soon as her aunt knew it, Owen had urged her (May) to tell Mr. Bragg also, feeling himself in a false position until the truth was revealed.

"I ought to have written to you yesterday," she said guiltily. "It's my fault, indeed it is!"

Mr. Bragg got up from his chair, and muttering something about "getting a little air," walked out on to the long platform.

There was certainly no lack of air outside there. A damp raw wind was driving through the station, making the lamps blink. Mr. Bragg had no great coat, that garment having been rolled up to serve as May's pillow. But he marched up and down the long platform with his hands behind his back, at a steady and by no means rapid pace, apparently insensible to the cold.

Owen Rivers! So the man May was engaged to was his secretary, Mr. Rivers! That was very surprising. Mr. Rivers was not at all the sort of man he should have expected that exquisite young creature to care about. But Mr. Bragg would have been puzzled to describe the sort of man he would have expected her to care about. He had never seen any man he thought worthy of her, and it might safely be predicted that he never would; seeing that Mr. Bragg was in love with May, and would certainly never be in love with May's husband, let him be the finest fellow in the world.

One suspicion he at once dismissed from his mind—that Owen had ever been in the least danger from Mrs. Bransby's fascinations. No; when a man was betrothed to a girl like May Cheffington he was safe enough from anything of that kind, argued Mr. Bragg. Indeed, his visit to the widow's house had given him a favourable impression of all its inmates. It was impossible, he thought, to be in Mrs. Bransby's presence without perceiving her to be worthy of respect. Searching his memory, he discovered that the first hint of her having any designs on young Rivers had come from Theodore Bransby, and now the motive of the hint began to dawn upon him. Theodore, as he had long ago perceived, hated Rivers. Mr. Bragg now understood why. He paced up and down the draughty platform, solitary and meditative, for full ten minutes. It was a dead time, and the whole station seemed nearly deserted.

Then he returned to the waiting-room, of which May was still the sole occupant. He stirred the fire into a blaze, and then sat down opposite to it as before. May looked at him nervously and anxiously. She did not venture to speak first.

"I'll tell you one thing, Miss Cheffington," said Mr. Bragg, all at once. "What you told me has been a relief to my mind in one way."

She looked up inquiringly.

"Yes, it has been a relief to my mind, and I'm bound to acknowledge it. I was afraid at one time—indeed, I'd almost made up my mind, though terribly against the grain—that you was engaged to some one else."

"Some one else!" exclaimed May, opening great eyes of wonder, and speaking in a tone which conveyed her naïf persuasion that, in that sense, there did not exist any one else. "Why, whom can you mean?"

Mr. Bragg reflected an instant. Then he said, "I'll tell you. Yes, I'll tell you, for he's tried to thrust it in people's faces as far as he dared. Mr. Theodore Bransby."

May fell back on her seat with a gesture of mute astonishment.

"Ah, yes; you're wondering how I could be such a blockhead as to think that possible. But if it had been true, you'd ha' wondered how I could be such a blockhead as to think anything else possible," said Mr. Bragg. It was the sole touch of bitterness which escaped him throughout the interview. After a brief pause he went on, "Not, you understand, that I mean to deny Mr. Rivers is far superior to young Bransby—out of all comparison, superior to him. I may, perhaps, consider Mr. Rivers fort'nate beyond his merits. That's a question we won't enter into, because you and me can't help but look at it from different points of view. But I must bear testimony that he's always behaved like a real gentleman in his duties with me; and, so far as I know, he's thoroughly upright and honourable."

May considered this to be but faint praise. But she graciously made allowances. Granny, however, knew better. When Mr. Bragg's words were repeated to Granny, she exclaimed, "Well done, Joshua Bragg! That was spoken like a generous-minded man."

By this time the engine which was to draw them to Oldchester was in readiness. Mr. Bragg inquired impatiently for the "good lady" of the waiting-room. And then May learned that that person was to accompany them on the journey, lest Miss Cheffington should need any attendance on the way.

"And, indeed," said Mrs. Tupp, afterwards, "if the young lady had been a princess royal, there couldn't have been more fuss made over her. S'loon carriage, and everything! Of course, it was an effort for me to go along with 'em at such short notice, and so entirely unexpected. But as they said to me, 'Mrs. Tupp,' they said, 'had it not have been for your kindness and attention, we don't know what we should have done.' And the gentleman certainly made it worth my while." As he certainly did!

At the present moment, however, Mrs. Tupp was by no means in a complacent frame of mind. She was seen hurriedly approaching from the extremity of the station, very breathless and exhausted, attired in her Sunday bonnet, and shawl to match, confronting Mr. Bragg, who stood, sternly, watch in hand, at the door of the carriage.

"I told you so, Miss Cheffington," said he to May, who was already made luxuriously comfortable within the carriage. "Now, ma'am! No, don't trouble yourself to explain, please. Because in exactly two seconds and a half we're off. Would you be so kind?" This to a guard who stood looking on beside the station-master. In a moment they had taken Mrs. Tupp between them, and, assisted from behind by a youthful porter, managed to hoist her into the carriage by main force. Mr. Bragg took his place opposite to May. The whistle sounded, and they glided from beneath the roof of the station, and at an increasing speed across the dark country through the streaming rain.

CHAPTER XII.

"And you got jealous! You actually were jealous of Owen and that poor, dear, pretty Mrs. Bransby?"

"Yes, Granny."

"And you were such a goose—I won't use a stronger word, though I could—as to pay any attention to what that idiot of an aunt of yours—Lord forgive me!—chose to say in her anger and disappointment?"

"Yes, Granny."

"And you let the jabber of poor Amelia Simpson—as kind a soul as ever breathed, but as profitable to listen to as the chirping of sparrows on the house-top—prey upon your mind, and bias your common sense?"

"Yes, Granny."

"Why, then, I'm ashamed of you, May! Downright ashamed—there now!"

"Oh, thank you, Granny!"

And May seized her grandmother's hands one after the other as the old woman drew them away impatiently, and kissed them in a kind of rapture.

This little scene, with but slight variations, had been enacted several times since May's arrival on the previous evening at Jessamine Cottage. May had ceased to make any excuses for herself, or to endeavour to describe and account for her state of mind. She was only too thankful to have her doubts treated with supreme disdain. To be scolded and chidden, and told that she did not deserve such a true lover as Owen, was such happiness as she could not be grateful enough for!

"Jealous of Owen because a parcel of mischievous magpies had nothing better to do than to dig their foolish bills into a poor widow's reputation? Why, I think you must have had softening of the brain!" Mrs. Dobbs would say. Whereupon May would kneel down, and bury her face in her grandmother's lap, and laugh and cry, and murmur in a smothered voice—

"Bless you, Granny darling!"

"Not but what," Mrs. Dobbs admitted afterwards in a private confabulation with Jo Weatherhead, "not but what I do think it's pretty well enough to soften any one's brain to undergo a long course of Mrs. Dormer-Smith. I thought I knew pretty well what she was, and I told you so long ago, Jo Weatherhead, as you must well remember. But, mercy! I hadn't an idea! Her goings on, from what the child tells me, and that fool of a letter she's written to me, display a wrongheadedness and an aggravating kind of imbecility that beats everything."

Mr. Weatherhead, for his part, was inclined to be seriously wrathful with everybody who had contributed to make May unhappy—not excluding Mr. Owen Rivers, who, said Jo, might have had more gumption than to rush to Mrs. Bransby's the moment he returned to England, and make such a fuss about her, just as though she, and not May, were the object of his solicitude and affection.

"And I think, Sarah," said honest Jo, "that you're too hard on Miranda. It's all very fine, but it seems to me that she had enough, and more than enough, to make her uneasy. What with disagreeable things being dinned into her ears from morning to night, and facts that couldn't be denied, interpreted all wrong, and no friend near to interpret 'em right, and her own modesty and humble-mindedness making her suspect that the young man had offered to her before he was sure of his own mind, and had begun to repent—take it altogether, I consider it's unkind and unfair to bully her as you do, Sarah, and so I tell you."

"You do, do you?" answered Mrs. Dobbs, who had listened with much composure to this attack. "Well, I'm not likely to quarrel with you for that. But you needn't worry yourself about May. I think I understand the case pretty well. If you doubt it, just try sympathizing with her, and telling her you think Mr. Rivers behaved bad and thoughtless. You'll see how pleased she'll be with you, and what a lot of gratitude you'll get for taking her part. Try it, Jo."

Mr. Weatherhead, on reflection, did not try it.

The unexpected legacy from Lucius Cheffington to his cousin was hailed by Mrs. Dobbs with heartfelt thankfulness. May's account of it at first was a very vague one. She had only imperfectly heard Mr. Bragg's communication in the railway carriage. And, indeed, at that moment, it had seemed to her an affair of very secondary importance. But now, when it occurred to her that this money would render them so independent as to put it out of the question for Owen to have to seek his fortune in South America, or any other distant part of the world, she was as elated by it as the best regulated mind could desire.

"And it isn't so very much money, after all, is it, Granny?" she said, with an air of satisfaction, which Mrs. Dobbs did not quite understand.

"Well," she answered, "it seems a pretty good deal of money to me. Between four and five hundred a year, as I understand."

"Yes; but it isn't a fortune. Mr. Bragg said it wasn't a fortune. I mean—it is very little more than Owen has with what he earns, Granny."

"Oh!" exclaimed Mrs. Dobbs, a light beginning to dawn upon her. "I see. Well, you can't have the proud satisfaction of marrying him without a penny belonging to you. But perhaps he might take a situation for five years on the Guinea Coast, so as to bring his income up above yours."

"Oh, Granny!"

"Why not? It would be quite as natural and sensible as his wanting to marry poor Mrs. Bransby and her five children. Things are getting too comfortable to be let alone. The least he can do is to undergo a course of yellow fever, and—"

"Granny, how can you?" And the young arms were round Granny, and the blushing face hidden in Granny's breast.

"Was I ever so foolish about Dobbs, I wonder?" murmured Mrs. Dobbs, as she stroked the girl's hair. "He was a good-looking young fellow, was Isaac, in our courting days, and a temper like a sunshiny morning, and we were over head and ears in love, I know that; and—yes, I believe I was every bit as soft-hearted and silly, the Lord be praised!"

Mr. Bragg called at Jessamine Cottage about noon the day after May's return. He asked to see Mrs. Dobbs, and remained talking with her alone for some time. He had made up his mind, he told her, to give Mr. Rivers a permanent post in his employment, if he chose to accept it. He thought of offering him the management of the Oldchester office, if, after a three months' trial, he found it suited him, and he suited it. There was no technical knowledge of the manufacture needed for this post: merely a clear head, honesty, the power of keeping accounts, and of conducting a large business correspondence.

"I think he can do it," said Mr. Bragg; "and, if he can, he may." Then he informed Mrs. Dobbs that he had telegraphed to Mr. Rivers to come down to Oldchester. He would there find, at the office in Friar's Row, a letter with all details. "As for me," said Mr. Bragg, "I shall cross him on the road. I am going to town by the three-thirty express. You needn't mention what I've told you to Miss C. I thought, perhaps, she'd like better to hear it—as an agreeable bit of news, I hope—from him."

What more may have passed between them Granny never reported. He went away without seeing May, merely leaving a message, "His kind regards, and he hoped she was feeling well and rested."

"Oh, I wish I had seen him!" exclaimed May, when this message was faithfully delivered by Granny. "I wanted so much to thank him again. It's too bad! I wonder why he went away without seeing me."

"Do you?" said Granny shortly. "Well, perhaps he thought he'd had bother enough with you for one while. He's got other things to do besides dancing attendance on young ladies who wander about the world, fainting from want of food, and requiring special trains, and all manner of dainties." Privately she observed to Mr. Weatherhead that innocence was mighty cruel sometimes, as could be exemplified any day by trusting a young child with a kitten.

"H'm! Mr. Bragg isn't exactly a kitten, Sarah," returned Jo.

"True, a kitten will scratch! He's a man, and a good 'un; and I'll tell you what, Jo, if Joshua Bragg wanted his shoes blacked, I'd go down on my old knees to do it for him."

May's legacy was a great piece of news for Mr. Weatherhead. He was not only delighted at it for her sake, but he enjoyed the importance of disseminating it. Jo went about the city from the house of one acquaintance to another. He also looked in at the Black Bull, where he ordered a glass of brandy-and-water in honour of May's good fortune. The item of news he brought was a welcome contribution to the general fund of gossip. The subjects of Mr. Lucius Cheffington's funeral, and how the old lord had taken the death, and whether Captain Cheffington would come back to England now that he was the heir, and make it up with his uncle, were by this time beginning to be worn a little threadbare; or, at all events, had lost their first gloss.

In this way it speedily became known to those interested in the matter that May Cheffington had arrived at her grandmother's house. Among others, the intelligence reached Theodore Bransby. Theodore had been frequently in Oldchester of late, on business of various kinds, chiefly connected with the approaching election. He had never relinquished the hope of winning May; and he believed that the death of Lucius was a circumstance favourable to his hopes. He did not doubt that the new turn of affairs would bring Captain Cheffington to England forthwith; and he as little doubted that many doors—including Mr. Dormer-Smith's—would be opened widely to Captain Cheffington now, which had been closed to him for years. Moreover, Theodore was convinced that one immediate result of her father's presence would be to separate May altogether from Mrs. Dobbs, and the unfitting associates who haunted her house, and claimed acquaintanceship with Miss Cheffington. May, he knew, had a weak affection for the vulgar old woman. But her father's authority would be strong enough to sever her from Mrs. Dobbs; and, for the rest, Captain Cheffington was his friend; whereas he was instinctively aware that Mrs. Dobbs was not. Latterly, too, ever since his father's death, May's manner to him had been very gentle.

He was meditating these things as he walked up the garden path to Jessamine Cottage. May caught sight of him from the window, and sprang up in consternation, crying to Granny to tell Martha he was not to be admitted. Mrs. Dobbs, however, told May to run upstairs out of the way, and determined to receive the visitor herself.

"I'm so afraid he will persist in asking for me! He is wonderfully obstinate, Granny!" said May, ready to fly upstairs at the first sound of the expected knock at the door.

"Ah!" rejoined Mrs. Dobbs, setting her mouth rather grimly, "so am I. Show the gentleman into the parlour, Martha."

Theodore was ushered into the little room, and found Mrs. Dobbs seated in state in her big chair. The place was far smaller and poorer than the house in Friar's Row, but in Theodore's eyes it was preferable. There was the possibility of some pretentions to gentility on the part of a dweller in Jessamine Cottage, whereas Friar's Row, though it might, perhaps, be comfortable, was hopelessly ungenteel.

Theodore, when he entered the room, made a low bow, which, unlike his salutation on a former occasion, was distinctly a bow, and not a nondescript gesture halfway between a bow and a nod. He had learned by experience that it did not answer to treat Mrs. Dobbs de haut en bas. He also made a movement as if to shake hands; but this Mrs. Dobbs ignored, and asked him to sit down, in a coldly civil voice.

She had been knitting when he came in, but laid the needles and worsted aside on his entrance, and sat looking at him with her hands folded in her lap.

Theodore could scarcely tell why, but this action seemed to prelude nothing pleasant. There was an air of being armed at all points about the old woman, as she sat there looking at him with a steady attention unshared by her knitting. But possibly the work had been laid aside out of politeness. In any case, Theodore told himself that he was not likely to be disconcerted by such a trifle.

"How do you do, Mrs. Dobbs?" he asked, when he was seated.

"Very well, I'm much obliged to you."

Here ensued a pause.

"It is some time since we met, Mrs. Dobbs."

"It's over a twelvemonth since you called at my house in Friar's Row, Mr. Theodore Bransby."

Another pause.

"There has been trouble in the Cheffington family since then," said Theodore, at length. "Ah, how strange and unexpected was the death of the eldest son! Lucius, of course, was always delicate. Still, he might have lived. His death has been a sad blow to Lord Castlecombe."

Theodore considered himself to be condescending and conciliatory, in thus assuming that Mrs. Dobbs took some part in the affliction of the noble family. In his heart he resented her having the most distant connection with them. But he intended to be polite.

"There has been trouble in other families besides the Cheffingtons," returned Mrs. Dobbs gravely, with her eyes on the young man's mourning garments.

"Oh! Yes. Of course. But no trouble with which you can be expected to concern yourself," he answered. He was annoyed, and preserved his smooth manner only by an effort.

"And, anyway," continued Mrs. Dobbs, "Lord Castlecombe's sons have left no fatherless children, nor widows, nor any one to be desolate and oppressed—like your poor father did."

Theodore raised his eyebrows in his favourite supercilious fashion. "Your figurative language is a little stronger than the case requires," he said.

"Widowhood is a desolate thing, and poverty oppressive. There's no figure in that, I'm sorry to say."

"Oh, really? I was not aware," said Theodore, nettled, in spite of himself, into showing some hauteur, "that Mrs. Bransby and her family had excited so much interest in you!"

"No; I dare say not. I believe you were not. I think it very likely you'd be surprised if you knew how many folks in Oldchester and out of it are interested in them."

The young man sat silent, casting about for something to say which should put down this old woman, without absolutely quarrelling with her. He was glad to remember that he had always disliked her. But he had come there with a purpose, and he did not intend to be turned aside from it. Seeing that he did not speak, Mrs. Dobbs said, "Might I ask if you did me the favour to call merely to condole upon the death of my late daughter's husband's cousin?"

This was an opening for what he wanted to say, and he availed himself of it. He replied, stiffly, that the principal object of his visit had been to see Miss Cheffington, who, he was told, had returned to Oldchester; and that, in one sense, his visit might be held to be congratulatory, inasmuch as Miss Cheffington inherited something worth having under her cousin's will. He did not fear being suspected of any interested motive here. Besides that he was rich enough to make the money a matter of secondary importance; his conscience was absolutely clear on this score. He had desired, and offered, to marry May when she was penniless; he still desired it, but truly none the more for her inheritance.

"Oh! So you've heard of the legacy, have you?" said Mrs. Dobbs.

"Heard of it! My good lady, I was present at the reading of the will. There were very few persons at the funeral; it was poor Lucius's wish that it should be private, but I thought it my duty to attend. There are peculiar relations between the family and myself, which made me desirous of paying that compliment to his memory. I think there was no other stranger present except Mr. Bragg. You have heard of him? Of course! All Oldchester persons are acquainted with the name of Bragg. After the ceremony Lord Castlecombe invited us into the library, and the will was read. I understood that the deceased had wished its contents to be made known as soon as possible."

This narration of his distinguished treatment at Combe Park was soothing to the young man's self-esteem. He ended his speech with patronizing suavity. But Mrs. Dobbs remained silent and irresponsive.

"I wish," said Theodore, after vainly awaiting a word from her, "to see Miss Cheffington, if you please."

Mrs. Dobbs slowly shook her head. He repeated the request, in a louder and more peremptory tone.

"Oh, I heard you quite well before," she said composedly; "but I'm sorry to say your wish can't be complied with."

"Miss Cheffington is in this house, is she not?"

"Yes, she is at home; but you can't see her."

Theodore grew a shade paler than usual, and answered sharply, "But I insist upon seeing her." He threw aside the mask of civility. It evidently was wasted here.

"'Insist' is an unmannerly word to use; and a ridiculous one under the circumstances—which, perhaps, you'll mind more. You can't see my granddaughter."

He glared at her in a white rage. Theodore's anger was never of the blazing, explosive sort. If fire typifies that passion in most persons, in him it resembled frost. His metal turned cold in wrath; but it would skin the fingers which incautiously touched it. A fit of serious anger was apt, also, to make him feel ill and tremulous.

"May I ask why I cannot see her?" he said, almost setting his teeth as he spoke.

"Because she wishes to avoid you. She fled away when she saw you coming," answered Mrs. Dobbs, with pitiless frankness.

He drew two or three long breaths, like a person who has been running hard, before saying, "That is very strange! It is only a few days ago that Miss Cheffington was sitting beside me at dinner; talking to me in the sweetest and most gracious manner."

"As to sitting beside you, I suppose she had to sit where she was put! And as to sweetness—no doubt she was civil. But, at any rate, she declines to see you now. She has said so as plain as plain English can express it."

"Your statement is incredible. Suppose I say I don't believe it! What guarantee have I that you are telling me the truth?"

"None at all," she answered quietly.

He stared blankly for a moment. Then he said, "Mrs. Dobbs, for some reason, or no reason, you hate me. That is a matter of perfect indifference to me." (His white lips, twitching nostrils, and icily gleaming eyes, told a different tale.) "But I am not accustomed to be treated with impertinence by persons of your class."

"Only by your betters?" interpolated Mrs. Dobbs.

"And, moreover, I shall take immediate steps to inform Captain Cheffington of your behaviour. He will scarcely approve his daughter's remaining with a person who—who—"

"Says, she'd rather not see Mr. Theodore Bransby."

"Who insults his friends. With regard to Miss Cheffington, I have no doubt you will endeavour to poison her mind against me. But you may possibly find yourself baffled. I have made proposals to Miss Cheffington—no doubt you are acquainted with the fact—which, although not immediately accepted, were not definitively rejected: at least, not by the young lady herself. And I shall take an answer from no one else. Miss Cheffington's demeanour to me, of late, has been distinctly encouraging. If it be now changed, I shall know quite well to whose low cunning and insolent interference to attribute it. But you may find yourself mistaken in your reckoning, Mrs. Dobbs. Captain Cheffington is my friend: and Captain Cheffington will hardly be disposed to leave his daughter in such hands when I tell him all."

He was speaking in a laboured way, and his lips and hands were tremulous.

Mrs. Dobbs looked at him gravely, but with no trace of anger. "Look here," she said when he paused, apparently from want of breath—"you may as well know it first as last—May is engaged to be married; has been engaged more than three months."

Theodore gave a kind of gasp, and turned of so ghastly a pallor that Mrs. Dobbs, without another word, went to a closet in the room, unlocked it, took out a decanter with some sherry in it, poured out a brimming glassful of the wine, and, placing one hand behind the young man's head, put the glass to his lips with the other. He made a feeble movement to reject it.

"Off with it!" she said in the voice of a nurse talking to a refractory child.

He swallowed the sherry without further resistance, and a tinge of colour began to return to his face.

"You haven't got too much strength," observed Mrs. Dobbs, as she stood and watched him. "Your mother was delicate, and I suppose you take after her."

She had no intention, no consciousness, of doing so, but, in speaking thus, she touched a sensitive chord. Any allusion to his mother's feeble constitution made him nervous. He closed his eyes, and murmured that he feared he had caught a chill at the funeral; that the sensation of shivering pointed to that.

Mrs. Dobbs stood looking down on him as he sat with his head thrown back in the chair.

"And so, my lad, you think I hate you?" she said. "Why, I should be sorry to be obliged to hate your father's son; or, for that matter, your mother's son either. She was a good, quiet, peaceable sort of young woman. I remember her well, and your grandfather, old Rabbitt, that kept the Castlecombe Arms when I was young. No; I don't hate you. Not a bit! But I'll tell you what I do hate; I hate to see young creatures, that ought by rights to be generous, and trusting, and affectionate, and maybe a little bit foolish—there's a kind of foolishness that's better than over-wisdom in the young—I hate to see 'em setting themselves up, valuing themselves on their 'cuteness; ashamed of them that have gone before 'em. I hate to see 'em hard-hearted to the helpless. Young things may be cruel from thoughtlessness; but, to be cruel out of meanness—well, I'll own I do hate that. But as for you, it comes into my head that perhaps I've been a bit too hard on you."

Mrs. Dobbs here laid her broad hand on his shoulder. He would fain have shaken it off. But, although the wine had greatly restored him, he thought it prudent to remain quiet, and recover himself completely before going away.

"You are but a lad to me," continued Mrs. Dobbs. "And perhaps I've been hard on you. There's a deal of excuse to be made. You love my granddaughter, after your fashion—and nobody can love better than his best—and it's bitter not to be loved again. You'll get over it. Folks with redder blood in their veins than you, have got over it before to-day. But I know you can't think so now; and it's bitter. But if you'll take an old woman's advice—an old woman that knew your mother and grandmother, and is old enough to be your grandmother herself—you'll just make up your mind to bear a certain amount of pain without flinching:—like as if you'd got a bullet in battle, or broke your collar-bone out hunting—and turn your thoughts to helping other folks in their trouble. There's no cure for the heart-ache like that, take my word for it. Come now, you just face it like a man, and try my recipe! You've got good means and good abilities. Do some good with 'em! Some young fellows when they're out of spirits, take to climbing up mountains, slaughtering wild beasts, or getting into scrimmages with savages—by the way, I did hear that you were going into Parliament—but there's your stepmother now, with her five children, your young brothers and sisters, on her hands. Just you go in for making her life easier. There's a good work ready and waiting for you."

Theodore moved his shoulder brusquely, and Mrs. Dobbs immediately withdrew her hand. He stood up and said stiffly, "I must offer you my acknowledgments for the wine you administered."

Mrs. Dobbs merely waved her hand, as though putting that aside, and continued to look at him, with a grave expression, which was not without a certain broad, motherly compassion.

"I presume the name of the man to whom Miss Cheffington has engaged herself is not a secret?"

"It is Mrs. Hadlow's nephew; Mr. Owen Rivers," answered Mrs. Dobbs simply.

He had felt as sure of what she was going to say as though he had seen the words printed before him; nevertheless, the sound of the name seemed to pierce him like a sword-blade. He drew himself up with a strong effort to be cutting and contemptuous. But as he went on speaking, he lost his self-command and prudence.

"Miss Cheffington is to be congratulated, indeed! Captain Cheffington will, no doubt, be delighted at the alliance you have contrived for his daughter! Mr. Owen Rivers! A clerk in Mr. Bragg's counting-house—which, however, is probably the most respectable occupation he has ever followed! Mr. Owen Rivers, whose name is scandalously connected throughout Oldchester with that of the person you were so kind as to recommend to my good offices just now! A person whose conduct disgraces my family, and dishonours my father's memory! Mr. Owen Rivers, who—"

"Hush! Hold your tongue!" cried Mrs. Dobbs, fairly clapping one hand over his mouth, and pointing with the other to the window.

There at the bottom of the garden was Owen, hurriedly alighting from a cab; and May, who had witnessed his arrival from an upper window, presently came flying down the pathway into his arms.

Theodore had but a lightning-swift glimpse of this little scene, for Mrs. Dobbs saying, "Come along here!" resolutely pulled him by the arm into a back room, and so to a door opening on to a lane behind the house. He was astonished at this summary proceeding, but he affected somewhat more bewilderment than he really felt, so as to cover his retreat. And he muttered something about having to deal with a mad woman.

"Now go!" said Mrs. Dobbs, opening the door. "I can forgive a deal to love and jealousy and disappointment, but that cowardly lie is not to be forgiven. To think that you—you—should be Martin Bransby's son! Why, it's enough to make your father turn in his grave!"

And with that she thrust him out, and shut the door upon him.

CHAPTER XIII.

Mrs. Dormer-Smith's affectionate letter to her brother produced a result which she had not at all anticipated when she wrote it. He arrived in England by the next steamboat from Ostend, and took up his quarters in her house. He had come ostensibly for the purpose of visiting Combe Park, and patching up a reconciliation with his uncle. This, indeed, was a pet scheme with Pauline. She had hinted at it in writing to her brother. Now that George and "poor dear Lucius" were gone, Lord Castlecombe might not dislike to be on good terms with his heir. He was old and lonely, and, as Pauline's correspondents had assured her, greatly broken down by the death of his sons.

Frederick scarcely knew which to regret the most—his niece's departure or his brother-in-law's arrival. He missed May very much, but very shortly he began to be reconciled to her engagement. Rivers was a gentleman and an honest fellow, and might be trusted to take care of May's money, which Mr. Dormer-Smith thought would be otherwise in imminent jeopardy from the arrival on the scene of May's papa.

That gentleman, indeed, who had at first taken the news of his daughter's engagement with supreme indifference, showed some lively symptoms of disapprobation on learning the fact of Lucius's bequest. A daughter dependent on the bounty of Mrs. Dobbs for food, shelter, and raiment, was an uninteresting person enough; but a daughter who possessed between four and five hundred a-year of her own, ought not to be allowed to marry without her father's consent. Frederick dryly remarked that May's capital was stringently tied up in the hands of trustees, whether she were married or single. Whereupon Augustus indulged in very strong language respecting his dead cousin; and declared that the terms of the will were a pointed and intentional insult to him, who was his child's natural guardian.

Still, although the capital was secure, Frederick knew that the income was not. And the more he observed his brother-in-law, the more he felt how desirable it was that May should have a husband to take care of her.

Captain Cheffington had not improved during his years of exile. He smoked all day long; and even at night in his bed, incensing May's chamber, which he occupied, with clouds of tobacco-smoke. He had contracted other unpleasant habits, and his temper was diabolical. He had not brought his wife to England with him. He would sit for hours with his slippered feet on the fender in his sister's dressing-room, railing at the absent Mrs. Augustus Cheffington in a way which was most grievous to Pauline;

for he showed not the least reticence in the presence of Smithson. Talk of "floating"—how would it be possible to "float" a woman of whom her own husband spoke in that way?

He had no very grave charges to bring against La Bianca after all. She had been faithful to him, and stuck to him, and worked for him. But he bewailed his fate in having tied himself to "a third-rate Italian opera-singer, without an idea in her head beyond painting her face and squalling!" It was just his cursed luck. Why couldn't Lucius die, since he meant to die, six months earlier?

At another time, he would openly rejoice in the death of his cousins, and express a fervent hope that the old boy wasn't going to last much longer. Pauline would remonstrate, and put her handkerchief to her eyes, and beg her brother not to speak so heartlessly of his own family: especially of "poor dear Lucius." But Augustus pooh-pooh'd this as confounded humbug. He was uncommonly glad to be the heir of Combe Park, and thought it about time that his family, and his country, and the human race generally, made him some amends for the years he had passed under a cloud! He would show them how to enjoy life when he came into possession of "his property," as he had taken to call Lord Castlecombe's estate. He planned out several changes in the disposal of the land, and decided what rent he would take for the house and home-park. For he did not intend to live in this d—d foggy little island, where one had bronchitis if one hadn't got rheumatism, and rheumatism if one hadn't got bronchitis. In one respect his visions coincided with his sister's, since he talked of having a villa on the Mediterranean coast, not far from Monte Carlo; but they differed from hers in several important points: notably in providing no place for her in the villa.

Frederick would sometimes throw a shade over these rosy dreams by observing doggedly that, for his part, he doubted the likelihood of Lord Castlecombe's speedy decease, and that, looking at them both, he was inclined to consider Uncle George's life the better of the two; so that, on the whole, domestic life in Mr. Dormer-Smith's smart house at Kensington was by no means harmonious. Meanwhile Pauline, with considerable pains and earnest meditation, composed a letter to her uncle on behalf of Augustus; she did not venture to entrust the task to Augustus himself. It would be impossible to persuade him to be as smooth and conciliatory as the case demanded. But she wrote a letter which, she thought, combined diplomacy with pathos, and from which she hoped for some satisfactory result. But the reply she received by return of post was of such a nature that she hastily thrust it into the fire lest Augustus should see it, and told him and her husband that "poor dear Uncle George was not yet equal to the effort of seeing Augustus, after the great shock he had suffered." Uncle George had, in fact, stated in the plainest terms that if Captain Cheffington ventured to show himself in Combe Park, the servants had orders to turn him out forcibly!

The object for which Captain Cheffington had come to England at that time being thus baulked, it would have appeared natural that he should return to his wife in Brussels. But day followed day, until nearly three weeks had elapsed since Lucius Cheffington's death, and still Augustus remained at Kensington. Every morning, with a dreadful regularity, Mr. Dormer-Smith inquired of his wife if she knew whether her brother were going away in the course of that day; and every morning the shower of tears with which Mrs. Dormer-Smith received the inquiry, and which generally formed her only answer to it, became more copious. Augustus, on the whole, was the least uncomfortable of the trio. He had contrived to raise a little ready money on his expectations; he was well lodged and well fed; the change to London (now that he had a few pounds in his pocket) was not unwelcome after Brussels; and as to his brother-in-law's undisguised dislike to his presence, he had grown far too callous to heed it, so long as it suited him to ignore it. Not but that he took note of it in his mind keenly enough, and promised himself the pleasure of paying off Frederick with interest, as soon as he should come into "his property."

All this time a humble household in Oldchester was a great deal happier than the wintry days were long. The news of Captain Cheffington's arrival in England had at first disturbed May. Perhaps he might insist on seeing her; and she shrank from seeing him. But she thought it her duty to write to him and inform him herself of her engagement; and neither Owen nor her grandmother opposed her doing so.

If May had any lingering illusion about her father, or any hope that he would manifest some gleam of parental tenderness towards her, the illusion and the hope were short-lived. The reply to her communications was a hurried scrawl, haughtily regretting that Mr. Owen Rivers had not thought proper to wait upon him and ask his consent to the marriage, which he totally disapproved of! And adding that although Rivers of Riversmead was undoubtedly good blood, it appeared that the traditions of gentlemanlike behaviour had been lost by the present bearer of the name, since he entered the service of a tradesman. The letter ended with a peremptory demand for fifty pounds.

May and Owen had planned that granny was to return to Friar's Row on their marriage. Mr. Bragg was willing to break the lease which he held, and to remove his office to another house hard by. And Mrs. Dobbs, with all her goods and chattels, was to be reinstated in her old home. As this scheme was to be kept secret from Granny for the present, it involved a vast deal of delightful mystery and plotting. Jo Weatherhead was admitted to the conspiracy, and enjoyed it with the keenest relish.

A word or two had been said as to Mrs. Dobbs taking up her abode with the young couple when they should be married. But this Granny instantly and inflexibly refused.

"No, no, children; I'm not quite so foolish as that! It's very well for Owen to take May for better for worse. But it would be a little too much to take May and her grandmother for better for worse!"

Of course it was not long before Owen took his betrothed to see Canon and Mrs. Hadlow. They walked together to the old house in College Quad, where, however, their news had preceded them. The Hadlows were very cordial. Both of them were very fond of May; and Aunt Jane loudly hoped that Owen appreciated his good fortune, and declared it was far above his deserts, though in her heart she thought no girl in England too good for her favourite nephew. The lovers were affectionately bidden to come again as often as they could, and brighten up the old place with the sight of their happy young faces.

They agreed, as they walked home together, that the home in College Quad seemed a little gloomy and lonely without Conny. Conny was still away. She had only been at home on a flying visit of a few days during several months past. She was now staying with a Lady Belcraft, who had a handsome house at Combe St. Mildred's. Mrs. Hadlow had told them so; and a word or two, uttered in the same breath, about Theodore Bransby being often in that neighbourhood, suggested a suspicion that Theodore might be thinking of returning to his old love. This idea annoyed Owen extremely. The hint which suggested it had been dropped almost in the moment of saying "good-bye" to Mrs. Hadlow, or he would have attempted at once to sound her on the subject.

He had interrogated his aunt privately—while May was being petted and made much of by the kind old canon—as to a rumour which was rife in Oldchester—namely, that Constance had been betrothed to Lucius Cheffington. But Aunt Jane positively denied this. She admitted that the gossip bad reached her own ears, and that she had spoken to her daughter about it.

"But Conny entirely disabused me of any such notion. She said that, in the first place, nothing was farther from Lucius's thoughts than love-making; and that, in the second place, it would have been a most imprudent marriage for her, since she could only expect to be speedily left a widow with a very slender jointure. Conny was never romantic, you know," said Aunt Jane, with a quick, half-humorous glance at her nephew.

Owen began to consider with himself whether it might not be his duty to acquaint Canon Hadlow with many parts of Theodore's conduct which were certainly unknown to him. All inquiries conducted either by himself or by Jo Weatherhead—who ferreted out information with untiring zeal and delight in the task—showed more and more plainly that the calumnies concerning Mrs. Bransby could be traced, for the most part, to her step-son, and in no single instance beyond him. May had long ago acquitted Constance Hadlow of speaking or writing evil things of the widow. Constance had not, in fact, expended any attention whatever on the Bransby family since their departure from Oldchester.

She was spending her time very agreeably. Her hostess, Lady Belcraft, was a widow. She was a great crony of Mrs. Griffin's, and delighted with Mrs. Griffin's protégée. Having, so to speak, retired from business on her own account (her two daughters being married and settled long ago), Lady Belcraft was still most willing to renew the toils of the chase on behalf of a friend. She and Mrs. Griffin had carefully examined the county list of possible matches for Constance Hadlow; and had agreed that there was good hope of a speedy find, a capital run, and a successful finish.

It so happened that on the same afternoon when May and Owen were paying their visit to College Quad, Theodore Bransby was making a call at the residence of Lady Belcraft in Combe St. Mildred's.

Ever since his interview with Mrs. Dobbs—now several days ago—Theodore had been considering his own case with minute and concentrated attention. We are all of us, it must be owned, supremely interesting to ourselves; but Theodore's interest in himself was of a jealously exclusive kind. His health was undoubtedly delicate. He had felt the loss of a home to which he could repair when he was ailing or out of sorts ever since his father's death. He found, too, that he was apt to become hipped and nervous when alone. He came to the conclusion that he needed a wife to take care of him, and, after grave consideration, he resolved to marry Constance Hadlow.

If he could by a word have destroyed Rivers and obtained possession of May Cheffington, he would have said that word without hesitation or remorse; but since that could not be, he did not intend to wear the willow. He would marry Constance. That she would have accepted him long ago he was well assured; and his circumstances were far more prosperous now than in those days. Canon and Mrs. Hadlow could not but be impressed by his disinterestedness in coming forward now that he was in the enjoyment of a handsome independence. And, on his side, he believed he was choosing prudently. If he were ill, the attentions of a wife—a refined and cultured woman, dependent, moreover, on him for the comfort of her daily life—would be far preferable to those of a hireling nurse, who would have the power of going away whenever she found her position disagreeable. But this was only one side of the question. When he grew stronger (he always looked forward to growing stronger) Constance would be an admirable helpmate from a social point of view. She had acquired influential friends, was received in the best houses, and would do his taste infinite credit, and whether as a politician or a barrister she might have it in her power to forward his ambitions.

It was as the result of these meditations that he called at Lady Belcraft's.

He had met her occasionally in society, and she knew perfectly who he was. But there was a distinct film of ice over the politeness with which she received him when he was ushered into her drawing-room. She thought this little attorney's son was taking something like a liberty in appearing there uninvited. She forgave him, however, immediately when, in his most correct manner, he asked for Miss Hadlow.

Really it might do, thought Lady Belcraft. The young man was very well off, and presentable, and all that, and dear Conny, though simply charming, had not a penny in the world (neither was dear Conny her ladyship's own daughter). Yes; she positively thought it might do! She was so sorry that Miss Hadlow was not within, but she expected her every moment. She was walking, she believed, in the park. "The Park" at Combe St. Mildred's meant Combe Park. Oh, yes; she was aware that Mr. Bransby was an old acquaintance. Playfellows from childhood? Really! That sort of thing always had such a hold on one—was so extremely—Oh, there was dear Conny coming up the drive.

Lady Belcraft sent a message by a servant, begging Miss Hadlow to come into the drawing-room, where she presently appeared.

She was dressed in a winter toilet of carefully-studied simplicity, and looked radiantly handsome. Theodore gazed at her as if he had never seen her before. Self-possessed she had always been, but she had now acquired something more than that—an air of conscious distinction—of "being somebody," as Theodore phrased it in his own mind, which he admired and wondered at.

"Here's an old friend of yours, Conny," said Lady Belcraft.

Constance had been pulling off her gloves as she entered the room, and she now extended a white, well cared-for hand to Theodore, with a cool little, "Oh, how d'ye do?" and the faintest of smiles.

Her hostess thought within herself that if there really was anything between her and young Bransby, Conny's behaviour was marvellous, and that all the training bestowed on her own daughters had left them far below the point of finish attained by this provincial clergyman's daughter.

"Did you walk far? Are you tired?" she asked.

"No, thanks, dear Lady Belcraft; I am not at all tired. I went to my favourite group of beeches. It's a capital day for walking. And what is the news in Oldchester, Theodore?"

Her calling him "Theodore" in the old familiar way seemed to have the mysterious effect of putting him under her feet; it implied such superiority and security. Theodore was conscious of this, but it did not displease him; she had doubtless resented his not making the expected offer earlier. He had thought when he met her in London that hurt amoure propre had much to do with her cavalier treatment of him. But he had a charm to smoothe her ruffled plumes.

After a little commonplace conversation, Lady Belcraft recollected some orders which she wanted to give personally to her gardener, and, with a brief excuse, left the room. Constance perfectly understood why she had done so, Theodore did not; but he seized the occasion which, he imagined, hazard had thrown in his way.

"I am very glad of this opportunity of speaking with you alone, Constance," he began very solemnly.

There was no trepidation such as he had felt in speaking to May. He neither trembled, nor stammered, nor grew hot and cold by turns. That chapter was closed. He was turning over a new and quite different leaf.

"Yes?" said Constance. "Really!" She removed her hat, smoothed the thick dark braids of her hair before a mirror, and sat down with graceful composure.

"I don't think we have met, Constance, since—" He glanced at his black clothes.

"No; I think not. I was very sorry. I begged mamma to give you a message from me when she wrote to condole with Mrs. Bransby."

"I merely allude to that sad subject in order to assure you that I am not unmindful of what is proper and becoming under the circumstances; and lest you should think me guilty of heartless precipitation."

He was beginning to enjoy the rounding off of his sentences—a pleasure he had never tasted in May's company; strong emotion being unfavourable to polished periods.

"Oh, I don't think you were ever guilty of precipitation," answered Constance quietly. But the mirror opposite reflected a flash of her handsome eyes.

"Nothing," continued Theodore, "could be in worse taste than to neglect the accustomed forms of respect. A period of twelve months would not be too long to mourn for a parent so excellent as my father; but six months could not be considered to outrage decorum. And I should not urge—"

He paused. He had been on the point of saying that he would not press for the marriage taking place before the summer, when he happily remembered that he had not yet gone through the form of asking Constance whether she would marry him or not. To him it seemed so like merely taking up the thread of a story temporarily interrupted, that he had lost sight of the probability that Constance's mind had not been keeping pace with his own on the subject. But it recurred to him in time.

Constance was sitting on a low couch near the fireside, at some distance from him. He now took his place beside her. There was a certain awkwardness in making a proposal of marriage across a spacious room.

"There can be no need of many words between us, Constance," he began, with as much tenderness of manner as he could call up. Then he stopped. Constance had drawn away the skirt of her gown on the side next to him, and was examining it attentively. "What is the matter?" he asked.

"I thought you had accidentally set your boot on the hem of my frock," she said. "And the roads are so muddy, although it is fine overhead! But it's all right. I beg your pardon: you were saying—?"

This interruption was disconcerting. He had had in his head an elaborate sentence which was now dispersed and irrecoverable. He must begin all over again. However, when fairly started once more, his eloquence did not fail him. He offered his hand and fortune to Miss Hadlow, "in good set terms."

She was silent when he had finished, and he ventured to take her hand.

"Am I not to have an answer, dearest Constance?" he asked.

She drew her hand away very gently and with perfect composure before saying, as she looked full at him with her fine dark eyes—

"You are not joking, then?"

"Joking!"

"Well, I know you are not given to joking, and this would certainly be an inconceivably bad joke; but it is almost more inconceivable that you should be in earnest."

He was fairly bewildered, and doubtful of her meaning.

"However," she continued, "if you really expect a serious answer, you must have it. No, thank you."

He stood up erect and stiff, as if moved by a spring. She remained leaning back in an easy attitude on the couch, and looking at him.

"I—Constance!—I don't understand you!" he exclaimed.

"I refuse you," she replied in a gentle voice, and with her best society drawl. "Distinctly, decidedly, and unhesitatingly. I think you must understand that. Won't you stay and see Lady Belcraft?" (Theodore had taken up his hat, and was moving towards the door.) "Oh, very well. I will make your excuses."

She rang the bell, which was within reach of her hand, and Theodore walked out of the room without proffering another word.

CHAPTER XIV.

Canon Hadlow had resolved that his daughter, when she returned to Oldchester for May's wedding, to which she was, of course, invited, should remain in her own home at least for some months. He had grown very discontented with her prolonged and frequent absences. Mrs. Hadlow, at the earnest request of Constance, backed by a polite invitation from Lady Belcraft, went to Combe St. Mildred's to remain there one day, and bring her daughter back with her.

But, instead of doing so, she sent a telegram home, desiring that a box of clothes might be packed and sent to her; and, most surprising of all, the box was to be addressed to Dover. This item of news was disseminated by the Hadlows' servant, whose duty it was to see the trunk conveyed to the railway station. And the woman declared she believed, from what she could make out, that her mistress was going to France.

Of course, the canon knew the truth. But the canon was not visible to callers. He had a cold, and kept his room. All the circle of the Hadlows' acquaintance—and the circle seemed to be immediately widened by the dropping into its midst of this puzzling bit of news, as a stone dropped into water is surrounded by a ring of ever-increasing circumference—were, however, spared further conjecture by the publication, in due course, of the supplement to the Times newspaper of Tuesday, the twenty-seventh of February. It contained the announcement of the marriage at the British Embassy in Paris, on the preceding Saturday, of Viscount Castlecombe to Constance Jane, only daughter of the Reverend Edward Hadlow, Canon of Oldchester.

The general public, or as much of it as had ever heard of the parties concerned—for that vast entity the general public is really as divisible as a jelly-fish; each portion being perfect for all purposes of its existence, when cut off from the rest—was ranged, as is usual in such cases, in two main camps; those who couldn't have believed it beforehand, though an angel from Heaven had announced it, and those who had all along had their suspicions, and were not so very much surprised as you expected. But only the nearest friends and relatives of the family enjoyed the not inconsiderable advantage for judging the matter, of really knowing anything about it.

Owen was the first person whom his uncle admitted to see him. The old man was greatly overcome. His daughter's marriage was a blow to him. It gave a rude shock to the ideal Constance, whom he had loved and admired with a sort of delicate paternal chivalry. There could be no question of love in such a marriage as this—no question, even, of gratitude, or reverence, or any of the finer feelings. To the pure-hearted, simple-minded old man, it seemed to be a sad degradation for his daughter. Not a soul except his wife ever fully understood his state of mind on the subject; for he spoke of it to no one. Mrs. Dobbs, perhaps, came nearest to doing so. She had a great reverence and admiration for the canon, and considerable sympathetic insight into his feelings. And when, afterwards, people said in her presence how proud and elated Canon Hadlow must be at his daughter's making so great a match, she would tighten her lips, and observe sotto voce that you might as well expect a Christian saint to be gratified by being decorated with the peacock's feather of a Chinese mandarin.

When Mrs. Hadlow came home, of course more particulars were divulged. Many came out by degrees in confidential talks with her nephew. Mrs. Hadlow spoke to him quite openly.

Constance had earnestly begged her mother to go to her at Combe St. Mildred's, and almost immediately on her arrival there had announced that she was about to marry Lord Castlecombe, and that everything was arranged for the ceremony to take place in Paris; since, under the circumstances, they both felt that it could not be managed too quietly. She much wished her mother and father to accompany her to Paris, in order that everything might be en règle.

When the first astonishment was over, Mrs. Hadlow impulsively tried to dissuade her daughter from taking this step. It was dreadful, it was really monstrous to think of her Conny marrying that old man, who was several years the senior of her own father! A man, too, of a hard, unamiable character—one who was much feared, little respected, and loved not at all! She was revolted by the idea. And as to the canon, she could not bear to think of what he would feel. He would never allow it! It was hopeless to think of gaining his consent.

When her mother's tearful excitement had somewhat subsided, Constance pointed out that she had a very sincere regard for Lord Castlecombe, who had behaved in every way excellently towards her; that as to "falling in love," as depicted by poets and novelists, she had her private opinion, which was, briefly, that all that was about as historically true as the adventures of Oberon and Titania; and that, at all events, she was sufficiently acquainted with her own character to be persuaded that she was incapable of that species of temporary insanity. Further, with regard to her father's consent, she deeply regretted to hear that he was likely to withhold it; since she would, in that case, be compelled to marry without it, which would be very painful to her. (And when she said that it would be painful to her, her mother knew that she spoke quite sincerely.) She was of full age to judge for herself in the matter, and could not think of breaking her word to Lord Castlecombe. She further pointed out that although, of course, Oldchester people would chatter about her—she spoke already, as though she were looking down on those common mortals from the serene and luminous elevation of some fixed star—yet there could be nothing scandalous said if she were known to be accompanied to Paris by her mother. As to papa, his health, and his duties, and many other excuses might be alleged for his not undertaking a journey at that inclement season.

Constance spoke with perfect calmness, and without the slightest disrespect of manner. But Mrs. Hadlow was made aware within five minutes that nothing on earth which she had power to say or do would, for an instant, shake her daughter's resolve to be a viscountess. There was nothing to be done but to put the best face possible on the matter, and go to Paris. She could not allow her child to travel thither alone. The bridegroom had already preceded them, to make all needful preparations.

Poor Mrs. Hadlow was in such a whirl of confusion and emotion as scarcely to know what she was doing or saying. "Had Lady Belcraft known of this?" she asked. Constance smiled rather scornfully, as she replied that nobody would be more surprised than poor dear Lady Belcraft when she should learn the news. No; Conny was not going to share the glory of her capture with any one. And, in truth, such glory as belonged to it was all her own.

Mrs. Griffin, on hearing the news, was at first half inclined to be sharp and spiteful at being kept in the dark. (Although, of course, she did not allow herself to continue in that vulgar frame of mind.) But Lady Belcraft was subdued, and almost prostrate in spirit before this gifted young creature. "She's a wonderful young woman, my dear—a wonderful young woman!" declared Lady Belcraft.

Just before they landed from the steamboat at Calais, Constance said to her mother, "Mamma, I do think you and papa are the most unworldly people I ever heard of! You have never thought of saying a single word about settlements."

Mrs. Hadlow started, and looked blankly at her daughter. She stood rebuked. "I have felt, ever since you told me, as if I had received a stunning blow on the head which deprived me of half my faculties," she answered. "But I ought to have thought of that. It is not too late now, perhaps, to secure some provision for you; is it, Conny?"

"I should not have thought of marrying Lord Castlecombe without a proper settlement, mamma. We might have been married a fortnight ago if it had not been for the delays of the lawyers; although matters were simplified for them by my having nothing at all! I am quite satisfied with the arrangements, and I hope you and papa will be so too. I think you will admit that Lord Castlecombe has been very generous."

Mrs. Hadlow was a woman of bright intelligence, and she had been apt to consider Conny a little below the Rivers' standard of brains; but now, as she looked and listened, she felt tempted to exclaim, like Lady Belcraft, that this was a wonderful young woman.

But what words can paint the effect of that fateful announcement in the Times on the family party assembled in Mr. Dormer-Smith's house at Kensington!

Augustus behaved so outrageously, used such vituperative language, and comported himself altogether with such violence, that his brother-in-law privately fortified himself by securing the presence of a policeman well in view of the windows, on the opposite side of the way, before requesting Captain Cheffington to withdraw at once from his house. Much to his surprise, and immensely to his relief, the request was complied with promptly. Captain Cheffington disappeared in a hansom cab, with a smart travelling-bag, and followed by a second vehicle containing two well-filled portmanteaus. Whereas, as James cynically remarked to the cook, a cigar-case and a tooth-pick was about the amount of his luggage when he arrived! James had not been fee'd. Augustus asserted his claim to be considered one of the family by swearing at the servants, and never giving any of them a sixpence. The explanation of this speedy departure was shortly forthcoming in the shape of a variety of bills, which poured in with astonishing rapidity. Augustus also, as has been stated, had been clever enough to raise a little money on the strength of his heirship. And Mr. Dormer-Smith had to endure some contumely from creditors who had looked to getting something like twenty-five per cent. above market-prices out of the captain, and were roused to a frenzy of moral indignation when they discovered that he was safe out of England, and beyond their reach.

To Pauline the blow was the more severe because she persuaded herself that she had been the victim of black ingratitude on the part of Constance.

"That girl!" she would murmur, weeping. "That girl, whom I held up as a model—and who really did behave perfectly when she was here—quite perfectly—to think of that girl being the one to turn round on the family in this treacherous way! I do not know how I shall endure to see her face again."

"Then don't see it," suggested Frederick. "If you think she has behaved so badly, cut her, and have done with it."

"Cut her!" exclaimed Pauline, sitting up from among the pillows in her chaise longue, with a vinagrette in one hand and a pocket-handkerchief in the other. "How can I cut my uncle's wife? She is now Lady Castlecombe, Frederick! You seem to have no idea that private feelings must give way to the duty one owes to society. I wonder who will present her. I dare say Mrs. Griffin will persuade the duchess to do it. It would not surprise me at all. Probably they will open the town house now, and come up every season. Cut her! Frederick, you talk like that Nihilist who is going to marry poor darling May!"

Frederick more than ever thought that "poor darling May" was to be congratulated on having secured the love and protection of the honest young Englishman to whom his wife persisted in attributing anarchical principles. He wrote a kind letter, in which he proposed to come down to Oldchester and give his niece away at the marriage, if that would be agreeable to her and Mr. Rivers. May's affectionate heart was overjoyed by this proposal. A joint letter, signed by May and Owen, was sent by return of post, in which both Aunt Pauline and Uncle Frederick were warmly invited to the wedding. And May put in a special petition that Harold and Wilfred should be allowed to be present. Granny would find a nook for them in Jessamine Cottage.

May also sent an invitation to Mrs. Bransby to be present, but she replied that she would not bring her black gown to be a blot on their brightness, but that no more loving prayers would be breathed for their happiness than those of their affectionate friend Louisa Bransby.

Neither did Aunt Pauline accept the invitation. She did not write unkindly. Her reply seemed to be, indeed, a sort of homily on the text—

"How all unconscious of their doom
The little victims play."

It was a sad business, but she was mildly compassionate and forbearing. But the best of all was that Harold and Wilfred were to be permitted to come. In fact, their father insisted on bringing them, to their inexpressible rapture. They took to Granny at once, and she had to keep a watch upon her tongue lest she should let slip before Mr. Dormer-Smith the words she had said on first seeing the children—

"Poor dear motherless little fellows!"

On the wedding morning a letter arrived for Mrs. Dobbs from Mr. Bragg. Mr. Bragg was about to sail for Buenos Ayres on a twelve-months' visit to his son. Before going away, he thought it would be agreeable to May and her husband, he wrote, to be the means of communicating something to Mrs. Bransby, which he hoped would be to her advantage. The new premises which he had taken for his office, now removed from Friars' Row, were to be furnished throughout, and a couple of rooms reserved for Mr. Bragg's use whenever he wished to come into Oldchester from his country house. Under these circumstances, a resident housekeeper would be required to look after the place and govern the servants. Mr. Bragg hoped that Mrs. Bransby would do him the favour to accept this post, and that she would find herself more comfortable among her old friends in Oldchester, than in the wilderness of London. Moreover, he enclosed a cheque for a handsome sum of money, as to the disposal of which he thus wrote:—

"The cheque I would ask Mr. Rivers to apply to paying young Martin Bransby's school fees for the ensuing year. And any little matter that may be over can be used for the boy's books, and so on. He is a fine boy, I think, and worth helping. Learning is a great thing. I never had it myself, but I don't undervalue it for that. I have thought that this would perhaps be the best way I could find of what you might call testifying my appreciation of Mr. Rivers's services to me. I hope he will accept it as a wedding present."

To May he sent no gift.

"I could offer her nothing but dross," he wrote, "and I don't want her thoughts of me to be mixed up with gold and diamonds, and such poor things as are oftentimes the best a rich man has to give. Some young ladies would be disappointed at this. I don't believe she will. When she's dressed and ready to go to church, just you please kiss her forehead with a blessing in your mind, and—you needn't say anything to her, but just say to yourself, 'this is from Joshua Bragg.'"

Of the wedding, it may be said that, although it was no doubt in many respects like other weddings, yet in several it was peculiar. And its peculiarities were in such flagrant violation of the regulations of society, that it was almost providential Mrs. Dormer-Smith escaped witnessing it.

In the first place, although Uncle Frederick was present, a welcome and an honoured guest, May insisted that Mr. Weatherhead should give her away. And, perhaps, nothing she had ever done in her life had caused Granny more heartfelt satisfaction. As to "Uncle Jo," the honour nearly overpowered him. His appearance in wedding garments, with an enormous white waistcoat, and a bright rose-coloured tie, was an abiding joy to all the little boys of the neighbourhood who were lucky enough to behold him.

Then the Miss Pipers fluttered into the church in such extremely bridal attire, with long white veils attached to their bonnets, as utterly to eclipse May, in her quiet travelling dress. May, however, wore two ornaments of considerable value: a pearl bracelet and brooch, which had arrived the previous evening. Inside each morocco case had been found a slip of paper bearing respectively the inscriptions:—"To Miranda Cheffington, with the good wishes of her great-uncle;" and "To dear May, with the love of her affectionate friend, Constance Castlecombe."

Lastly, Amelia Simpson was so florid in her raiment, and so exuberant in her delight, as to be the observed of all observers. In her excitement, she backed heavily upon people behind her, and trod upon the gowns of people before her; knelt down at the wrong moment, and then, discovering her mistake, jumped up again at the very instant when the rest of the congregation were sinking on to their knees; dropped her metal-clasped prayer-book with a crash in a solemn pause of silence; lost her pocket-handkerchief, and, in her near-sightedness and confusion, seized on Miss Polly Piper's long white veil to wipe her tear-dimmed spectacles; and was, altogether, a severe trial to the nerves of the officiating clergyman.

Many other friends were there. Major Mitton, with his amiable face, and erect, soldierly figure; Dr. Hatch, who said he doubted whether he could snatch a moment to witness the ceremony, but who remained to the very last, to wish the young couple God speed! when they drove away from the door of the church on their honeymoon trip. Even Sebastian Bach Simpson was in a softened mood. The entire absence of pretension about the whole affair conciliated his good will; and he played Mendelssohns' "Wedding March" as a voluntary, when the bride and bridegroom walked down the church arm-in-arm, with unusual spirit and heartiness. And so May and Owen began their voyage of life together, followed by many good wishes, and by less of envy, hatred, malice, and uncharitableness, than perhaps fall to the lot of most mortals.

Marriage, which is the end of most story-books, is but the beginning of many stories; but this chronicle cannot follow the personages who have figured in it much beyond that fateful chapter of the wedding-day.

One or two facts may, however, be told, and a few outlines sketched in, to indicate the course of future events on a more or less distant horizon.

For a long time Pauline clung, with the soft pertinacity which was part of her character, to the hope that "poor dear Augustus" might yet inherit the Castlecombe acres, and resume his place in society. Uncle George could not live for ever! But one fine day the bells of Combe St. Mildred's rang a merry peal, and the news spread like wildfire through the village that an heir was born in a foreign city called Naples; and that my lord and my lady—who was doing extremely well—and the all-important baby were coming home to Combe Park as soon as ever my lady was strong enough to travel.

Then, indeed, Pauline felt that Providence had decided against her brother, and that her own duty to society lay plain and clear before her.

During the following year or two she suffered considerable persecution in the shape of appeals for money from Augustus. The first were in a haughty strain, but before long they sank into the whine of the regular begging-letter writer. She gave him what she could, for to the last she had a soft place in her heart for her brother. But her husband, finding the case hopeless, forbade her to give any more, and, as far as he could, prevented Augustus's letters from reaching her.

Captain Cheffington then brought his wife to London. He had little fear of his creditors, having by this time sunk so low as not to be worth powder and shot. He got his wife engaged, under her real name, at a music-hall of the third class, and caused paragraphs to be inserted in sundry sporting and theatrical prints to the effect that "the Mrs. Augustus Cheffington, whose Italian bravura-singing was so successful a feature in the nightly entertainment," etc., etc., was the niece by marriage of a peer of the realm—Viscount Castlecombe of Combe Park; and he furnished his relations liberally with copies of these papers. Probably he had some hope that they would buy him off to save the honour of the family, but in this he was totally at fault. The old lord who, in the joy of his little son's birth seemed to have taken a new lease of life, merely chuckled at "Gus's making such a confounded ass of himself," and cared not a snap of the fingers for anything he could say or do.

Owen Rivers privately supplied his father-in-law with all the necessaries, and some of the comforts, of life, on condition that he was never to annoy May by making any kind of appeal to her; on the first infringement of this condition the supplies would be withdrawn. And in order to secure its not being all lost at the gaming-table, Owen paid the money into the hands of La Bianca, who, according to her lights, was by no means a bad wife, and was certainly a much better one than her selfish and graceless husband deserved.

Mrs. Bransby gratefully accepted the position offered to her, and fulfilled its duties entirely to Mr. Bragg's satisfaction. Indeed, when the latter returned from Buenos Ayres, he took the habit of spending a good deal of time in the apartment reserved for him over the office. The house—one of the roomy, old-fashioned mansions in Friar's Row—contained ample accommodation for Mrs. Bransby's family. Miss Enid completed, and maintained, her conquest of Mr. Bragg; and some persons thought that it was this young lady's personal attractions which caused him to spend so much of his time in Friar's Row; but other observers thought differently. And, indeed, quite latterly, Mrs. Dormer-Smith has had her ill-opinion of Mrs. Bransby strengthened by certain rumours touching the likelihood of that lady's promotion to a higher position in Mr. Bragg's household than that of paid housekeeper.

"If that should ever come off," says Mrs. Dormer-Smith, "I suppose poor dear foolish May's eyes will be opened at last; and she may repent when it is too late having thrown away her magnificent opportunity, to be picked up by that designing woman."

When these mysterious forecasts are imparted to Lady Castlecombe, she only smiles faintly, and says in her quiet, well-bred way, "Well, but why not?" My lady has her own views on the subject—views in which the discomfiture and mortification of Theodore Bransby form a conspicuous and pleasing feature. But hitherto nothing has happened to justify the previsions of either lady on this score.

Theodore is not often seen in Oldchester now. The place is full of disagreeable associations for him. His political candidature was a failure: the Castlecombe influence on his behalf having been suddenly withdrawn after his lordship's marriage—greatly to the perplexity of his lordship's agent!

Nevertheless, Mr. Theodore Bransby by no means despairs of being able to write M.P. after his name at some future time. But if he ever does enter Parliament, it will probably be on what our Continental neighbours term "the extreme Left of the Chamber." For Theodore's political opinions have undergone a great revulsion, and he is now loftily contemptuous of the territorial aristocracy. In fact, he has been heard to support advanced theories of an almost Communistic complexion—stopping short, however, at the confiscation of other people's property, and maintaining the inviolability of Government Stock, of which he is a large holder. This sort of theory he finds to be quite compatible with the pursuit of fashionable society.

Although surrounded by every luxury which can minister to his personal comfort, he is not at all extravagant, and, indeed, saves more than half his annual income. This he does, not from positive avarice, but because he feels ever more and more strongly that money is power. Moreover, it will be well to have a handsome sum in hand whenever he marries: for he is still firmly minded to find a wife who will devote herself to taking care of him. Quite recently a paragraph has appeared in the Oldchester newspaper announcing the probability of a marriage between "our distinguished townsman, Mr. Theodore Bransby, whose career at the Bar is being watched with pride and pleasure in his native city, and the Lady Euphemia Haggistown, daughter of the Earl of Cauldkail, etc., etc., etc."

Lady Euphemia is a faded, timid, gentlewoman of some five or six-and-thirty years of age, with neither money nor beauty. She is sometimes haunted by the ghost of a romantic attachment to a penniless young navy officer lost at sea hard upon twenty years ago. But she has a soft, submissive desire to win the kindly regard of the remarkably stiff and cold young gentleman whom her father has decided she is to marry whenever he shall see fit to ask her. But poor Lady Effie does not succeed in softening the implacable correctness of her suitor's demeanour into anything very humanly sympathetic. Theodore is quite certain to make the most of his wife's title and social standing in dealing with the world in general, but it is to be feared that he may think fit to balance matters by tyrannizing over her in private with some rigour.

Mrs. Dormer-Smith often moralizes her family history, entangling herself in many metaphysical knots in the course of her cogitations as to what would have happened if something else had happened which never did happen!

Of course, if poor dear Augustus had not thrown himself away on Susan Dobbs things would have been very different. But even in spite of that, much might have been retrieved had he not made a second and still more shocking mésalliance with a strolling Italian singer; because, probably, if Augustus had come home after the death of his cousin Lucius in a proper spirit, and under not discreditable circumstances, and had conducted himself so as to conciliate his uncle, the old man would never have thought of marrying again. Constance Hadlow would never have become Viscountess Castlecombe, and no heir would have appeared to thrust Augustus from his inheritance.

There was an ever-recurring difficulty in fixing the exact point at which "poor dear Augustus's misfortunes" had become irretrievable. So that, although Pauline was on perfectly civil terms with the Castlecombes, and although Frederick was asked down to Combe Park for the shooting every season, and although my lady was happy to receive the Dormer-Smiths (with the least little indefinable touch of condescension) whenever she was at her house in town; yet, in her confidential moments, Pauline's intimate friends were never quite sure to which of the three momentous alliances she was alluding, when she talked plaintively of "That Unfortunate Marriage."

Frances Eleanor Trollope – A Short Biography

Frances Eleanor Trollope, née Ternan, as most probably befits a writer, was born in August 1835 on board a paddle steamer in Delaware Bay. Her parents were on a three year acting tour of North America after their marriage in Edinburgh earlier that year. Frances was to be the eldest of three surviving daughters to Thomas Lawless Ternan and Frances Eleanor Ternan (née Jarman)

On their later return to England her father became the manager of the Theatre Royal in Newcastle upon Tyne where her mother was a leading actress. The three daughters were occasionally included in some of the stage productions to show off their skills.

In adult life Ellen, her younger sister, had become the mistress of England's famed novelist Charles Dickens. Dickens helped to arrange an interview for Frances to become the governess to the child of the widowed writer Thomas Adolphus Trollope. Thomas lived in Florence, often working in collaboration with his mother, the social justice writer, Frances Milton Trollope.

Her relationship with Thomas grew very rapidly and, despite an age difference bordering on a quarter of a century, she married him within five months of becoming his child's governess.

Thomas Adolphus had built a successful and prolific career. The villa he had established with his former wife, Theodosia, was both beautiful and a meeting place for the literary and expatriate circles.

Soon Frances and Thomas decamped from Florence to Rome where they again entertained a wide literary circle of friends as they built a beautiful estate to encompass their lives.

By this marriage she became also the sister-in-law of the world famous Anthony Trollope and daughter-in-law of Frances Milton Trollope, whose biography Frances Trollope: Her Life and Literary Work from George III to Victoria she would later author.

Frances Eleanor also wrote many novels. Her fiction is peopled by eccentric cosmopolitan Londoners, Italian and French visitors, and motherless, bright, and educated young women trying to carve out niches for themselves within the boundaries of the middle and upper-middle classes, with varying degrees of success.

She also contributed pieces to many periodicals, predominantly travel writings which showcase her sustained interest in the art, culture, and history of Italy.

With Thomas Adolphus serving as editor she translated plays and travel books from Italian and German origins.

Their time in Italy endured from their marriage in 1866 until 1890, when they returned to England. Sadly Thomas Adolphus died in 1892.

Frances Eleanor Trollope died on August 14th, 1913 at Southsea, where she had been living with her sister Ellen.

Whilst her works are, of course, overshadowed by Anthony Trollope and other family members they were well regarded at the time and although they fell out of public view they are now coming back into favour and deserved recognition.

Frances Eleanor Trollope – A Concise Bibliography

Novels
Aunt Margaret's Trouble (1866) (as by "A New Writer"; all her other books carried her own name)
Mabel's Progress (1867)
The Sacristan's Household (1869)
Veronica (1870)
Anne Furness (1871)
A Charming Fellow (1876)
Black Spirits and White (1877)
Like Ships Upon the Sea (1883)
That Unfortunate Marriage (1888)
Among Aliens (1890)
Madame Leroux (1890)
That Wild Wheel (1892)
The Fate of Fenella (co-written, 1892)
The Sacristan's Household

Non Fiction
Frances Trollope: Her Life and Literary Work from George III to Victoria (1895)

Printed in Great Britain
by Amazon